THE CLOCK ON THE WALL TICKED DOWN THE SECONDS AS HE STARED INTO THE CAMERA.

This was it. In a matter of minutes, his life would change. Everyone's life would change.

He rehearsed his lines, though he knew them by heart. There would be no teleprompter. There would be no script. There would only be him. And the camera, of course. And the person who would receive this message.

A small television sat off to the side, monitoring the feed. He could see his image staring back at him. He watched as the second hand ticked off the final seconds. *Tick. Tick.* And then it was time.

The red light above the lens flicked on. With the remote in his hand, he zoomed in and watched the monitor. This was it. No turning back.

He closed his eyes for a moment and took a deep breath and let it out again. His heart was pounding through his chest. He opened his eyes and set his jaw firm. And then he began.

"Good evening, Mr. President. I am the Prophet. And I have been commanded to give you a message."

THE 13: FALL

BOOK ONE

ROBBIE CHEUVRONT AND ERIK REED

WITH SHAWN ALLEN

BARBOUR
PUBLISHING

To Whom It May Concern,
According to the Purposes of His Will;
According to Those Who Have Been Called

"*The man must be bad indeed who can look upon the events of the American Revolution without feeling the warmest gratitude toward the great Author of the Universe whose divine interposition was so frequently manifested in our behalf. And it is my earnest prayer that we may so conduct ourselves as to merit a continuance of those blessings with which we have hitherto been favored.*"

—George Washington

"*I have lived, sir, a long time, and the longer I live, the more convincing proofs I see of this truth: that God governs in the affairs of men. And, if a sparrow cannot fall to the ground without His notice is it probable that an empire can rise without His aid? We have been assured, sir, in the sacred writings, that 'except the Lord build the house, they labor in vain that build it.'*"

—Benjamin Franklin
(as quoted by Jarod Sparks,
The Works of Benjamin Franklin, 1837)

AUTHORS' NOTE

The 13 is a story that we came upon through a great friend and copastor of ours at The Journey Church, where we pastor. Shawn Allen is an amazing, godly man who has been gifted with a great imagination, and we have loved working with him on this novel.

The Journey Church is a multisite church, and Shawn is our pastor at our Hartsville, Tennessee, campus. Before being called into full-time ministry, Shawn was a police officer with the Metro Nashville police force. He is a graduate of Bethel University and is currently attending Southern Seminary. He and his wife, Miranda, live in Lebanon, Tennessee.

In the middle of writing *The Guardian*, our first novel (also available from Barbour Publishing), Shawn came to us with an idea for a story that was ripped right from the headlines of today's newspapers. Erik and I were immediately intrigued and couldn't wait to finish *The Guardian* so we could begin working, with Shawn, to bring *The 13* to life.

Though his name may not be on the cover of this book, make no mistake, Shawn is as much a cowriter of this novel as Erik and I are. His imagination and ability to bring life to characters have been an intricate part of *The 13*. We could never have written this book without him, and we look forward to partnering with him in our next adventure: book two of *The 13*.

Thank you, Shawn, for partnering with us on this great adventure. You are our best friend in life, and in our work.

Robbie & Erik

PROLOGUE

Hidalgo County Sheriff's Department
Edinburg, Texas, July 2, 2025; 10:30 a.m.

Becky Sayers looked at the discolored, flat-screen plasma TV and silently cursed her boss. "You'd think in this world of technology, we could find a TV that wasn't made before I was born," she mumbled to no one. "I mean, this thing's not even in 3-D." A rerun of *Everybody Loves Raymond* was playing—the one in which Raymond fakes going to the doctor so he can play golf. She'd seen it at least four times, but it was one of her favorites.

She pushed back from her desk and stretched her legs. The switchboard had been quiet most of the afternoon. A few drunk-and-disorderlies and a domestic dispute. The holiday weekend usually meant a boring few days at the Hidalgo County Sheriff's Department. But even though Hidalgo County seemed like half a world away from Washington, DC, the impact of the last two weeks' events were being felt. It seemed that everyone was waiting to see what would happen next.

The green light flashed on her board. She placed the earpiece in her ear and said, "Thank you for calling the Hidalgo County Sheriff's Department. This is Becky. . . ."

The caller made her complaint and hung up abruptly. Her neighbors were setting off illegal fireworks; could a deputy come by and take care of it? All of south Texas had experienced a horrible drought these last few months. The governor had issued a decree, suspending all fireworks throughout the entire state. Residents weren't happy, but they understood. Brushfires this time of year were common and could lead to damage in the billions of dollars.

Becky keyed her microphone. "Roy, this is Becky. I need you to go out to Ms. Dobson's farm, out on Highway 83. Neighbor kids are shootin' off sparklers or something."

She waited for the grumpy complaint that was sure to come. Roy hated dealing with neighborly disputes. He always tried to pawn them off on one of the other deputies.

Nothing.

"Roy, this is Becky—come in."

Nothing.

"Roy! I ain't playing! Pick up that radio or else!"

Still nothing.

She switched over to another channel. She couldn't figure why one of her deputies would switch channels, but she was starting to get a little worried. Roy was dependable, if nothing else. He'd never not answered a call while he was out in the field.

"Roy, this is Becky. You change channels on me to try and get some R and R?"

Nothing.

Now she was getting worried. She switched the channel back. "Clay, this is dispatch. Check in—over."

Nothing.

"Marcus, check in—over."

Nothing.

She walked down the hall and found her boss, told him what was going on, and waited for a response. He told her not to worry. It was probably just weather related. "Probably a sunspot or something, messin' with the radios," he said. "Try again in a few minutes."

Back at her desk, she waited, watching the end of the show. As the credits rolled she picked up her microphone. After five minutes of going through the motions again, she decided this was no sunspot.

She grabbed the phone and called the Cameron County Sheriff's office—the next county over. She told them what was going on and asked if they were having any trouble. Gina, the dispatcher over there, said none of her deputies had checked in or returned back to HQ either.

Becky hung up and called Star, Zapata, and Webb Counties. All three reported the same goings-on. At that point, she dismissed paranoia and called the state police. She was told that they, too, had a few officers who weren't responding, but all of the state police vehicles were equipped with GPS and were being located as they spoke. The young man at state police HQ offered to send a few officers her way to check on her deputies as well. She thanked him and told him where her deputies were last known to be.

★

July 4, 2025; 12:00 p.m.

Becky stood in front of her fourth TV camera in the last hour and told her story again. This time it was Fox. NBC and CBS had already been by.

The mysterious disappearance of her deputies two days ago was making national news. Several sheriff's deputies, border patrol agents, and state and local police officers had all turned up dead, all across the border towns in Texas. Over the last two days, New Mexico and Arizona had reported similar tragedies.

Becky was one of the first to discover the disappearances across the border, therefore she was a hot commodity with the news anchors.

The pretty, blond reporter smiled and nodded as Becky told her story. She opened her mouth—Becky figured she was about to ask another question—and then slapped her hand over her left earbud. Her smiled faded and gave way to a look of disbelief, shock, then horror. Tears filled her eyes and her face turned ashen. Her arm dropped to her side, taking the microphone with it.

"What's wrong?" Becky had never seen a television personality act like this.

The reporter turned to her, eyes wide. She moved her mouth but nothing came out.

Becky grabbed the woman by her shoulders and shook her. "Hey, what's wrong?"

The reporter looked at Becky blankly and said, "Bomb. . . They're all dead." Her knees gave out, and she slumped to the hard, dry ground.

Becky ran back inside to the flat-screen TV.

★

Hidalgo County, Texas
July 4, 2025; 11:30 a.m.

Jonathan Keene pulled his car off the road onto the dirt path, according to the directions he'd been given. After a mile, he came to the fork in the road. Up ahead, on the left, there stood the house.

He parked the car, got out, and surveyed the area. Nothing. No sign of anyone. The house was a typical single-family home. It needed a coat of paint, and the railing on the front porch had seen better days. The lawn was unkempt, but a somewhat new-looking satellite dish sat mounted on the corner of the roof.

Walking into the house, he noticed the reflection of light coming from the hillside off to his left. He waited ten minutes. Then, as per his instructions, he left through the back door and walked slowly up the hill toward the reflection.

Once at the top, he got to his knees, placed his hands behind his head, and interlocked his fingers. This was the unsettling part. Out in the open. No cover. The sun blazing in his eyes. The wind blowing dust everywhere. It was hard to see anything past twenty feet. He did feel better, though, knowing that strapped to his back, under his loose shirt, was his Glock 9mm. It lay inches from his fingertips.

After nothing for five minutes, he heard the faint hum of motorcycle engines. Within seconds he was surrounded by a half dozen, armed Mexicans. One, covered with tattoos and a scar across his left cheek, moved toward him. According to the description he'd been given, this was his informant.

"*Hola*," the young man said. "Welcome to Mexico."

Though the walk uphill had been a short one, Keene knew that in doing so, he'd illegally crossed the invisible border into the gangbanger's country.

"*Gracias*." Keene shifted uncomfortably and squinted upward. "You must be Hector."

"Do I need to search you?"

"Not unless you want to find the nine mil I got strapped to my back," Keene said.

Hector laughed. "Stand up."

"So what's so important that you need to talk to the CIA?"

"Follow me." Hector began walking down the hill toward the house.

Keene followed the men back into the house, thankful to be back on sovereign US soil.

"I know what happened to those sheriff's deputies," Hector said.

"Yeah, so. Call the police."

"Nah, CIA, *la policía* don't want none of this."

"None of what?"

"That's a nice watch. Where was that made? China?"

"Yeah," Keene said. "What's that have to do with anything?"

"Lots of stuff in your country made by China."

"Yeah, so?"

"Funny thing. In the last two months, I been seeing lots of Chinese people 'round here."

"Maybe they like the food."

"Maybe," Hector answered. "But these Chinese been coming in droves. In big military trucks. From down south."

"Interesting." Keene gave this some thought.

"You want to know what's really interesting?"

Keene shrugged.

"These Chinese, they got guns."

"So?"

"And tanks. And airplanes."

"What?"

"You heard me. They got an army down here. They been bringing it up here to the border for the last two months."

"Impossible. We would've known about it," Keene said. This guy was unnerving him.

"You wanna know what happened to your cops? About three hundred Chinese foot soldiers, with automatic weapons, crossed your border and took them out. I got boys all up and down the border saying they see it, man. Now, I don't know what's up with a hundred thousand Chinese being in my—"

"What did you say? How many?"

"From what I hear, about a hundred thousand."

Keene's jaw went slack. There was no way a hundred thousand Chinese soldiers were living across the border without the United States knowing about it. Something was wrong.

"You look like you seen a ghost."

"Why are you telling me this? Why now? Why not two months ago?"

" 'Cause two months ago, I couldn'ta cared less. You Americans don't know what goes on down here. You come to your vacation spots and get treated like kings. Then you go back home and don't care what happens to the rest of us. Well, guess what? These Chinese start showing up and doing nice things for our communities. Nobody says anything 'cause they like it. Then, without warning, they start taking over. And our *policía* don't care. They getting paid off. Next thing I know, I start seeing guns, tanks, and fighter planes. And then they come into town and line up five men and shoot them in the head. They say, anyone talks or tries to do anything, they kill the whole town."

"This is—this is ridiculous!" Keene said. "I don't know what your game is, but this isn't funny. You could get into a lot of trouble—"

"I ain't playin'!" Hector shouted angrily. "They kill my little brother, man! And something bad is about to happen! I'm telling you as a favor." He hung his head and wiped his eyes. "I don't know why your government don't know about this, CIA, but I'm telling you. Someone had to mess up big to miss this."

Keene stood there dumbfounded. There was no way this could be true. An entire army couldn't march on the United States' border and not be detected. He had to call Jennings. He reached for his phone and felt the buzz against his leg. He looked at the display. *Funny*, he thought.

"I was just getting ready to call you," he spoke into the mouthpiece.

"Get back here immediately," his boss, Kevin Jennings, ordered.

"Yeah, about that," Keene said, "I think I need to stay here awhile. I need to check something out."

"No, you need to get back here immediately. Turn on the TV."

"What's happened?"

"Just do it!" came the reply.

Keene pushed past the group of men and pushed the button on the television sitting on a makeshift stand. It only took a few moments for him and the others to see what was happening.

Every channel had interrupted programming, now covering the breaking news. Plumes of black smoke rose into the sky from devastated buildings. Bridges and highways melted into a pile of searing red metal. Ash and debris covered the entire landscape. Cars were turned over and blown to bits. Then the camera changed. A new city. Same result. Then another. Then another. Finally the images ended. The cameras returned to the news station. A disheveled-looking man in blue jeans and a sweater sat in front of the camera. He opened his mouth and said the words that would change the course of history.

"Ladies and gentlemen, less than ten minutes ago, the entire West Coast of the United States of America was attacked. It appears to be a nuclear strike. Every major city from San Diego to Seattle. The death toll has to be in the millions. . . ."

PART 1: THE PROPHET

CHAPTER 1

The man sat in front of the small camera, rehearsing what he was about to say. Behind him, the wall was dotted with computer monitors, all displaying different news websites, with the screens zoomed in showing today's date. A bead of sweat rolled down the side of his cheek as he bit into his lower lip, trying to calm himself. He was moments away from doing something that couldn't be undone.

He'd wrestled with himself the last three days, knowing what would happen if he didn't do as he was instructed. He'd cried out in desperation, begging that he wouldn't have to be the one. He'd even tried to bargain his way out of it. But it was no use. This would be done. If not him then someone else. But no. It was his charge. Given to him with explicit instructions. He would be obedient and do as he was instructed.

The clock on the wall ticked down the seconds as he stared into the camera. This was it. In a matter of minutes, his life would change. Everyone's life would change.

He rehearsed his lines, though he knew them by heart. There would be no teleprompter. There would be no script. There would only be him. And the camera, of course. And the person who would receive this message.

A small television sat off to the side, monitoring the feed. He could see his image staring back at him. He watched as the second hand ticked off the final seconds. *Tick. Tick.* And then it was time.

The red light above the lens flicked on. With the remote in his hand, he zoomed in and watched the monitor. This was it. No turning back.

He closed his eyes for a moment and took a deep breath and let it out again. His heart was pounding through his chest. He opened his eyes and set his jaw firm. And then he began.

"Good evening, Mr. President. I am the Prophet. And I have been commanded to give you a message."

CHAPTER 2

The sun had begun to set over Washington, DC, as the streets bustled with the commuters going home from work. Slivering rays of light pierced their way through the buildings, making way for the cool early summer breeze that wound its way off the Potomac and into the city streets. Soon the breeze would give way to the hot midsummer. Soon you would be able to see, as well as feel, the heat wafting up from the pavement, making DC inhabitants wistful for the pleasantries of June.

The president was just a few minutes away from giving his highly antici-pated speech on health-care reform. Rarely did a president call together both chambers of Congress for the purpose of an address to the nation outside of the State of the Union address. But since President Calvin Grant had taken office, it had been one of his major priorities to put an end to all of the infighting with the health-care industry once and for all. This speech was to be the exclamation point at the end of a three-year, grueling bipartisan reform effort. Though it was no secret that the president had been working on the new policy, details of it were. The only thing that had been leaked so far had been the fact that President Grant had successfully achieved what none of his three predecessors could, a comprehensive bill with regulation that all parties agreed upon. Outside of that, not even a hint of what was to come had been available, which had every news anchor and pundit both frustrated and in anticipation.

The news anchors outside the Capitol seemed to be in deep conversa-tion with their cameras, floating their ideas and predictions of what was to come. And then, as if being led by a conductor, they all nodded in unison, each to his respective camera, signifying the president's speech was about to begin.

Inside the chamber of the House of Representatives, significant lead-ers, from both parties, lined the aisleway, hoping to get a photo opportu-nity with President Grant as he passed by. The room, as was typical for this sort of event, was a cacophony of noise as everyone continued conversations and settled in. Finally the outer doors to the House chamber swung open, and the sergeant at arms entered. Immediately the room quieted, as if someone flipped a switch. Then came the announcement.

"Mr. Speaker, the president of the United States!"

As was traditional, the room was again flooded with noise as the members of the Senate and House, along with everyone else in attendance, stood and applauded as the president slowly made his way to the floor of the chamber, shaking hands, signing autographs, and posing for pictures along the way. Finally, with the business of being sociable behind him, President Grant held his hands up to quiet the almost eight-minute opening ovation.

Only a few moments later and the speech was in full swing, and the president had wasted no time in commanding the attention of the entire nation. So far, the speech had lived up to its expectations. With the news of his wife being diagnosed with cancer only a few weeks earlier, he was expected to deliver a stunning blow to the health-care reformers. And with the content of the speech being perhaps *the* closest-kept secret in all of Washington, the entire room, as well as the rest of the country waited on bated breath to hear what the president had to say. That and the fact that President Grant was thought of as perhaps one of the most beloved presidents in recent history, it was a sure bet that this address would go on record as being one of the most viewed events in all of television history, not just presidential history.

Homes all across the country were tuning in to hear what the president would say. Ratings were already pouring in from all over the country. Indeed, this was already a record-setting event. Within the first ten minutes, the reports were already surpassing the collective quarterly ratings. President Calvin Grant had the nation waiting on bated breath for his next thought.

The speech was just over forty-five minutes when, just as promised, President Grant landed his final blow. The news was simple. He had already been working with members of Congress and had the support needed to change the health-care system. His plan would strip away the potential for many of the frivolous lawsuits that plagued the industry. New law was being introduced to allow Americans unprecedented access to good health insurance. And there were major stipulations being put on the insurance companies, regulating how they underwrote policies and collected revenue. No longer would there be massive abuses, deterioration of services, and rising costs. The message was simple. There was about to be a complete overhaul of the American medical system. An overhaul that would eliminate the government-run policies of previous administrations and give the medical field back to the private sector, but with some "seat belts," as President Grant liked to call it.

The speech ended in thunderous applause. And though there had been some lines drawn previously in the speech between parties, the final five minutes brought both sides of the chamber to their feet in rousing cheers.

★

After the speech, President Grant made his way through the chamber, once again pausing for photos and signing autographs. He tried to be as pleasant as he could, but there were bigger things on his mind right now. Tess, his wife, was at home, lying in bed. He wanted nothing more than to get home and see how she felt.

After another fifteen minutes of meet-and-greet obligations, he finally excused himself, reminding everyone where he really needed to be right now. He asked the Secret Service agent in charge of his detail to make ready the motorcade. He wanted to leave in the next few minutes.

The drive back to 1600 Pennsylvania Avenue was quiet. He waved to the guard as the car passed through the security entrance. Once inside, he headed straight upstairs to the private residence.

Tess was lying in bed and greeted him with a huge smile.

"You were amazing, Calvin. I'm so proud of you."

"Nah," he brushed it off. "Just a bunch of no-good politicians trying to make things worse is all we are!"

"I wish I could've been there."

"Me, too, Tess," he said, sitting down on the edge of the bed. He took her hand in his and kissed it gently. "I love you."

"I love you, too," she said.

"I'll leave you to rest," he said, standing back up. "Besides, I'm going to go surf the net and see all the good stuff they're saying about me!" He winked.

Tess smiled back at him and said, "Don't stay up too late. You need your rest."

"Look who's talking."

He left her to sleep and stepped into his private office. He sat down and turned on the monitor to wake up the computer. In just a few moments, the desktop came alive. He opened a browser window and typed in his search. Already, there were over twenty-five thousand results for his speech.

He was looking down the list when he heard a *ding*. His private e-mail.

He assumed it was one of his staff, congratulating him on a successful speech. He decided to check it because, well, he thought at least one positive response would be nice before he started sifting through all the negative ones.

Opening the mail server he saw the new message. There was no subject. There was no return address. He didn't think much of it, so he double-clicked the icon and watched it open. It was a video. And it definitely wasn't from one of his staff. But he was afraid that he knew who this was. And what this was about. He had heard from this man before. Just not like this. *How did you get into my private e-mail?* he thought. He stared at the still image of the man on the screen. Should he call for Agent Green? Should he just step away from the computer and not touch anything? No, he decided. He wanted to see it. He pushed PLAY.

The man sat still on a stool and stared into the camera. A bead of sweat rolled down his forehead and clung to the top of the bandana that covered every inch of his face below the eyes. He wore a plain, long-sleeved, white T-shirt and blue jeans. His shoes were everyday work boots. All in all, a very nondescript, average-looking man—with the exception of the face, of course. Behind him stood a white wall with what appeared to be computer monitors with websites showing today's date.

A few seconds, which might as well have been hours, passed as the strange man closed his eyes and took a deep breath. As he opened his eyes again, he began to speak.

"Good evening, Mr. President. I am the Prophet. And I have been commanded to give you a message."

The man swallowed hard and then continued, "I am a servant of the Lord Most High. And I have been instructed to warn you. Since the days of our forefathers, the United States has become a prosperous nation, strong in her defenses. She has done great moral things in the name of peace and freedom. She has been an open door for those who are in search of something greater. And she has brought stability to the world."

The man blinked hard and wiped the sweat from his brow.

"But," he continued, "'I have this against you,' says the Lord. 'That you have abandoned the love you had at first.'

"Therefore, thus says the Lord, 'Behold, the day of the Lord comes, cruel, with wrath and fierce anger, to make the land a desolation and to destroy its sinners from it. For the stars of the heavens and their constellations will not give their light; the sun will be dark at its rising, and the moon will not shed its light. I will punish the world for its evil, and the wicked for their iniquity; I will put an end to the pomp of the arrogant, and lay low the pompous pride of the ruthless. I will make people more rare than fine gold, and mankind than the gold of Ophir. Therefore I will make the heavens tremble, and the earth will be shaken out of its place, at the wrath of the Lord of hosts in the day of his fierce anger. Behold, my anger and my wrath will be poured out on this place, upon man and beast, upon the trees of the field and the fruit of the ground; it will burn and not be quenched.'

"Yet fourteen days, and the United States shall be overthrown!"

CHAPTER 3

Jon Keene started every day the same. Up at five fifteen, dressed by five twenty-five, and out the door by five thirty. He usually tried to keep at least a seven-minute mile pace, but lately he was beginning to feel the effects of his thirty-seven-year-old body. A couple minor football injuries in his teens, several combat tours in his midtwenties, and a sore back from a recent golf outing were all barking at him right now as he pushed himself through the last quarter mile of his daily run.

He saw the black SUV parked in his driveway from two hundred yards out. Not a big deal. He was used to it. Jennings sent people to fetch him all the time. But not this early. No matter, he wasn't going anywhere without a shower and a quick bite to eat. Whoever it was, probably some errand runner, would just have to wait.

The back window of the Tahoe slid down as he slowed his pace to a walk and made his way alongside the drive.

"Good morning, Jon," the man said.

"Yeah. . .it was." Keene folded his arms and stood stiff.

The door opened and Kevin Jennings, director of the Central Intelligence Agency, stepped out.

"We need to go. I'll give you ten minutes to shower and change."

Keene feigned a smile at his boss. "I'm touched that you came yourself. What? Couldn't find a staffer to come pick me up?"

Jennings dismissed Keene's mock humor. "Ten minutes. And make them good. We're going to see the Man."

Keene noted Jennings's seriousness and turned toward the house without another word. He unlocked the door and went inside.

He took the stairs two at a time, shedding clothes along the way. He had been to the White House a couple times. But never at six o'clock in the morning. Never to meet the president—usually just to pick up a dignitary of some sort. And never escorted personally by the director of the

23

CIA. *Surely this couldn't have anything to do with that quack who hacked the Black-Ops list last week from the CIA,* he thought. "Nah," he said aloud to no one, "probably sending me to bring in some high-level asset from Iran or something."

He turned the lever on the shower and didn't even wait for the water to warm before jumping in. This, too, was part of his ritual. The initial shock to the body of the cold water got his blood pumping and woke him up mentally.

Nine minutes later, Jon Keene stepped out of his house, shirt untucked, tie draped over his shoulder, and a blueberry muffin dangling from his mouth, as he held his coffee in one hand and his keys in the other.

"You could've finished getting dressed," Jennings said.

"You said ten minutes," Keene answered opening the door on the other side.

CHAPTER 4

President Grant checked himself in the mirror and straightened his tie. He had already been up for an hour and a half, not that he'd slept any last night. The video from the man calling himself the Prophet had left a foul taste in his mouth. And not because this Prophet was giving him orders, or trying to. Calvin Grant was not a man given to ego. Yes, he took himself seriously, but only in the sense that he was charged with the most powerful office in the world. In actuality, the office served to humble him.

Calvin Grant, born Calvin Lincoln Grant, was the cliché American dream. He'd spent his youth living in the projects of Nashville, Tennessee, fighting just to stay out of trouble long enough to get the education his mother had begged him to understand was vital to change his life and his economic situation. He had listened to her. And along the way, he quickly learned two important lessons: Those who sought to achieve great things, more often than not achieved great things. But those who sought to serve their fellow man achieved something that no title or amount of money could buy.

He had been in his third year at Middle Tennessee State University when he met his wife. Tess, short for Tessania, had wrecked his world from the moment he laid eyes on her. He had been walking across campus with his head down when he ran into her. Literally. After he knocked her and her books to the ground, he bent down to help her pick up the mess, stringing together a line of apologies. That is, until he looked up and saw her for the first time. Her smile, her eyes, her hair, all captivated him and held his tongue ransom for words.

She had finally broken the silence by introducing herself. He took her hand to shake it and noticed the book she had been holding. A Bible. Before he could turn and leave, she took the initiative and asked if he went to church. He told her that he had, sometimes. On Christmas and Easter, for sure. The look she had given him was one of pity. Then she invited

25

him to a Bible study at a friend's house that night. And the rest, as they say, is history.

Twenty-eight years of marriage, a masters in public policy from Georgetown University and then a law degree from Pepperdine, three kids and a grandchild on the way, and two terms as governor of the great state of Tennessee later, Calvin Grant occupied the highest office of the land. And having just finished his morning quiet time in the scriptures, he was about to walk into a meeting that scared him for sure. One that he had asked for, but nevertheless the subject of this meeting shook him to his core. It would not be fun. For anyone present. For what he was about to suggest would immediately call into question his sanity, and quite possibly his ability to run the country.

President Grant stepped out of the bathroom, bumping into the door frame, and back into the bedroom, where Tess was stirring.

"You look beautiful this morning, darling."

"And you are still a handsome old klutz," she said as she sat up smiling. "Come here and let me fix that tie. You can't go anywhere looking like that."

President Grant shuffled over to the bed and sat down. He let Tess straighten the Windsor before he reached for her hands.

"Pray with me, Tess. This meeting is going to get heated. Fast."

The seriousness was not lost on his wife. She held his face in her hands and said, "Calvin, you are the most God-honoring man I've ever met. You have been blessed by the Lord with this position. You and I both know that He has ordained this. Whether this guy from last night is a crazy person or for real, you are the right man to be in this office right now. You just go in that room and lead those men. Trust that God will give you wisdom. And at the end of the day, God's will most definitely will prevail. Now, let's pray."

Holding his wife's hands in his, he bowed his head.

CHAPTER 5

Megan Taylor sat in her green Volkswagen Bug on the DC beltway in bumper-to-bumper traffic. Not even seven a.m. and already traffic was backed up as far as the eye could see. Oh well, that's what she got for living outside the city. Sure, rent was a lot cheaper, but some days she wondered if it was worth sitting for over an hour each way in this mess.

It wasn't like it truly mattered, though. She had no personal life. What life she did have, she spent losing countless hours of sleep, poring over data that was supposed to keep things like what happened last week with the CIA Black-Ops list from happening.

Megan had known from the age of thirteen she wanted to be an FBI agent. She had read several novels depicting a heroine FBI agent who somehow always seemed to save the world right at the last minute. She was hooked after the first novel. She spent her teenage years learning everything she could about the Bureau. She became heavily entrenched in team sports. Lacrosse, swim team, and softball were all favorites. But it was soccer that won her the most attention. And it was soccer that landed her a full ride to Harvard, where she took advantage of the free education. Somewhere along the line, Megan realized she had a knack, a gift actually, for computers. And it was this gift that got her noticed by the same agency she had set out to conquer in the first place. They took notice, all right. Just not the way she had intended.

Megan had opened her door one night to a sorority sister who looked like she'd been up all night crying. It seemed that the friend's ex-boyfriend, a computer savant himself, had taken it upon himself to share with the entire Harvard faculty a few photos her friend had never posed for. The pictures had been doctored to look like she was stealing and then copying student records from the records office. Once Megan had identified the program the hacker had used, she turned it around on him. But in her version, not only was he the one who now seemed to be the thief, but some of the people he seemed to be selling to were known drug dealers and criminals in the area.

Typically, the two students would've found themselves being dragged before some committee that would decide their fates. However, the fact that the ex-boyfriend was the FBI director's son gathered a little more attention than she had planned for. But in the end, she had impressed the man so much with her skills that he offered her a job. Two weeks after graduating, she took him up on his offer.

That seemed like a lifetime ago. It was mind-blowing how quickly eight years could pass, she thought, as the traffic slowly began to move. She had just put her turn signal on to make her way to the exit lane when her phone rang.

"Taylor," she said, wedging the phone between her shoulder and her ear. The little stick shift was fun and convenient to drive in almost every case, except in traffic and on the phone.

"Pull over," Bill Preston, director of the FBI ordered.

"On the Beltway, sir?" she asked confused. "I'm about to get off the exit for the office."

"Not anymore," Preston said.

She immediately felt uncomfortable. "Sir, I don't understand. Is something wrong? Am I in trouble for something?"

Preston laughed into the phone. "No, you're not in trouble."

"Then what? I mean, is there something going on at the office?"

"No. Everything's fine. Just pull over to the side of the road."

"Director Preston, I really have a lot going on this week. I have a deadline for that job over in Georgetown."

"Yeah. . .you can maybe get to that in a little while. Right now, change of plans. Your presence is requested at 1600 Pennsylvania Avenue in fifteen minutes."

"Ha! First of all, that's funny! I mean, really. That's cute, sir. But even *if* it weren't a horribly bad joke, it would take me an hour at best to get to the White House. And why the White House, anyway?"

"Can you see behind you in your rearview?"

"Yes, sir. Why?"

"Keep watching."

Megan stared into the mirror and saw two black SUVs approaching from the shoulder of the road at a quick clip. They were about half a mile back.

"You see them?" Preston asked again.

"I see two Bureau trucks coming down the shoulder. Coming up fast."

"Good, I want you to pull your car onto the shoulder and wait for them."

Megan laughed. "You're kidding, right? I'm *seriously* going to the White House?"

"Agent Ross will take your car. He'll drive it to work for you. You get in the second truck. I'll brief you on the way."

The conversation was over because the line went dead. No matter. She was at a loss for words anyway, so she just followed orders and pulled onto the shoulder of the road and turned her flashers on as the SUVs pulled in behind her. The passenger door on the second truck opened; Preston stuck his arm out to help Megan in then closed the door. The big truck was already moving.

"So, you're serious?"

"He asked for you by name," Preston said.

"But I've never even met the president." Megan shook her head.

"Well, I might have had something to do with that," Preston nodded to her.

CHAPTER 6

The driver of the lead SUV flashed his credentials out the window as the two-car motorcade entered the grounds of possibly the most secure facility in the world. The armed security guard looked them over and motioned him on through. Jennings lowered the window knowing they were next.

"Director Jennings," the guard nodded. "Good morning, sir."

Jennings nodded back. He thumbed at Keene and said, "He's with me. Grant is expecting us."

"Yes, sir. You know the way."

The guard stepped aside and motioned their driver to move ahead. The big truck carried on for a few feet before coming to a stop. Keene immediately fell in behind Jennings as they moved through the security check into the West Wing. Chief of Staff Lewis Hardy met them in the hall passing the Rose Garden.

"Lewis." Jennings shook the man's hand.

"Kevin." And then to Keene, "And that would make you Jon Keene."

"Nice to meet you." Keene offered his hand.

"This way, gentlemen. President Grant is expecting you."

Keene shot his boss a sideways glance when they continued on past the Oval Office. Jennings shrugged his shoulders as if to say, *I don't know.* As if reading their minds, Hardy looked over his shoulder and said, "Your meeting will be taking place in the residence this morning, gentlemen."

This time it was Jennings who gave the bewildered look. Keene shrugged it off. *What's the difference,* he thought. *It's his house. He can hold a meeting wherever he wants, right?*

The three men turned the corner and entered the elevator that would take them to the private residence. The doors opened and they stepped out. Down the hall and through a door they found President Grant sitting, sipping what smelled like a fresh cup of coffee. Immediately he stood and greeted his guests.

"Kevin. Thank you for coming. And you must be Mr. Keene."

"It's a pleasure to meet you, Mr. President," Keene said taking the firm handshake.

"Please, call me Calvin. In here, I'm *Mr. Tessania Hall.*" He smirked and laughed.

"I heard that, Calvin."

"I know you did, dear. I said it for you!" Then in a hushed voice to the men standing with him, "Key to a successful marriage: always let her think she's the boss." Again he let out a small snort.

Tess came around the corner and gave him the *what-for* look. "I heard that, too, *Mr. Tessania Hall.*" She entered the room and said her hellos to everyone. Then, giving her husband a kiss on the cheek, she dismissed herself.

"Kevin, Mr. Keene," President Grant turned his attention back to his guests, "you two make yourselves at home. Can I get you a coffee or something while we wait?"

"Uh, I'm fine, Mr. President," Keene said. "I'm sorry. I guess I didn't understand, we're waiting for someone else to join us?"

"Three, actually," the President replied.

"Three. . .other people?"

"Yes, Mr. Keene." As if on cue, the door to the private office opened up, and in walked the director of the FBI followed by someone Keene had never seen before. "And here are the first two now."

"Gentlemen," President Grant said to Jennings and Keene, "I believe you all know Director Preston of the FBI." The men exchanged greetings. "And this," Grant continued, "must be Megan Taylor. Computer software technician extraordinaire."

Keene watched as the woman introduced herself to the president and Jennings. She was very attractive—seemed to be in her late twenties, early thirties. Her shoulder-length brunette hair was feminine, yet business professional. She had the look of someone who didn't have a hard time getting what she wanted—and at the same time, she had that *don't-mess-with-me-or-I'll-put-you-in-your-place-quickly* look. He thought she looked to be somewhat athletic, for a computer nerd. Not the typical horn-rimmed glasses and braces on the skinny beanpole frame of a girl. He noticed that she didn't wear any jewelry other than a small pair of earrings in the shape of a cross. No wedding ring. That didn't surprise him, given his assessment of her. She looked like she could be a royal pain in the—

"Hello, I'm Megan Taylor." She stuck out her hand and was waiting for Keene to shake.

He took her hand and immediately regretted underestimating the woman's grip. *Definitely a pain in the—*

"If you all would," President Grant interrupted, "please go ahead and take a seat. Our final guest should be arriving any second."

The others sat down as the door to the private office opened again. And again, someone Keene had never seen before entered the room.

The man looked to be in his early forties. He had a quiet demeanor but a strong gait to his walk. He was casually dressed, wearing a pair of khaki pants and an untucked button-down shirt. He had boots and a watch that said military, but Keene was sure it was formerly, not currently. He knew the type. Glad to be out, but somehow just couldn't let go of that fashionable military look. He took note of the ink that peeked out from under the man's rolled-up sleeve. He'd seen tattoos like that before. Had one himself, though slightly different: Special Ops, no one he'd crossed paths with. And that made this man even more intriguing.

President Grant opened his arms and embraced the new guest. They stood together in a big, manly bear hug for several seconds. Finally Grant let the man go and said, "Boz, I'm so glad you're hear."

"Glad I could make it, Calvin."

"Everyone, this is Bozwell Hamilton. Boz. He is a very dear friend of mine. We've known each other for quite a while and have a long history together. But we'll get into that later."

They all stood again and took turns introducing themselves to the stranger called Boz.

"Now then," Grant finally continued. "If everyone's ready, let's get to it."

CHAPTER 7

The Prophet finished his morning prayers and stood from his knees. He half expected someone to break down his door any minute now. If he was honest, he'd half expected it to happen while he was taping his message last night.

He had never been assured of his safety. But to be honest, safety was never part of the deal. And he knew that. He accepted that the day he gave his life. None of his predecessors had been guaranteed safety. Why should he? If he had to really take inventory of his situation, the possibility truly existed that he, too, would be persecuted.

No matter. The message was to be given. That was the command. Tell them. And that's what he would do.

He had been fasting for seven days leading up to the taping. Today he would break his fast. He set about fixing the small meal of oatmeal and toast. His body was weak. He needed the food. And he wanted more. But he also knew that if he were to eat a big meal, he would be sick. His system wouldn't be able to handle it after seven days of just water. So he bowed his head and gave thanks for the food set before him.

He ate slowly, so as to not upset his stomach. Though he was in great physical condition, he could feel the effects of the fast. His muscles felt atrophied. Weak. His skin looked pale. Clammy. His head was still pounding from the headache he'd suffered the last two days. Slowly, bite by bite, he could feel his energy begin to return.

He finished and set the bowl and cup in the sink. The small breakfast was a good start. He would make sure to have a bigger lunch. And a protein bar for a snack in between. Or two.

Feeling a little better, he turned from the small kitchen and walked the three steps into the living area. He grabbed the book and thumbed through the pages. Its bindings were coming loose. He had scribbled notes and references throughout. If he hadn't known its contents so well, he might not have been able to make out the words.

He spent the next hour flipping through the worn pages, reading the contents both silently and aloud. He went through his favorite passages and then settled on a particular title. This was perhaps his favorite section. It spoke boldly. It brought condemnation but offered refuge and salvation. He felt the tears well up inside as he read. No matter how many times he read it, it always had the same effect on him.

After the reading, he spent another hour in prayer. His knees hurt from the hard wooden floor. The carpet had been torn up long ago. The previous tenants of the small apartment all but destroyed the place. Some would say it wasn't fit for someone to live in. But it was cheap. And it was unassuming.

And he needed to stay that way. Because last night was not the first warning. There had been three previous ones. And, he was sure, there would be more.

CHAPTER 8

Keene took his seat, along with the other two guests, as President Grant had asked. The two directors, however, remained standing. Keene thought that odd. He guessed they were going to speak, too, about whatever it was that brought him here at this ridiculous hour in the morning. But then something different happened. President Grant thanked the two men for bringing Keene and the FBI girl in. And he walked them back to the elevator.

"Any idea what's going on here?" Taylor whispered to him and the other guy.

Keene shrugged his shoulders. Hamilton shook his head.

When he returned, the president reached into his desk. "Before we start, I think it's important that the two of you know"—he nodded to Keene and Taylor—"that Jennings and Preston are aware of the content of our meeting this morning. They are not staying because they have a debriefing with Director Levy this morning. And you all are probably wondering why I've called you here today. So let's get to it." President Grant leaned on the front of the desk, facing his three remaining guests. In his hands were three envelopes. Nothing significant, just plain white number-ten envelopes.

Keene watched as the man called Boz shifted in his seat and produced a little worn book and began thumbing through the pages.

"You all know my thoughts on God and faith," the president continued. "I've never tried to hide it. I've never backed down from it. I talk openly about it. Ever since the first night I met Tess and went to that Bible study, my life has been different."

He passed an envelope to each of his guests. Each one had written on it, *To the President of the United States.*

"What you have there are three separate letters. Each written, I believe, by the same person."

Keene opened his envelope and carefully took out the single, letter-sized page. He quickly skimmed the contents. The words were scribbled but legible. Two short paragraphs.

"Beginning three months ago, I received the first one, the one you have in your hands, Mr. Keene. One month to the day I received the next." He motioned to Taylor. "And then, one month ago yesterday, I received that one." He nodded to the man called Boz.

Keene looked at the FBI agent and the stranger. Taylor seemed as confused as he was, but the man called Boz looked as if he had a better grasp on what was going on.

"Excuse me, Mr. President," Keene said. "Why are you showing these to us? Wouldn't this be an FBI thing?"

"Because, I believe it's the same man who sent me this last night. I'll get to *why you* in a minute." He reached behind him and turned the monitor of his computer around to face them. The video was up and ready to go. He pushed PLAY.

The three of them sat silently watching, listening to the man on the screen. When it finished, Keene was already fidgeting in his chair. The president held up his hands and continued.

"I know what you're thinking, Mr. Keene. I can assure you. I'm taking it seriously now. But do you even know how many letters like this the White House gets every day?"

Keene didn't answer. He did know.

"Usually," Grant continued, "these don't even see the light of day. Someone sends them over to the FBI, and that's that. If there's a credible threat, I get a briefing and we move forward."

"But these did." It was Taylor.

"Yes, Ms. Taylor. But not because someone over at your agency thought they deserved special attention. These three letters"—he reached out and took them back—"never made it to any agency."

"I don't understand," Taylor said.

"Four months ago, I came downstairs, as I always do, and met Chief of Staff Hardy in the hallway. As we always do, we walked to the Oval Office and I listened as he gave me a brief summary of the day's events. Then, as is my routine, I went into the office, where I spend fifteen minutes every morning in prayer and reading my Bible. As I sat down at the desk, I noticed this"—he singled out the first envelope—"sitting in the middle of my desk.

"Naturally, I flipped it open and read it. As you saw, it was a warning. I don't know why, but I decided not to say anything then."

"With all due respect, sir," Keene said, "that was irresponsible."

"I'm well aware of that, Mr. Keene." The president's glance was a warning. "Usually, the first thing I would do is call Lewis Hardy in here and begin asking questions. For some reason, one that I cannot explain right now, I didn't feel the need to take it any further. I placed the letter inside my jacket pocket, and two minutes later my first appointment walked through the door."

"What about the others?" Taylor asked.

"The second one came in the same way—I found it on my desk. One month later, to the day."

Keene raised his eyebrows and blew out a long, loud breath.

Grant gave him a stern look. "I understand your disapproval. I will remind you again that you are here at my request. Please, let me finish."

Keene shifted his gaze and lowered his head.

"Thank you," the president continued. "All that matters at this point is this: I believed these letters to be of no threat. I kept them to myself because, well, whoever wrote them is right! This nation has lost its way. We are all but morally bankrupt as a nation. I kept them to myself to remind me that we—I—have work to do in this office.

"I'm well aware of the path America is on. And this man is right. If something doesn't change soon, we are no longer going to be the country that our forefathers bled and died for! I kept the letters as a reminder to me that we are all at God's mercy. And I wanted to use them as motivation for me to help lead this country back to where it came from."

"So then. . ." Taylor began, waiting to see if she'd be barked at for speaking.

The president nodded for her to continue.

"So then. . .why not just send these over to the FBI? I'm sure Director Preston—"

"Because," the president interrupted, "last night changed everything."

Finally! Keene thought. The president was coming to his senses.

"As far as the nation is concerned," Grant continued, "this goes no further than this office. Do you understand?"

Keene was standing up to go. He was about to lose his mind. He wanted to be out the door five minutes ago, looking for this guy.

"Let me finish what I want to tell you and the others, Mr. Keene, and I'll gladly hear your thoughts and objections."

Keene forced himself back down into the chair and sat still.

"Mr. Hamilton." President Grant shifted to his friend. "Would you please. . ."

The man flipped through the pages of the little book he had taken out earlier and began to read. "Behold, the day of the Lord comes, cruel, with wrath and fierce anger, to make the land a desolation and to destroy its sinners from it. For the stars of the heavens and their constellations will not give their light—"

"That's what that kook just said on the video," Keene said. He narrowed his eyes and leaned in. "Who are you?" He glared at Hamilton.

The president held up a hand.

Keene broke his stare and looked back to Grant. "My apologies, sir."

"It's scripture, Mr. Keene," Boz said.

"From the book of Isaiah," Taylor added.

"That is correct, Ms. Taylor," Boz said. "Isaiah thirteen. Verses nine through thirteen. And then Jeremiah, and then, though the number of days is changed, Jonah."

"I don't understand," Keene said.

"The speech," President Grant explained. "The Prophet's speech on the video is a collection of Old Testament prophets' words. Warnings to nations to repent or have God's wrath poured out on them."

"Fourteen days means the Fourth of July," Taylor said.

"Yes, it does, Ms. Taylor," President Grant said. "And that is why I've called you all here."

"But isn't this different from the letters?" Keene asked. "And I don't know that I'd go ahead and give this guy a nickname just yet. *The Prophet?*"

"I agree," Taylor spoke up.

"I can promise you, as of now, I am taking this seriously, though as far as the American public is concerned, we aren't. There's no need to panic them. But our country will celebrate Independence Day in two weeks. If this man is a terrorist and threatening our country, I want you to stop him before it happens."

"What do you mean? If?" Keene asked.

"You three are the best at what you do," Grant said. "You don't know him, but Boz here has military experience. I'll let him tell you about that. But what you both need to know," he nodded at Keene and Taylor, "is that Boz is a pastor. He still works with the army, now and again, but not as a soldier. As a pastor. He is a good friend of mine, and I trust his judgment on all matters of faith."

Keene tried not to make a sour face. He was beginning to have a good idea of where this conversation was headed. And he didn't like it. Not one bit.

"I have decided," Grant continued, "that the three of you will work together on this. To personally report back to me and answer to no one else *but* me. You will have the full resources of both your agencies and this office. I want you to find out everything you can about this *Prophet*. Everything. Who he is, where he came from, how he did this, all of it."

"What about Homeland Security?" Taylor asked. "We'll need to get this cleared by Director Levy. Won't we?"

"You let me worry about Marianne Levy," President Grant said. "It is still within my purview to use agents at my discretion. You three do what I've asked you to."

Keene spoke up. "With all due respect, sir, I understand why I would be put on an assignment like this. And I'm at your service, sir. But I don't need these two to help me find this guy. Give me a week, and I'll have everything from where he was born to where he used the bathroom last. They'll just get in my way."

President Grant took a deep breath. "*With all due respect*," he said smiling, "I'm very intimate with your file. I have no doubts of your abilities. But I also know their limits. This man hacked into my private e-mail. Last time I checked, you weren't a computer genius. Ms. Taylor here is the best. And unless you can tell me how he did it, Ms. Taylor is with you. If she can't tell us how this guy did it, then I'm forced to consider other options."

Keene still disagreed with the man, but he was the president of the United States. He would take this up with Jennings after he got out of here. "And what other options would those be?"

"Me," Boz answered.

Keene gave a confused look. "I don't understand. I'll concede the computer thing, for now. But I don't need a preacher to help me catch a terrorist who has decided to use some ancient Bible mumbo-jumbo to scare people and threaten our country."

"Mr. Keene," the president looked for the first time like a worried man, "did you ever stop to think, even for a second—as far-fetched as it may sound to you—this man may not be a terrorist?"

CHAPTER 9

"This is ridiculous!" Keene said. He walked back and forth in front of Jennings's desk, scuffing the newly polished hardwood. "I'm not about to go traipsing around the city with a computer nerd and a chapy trying to find him—"

"Hey!" Jennings stood up and put a halt to his operative's rant. "Sit down," he said, motioning to a chair.

Keene was still fuming and just looked at his boss.

"I said, sit down!" Jennings said, matching Keene's tone.

Keene reluctantly took the seat.

"Let me tell you something," Jennings continued as he sat back down. "When the president of the United States calls you at three thirty in the middle of the night and tells you—not asks, *tells* you—to bring someone to see him, you don't ask questions. You do it! This is top priority, as far as he's concerned. He asked me who the best guy I had was. Unfortunately, for both of us, that's you! And if he decides to send you and this computer girl and this. . .this. . ."

"Chapy."

"What?" Jennings looked at him.

"Chapy, chaplain. Military pastor."

"Whatever. Then the three of you are going to do exactly what he asks. Do I make myself clear?"

"There's something you need to know, man." Keene stopped and chose his words carefully. "I think the president may be a little misguided on this."

"What's that supposed to mean?"

"Man, you know!" Keene said, waiting for Jennings to catch on.

Jennings stared blankly at him.

"C'mon, Kevin. Look, I'm not trying to suggest that the president is some religious zealot. But everyone knows his stand on faith and God. He actually suggested that this *Prophet* might not be a terrorist."

Jennings stood back up, "I don't care if this guy thinks he's Moses himself. The president has asked—no, *told*—you that you're on this. Whatever thoughts you have about God and faith are your problem. *Our* problem is finding who this guy is and what organization he belongs to before he does it again. Or worse. And that means you do whatever you need to do to get it done. Understood?"

Keene watched as Jennings walked over to the door and opened it.

"This is ridiculous!" Keene said, leaving the office the same way he came in.

CHAPTER 10

Bill Preston looked up as the door to his office opened.

"How did the rest of your meeting go?"

"Oh, it went great!" Taylor said, her words dripping with sarcasm.

She plopped herself down in the chair in front of her boss's desk. Preston continued looking over the document he had in front of him.

"Sir, he wants an answer for how this happened."

"Okay, so give him one." When Taylor said nothing, he finally put the document down and looked at her. "Actually, I'd like one, too. Care to share?"

"Funny." Taylor grimaced. "You and I both know this is going to take some time. I've got to reverse-engineer the pathway and find out where it came from. Maybe then I can tell you more."

"Well then," Preston said, "better get to it."

"Let me ask you something, sir."

Preston nodded to her.

"How well do you know the president?"

"How do you mean?"

"I mean, how well do you know him? Are you purely business? Do you ever see him socially? Do your wives know each other? Are you—"

"Friends?" Preston finished her sentence for her. "No, not really. I mean, I've been to several of his functions. We've seen each other, on occasion, outside of federal business. He's the president of the United States, Taylor. It's not like he just goes out and hangs with the guys. Why?"

"I don't want you to think I'm jumping to conclusions. . . ."

"But?"

"But, well, the president has known about this guy from the video for three months now and hasn't said anything to anyone."

Preston just looked at her.

"Don't you think that's a little strange?"

Preston pursed his lips. "Strange? No. Breach of protocol, yes. But

Grant has his reasons."

Immediately she regretted saying anything. If her boss new about this and didn't follow up with it, it could mean congressional hearings if something else were to happen as a result of keeping it quiet.

"Sir, I don't want to start any trouble."

"Too late for that now, Taylor. What are you talking about?"

Taylor felt the buzz inside her jacket. She fished the phone out and hit the button, grateful for the interruption.

"Taylor here."

"It's Keene."

"Hold on."

She pulled the phone away and covered it with her hand and whispered, "It's that Jon Keene guy. From the White House this morning. I probably should take this."

She backed out of the door and put the phone back to her ear, leaving her boss sitting where she found him.

"I'm back, what can I do for you, Mr. Keene?"

"First of all, it's Jon. Or Keene. Either one of those is fine. Never Mr. Keene, got it?"

"Yeah, sure." She pulled the phone away and looked at it and mouthed, *Whatever!*

"Where are you?"

"At my office. Why?"

"Good, I'm outside. Black Pathfinder with black wheels. I'm in the visitor spot. Let's go."

"Go where? I'm not going anywhere with you."

"You heard the man. We're on this together. And you also heard him say I'm lead on this. Now let's go. We're going to see a guy. If you're not out here in five minutes, I'm going by myself, and I'll tell Grant you chose not to participate."

The line went dead.

Taylor went from zero to fuming in a snap. First, she'd been in the same room with Keene and the president. She had not even once heard the president say Keene was in charge. Second, she had other things to be doing right now. Trying to find the source of that recording from last night, to start with. Not riding around in a car with some CIA macho wannabe superspy.

Nevertheless, the CIA was known for turning up people who didn't want to be found. She needed to know who this particular someone was and if he was going to shed any light on the situation.

She grabbed her bag from her desk and headed out the door.

CHAPTER 11

Lewis Hardy, the president's chief of staff, stood in front of his boss, pleading his case for the third time. It really was a matter of perception, he argued. The American people deserved to know that there was a possible threat.

"I'm not about to go out there and tell the people some guy sent me a private e-mail threatening this nation. Have you lost your mind?"

"I'm not suggesting that, sir," Hardy said. "But if you at least let *me* go out there and just announce that we've had some chatter increase and we're raising the threat level in order to take all precautions, we'll at least be covering our butts if something should happen."

"And Marianne Levy will drag me before some judiciary committee and try to impeach me."

"Mr. President, this could be serious."

"I'm well aware of that. And I will meet with Director Levy and ask her if she is aware of anything out of the ordinary. We'll take it from there."

"And if she agrees with me?"

"Then we'll revisit this and decide how to inform the American people."

"And I'll twist his arm to make sure." Boz, silent until this moment, spoke at last.

Hardy looked relieved. "Yes, sir. Thank you!" Then to Boz, "And thank *you*."

Boz nodded to him and smiled as Hardy turned and left the room.

"You're not telling Levy anything. Are you?" Boz asked as Hardy disappeared.

"Nope."

Boz laughed and said, "But we both know Lewis is right. You don't go out there, and this becomes a whole 'nother level of big deal. . . ."

"Yeah, you're probably right. But what if it *is* a whole 'nother level?"

Grant made the fake quotation marks with his fingers.

"That's why I'm here, isn't it?" Boz said, already knowing the answer.

"Boz, I don't want to scare anyone, but you and I both know that if this is not some terrorist making threats, we have a big problem on our hands."

"Correction," Boz said. He walked to the window and pointed outside. "If this guy isn't a terrorist. . ." He let it hang there for a moment. "That's a lot of people out there, Calvin." He paused, looking out at the city. "We'll all have a big problem."

CHAPTER 12

So where are we going?" Taylor asked. Keene drove the black Pathfinder with a race car driver's skill, swerving in and out of traffic. "And why are we driving like this?"

"We're going to see a friend," Keene answered.

She was silent again. This was how it had been since he picked her up. A few short exchanges and then nothing. Keene wasn't giving out any information, and he could see it was beginning to frustrate her.

"Hey, let's get something straight, okay?" she said.

Keene noted the tone in her voice. "What's that?"

"I know you're not that excited to be working with me. That's fine. I'm not that keen on working with you either. No pun intended."

Keene showed a hint of a smile. "That's actually funny. I've never heard that before."

She looked at him sourly.

"No, I'm serious," he laughed. "I've never heard that. You would think with my last name, someone would've used it before. Never heard it."

"Glad I could amuse you."

"Hey, look. I'm not trying to be confrontational here. I'm just saying. Jeez, lighten up, Taylor. It's no wonder no one likes working with you."

Taylor whirled around on him. "What! Where did you hear that? I'll have you know, I get along with everyone! And in my job, I don't work with anyone because my work doesn't require me to!"

Keene didn't know anything about her. But he was finding out everything he wanted right now.

CIA operatives are taught many things; one of the first things is how to read people. Information can be elicited just by introducing certain topics to a conversation without ever asking a direct question. And right now, Keene was confirming what he already knew. This Taylor was a close-kept, smart woman who wasn't afraid to mix it up with anyone. Maybe he was going to like her after all.

"Look," Keene said. "I think we got off on the wrong foot."

He stuck his hand out to her.

"My name's Jon Keene, CIA."

She looked at the offered hand and took it reluctantly.

"I'm going to be honest with you, Taylor. First of all, I'm not too excited about you and this chapy being on my team."

"Chapy?"

Keene blew out a big sigh. "Doesn't anyone know what a military preacher is called? Chaplain, chapy. Whatever! I mean, I don't even go to church and I know this!"

Taylor didn't say anything.

"Anyway," he continued, "I know you aren't crazy about working with me, either. But that doesn't change the fact that Grant has us together. So here's the deal. In my line of work, you get paired with someone, you don't trust him with anything. 'Cause if you do, you usually end up getting burned. I trust my boss, Jennings. And that's about it. And he tells me I have to trust you and this chapy. So whatever. We're here, and that's that. Any questions?"

"Just one," she said. "I don't remember Grant putting you in charge."

"That wasn't a question."

"Okay. How 'bout this. Are you going to be a pain my rear end the whole time we're working together?"

Keene smiled as he pulled the car into the alleyway. He watched as Taylor unbuckled her seat belt and reached behind her and pulled out her gun. She checked her magazine, put it back in, and then racked the slide. She put it back in the holster and looked at him.

"So who we going to see?" she said with an impatient look.

"Planning on shooting someone?"

"I thought all you CIA boys liked to play with guns."

Keene reached back and pulled out his own weapon, repeated the same process she just had and said, "Only when they won't give us grenades. Let's go."

He opened the door and got out. He watched as she bent down and unnecessarily tightened the laces on her shoes, giving herself a few seconds to visually sweep the area. Maybe she wasn't just a computer geek, he thought. She at least had some sense about her. He was starting to like this girl. Even if he didn't like the situation. He decided she was okay.

"Don't worry, Taylor," he tried to assure her. "If I thought someone was going to come out gunning for us, I wouldn't have brought you."

That was a lie. This area of town was not the kind of place that anyone wanted to be. Including the people who lived here.

He was actually kind of glad he had seen Taylor check her gun and her reaction when she stepped out of the truck. For all he knew, the guy they were here to see. . .was probably going to answer the door with his own gun.

Now all he had to do was try not to get her killed.

CHAPTER 13

The Prophet finished his sandwich and tea. He left the cup and plate on the table. He had wanted to wait until lunch to actually eat. But after the small breakfast so early in the morning and his system slowly coming around to the idea of solid food again, it wasn't long before his insides felt like they were trying to eat themselves. Figuring the effects of the fast were quickly subsiding, he allowed himself to eat the sandwich.

This time his body quickly responded with a burst of energy. He no longer felt weak and lethargic. He could feel the blood pumping through his veins. He felt alive! He grabbed his coat and hat and stepped out of the small apartment.

Chicago was unusually cool for this time of year. Just last week, they had had a cold front drop in from Canada, and the temperature had dropped back down into the sixties. You never knew what you were going to get in the Windy City.

It was three blocks to the train station and then a twenty-minute ride into the city. It would give him time to read the papers and see what everyone was saying. He had to admit, he was curious to see how the people would take it.

He passed by a newsstand on the corner and picked up the *New York Times*, the *Chicago Sun-Times*, *USA Today*, and two tabloids. He tossed the attendant a twenty-dollar bill and told him to keep the change. He pulled his jacket collar up and kept walking.

On the train, he found a seat in the back and lay the papers down beside him. He got situated and grabbed the top one, the *Times*. The headline was: "President Grant's Health-Care Bomb: Pipe Dream?" He continued thumbing through them, sure that something would be there. But there was nothing. Why was the president still ignoring him? He didn't understand.

When he was chosen and told to do this, he was told President Grant was a good man, one who loved his God and his country. That he understood America had changed and was far from what her forefathers had intended her to be. Why, then, would he not listen?

The train stopped and he got out. He walked a few blocks over and entered a diner. His appetite was coming back with a vengeance. He sat down, ordered some coffee and a sandwich, as he continued to try and think about what was happening. He didn't understand. But he would do as he was told.

He was more saddened than anything. He knew what was coming. He had been told. And it broke his heart. It wasn't a joke. It wasn't a hoax. And unless the president took his warnings seriously, it definitely wasn't going to be stopped.

CHAPTER 14

Who did you say this is?" Taylor asked, falling in behind her new partner.

"I didn't," Keene said.

They made their way around back to a metal door. Taylor continued to look around as Keene rapped his knuckles on the big steel frame. The fact that he had his other hand behind him, his fingers lightly resting on the gun tucked in his waistband, was not comforting to her. She quickly did the same.

"Open up, Artie!" Keene shouted. "I know you're in there!"

A few seconds passed and then a muffled voice.

"Who is it?"

"It's your mom!" Keene shouted back. "Open up or I'll kick it in!"

The sound of several latches could be heard on the other side of the door. Then it opened up a few inches, still attached to a chain.

"Aw, man!" the squeaky voice said. "C'mon, Keene. What do you want?"

Apparently, Taylor thought, she wasn't the only one Keene had this effect on.

"Open the door."

The door opened and a skinny man with a scraggly beard stood there. He wore an open bathrobe and slippers; underneath he sported a T-shirt with a picture of a Commodore 64 computer on it that read *Old School*. His Nike gym shorts were baggy, and his legs looked like toothpicks sticking out from them.

Taylor laughed and pointed at his shirt. "My dad had one of those."

"Got one in the back," Artie said proudly. "Still play some of the old games on it."

Inside, the door gave way into a dimly lit open space. It looked like a warehouse, but given the décor—what little there was—it was obvious Artie lived there.

"I guess you can come on in," Artie said as Taylor watched Keene push his way past the little man.

"This is Taylor," Keene said. "She's with the FBI."

"Aw, man," Artie said incredulously. "What's wrong with you? How you gonna bring FBI in here, bro? I thought we were boys."

"Artie," Keene said, "you're a computer hacker and a lifelong criminal. I'm a government agent. We aren't, nor have we ever been, *boys.*"

"C'mon," Artie said. "Why you busting my chops? I ain't done nothing."

"That's exactly why we're here."

"What?" Artie stared at them with a confused look. Taylor got the joke.

"Double negative. *Ain't done nothing.* Means you have done something."

Artie looked even more confused.

"You're not that bright. Are you?" Taylor said.

"Don't let him fool you," Keene said. "Artie here's smarter than he looks. And he's got a lot of cool toys."

"Yeah, so?" Artie said defensively. "Ain't no law against having computer equipment."

"Yeah," Taylor said, "but what do you do with all this computer equipment?"

"None of your business, lady," Artie snapped.

"You better watch it," Keene warned. "She's not playing. If she shoots you, I'll just say you drew down on her."

"Oh yeah, right! With what? My finger?"

"No," Taylor said. "With that .38 you got tucked in your shorts."

She could see Keene grinning out of the corner of her eye; she had just impressed him. But even a first-year probationary agent would have noticed the bulge in the small of Artie's back, under the robe, when they came in.

"Look," Artie said. "I haven't done *anything.* What do you guys want?"

"That's a good question," Taylor said. "What *do* we want, Keene?"

"Well," Keene said, "like I said. Artie's got a lot of cool toys. Thought he might want to help us out with that video."

Taylor grabbed Keene by the arm and led him away from Artie. "Can I talk to you for a minute?" she said, fuming mad. "What in the world are you doing!"

"Relax," he said casually.

"Relax? Did you not hear President Grant? We can't show this criminal that video."

"Calm down. I'm sorry. I should've told you why we were coming here. But do you think I'm a complete idiot? Do you think I would risk showing this thing to anyone if I thought it was going to get out before we knew what was going on?"

Taylor just looked at him. She had to assume he could at least be trusted. She hoped.

"And what do you suppose this guy is going to be able to help us with?" she asked. "I have all the same gear back at the Bureau. We could've just stayed there."

"Yes, we could have," Keene said. "And what if someone came by asking what we were doing? What if someone else is monitoring your station? I've been around enough stuff like this to know you don't just drop off letters to the Oval Office unnoticed. You don't just hack into the president's private e-mail."

"Are you suggesting that someone on the inside is helping this guy?"

"Don't know. But until we do, we can't take a chance that anyone other than us knows about this."

"And, apparently, Artie."

Keene let out a laugh. "Trust me. This guy has skills. If there's anything on that video you want to look at, he can find it."

She wasn't happy about it, but she knew he was right. And until they discovered if and who, they needed to stay under the radar.

"Okay," she said. "We'll do it your way."

Keene nodded and stepped away. But she grabbed him by the arm one more time.

"But if this comes back to bite me in the rear end, I'm gonna have your head on a stick!"

She followed Keene back over to where Artie was waiting.

"We're going to show you a video," Keene said. "I want you to tell me what you see."

"What kind of video?" Artie asked.

"The kind that can get you killed if you ever talk about it," Taylor said.

"Then I'd rather not," Artie said.

"Shut up and sit down," Keene said, grabbing the frail man by the shoulders. He pushed him into the next room and down into the chair sitting in front of a wall of computer towers and monitors.

"Welcome to my lair," Artie said, looking at Taylor.

She had to admit, she was impressed. She was familiar with every piece of gear sitting here and had most of it in her office. She handed him the thumb drive and said, "It's the only thing on there."

Artie pushed the thumb drive in and began to click around on the keyboard. Instantly the video appeared. Keene reached out and grabbed his hand, stopping him from pushing PLAY.

"No audio. Just watch."

"Man, c'mon!" Artie protested. "You asked for my help. Remember?"

"Just watch," Keene said again.

Artie muted the audio output and pushed PLAY. Once again the video of the man sitting on the stool played.

"What do you see?"

"Nothing, man. Just some dude on a stool with a bandana on his face. What am I looking for?"

"Can you tell me where this was filmed?"

"Universal Studios," Artie said sarcastically. "Seriously! How am I supposed to know that?"

"Look around. Anything there that can identify where this is?"

Artie froze the image and studied it for a few minutes. "Man, I've got nothing."

"There's something," Keene said.

"There's nothing! Dude's in a room, on a stool, with computer monitors behind him. What do you want from me?"

"I want you to tell me if there's anything in there that tells me where this guy is."

"Maybe if I could hear the audio."

"How?" Keene asked.

"Because you can filter out noises and isolate others," Taylor said. "And that may give us something."

"Okay," Keene said. "Do it."

"Keene!"

"It was your idea," Keene said.

"Yeah, so take Artie out for some ice cream, and I'll do it."

"No way," Artie protested. "No one touches my gear 'cept me."

"Trust me," Keene said. "Artie has helped me before. He may not be the best law-abiding citizen out there, but he's solid. We can trust him."

Taylor hoped she didn't live to regret this. "Okay. But you're on the hook for this."

"You hear that?" Keene said to Artie. "That means that if you burn me on this, I'm going to come back here and shoot you."

"You worry too much," Artie said.

Keene spun the small man around in his chair so they were eye to eye. "Artie," he said in a menacing voice, "I'm serious. This is national security stuff. You even open your mouth to your dog—me, or someone like me, will show up here and kill you. You understand?"

Artie swallowed hard. "Yeah, yeah. I get it. Not a peep."

"Go ahead," Keene said, spinning him back around to face the computer.

Artie reset the play head and started the clip again. This time the Prophet's words echoed through the open room. When it was finished, Artie started tapping away.

"Man, you weren't kidding, huh? This is like some terrorist stuff, right?" He held up his hand. "I know. I know. Not a peep."

Artie tapped away again on the keyboard. Taylor watched him bring up an audio shelving software, complete with compressor and graphic equalizer plugins. She had an app very similar to this—but this one looked like it had a few more bells and whistles.

"Okay," Artie said when he was done pointing and clicking. "What I've done here is, I've muted the dude's voice and opened up some bandwidth that should allow us to hear the surrounding sounds. If there's anything going on, we should be able to hear it."

This time the video played and the Prophet's voice was silent. In its place, a myriad of noises could be heard in the background. They listened through once without anything jumping out. They played it again. And then again a third time. Halfway through, Taylor spoke up.

"Right there! Stop," she said. "What was that?"

"What?" Artie asked.

"That dinging sound. Back it up."

He did and then played it again.

"There!" she said. "Can you isolate that?"

"I think so," Artie said, tapping away at the keys. He rolled it back and played it again.

"That's it."

"That's what?" Keene asked.

"That's a train," she said smiling.

"Oh. . .okay," Keene said. "Yeah, that helps a lot."

"Isolate it," she said, dismissing his tone.

"That's going to be tough," Artie said.

"Yeah," she said. "Maybe for you. Move over and I'll do it."

Artie smacked her hand away. "Like I said. No one touches my gear but me. Give me a second."

He clicked a few more buttons and played it again. The train's audio now came to the forefront.

"That's good," she said. Then, "Roll it back again. See if you can hear anything before that."

Artie did and started the video again, with the current filters in place. A lot of screeching and clanging was heard, but there was also something else.

"Right there!" Taylor said again.

"Yeah, I heard that, too," Artie said. "Let me see if I can clean it up."

Again, he tapped away for a few seconds. Pushed PLAY.

A computerized voice could be heard over what apparently was a PA-system announcement. And now, after all the shelving of the frequencies, they could hear what the female voice was saying:

The train is approaching. Please stand clear of the platform.

After that came another succession of screeches and clangs. A train was coming to a stop.

"Hey can you boost that?" Taylor said hurriedly.

"Yeah."

This time it was a different voice.

"What's that?" Keene asked.

"It's the conductor of the train," Taylor said. "The doors must be opened, and he's announcing where they are and where they're going. Boost it some more."

Artie did and ran it back.

"*. . .Blue line. Next stop, UIC-Halsted, then Clinton-Blue.*"

Taylor was getting excited now. "We need to—"

"Already on it," Artie interrupted.

He opened his browser. He typed in a search. Seconds later they were all looking at a transit authority map.

"There," said Keene, pointing to the screen. "Racine Station! Chicago." He gave Artie a friendly smack on the back of the head and said, "Good job. We owe you one."

"Yeah," Artie said, "just don't kill me, and we'll call it even."

CHAPTER 15

The Prophet was confused. While he was under no assumption that he would be safe—in the sense that his calling didn't mean a safe life—he didn't think that he would be in any physical danger. Not that that would dissuade him. He was committed. He would follow whatever direction he was led in. And if it meant his head being served up on a platter, then so be it. But if what he'd been told was the case, then how would he continue his mission? *Well,* he thought, *I guess that's what living by faith means.*

So. . .there would be someone coming for him. And while he wasn't told who or when or how, he was to avoid being caught at all cost. And that was going to be the trick. Wasn't it? Don't get caught by the person or people who are coming for you, though you have no idea where they are or when they're coming. He smiled to himself. Not that he found it amusing. Just that now he had more to be concerned with. He pulled the collar of his coat up, to shield his face from the bitter wind that howled outside, and left the diner.

Two blocks up he entered another small café. The hoodie was pulled tight, and he turned his head as he passed the front counter, avoiding the small camera above the clerk. He made his way to the back and sat down at an open space. He quickly glanced around to see if anyone was paying him any attention. No one. Nor would they. Most people here were already busy typing away on the many keyboard stations around him. He chose this particular Internet café because it was usually filled with people who were out of work and didn't have Internet of their own. Most of them were probably revising their résumés. Some others were just young kids skipping school, playing games.

He pulled the disposable credit card out of his pocket and inserted it into the receptor. The monitor came to life, and he began typing. Nervously, he felt inside his jacket pocket for the thumb drive. Still there. That made him feel a little better.

He finished typing his letter, pulled the thumb drive out, and stuck it in the machine. He dragged the file over to the icon on the screen and watched the little blue line streak across as the file was copied. Clicking on the icon, he watched as it opened and showed the contents of the small drive. There was his letter. And right next to it, another program. He double-clicked and watched again as the blue streak told him the program was opening. A little white box appeared with the words LAUNCH SWEEP? on it. He clicked YES and ejected the thumb drive.

As he walked out the door, he could hear the patrons' grumbles. Two seconds later, he heard the snap and sizzle as sparks flew from the desks of computers. The entire café had been fried.

CHAPTER 16

So how do you know him?" Taylor asked as they drove.

"Who? Artie?" Keene said.

"No, President Grant," she said. "Yes, Artie."

Now there was a complicated story. One that he didn't really have the desire to get into with her. He had used Artie on a number of jobs, jobs that he was neither authorized to talk about, nor did he want to. Shortly after leaving the SEALs and newly with the CIA, he had been introduced to Artie by his mentor, Sam. Sam had tried to explain to Keene, who was fresh off the Farm—the CIA's training facility—that there were assets, and then there were *assets*. Artie was the latter: a pure genius who, from a technological perspective, could get you anything you needed. However, unless he felt his life was in danger by you, you couldn't trust him farther than you could throw him. Keene only hoped he had instilled that level of fear in the little computer nerd before they left.

"We go way back."

"Seriously, Keene. Can we trust him?"

"He better hope so," Keene said as he reached into his pocket. Pushing the button, he put the phone up to his ear. "Keene here."

It was Artie.

Suddenly, he jerked the wheel and crossed two lanes of traffic, pulling the truck over to the side of the road.

"Hey!" Megan shouted. "A heads-up next time?"

Keene shushed her with his hand and said, "Hold on. I'm putting you on speaker." He put the truck in park and pushed the little speaker icon on his screen. "Go ahead."

"Okay," Artie said. "What I was trying to say was, listen to me before you just start yelling and geting mad at me."

Keene pinched the bridge of his nose. *Please*, he thought, *please don't make me have to go back there and kill him.* "What?" he said impatiently.

"Okay. So I kinda made a copy of the video."

"You did what!" Taylor screamed.

"Artie," it was Keene now, "you better—"

"Hey!" Artie shouted over them. "You can come back here and shoot me if you want. But after I'm done telling you what I found."

Keene looked at Taylor. He could see the curiosity in her eyes, too. "Go ahead."

"Okay," Artie continued. "So like I said, I made a copy. Don't ask. Trust me. I'm just that good."

"Speed it up!" Keene's voice rose.

"Okay, okay. I'm getting there. So I went back and just looked at some different things. First, I just watched the dude sitting on the stool. Then I took time to zoom in on all of the monitors behind him. They're all national networks, so I figured that's not going to help. But I kept looking anyway, 'cause, you know, never know what you may find right? Right. So, I kept going and still didn't find anything."

"That's it, I'm turning this car around!"

"Okay, okay. Jeez, hold on. I'm getting to it. So I started to just look around the room. And I noticed something."

"What?" Keene asked.

"So, like, there's not a lot of light around this guy. Just what looks like natural daylight. But I noticed that it wasn't coming from any of the sides. It was coming from above."

"How did you see that?" Taylor asked.

" 'Cause I threw a couple gamma ray filters in there and diffused it. I can see sunlight rays coming from above and at an angle. Like skylights or windows up high. So I used a couple other filters I have, and I was able to get some shadows. Looks like a tic-tac-toe board shadow being cast over the wall of newspapers."

"So?" Taylor said. "What's that got to do with anything?"

"It's a warehouse," Keene said.

"It's a warehouse!" Artie repeated. "Exactly! So I got back on the net and started looking for warehouses around Racine Station. Turns out, there's a whole neighborhood of them there."

"That doesn't help," Keene said.

"Yeah, but maybe this will," Artie said. "So this neighborhood only has a few small buildings like the one this guy is in with that kind of blueprint. Don't ask. I pulled the records. So anyway, there's like twelve of these warehouses that were built with plans that match what we were looking at. All of them have been renovated in the last ten years. And all of them were either turned into some kind of boutique store or apartment building. In the last couple years, with the bad economy, four have been abandoned."

"Okay," Keene said, his interest rising.

"Only one of them is close enough for us to have been able to get that audio," Artie said.

"So you found it," Keene said.

"I found it!" Artie said.

"Good job," Keene said. "I told you there was something. Text me the address. Oh, and—"

"Yeah, I know. Delete the video. I already did."

Keene clicked off the call and put the truck in gear. He stepped on the gas and shot out into the street, pulling a complete U-turn.

"Hey!" Taylor shouted again. "I thought you were going to warn me when you did that."

"Sorry," he said.

"Where are we going?"

"Your place."

"For what?"

"To pack a bag. We're going to Chicago."

★

"Why Chicago?" Director Preston asked.

"Found a lead," Taylor answered, gripping the handle above her window with her free hand as Keene swerved in and out of traffic. "Keene seems to think we should go."

"Anything big?" Preston asked.

"Don't know yet. One of Keene's buddies," she watched as Keene made the face again, "is a computer hacker. Pretty good one, too. Has some gear that he shouldn't have. But that's neither here nor there. It's a good lead, and we're going to check it out."

"Anything you need me to do?"

"Nah. I'll keep you posted."

"Check in when you get there."

"Will do."

Taylor clicked off the call as the truck pulled into her driveway. She undid her seat belt and opened the door.

"I'll be a couple minutes. You can come inside if you want."

"I'll wait out here," Keene said. "I'll call Jennings and let him know."

"Suit yourself," she said. "Give me ten minutes."

Inside, she ran to the bedroom and grabbed her overnight bag, stuffing it with underwear, jeans, T-shirts; a toothbrush followed. She zipped up the bag and headed into the kitchen where Barney, her Jack Russell, was sitting on his doggie bed. *Shoot*, she thought.

"Sorry, buddy. I almost forgot about you."

She pulled out her phone to call the neighbor, but as she did, it buzzed.

"Taylor here," she answered.

"Ms. Taylor, it's Boz."

"Oh hey, Boz. What can I do for you?"

"I'm still at the White House, but I wanted to try and catch up with you and Mr. Keene. Where are you?"

"Ah," Megan paused, unsure what to tell him. "At my house. But I'm about to leave."

"I see," Boz said.

Megan could hear the questioning tone. She figured she might as well tell him.

"Keene and I are on our way to Chicago. Seems there may be something worth checking out. We're leaving right away."

"Great. I'll come with you."

Aw, man, Taylor thought. No way this was going to go over well with Keene. "Tell you what, Boz. Keene and I are in a pretty big hurry. What if I just call you and keep you updated?"

"I really don't think that will work. But I also don't want to be the cause of any friction between you and Mr. Keene. So if you'd like, you can keep this conversation between us, and I'll just meet you at the plane."

Megan was about to try and protest again, but the line went dead. She opened the cupboard and grabbed the bottle of ibuprofen, took two out for the headache that was now pounding in her temple, chased them down with a glass of water, and threw the rest of the bottle into her bag. She quickly called the neighbor and explained her unexpected trip. The neighbor promised to take Barney out and feed him for the next couple days. Taylor left a twenty on the counter with a note that read, *Thanks a bunch! I owe you one!*

She barely got the bag in the backseat and her seat belt buckled before Keene pulled out onto the road again.

CHAPTER 17

Boz clicked off the phone call from Taylor as President Grant came back into the room. He had been left there by himself while the president attended to a quick briefing. While alone, he tried to think through everything Grant had shared with him the last couple days. First there were the letters. Then there was the video. And finally, there was Jonathan Keene and Megan Taylor.

There really wasn't any good explanation for how he'd found himself here. It all seemed surreal. He had been an Army Ranger, before. And if there's one thing that Ranger school had taught him, it was that everything had an explanation. There was no such thing as coincidence, or chance. Strangely, his current role as a pastor had affirmed that way of thinking. Therefore, no coincidence. No chance. And that made him feel all the more uneasy about what was going on here. He had shared his concerns with Grant, who had as much as agreed with him. But there was the idea that maybe they could somehow stop what this Prophet was warning them about. Perhaps, in His providence, God was using them to bring about some much-needed change.

"I need to know where Keene and Taylor are leaving from," Boz said to the president as he reentered the room.

President Grant crinkled his brow. "I'm not sure I know what you mean."

"Oh, yeah. Sorry," Boz said, realizing that he had started in the middle of the conversation. "Keene and Taylor are leaving for Chicago. I need to go with them. Where would they be leaving from?"

President Grant nodded and picked up the phone.

"Director Jennings. . . . I'm fine, thank you. I need some information, if you would be so kind. . . . Thank you. Mr. Keene is leaving for Chicago, I understand. . . . Yes, I would like to know where from. . . . Thank you."

President Grant placed the receiver back in its cradle and smiled at his friend. "Being the president does have its perks every now and again."

Boz smiled, knowing that his friend was a very humble man who would never use his office for personal gain. Even so, he had to agree with him. It did have its advantages.

"Reagan National," President Grant said. "Private terminal, hangar three. Gulf Stream-5. They're leaving in less than an hour."

"Then I'll bid you good day, Mr. President."

"I'll have one of my detail take you there. You'll be there when they arrive."

"Thanks. That's probably not a bad idea, seeing how they don't know I'm coming." He smiled.

★

Keene pulled the Pathfinder through the security gate, flashed his ID and made his way to the newly added private hangars at Reagan National. The airport had been under reconstruction for more than a decade and now was fully operational. The big hangar's doors were swinging open as Keene pulled the truck over to the side and parked. He and Taylor jumped out and walked to the waiting Gulf Stream jet. He was not at all happy at what he saw standing at the top of the stairs.

"Hello!" Boz shouted over the whining of the jet engines. "Good to see you again!"

Keene pushed his way past the man and threw his bag onto one of the empty couches that lined the side of the midsized jet.

"What are you doing here?" Keene asked.

"Well, unless I'm mistaken," Boz said, "I'm going to Chicago with you."

"And how, exactly, did you come to find out where we are going?" Keene shot a cross look at Taylor, who shifted her eyes away.

"You could say I'm very resourceful, Mr. Keene," Boz answered.

Keene fumed. Taylor must have talked to the man and told him where they were headed.

The personal flight attendant for the aircraft secured the door and knocked on the door to the cockpit to let the pilots know they were ready. Keene moved past her and took his seat beside Taylor. He leaned over and whispered in her ear.

"You do this to me again, I don't care what the president says, I'll be working this on my own. We clear?"

He pulled back and gave her an icy stare. Impressively, she didn't budge. Rather, she matched his glare with one of her own. And leaned over to reply.

"You threaten me again, Keene, and I'll get out my laptop and personally make sure that every agency in the world has you on their number-one priority list. Are *we* clear?"

The plane rocked back and forth as it made its way out onto the runway. Keene and Taylor sat back in their chairs, avoiding each other's gaze. Boz, who had been in the back, came up front and sat down in the chair facing them. He had some bottled water in his hands and tossed one to each of them, as he sat down and buckled up.

"Make sure you drink plenty. Chicago's cold and dry. And we're going to be flying at forty thousand feet. Wanna make sure we're plenty hydrated, in case we need to chase someone down."

Keene huffed to himself.

"What's that, Mr. Keene? Did you say something?" Boz asked.

Keene just looked at the man and twisted the cap off his water. "Thanks, chapy."

Aside from the roar of the engines, the cabin was silent. No one spoke as the plane took off and climbed altitude. After five minutes, the captain came on the loudspeaker and announced they were at cruising height.

Taylor unbuckled her belt and stood up.

"I'm gonna go freshen up. Been a long morning."

She made her way back to the rear of the plane and into the lavatory, leaving Keene and Boz to themselves. Several seconds passed before either spoke.

"So, chapy, what's an ex-Ranger like you doing in a place like this?"

Boz smiled. Keene tried to get a read on him, but there was nothing.

"Haven't been called that in a while," Boz said. "Guys in my old unit used to call me that. Even before I went into the pastorate."

"Yeah," Keene said, "we used to call all you Bible-thumper guys chapy."

"Bible thumper. Interesting," Boz nodded. "So these guys, these *Bible thumpers*. . . Ever see any of them running around beating on their Bible?"

"What?"

"I mean, you call us Bible thumpers. Ever see anyone running around beating on their Bible? You know. . .smacking it around?"

Keene chuckled. "Nothing personal. It's just an expression."

"You think your president is a *Bible thumper*?"

"Look," Keene said, "the president is my commander in chief. What he does on his own personal time is his business. It's just a joke. Lighten up."

"Jon—you mind if I call you Jon?"

Keene shrugged. "Whatever you like. Mind if I call you chapy?"

"Not at all," Boz said. "I'm not here to watch over your every move. I'm here because your commander in chief asked me to help out. Regardless of what you think, I'm fully capable of taking care of myself. And the two of you if need be, for that matter."

Keene let that hang there for a moment. The guy was a former Ranger. He was Special Ops. And so it wasn't a matter of whether or not the guy could handle himself. It was a matter of why he was here in the first place.

"Let me ask you something," Keene said.

Boz nodded.

"Why *are* you here? I mean, what do I need you for?"

Boz smiled. "I'd like to think that I'm here for several reasons. The first of which is probably you."

"What's that supposed to mean?"

"Not what you think. We can talk about that later. Right now, you need to know that I, and the president, think that this is not as black and white as you think it is. And I know you're probably going to think I'm crazy, or he's crazy, but I'm not convinced this guy is a terrorist."

"Then what is he?" Keene asked.

"We'll just have to wait and see," Boz said. "But right now, I have insight into how this guy thinks. And if you're going to track him effectively, you need me."

"And why do you have insight into this nut job? You a nut job, too?"

"You married?"

"Was. What's that got to do with anything?"

"Yeah, I know about your first wife. I meant now. Married? Anyone special in your life?"

Keene sat up straight. He didn't like where this conversation was going. He didn't bring up the past. "No. Not married."

"It's hard, isn't it?" Boz asked.

"What's that?"

"Losing a wife like that. I'm sorry."

Keene was now starting to get agitated. "Nothing to be sorry about. She was killed by a terrorist."

"Uh-huh," Boz said.

"And now I hunt down terrorists and kill them back," Keene said. "It's that simple."

"Is that why you joined the CIA after you left your unit?"

Okay, Keene thought, *now this guy is really starting to make me mad.* "You trying to shrink me, chapy?"

"Shrink you?" Boz laughed.

"Yeah, you know. Like a psychiatrist, a shrink?"

66

"Oh." Boz chuckled. "No, I'm not trying to *shrink* you. Just trying to get to know you."

"Well, don't," Keene snapped. "I don't live in the past."

"Fair enough. You and I actually have a lot in common. I don't live in the past either. Doesn't do you any good."

"Exactly."

"You know I lost a wife, too?"

Keene raised an eyebrow.

"Yeah. And my daughter. Car accident."

"I'm sorry." Keene had a moment of remorse.

"Thanks." Boz finally spoke. "It was an accident. Rainy night, wet roads, bad brakes."

"Yes, it's hard," Keene said.

"I used to be just like you. A hard, angry man."

"You don't know me."

Boz leaned forward, his eyes icy, his face expressionless. He pointed his finger.

"Let me tell you something," Boz said in a tone completely changed. "You think you're a bad man. You think you're tough. But I've got news for you, kid. Your Bosnia mission, I prepped that. That six-month stint you did in Tehran, you were there because I laid the groundwork ten years before. You think that just because you lost four men in Karbala—because you should've seen it coming—makes you some kind of special, horrible person? Those men you lost. . .they knew the risk. And yeah, I know you think you messed up. You could've pulled back earlier. But the job wasn't done. And you don't leave the job undone! But you're not the only team leader to ever lose men. We've all lost men. So don't sit there and dishonor their sacrifice by acting like their deaths were meaningless. You think you've got the market cornered on vengeance and anger? I traveled that road for a long time, kid. And I can tell you that the only place it's going to lead you is down a deep, dark hole."

Keene's eyes widened.

"Yeah, that's right. I know you. I know all about you, because I was you. I was you before you even knew who *you* were. I wasted a good part of my life trying to fix things that I had no control over. So don't sit there with that sanctimonious smirk on your face thinking some middle-aged *chapy* is cramping your style by being here. Neither one of us knows for sure what we're walking into. And if there's anything we can do to stop it, then I can promise you I'll do whatever it takes to make that happen. But if I'm right and we can't, then we need to find this Prophet and get some serious information out of him."

Keene hadn't been put in his place like that since Basic Underwater Demolition school. And he didn't much like it, but this chapy was no joke. He'd seen that look before. You don't mess with that look. That look can get you killed. He knew. 'Cause he'd given that same look to many unfortunate souls in his time with the unit.

"So if there's nothing we can do to stop this coming attack, as you say, then why bother to find him?"

"I know this will sound like lunacy to you," Boz said, appearing to return to his normal state of calm, "but I believe that this Prophet may actually be real."

Keene didn't know what to say. Everything in him wanted to call his boss and the president and tell them that this chapy guy was a quack. But then there was the respect he had for the man's military record. He couldn't just dismiss it. And as bad as he hated to admit it, there was something niggling at the back of his brain telling him there was more to this than met the eye.

"And if he's real," Boz continued, "then it won't be an isolated event."

"How do you know that?"

"Because. When God allowed something like this to happen to a nation in the Bible, namely, Israel, it wasn't just a single attack."

"How do you mean?" Keene asked.

"I mean, God would give the entire nation over to another nation. We need to find him, assure him we're not going to *kill* him, and then find out what he knows. Before we completely lose our country."

PART 2: CONDEMNATION

CHAPTER 18

The woman, dressed in a casual, stylish business suit, got out of the car and walked silently into the deserted warehouse. As with any meeting, she was fifteen minutes early—which, in her opinion, was on time. Punctuality was something she held in high regard. To be late to a meeting, she thought, was a slap in the face to your counterpart. Being late was as good as saying, *My time is more valuable than yours.*

The first of the visiting limos—fifteen minutes late—arrived, two armed guards stepping out and surveying the area. Once they were satisfied they were alone, one of the men spoke into a radio and watched as the remaining vehicles approached.

Three more limos lined the curb, and several armed guards stepped out, all checking the area. Finally, a small, elderly man exited the next-to-last vehicle. He wore a finely tailored Italian suit, accented with a red Hermès tie. A gold Rolex rested securely on his left wrist. Fine, hand-tooled leather Italian shoes completed the ensemble.

After a short pause to check out the surroundings, the elderly man walked inside the warehouse. The woman was waiting impatiently for him at a small table, set with two chairs. He nodded to the other man and sat down.

"Mr. Chin." She nodded.

"Ms. Smith."

Ms. Smith leaned back in her chair. "I must say your people's lack of punctuality is disappointing. I thought that with business and money being your god, you would respect its nuances."

The man smiled a perfunctory smile. "Madam, I apologize for our tardiness. One can't be too careful when meeting like this."

"No, I guess not."

"Then let's get down to business, shall we?"

The woman nodded as Chin took his seat.

"Is everything in order?" Chin asked.

"Everything is as I said it would be. Do you have my money?"

The diminutive man turned in his chair and took the laptop from one of his men. He set it on the table and opened the lid. After a few seconds, a screen appeared that had a box in the middle with a waiting cursor.

"Just type in the account number and the funds will be transferred," Mr. Chin said.

The woman carefully took her hands out of her coat pocket and produced a set of latex gloves. She pulled them on and brought the laptop closer.

"Can't be too careful." She raised an eyebrow.

Chin smiled and nodded.

She typed on the keyboard, hit ENTER, and scooted it back to the man. "So I guess our business here is done."

Chin stood up and took the laptop. "For now, Ms. Smith. Good day."

He gave a slight bow and walked back to the waiting car.

The woman watched as the small caravan of cars pulled away. She waited a few more minutes and then pulled out the disposable phone she'd purchased a month ago. She punched the numbers in and waited until it was answered.

"It's done," she said.

CHAPTER 19

Taylor returned from the lavatory to the front of the plane, where she'd left Keene and Boz. More than anything, she'd wanted to give the men time alone to do whatever it was that macho former military men did when they obviously didn't like each other and were thrust into working together. She'd been sure fireworks were coming and just didn't have the energy to listen to it. So she'd excused herself.

What she found was a surprise. She had heard about these Gulf Stream jets before but had never been on one. The bathroom was ridiculous! It was nicer than her first apartment.

She sat back down and looked at the two men she'd left a few minutes earlier. They were both still alive, and there wasn't any blood, so she thought that was good.

"You two have a nice chat?"

"We're fine," Boz said. "Aren't we, Jon?"

Keene nodded. "All good."

Boz undid his belt and stood up. "I'm gonna grab some shut-eye on the couch. Rule number one."

"What's that?" Taylor asked.

"Always eat and sleep when you can," Keene said. "Never know when you're going to get the chance to do either again."

Boz smiled. "That's right." He stepped out from the seats and moved around to the back. "Wake me up if you need me."

Taylor sat there for a few minutes, looking out the small window at the vast openness. She wondered how it was possible that this Prophet had been able to pull off what he did. The enormity of it was mind-boggling. She really didn't want to accept that this video was somehow untraceable. And though she was a woman of faith, she shuddered at the thought that this Prophet could actually be what he said he was.

She snapped back from her thoughts and turned to Keene.

"I'm sorry I didn't tell you he was coming."

Keene looked at her with that blank expression he'd had earlier.

"Look, man. . ." she began.

"It's all right," Keene interrupted. "Boz is okay. I just don't like finding things out like that."

Taylor was taken aback. First time Keene had acted like a normal human being since she met him. "Yeah, sorry 'bout my attitude, too."

Keene sat up in his chair. "For better or worse, we're stuck together. We have to work this, all three of us. I don't know what we're up against, but I don't know that I can just buy into what he says either."

"And what's he say?"

"That this guy may be some messenger from God."

"And why's that so hard for you to believe?"

"Really? You, too?"

"Well, I mean, God has spoken to people throughout history. Why not this guy?"

"Seriously?"

"What? I'm a Christian. Why *wouldn't* I believe that this could be happening?"

"Listen, Taylor. This guy's either a terrorist or he works for terrorists. Probably HAMAS or something. We just have to figure out who. It's that simple. And if he has information about an attack on our soil, I'm going to find him. And when I do, he'd better hope he's close with God."

Taylor leaned down and took the bag out from under her seat. She grabbed her laptop and opened it.

"What are you doing?" Keene asked. "Can't get Internet up here."

"*You* can't get Internet up here," she corrected him. "I, on the other hand. . ."

"Isn't that, like, dangerous to the plane?"

"You can already get Internet on most commercial flights. If you pay enough. So no, it's not dangerous to the plane, unless their navigation and controls are using encrypted satellites—which is what I'm about to tap into."

Keene looked at her.

"They're not using encrypted satellites. We're fine."

"What are you looking for?"

"I'm going to pull up satellite imaging of the area where Artie said the warehouse is. See what's there."

"All right. Well, I'm going to rack out for a few until we land. Wake me up when we get there."

Taylor watched as Keene tilted his head back and closed his eyes.

Within seconds, the man looked like he was asleep. *Must be a military thing*, she thought. And then she was jealous. It took her forever to fall asleep at night. She wished she could just turn it all off, like a light switch, and fall off to sleep.

She logged on to the secure satellite server and pulled up a handful of maps for the Chicago area. She had, in front of her, a detailed Public Transit map, one for street names, and then a satellite imagery map. She studied all three, trying to decide what would be the best way to approach. She also looked at the surrounding areas to see if perhaps she could pinpoint a couple places that the guy might use frequently. Maybe a Laundromat, some restaurants, local markets, and so on.

After forty minutes or so of staring at more than ten different maps, her eyes were burning. She was mapped out. She had some thoughts, but that's all they were. Thoughts and hunches. She would share what she'd found with Keene and Boz after they woke up. She looked at the clock and realized they didn't have much time left in the air, so she decided to shut it down and try to at least rest for a few minutes, even if she couldn't fall asleep. But before she closed the lid, she decided to check her e-mail, since her phone was dead up here.

She opened the server and waited for the little blue line to move across the screen as her mailbox chimed. Three new messages. The first two weren't anything. Just an online coupon and an invite from someone at the office to a coworker's birthday party. The last one, though, caught her attention immediately.

It had a little red flag next to it, indicating that it was a secure e-mail, sent from an unknown sender. Always aware of viruses, she did a reverse check on the IP address and saw that it came from an Internet café in Chicago. Her pulse quickened as she clicked the heading to open the contents. Immediately the screen filled with the message.

She read it and then read it again. She quickly opened another secure e-mail. She typed her message with several exclamation points at the end and hit SEND.

She took a deep breath and looked over at Keene. Definitely asleep. Well, not for long. She nudged his arm and said, "Hey, wake up. You need to see this."

Keene smacked his lips and stretched his arms and said, "What?"

"This," she said, turning the screen around so he could see.

Keene stared at the screen and read the first line of the e-mail.

Ms. Taylor, this is the Prophet. I understand you are looking for me.

CHAPTER 20

Ms. Smith pulled her Mercedes into the parking garage, showed her ID, nodded and smiled to the guard, and then proceeded to her assigned parking space. She repeated the ID process as she entered the building, made her way to the elevator, and pushed the button for the top floor.

When the doors opened, she was greeted by one of the secretaries, who told her she was expected and to go right in. She walked past the desk and stopped to look out the huge, floor-to-ceiling window; the city landscape spread before her. The tip of the Washington Monument could be seen reaching up to the sky over the other buildings. Such a picturesque icon of the American spirit. *Oh well,* she thought, *all good things must come to an end.*

She continued on past the other desks and computers to the end of the hall. She knocked quietly on the door and turned the knob. Inside, another woman, sitting behind the big desk and talking on the phone, motioned for her to come in. She closed the door behind her and sat down. The other woman ended her phone call and turned to see her.

"Any problems?" the woman behind the desk asked.

"None," Ms. Smith answered.

"Good. Then everything is scheduled as planned?"

"Yes."

"Okay, then."

"Okay, then," Ms. Smith repeated.

The woman behind the desk folded her hands under her chin and looked at her with great concern. "I need to ask you something."

"Go on."

"Let's say I have a special need for an operative for a top secret assignment. Who would you ask?"

Ms. Smith looked at the woman and said, "Me, of course." Then, "Let me ask *you* something. May I?"

"Go ahead."

Ms. Smith folded her arms and said, "Why, all of a sudden, are you interested in another operative?"

"I'm not. But apparently the president is."

"Oh, I see. And he's asked you for a recommendation?"

"Not exactly. He went around me."

This caught her off guard. "Correct me if I'm wrong, but I thought you were the director of Homeland Security, Ms. Levy," she said.

"I am!" Levy snapped, evidently not sharing her affinity for dry humor.

"Then why is the president going around asking about operatives for a secret assignment without your knowledge?"

"I intend to find that out, Ms. Smith. In the meantime, I'm asking you. Who would Jennings send him?"

She had crossed the paths of several agents over her career. Some she knew. Others she had only heard of. And then there were those who weren't supposed to even be known about. And she only knew of one that was rumored to still be active. And he was bad news. She kind of hoped it was him. *That would make the game interesting*, she thought.

"Jon Keene," she finally said.

"Never heard of him," Director Levy said. "I would know about him if he were around."

"Would you?" Smith asked. "From what I understand, there are those who don't care for your new position, Madam Director. I believe the president and Kevin Jennings fall into that category. So let me ask you something. If I were Kevin Jennings and had an asset at my disposal that my boss didn't know about, and I really didn't like my new boss, you think I would tell?"

Ms. Smith watched as the woman mulled that over.

"No, I guess you wouldn't. Then I guess it's a good thing I have you. Isn't it?"

"I would say it is to your benefit," she answered.

"Good. Then I want you to find out everything you can on Jon Keene."

"I need to take care of a couple things first."

"Then I guess you can take the rest of the day for yourself," Levy said.

Ms. Smith stood to leave. "I'll be in contact with you."

"No, don't. I'll find you."

"No, you won't. That's why you hired me." She let that hang there for a second. "I'll check back in two days."

"Where are you going?"

"Home."

"Yes, home. . ." Levy's eyes narrowed. "We never *have* established where that is exactly. Now have we?"

"Oh, I'm quite aware of where home is," Smith said.

Levy gave a short laugh. "You are quite enigmatic, Alex. Alex. . . What did you say that was short for again?"

"I didn't."

"Oh, yes. I guess you never did."

"If that will be all?" Smith asked.

"That will be all. I have a meeting with him in just a few minutes. I'll be done for the day after that, if you need to get in touch with me."

"You meeting him here? Or are you going there?"

"There. Supposed to be there in ten minutes. Not gonna happen."

Smith cringed again at this whole idea of being late to meetings. No matter, it wasn't her that was going to be late. She was right on time. Her flight left in a little over three hours. She was packed and ready to go. And she was looking forward to a couple days to herself.

"Let me ask you something, Ms. Levy," Smith said.

"Go ahead."

"Are you sure about this?"

"About what?"

"You know. . ."

"It was an inevitable conclusion to things. I'm just playing my part."

"Okay, then."

Levy came around and put her hand on her shoulder. "I'll walk down with you."

★

Thirty minutes later the door to the Oval Office opened, and Director Levy walked in. She had, under her arm, a manila folder that carried the weekly threat assessment. She walked over to the desk and dropped it on top, clearly agitating the president who was on the phone. He gave her a sour look and motioned for her to sit.

She did and waited another three minutes before the president finished his call. When he hung up, he looked at her as if he were disappointed.

"Ms. Levy," he said, "I believe our meeting was for thirty minutes ago."

"Twenty," she corrected. "And I am sorry, Mr. President, but it couldn't be helped."

The president just looked at her. She was enjoying this. There was no love lost between them. They saw completely differently on just about every issue imaginable. He probably would have fired her if his predecessor hadn't made it nearly impossible.

During the previous administration, communication had degenerated so badly between agencies, the president held a summit. All of the directors of the agencies, as well as law enforcement attended. It was decided that a single agency should head up all Intel, foreign and domestic. And while each agency would still operate in its own arena, an executive order was proposed that would give the Department of Homeland Security dominion over every law enforcement and intelligence agency in the nation. Everything but the nation's military. In effect, creating a sort of *super* cabinet-level position. One that still had to answer to the president but with a lot of autonomy, nonetheless. The president of the United States would still be the commander in chief of the nation's military. But every other law enforcement agency would get its marching orders from Homeland Security. And as a point of emphasis, the appointed director would function much in the same way as a Supreme Court justice: the director would serve a lifetime appointment. He or she would have to be vetted and confirmed by Congress but a lifetime appointment, nonetheless. This was to eliminate mass confusion at the turn of a term limit of an administration, as inevitably, each new director would want to change a number of things, causing more confusion and problems than when the agencies had operated autonomously.

The proposal was agreed upon and signed into law a month later. It was the lame-duck president's swan song, so to speak. Marianne Levy was not everyone's first choice, but she did appear to be qualified, having been a career National Intelligence Agency employee who eventually rose to the rank of director. Though she was shrewd and had made many enemies within the agency and in Washington, she was good at her job. And the fact that Levy had been sleeping with the former president for more than a decade, known only by a handful of people, had everything to do with the fact that she got the appointment, a fact of which the current president was well aware. Levy and President Grant did not like each other one bit.

"Ms. Levy, I'm sure you are a busy person. But you can rest assured, I'm busier. Please try to be on time next time."

"Calvin. Calvin, Calvin, Calvin," she said. "You've been a very secretive boy. I heard you had Kevin and Bill over here this morning. Without telling me? I'm hurt."

"Marianne, I'm the president of the United States. I don't have to clear my meetings with you."

"Fair enough. But Kevin and Bill work for me now. Remember? And I don't appreciate finding out from my staffers that my directors of the CIA and FBI had a secretive meeting with the president before the rest of the world had even had breakfast."

"It was nothing," the president said. "I asked them here to discuss this implementation of the new weapons training that you've asked them to adopt. I merely wanted their assessment on the brief you wrote."

"Yes, I talked to them. They both said the same thing."

"Why wouldn't they?"

"Because, Calvin, we both know they hate me. You hate me."

"I don't hate you, Marianne."

"And there's nothing the three of you would like better than to find a reason to get rid of me, so you can put things back the way you like them."

"You know, Marianne, you're right. I don't like the fact that you're in charge of every bureau and agency in law enforcement. I don't like the fact that you think for some reason that somehow elevates you over the office of the presidency. I don't like the fact that if you are all of a sudden unreachable, lots of people could lose their lives, because they are waiting around for your go-ahead. You're right. I don't like it. And I've made no bones about it. I will do everything in my power to get that law in front of the Supreme Court and repealed, or whatever I can do."

"For someone who professes to be the kind of man you are, you sure are mean and angry."

"You can call it a righteous anger, Marianne. I asked you here as a courtesy. So *I* could tell you that I had Kevin and Bill in here. And that *I* have asked them to keep me informed, something you seem to think is optional. I don't need to clear any of that with you. You may head up the agencies, but I still appoint the directors. And you may have complete autonomy as to how they operate, but in the end, you still answer to me. Don't forget it."

It took everything she had not to reach out and slap the man in the face. She loathed him. She loathed everything he stood for. And if he thought he was going to take away what she had worked so hard for, he had another think coming. He had no idea. She was about to be more powerful than any president in history.

She grabbed her purse and turned on her heel. "I'll show myself out."

CHAPTER 21

Keene stared at the screen of Taylor's laptop as he read and reread the e-mail. It was short and simple.

> *Ms. Taylor, this is the Prophet. I understand you're looking for me. But you need to understand that I am not the one you need to seek. I am just a messenger. Your and Mr. Keene's attempt to stop this is futile. The Lord has spoken. Tell the president to tell the nation the truth. He must instruct the nation to repent and return to the Lord. Otherwise, this nation will face its most dire hour.*

He looked at Taylor and asked, "How did he get your e-mail? Better yet, how does he know who you and I are?"

"I—I have no idea," she stammered. "My e-mail is secure. He shouldn't have been able to get in, let alone know who we are."

Boz, who had stirred awake from the commotion, was now standing over the back of the chair, also looking at the screen. "Looks like someone's got the jump on us."

"And how do you suppose that happened?" Keene said.

"Dunno." Boz shrugged. "But if he's really a prophet. . ."

"Can we please stop with the Prophet thing?" Keene snapped. "This guy is a terrorist. It's our job to catch him. Can we just focus on that?"

"Jon—" Boz tried to start but was interrupted.

"Guys! Enough!" Taylor said. "I ran a back trace on the e-mail. I have the location that it was sent from. He didn't try to hide that. It's an Internet café downtown. I called it in, and there are agents on the ground waiting for us when we land. I told them not to make a move before we get there."

Keen clenched his fists. "You did what!"

"What? What are you so jacked up about?"

"There's no way those boys are going to wait for us. They're probably storming the place right now!"

"I gave them an explicit order not to move," she said.

Keene looked at Boz, who was pinching the bridge of his nose.

"See!" he said. "Even he knows!"

"He's right, Ms. Taylor," Boz said. "I would be very surprised if they wait."

"I'm so glad you guys think so highly of the FBI and our protocols," she said.

The plane dipped and banked hard to the right.

"I guess we'll find out in a few minutes," Keene said as the plane began its descent.

★

On the ground they were met by two men, both wearing off-the-rack suits and black loafers that screamed FED. Though it wouldn't have mattered anyway, since they were also wearing the standard-issued blue coat with the stenciled FBI on the back. The men introduced themselves as Special Agent Franks and Special Agent Graham and ushered them into the waiting Suburban.

Inside the truck Keene spoke first.

"Give me the sit-rep," he said.

"Got two guys outside in plainclothes," Graham answered. "We were told to hold and just observe."

"And you guys just sat tight? Just like that?"

"Came straight from Director Preston's office. So yeah, we're just sitting on it."

Keene could feel the burn of Taylor's glare.

"And nobody's moved?"

"Oh, lots of people moving," Franks said. "There's all kinds of electricians and what looks like computer geeks in and out of the place. Got a power generator outside, and it looks like the place is under renovation."

"That doesn't make sense," Taylor said. "The e-mail came from there."

"Don't know," Graham said. "Looks like they've had some kind of huge power outage there that fried everything. Don't know when it happened. But when we showed up, all that was going on."

"How far out are we?" Boz asked.

"Fifteen minutes," Franks answered.

"Let's make it ten," Keene said.

★

Outside the Internet café, the group watched as technicians and electrical company personnel moved in and out of the building. Computers were being taken in and out and loaded into and out of a truck. Keene observed for a few seconds before deciding to move.

"It's obvious that if this is the place that e-mail was sent from, he's no longer here. Taylor, let's you and me go see what's going on."

"I'm in," Taylor said, unbuckling her seat belt.

The two exited the vehicle and moved across the street to where the caution tape was draped in front of the café. Taylor pulled her badge and grabbed one of the guys carrying a laptop.

"Hey, Megan Taylor, FBI. Who's in charge here?"

"What's the FBI doing here?"

"Guy in charge?" she repeated.

"Over there," the man said. "Tall guy with glasses."

Keene didn't wait for Taylor. He stepped over the tape and made his way inside to the man that had just been pointed out to them. He grabbed the man by the arm and started to lead him away from the others.

"My name is Jon Keene," he said. "Is there someplace we can talk?"

The guy with glasses looked instantly nervous. "What? What's going on here?"

By that time, Taylor had joined him and produced her badge.

"We're with the FBI. We just need to ask you some questions," she said.

"Sure," the man said. "In here."

He led them to the back of the room and into what looked like a makeshift office. It had a small door that led to an even smaller desk with two chairs. The chair behind the desk faced a window that looked out into the café.

"This is the manager's office," he said. "I try to spend as little time in here as I can, for obvious reasons."

Keene gave a courteous smile. "Obviously." He closed the door behind them.

"Something I can do for you two?"

"Do you know the people who use your Internet café?" Taylor asked.

"I know some of them," the man answered. "But this is a big city. Lots of people. Hard to know everyone."

"What happened here?" Keene asked.

The man's nervous look turned to one of disgust and anger. "Some punk uploaded a virus that fried my whole café. Literally!"

"When you say fried. . ." Keene began.

"I mean fried!" the man said. "Thousands of dollars of damage! Every computer in here lit up like the building got struck by lightning. I've never seen anything like it before. I mean, everything started sparking and then smoking and then just *bzzzt*! Gone!" His eyes narrowed. "Hey. . .what's going on here?"

"Classified," Keene said. "You got security cameras here?"

"Of course!" the man said.

"Can we see them?" Taylor asked.

"Nope."

"What do you mean, *nope*?" Keene asked.

"I mean, everything was being backed up to hard drives. They're all gone."

Keene did little to hide his frustration. Technology was great until something like this happened.

"See anyone unusual this morning?" he asked the man.

The man thought for a minute and said, "Nah, pretty much everyone in here today I've seen at least a couple of times." He nodded his head but then stopped short. "Hey, wait a minute. There was this guy."

"Who?" Keene and Taylor spoke simultaneously.

"Yeah. . ." he said. "This guy came in about an hour or so ago. Had a hat on and a hoodie pulled up over his head. I remember 'cause I was thinking I might need to keep an eye on him."

"Why's that?" Keene asked.

"Couple months ago, I had a couple kids come in here acting all weird, just shuffling around. And then just like that"—he snapped his fingers—"they grabbed a couple laptops and booked it outta here. I just thought the guy looked suspicious for a minute. But he just walked over to one of the terminals and started working."

"So you didn't pay any attention to him after that?"

"No. Once I saw him sit down and start typing, I let it go. Just figured he was normal."

"What computer?" Taylor asked.

"That one right there," the man pointed as one of the technicians was disconnecting the cables to take it away.

Taylor nearly leaped over Keene as she bolted out the door.

"Hey! Wait a second," she shouted to the guy. "Don't touch that! FBI!"

The guy stood frozen, as if in a panic.

Keene stepped out of the office and over to the terminal where Taylor was. "We should get it printed."

"Do you know how many sets of prints are going to be on this keyboard?" she asked rhetorically. "Besides, he wore gloves."

"Really? And how do you know that?"

"Wouldn't you?"

Keene realized she was right.

Taylor took the computer from the guy and set it back down at the station. She moved her eyes around like she was looking for someone.

"Hey you, electrician guy."

The man she spoke to turned and said, "Who me?"

"Yeah, you. How long till you get power back up to this store?"

"Aw man, this place is a mess. Whole junction box is fried. Probably going to take a week, at least."

"A week!" It was the manager.

"Sorry, man," the electrician said. "Someone did a real number here."

"We need to get this to an FBI office," Taylor said to Keene. They can have an analyst try to recover the hard drive and see if there's anything on it that will help us."

"Then let's do it," Keene said. He turned to the manager. "We'll be confiscating this computer. We'll get you a receipt."

"Hey," the manager said. "You can't just take that. And what's going on here?"

"We can and just did," Keene said. "We'll be in touch if we need anything else."

As he and Taylor stepped outside, Boz was waiting for them.

"See that, over there?" he said.

"See what?" Keene asked.

"That bank," Boz answered. "See what's in front of the bank?"

"The ATM!" Taylor said.

"Surveillance camera," Keene said. "That's good. We've got a possible description, if that's what you want to call it. Maybe that camera caught our guy going in or coming out."

"That's what I was thinking," Boz said.

"Here," Taylor said, handing him the computer. "Take this back to the truck. Keene and I will go find out about our camera."

Boz took the computer and walked back to the truck. Keene and Taylor crossed the street to the bank.

Inside, Keene found the bank manager and told him who they were. Though the manager had questions, Keene couldn't tell him much. The manager voiced his reluctance but ultimately gave his permission to look at the ATM footage. It, too, Keene learned, was captured digitally, and the feed came directly to the security suite on the second floor. The manager led them to the elevators, swiped his key card, and escorted them to the security suite.

"This is Davies," he said of the suit in the chair behind the desk. "Formerly a detective with the Chicago PD."

"Nice to meet you." Keene shook the man's hand.

"What can I do for you?" Davies asked.

"We'd like to take a look at the footage from the ATM camera over the last couple hours," Taylor said.

"Sure," Davies said. "Let me pull it up over there." He pointed to a large flat screen on the side wall. It sat in the middle of at least ten other smaller screens. Each one revealed a video feed from somewhere in the bank.

"Nice setup you have here," Taylor said.

"It's the cost of doing business," Davies said.

He punched a couple buttons on the keyboard and the flat screen flicked. In another second, an image of the Internet café across the street came into focus.

"Take it back to three hours ago," Taylor instructed.

The video came up and started moving forward. Fortunately, there were only two ATM customers during the footage. Even then, the camera was situated so as to allow at least partial view of the front door to the café across the street.

Several minutes of footage passed by in fast motion without any luck. But at almost two hours into the time code, there he was. A man wearing a ball cap and a hoodie approached the café.

"There!" Keene said. "Slow it down."

Davies did as he was told and slowed the speed to less than normal.

"Can you zoom in?" Keene asked.

"It's a fixed camera," Davies answered. "Best I can do is isolate an image and blow it up. And for all the money they've spent putting eyes and ears inside this place, they never touched the ATMs. That camera out there is old. And it's going to get pixelated fast, depending on how big you blow it up."

"Perfect," Keene said. He looked at Taylor. "Just keeps getting better, doesn't it?"

Davies slowed the video down to almost a complete stop. The man in the hat pulled it low down over his eyes and then pulled the hood up over his hat. He stopped before entering and turned his head, as if to check to see if anyone was paying him notice. As the man turned, Davies stopped the camera just as the man's full face came into view.

"There!" Taylor said.

The camera froze on what seemed to be a man in his mid-to-late thirties. He appeared to be of medium build and had a scraggly beard.

"Go ahead and blow it up," Keene said.

"This is actually a good picture," Davies admitted. "I may be able to give you something here."

With a few clicks the man's face filled the screen. The pixilation indicated the camera's age, but it was still clear enough to get a good look.

"You think that's him?" Taylor asked.

"I'd bet my life on it," Keene answered. "Can you print that out for us?" he said to Davies.

"Also," Taylor said, "can you e-mail it to me? I have some software that may be able to fill in the pixilation."

"Sure," he said and clicked a few more buttons then handed Keene the image as it rolled out of the printer next to his desk.

Keene grabbed the photo, shook the man's hand, and said, "Thanks a bunch. You've been very helpful, Detective Davies."

Davies nodded and said, "Glad I could help."

CHAPTER 22

The Prophet stood across the street, leaning against the side of a corner market. There were lots of people going in and out of the store, so he wasn't that noticeable. And he really wanted to not be there, but he was instructed to stay and watch. He was to see who was looking for him. He knew the names but not the faces. This would help him to avoid them until it was time.

See, that was the thing. At some point, he would come to them. He was told they would need him. And they would look to him for guidance. But for now, he was to observe and just be the messenger.

So he watched as the FBI vehicle pulled up to the café. He observed the two people who got out of the truck. The girl looked to be athletic and capable. The guy looked cold and calculated. Both immediately were aware of their surroundings as they got out of the vehicle, surveying the area, looking for anything that appeared to be suspicious.

And that's why he decided to leave. He had seen them. Knew their faces now. And that was enough. But as he pushed off the side of the building to go, another man emerged from the vehicle. This man looked different. He carried himself the same as the first man but was different somehow. This must be the one, he was told, who was the believer. *Good*, the Prophet thought, *they'll need him.*

Just then the man he had been observing turned in his direction. And it only happened for a split second. But they locked eyes. He froze for a moment, a slight panic coursing through his veins as the man took two steps closer to him, still looking. But then he stopped and turned back to face the café. Keene and Taylor had emerged and were carrying a computer. The three of them had a brief conversation and then split up again.

That was enough. He should have left minutes ago. Without a second thought, he turned and pulled the hoodie back up over his hat and turned down the other street.

CHAPTER 23

Marianne Levy left the White House and headed back to her office at Homeland Security. When she got there, she checked in with her secretary and cleared her schedule for the rest of the day. She went inside her office and closed the door.

Sitting down at her desk, she opened her laptop, typed the address in the search bar and waited for the site to come up. She entered her secure password and waited for the page to appear.

The website was an online banking system in Switzerland in which she was an account holder. She scrolled down to the bottom of the page to look at it one more time. It was the fourth time she'd done it since meeting with Ms. Smith. There it was, two hundred and fifty million dollars. Untraceable. In a secure Swiss bank.

It wasn't that she hated her government, it was just that she really loved money. And this was a lot of it. And not even all of it. This was just the first payment. And the reality of it was, if one had enough money, governments didn't matter. And the deal she'd made was going to ensure enough money.

She was going to need to leave for a while, though. Once it happened, there would be no telling what the fallout would be or how long it would take. That also created a problem. She would pretty much be serving herself up as the culprit. But she was pretty sure that with two hundred and fifty million dollars already, and another one hundred still to come, she could provide herself with some safety. And besides, in just a few days, there would be so much chaos, she would be the least of anyone's worries.

She closed the laptop and packed it inside her briefcase. She left her office and drove home to Arlington. She parked the car in the drive and looked at the house, a beautiful historic Georgian, over a hundred years old. She would miss this place. She had spent nearly a decade renovating it. There were a lot of good memories here. She quickly dismissed the thought. Three hundred and fifty million dollars could buy some pretty good memories, she decided.

She let herself into the house and placed her keys and phone on the table by the front door. She walked through the foyer toward the kitchen to pour herself a glass of wine. Time to celebrate. Instead, she was met by an unannounced visitor standing by the counter.

"Ms. Smith," she said, startled. "What are you doing here? How did you get in?"

"Really?" Ms. Smith sighed.

"Never mind." She had forgotten, for a moment, Smith's talents. "What are you doing here? I thought you were going home."

"I'm on my way to the airport. I just needed to stop by and tell you that Mr. Chin called."

"And?"

"And he says they're going to need more."

"What! No! I've given that man everything he needs."

"He says they do have what they need. For the initial agreement. But he wants to talk about something more involved."

"Like what?"

"He wants to move some things south of the border."

"What things? And why does he need me for that? I don't run Mexico."

"I'm not sure. He wouldn't tell me. He wants to meet with you."

"Listen, I've given him everything he needs for North Dakota, South Dakota, and Montana. That was the deal."

"So what do you want me to tell him?"

"Nothing."

"So you want me to tell him no?"

"No, I want you to tell him nothing. I'll tell him. When does he want to meet?"

"A week from today. Same place."

"Tell him I'll be there, eight o'clock."

"I'll give him the message." Smith turned and walked toward the front door.

CHAPTER 24

The sun had begun to set by the time they left the bank. They spent a little time, just showing the photo around to the people in the area. No one had noticed the man, although Boz thought he'd seen someone who looked like that at the market across the street. So they tried the guy behind the counter, but he was no help either. Whether it was the Prophet or not, they decided that he was long gone by now, and so they decided to head to the warehouse—the reason for their Chicago trip. So they packed it up and headed out.

The FBI Suburban turned north on North Michigan Avenue and headed to West Madison Street, to a warehouse district known as the West Loop. It was decided that Special Agent Graham would take the computer from the café to the Bureau's field office nearby, while Special Agent Franks would take the three of them to the warehouse.

On the way, Franks told them the West Loop was, at one time, one of the up-and-coming neighborhoods in Chicago. Several years ago it had been renovated from an industrial area and had, over the years, become a trendy neighborhood—though with the down-turning economy over the last few years, many of the warehouses were abandoned once again.

The warehouse in question was a small one nestled in between larger buildings, off one of the side streets. It looked to have been a small boutique store. As the vehicle slowed down, Keene spoke first.

"Taylor, you and I can take the front. Boz, why don't you and Franks go around back."

"Just don't shoot first, Jon," Boz said.

"I'm not going to shoot him. I'm CIA, remember? We torture them first." Keene winked.

Keene and Taylor got out of the car, drew their weapons, and proceeded to the front entrance, as the Suburban drove around back.

"What makes you think he's still here?" Taylor asked.

"I don't think he's here," Keene admitted. "But you never know. Maybe we'll at least find something in here that will lead us to him."

"Jon, wait."

It was the first time she had called him by his first name. *A little strange but whatever*, he thought.

"What?"

"I have a bad feeling about this."

"What do you mean, a bad feeling?"

"I don't know. I just don't. . ."

"Just stay on my six and keep your eyes open."

"Listen to me," she said.

Her seriousness gave him a slight pause. Something really was bothering her about this.

"Megan, look." He noted that calling her by *her* first name got no negative reaction, so he continued. "This guy has made a threat against the United States of America. You said he probably did it from here. We have to go in there. Besides, like you said, he's probably not in there anyway."

He didn't give her any more time for objection. He leveled his gun and opened the front door.

The place was dark. The front of the building had been outfitted to be an office, so there were walls and drop ceilings. The only light was from the open doorway. Keene reached for his flashlight and clicked it on. The beam illuminated an entryway with a long hallway leading down a corridor. No offshoots were found for the first ten paces or so, but then two doors on either side of the hallway appeared. Carefully, they checked each one only to find small abandoned offices. Continuing down the hallway, they found themselves against another door, this one bringing a dead end to the hallway. Keene motioned for Taylor to go low, signaling that he would stay up as they entered the door. He turned the knob.

Sweeping left to right, high and low, they moved through the door. Inside they found themselves in the main warehouse area. It was a room about the size of a four-car garage. Probably used for some type of manufacturing in the past. Now it was just an empty shell. But it wasn't completely empty. In the middle of the room sat a single stool. On it was a piece of paper. After securing the room, Keene took the paper from the stool and read it.

Mr. Keene and Ms. Taylor, you are seeking the wrong thing.
What you look for is not here. Please, Please! Tell the president to do

as the Lord has instructed him. He is a good man and knows the truth. And now you need to leave.

I have rigged this place with explosives. When you came into this room, you triggered the countdown. I have done this because it is not time for you to find me yet. And so I cannot take the chance that I left something behind that would help you. It has been set to five minutes. I tell you this so you can leave, safely. I wish you no harm. Please leave the building now.

"It's a bluff," Keene said, more to himself.

"I don't think so," Taylor said.

"What do you mean?"

"Look!"

She pointed to a small camera in the corner of the room. It had a little red light on it, signifying that it was on.

"He's watching us," she said. "Let's get out of here. Now!"

"He said five minutes. We've been in here less than two. Look around for anything quickly."

"What! Have you lost your mind, Keene?"

So much for first names.

"Fine!" he snapped. "Then you go, and I'll stay."

Keene holstered his gun and started moving around the room. It was empty. He trained his flashlight beam around the edges of the room, hoping to find anything that may have gotten left behind. There were a couple fragments of newspapers. He remembered that the video of the man showed a wall of computer monitors behind him, confirming the day of the broadcast. But nothing else. But now the place was empty. Next he pushed the light upward along the rafters. Wires. And lots of them. Strung from one beam to another.

"Look around. There's nothing here but this stool and this note," Taylor said finally.

"And those," he said, pointing up to the rafters.

"Okay, let's go," she said finally.

Just then, a beeping sound could be heard. First it started slow then sped up. Rapidly.

"I think our five minutes just got cut short," Taylor said.

"Either that or your watch is broken. C'mon!" he said grabbing her arm.

He had no idea what kind of explosives this nut job had used on this building or how big the explosion would be. But he had learned one thing in his time as a SEAL. When the beeping got faster, you didn't stick around to find out. Especially if you weren't the one who set the charge.

The beeping noise continued to speed up as he pulled her toward the door of the open room. He reached out and grabbed the handle and pulled it open. Just then the beep stopped speeding up. Now it was a continuous tone.

"Get down!" he shouted as he pushed her through the doorway.

First, there was a giant white flash. Then, like a giant vacuum, the air around them sucked back into the room. Then with deafening thunder, the room exploded. The concussion wave threw both of them down the hall as the building went up in flames.

CHAPTER 25

President Grant said good-bye to the students as they filed out of the Oval Office. Some fifth graders from Baltimore were cashing in on a contest they had won—part of an initiative the First Lady had started. The pinnacle of the trip, a meeting with the president. This was his last appointment for the day before going upstairs to check on Tess. She hadn't been feeling well these last few days. He had lost an uncle to cancer when he was young. And now seeing his wife go through this was pure agony. The good news, though, was that the doctors had discovered it in the earliest stages. They had been sure that during the operation they got it all. Now it was just the pain and sickness from the chemotherapy. She was expected to make a full recovery. That didn't surprise him. Tess was the strongest person he had ever met.

He made his way to the elevator that led to the private residence. Upstairs he found his wife lying on the couch reading a magazine.

"Hello, my love," he said, bending down to kiss her forehead. "How was your day?"

"Better than yours," she joked. It was their customary greeting each evening. "How's everything downstairs? Any word on what happened last night?"

"Nothing yet," he said. "But I have some really good people looking into it. How are you feeling?"

"As good as can be, I suppose. But I'm feeling better every day. That's enough about me. So what are you going to do about this Prophet?"

"Honestly, I don't know. I mean, what if this guy is really just a whack job trying to scare people? On the other hand, what if he's not?"

"Do you believe that?"

"What?"

"That he's a whack job, as you put it."

"Everything in me says yes. But what if I'm wrong? Boz seems to think he may be for real."

"Honey, you're the president. If there was an impending threat against this nation, don't you think you'd know about it?"

He laughed out loud. "You'd think! But with Marianne Levy running everything over there, it's hard to tell what she knows and doesn't."

"Can't you find out from the Pentagon or something?"

"It has been my mission, since I took this office to get this whole thing reversed. Eight years of a president that abdicated his responsibility as commander in chief has left us this mess. Right now, Marianne holds the keys to this nation's security. The law was almost unanimously passed in both the Senate and the House, for goodness' sake!"

He knew he was letting his temper get the best of him. And he didn't want to upset her, knowing she wasn't feeling well. He took a long deep breath and sighed.

"I'm sorry. You don't need to hear all of this."

"Your problems are my problems. I want to hear it."

"The woman thinks she's beyond the scope of this office. I have to repeatedly remind her that she still serves under me."

"Have you talked about this Prophet with her?"

This was a tricky subject. By all rights, he still was the president and was able to control certain operations. He was well within his authority to task Jon Keene and Megan Taylor to investigate this. But technically, he was supposed to advise the director of Homeland Security on all matters domestic and seek her cooperation.

"No," he answered. "I haven't. But she knows. She made it a point this morning to come into my office and tell me as much."

"You need to talk to her. You don't need to make her any more of an enemy to you than she already is. Last thing you want is to be dragged in front of a congressional committee."

He knew she was right. He just hated the thought of having her stick her nose in this, given what was at stake. He didn't care if she *was* head of all the agencies. The reality of it was, both the CIA and FBI directors didn't trust her either. They both made that adamantly clear to him. But rules were rules.

"You're right. I'll call her into my office tomorrow."

"You know," Tess said, "you could just go there. Might be a nice gesture."

"Hmph."

"Hmph, indeed," she quipped back. "So what about this Prophet?"

He thought about that for a minute. On one hand, he wanted to get on television and tell the American people that they, he—all of them—needed to do what the man said: start working on fixing this nation. On the other hand, he knew that he would jeopardize his job if he did. And it wasn't that he was afraid of losing his job. The job was only temporary anyway. But he also knew that the next guy may not share his convictions. And he really was set on changing this country. He looked at his wife with genuine uncertainty.

"I don't know, Tess. I just don't know."

Just then the phone rang in the hallway. Grant walked over and lifted the handset.

"Yes?"

"Calvin, it's Boz. There's been an accident."

CHAPTER 26

Boz and Special Agent Franks were sitting outside the warehouse, behind the building, making small talk as they waited for word from Keene and Taylor. Boz had just asked Franks to check in with them on the radio when it happened.

First there was a low growl. Then the ground rumbled slightly. Boz knew instantly what was happening. He jumped across the hood of the SUV and grabbed Franks by his coat. He pulled with all his strength and dragged the man down to the ground.

Glass flew everywhere as the blast blew out the upstairs windows. A huge fireball reached up and licked the sky as black smoke plumed out of the now gaping rooftop.

Boz, who was now lying on top of Franks, rolled onto his back, flat on the pavement.

"You okay?"

"Yeah? You?"

"I'm good. Other than a few scratches."

Suddenly Franks jumped to his feet. "Keene! Taylor!"

He started to run into the building, but Boz grabbed him and pulled him up short.

"Don't!" he said. "This whole place is going to come down in a few seconds. Try to reach them on the radio. I'll go around front."

"We have to go in there!" Franks argued.

"Listen to me," Boz said. "I've seen that kind of charge before. That whole roof is coming down in the next few minutes. You go in there, you're probably not coming out. Stay here and try to get them on the radio."

Boz didn't wait for the man to argue any further. The flames were getting higher, and he could already hear the sirens from the first responders. He needed to get to the front and check on Keene and Taylor. He ran as fast as he could around to the front.

The front of the building looked much better. The blast seemed to have been contained in the rear of the building. Huge plumes of white smoke were the only thing happening up here. He pulled his shirt up over his face, leaving only his eyes exposed and kicked in the door.

He couldn't see much. A thick layer of haze blanketed his view. Turning on his flashlight, he dropped low and crawled down the long hallway. He had only gone about a third of the way down before he saw them. Keene and Taylor were lying on the floor, Keene lying on top of Taylor.

Quickly, he checked over them and found no apparent injuries. They were just unconscious, it appeared. Boz pushed Keene off of Taylor and smacked his face. Hard.

"Jon! Jon! Wake up! Can you hear me?"

As if someone flipped a switch, Keene's eyes popped open as he gasped.

"You okay?" Boz asked.

"Yeah, I'm good."

"C'mon! Let's go."

Boz grabbed Taylor, held his breath, and stood up. He threw Taylor over his shoulder and headed back down the hallway. Keene was already in front of him.

As they exited the building, Franks was there waiting. He grabbed Keene as he stumbled out the door and helped him across the street, lying him down on the sidewalk. Boz arrived a second later with Taylor. He checked her pulse. It seamed to be good, but she was still unconscious. Just then an ambulance turned the corner, followed by two fire trucks. Boz waived down the paramedic as the firemen went to work on the building.

One paramedic checked Taylor's vitals as the other placed an oxygen mask over her face. A few seconds later, her eyes fluttered open. Keene, Boz, and Franks all stood silently, waiting for the word.

"She's going to be okay," the paramedic said. "Just looks like she got some smoke inhalation."

Boz breathed a sigh of relief. Last thing he wanted was to have to call Calvin and tell him he let one of these kids get killed.

"We're going to have to take her to the hospital just to be sure," the paramedic added. "What happened here?"

Boz looked to Agent Franks and nodded. Franks stepped forward.

"Special Agent Franks with the FBI. Sorry, but you don't need to know that. Just take care of the girl."

"I'm okay," Taylor coughed, trying to take off the mask.

Boz reached over and stopped her. "Just sit tight, Megan. Let them check you out."

She tried to sit up but closed her eyes and grabbed her head.

"Ugh!" she grunted, lying back down. "Okay. Maybe I'll lay here for a minute."

Boz looked at Keene, "You need to let him give you the once-over, too."

"I'm fine," Keene said.

"Now." It was an order, not a suggestion. It was the first time he had spoken with any kind of authority, and Keene seemed to be taken aback.

"You can jump in the back here with her," the paramedic said. "And you two can follow."

Franks looked at Boz, "Ah, I'm going to have to stay back here and explain all of this."

"Yeah, about that," Boz said reluctantly. "What are you going to tell the locals?"

"Just what I know. It's classified, and it's an FBI matter. For now, anyway. I'm probably going to have to give them more than that soon."

"I'll make some calls," Boz said. "Don't worry about it. Just keep them at bay for a little while."

"Okay," Franks said. "I can do that."

Boz turned to the paramedic and said, "I'm going to ride back there with them."

"You can ride up here with me. No room back there."

Boz gave the man a hard stare.

"Or you can just ride back there with them," the paramedic said, swallowing hard.

They helped Megan into the back of the ambulance, and then he and Keene jumped in with her and the other paramedic. The doors closed, and the ambulance took off. Boz took out his phone and punched some numbers in.

"Who are you calling," Keene asked.

Boz held up a finger to hold him off as he waited for the call to connect.

"Calvin," he said. "It's Boz. There's been an accident."

CHAPTER 27

The doctor on call checked Keene and said he was okay. Just needed some rest. Taylor, however, had breathed in a good amount of smoke and was going to need to stay overnight. Keene and Boz decided to just stay there with her for the night. The doctor said they could make use of one of the doctor's lounges: there were a couple cots, and they could just make themselves as comfortable as they could.

Special Agent Franks had stopped by and brought them their overnight bags from the plane. He offered to let them come back to the FBI station, or even put them up in a safe house for the night. But they declined, saying they wanted to stay close in case anything changed with Taylor.

Keene's head was still pounding from the headache. He put his bag down next to one of the cots and pulled out a bottle of ibuprofen. He took two and swallowed them down. He still couldn't believe he'd been dumb enough to let this happen.

"It's not your fault," Boz said out of nowhere.

Keene just looked at him.

"I mean it. It's not your fault."

"I never said it was."

Boz laughed. "You didn't have to."

"Yeah, well. . ."

"Yeah, nothing," Boz said. "Want to tell me what happened?"

"Nothing to tell. Guy had the place wired. He left this."

Keene handed Boz the note the Prophet had left on the stool in the room. Boz read it and handed it back to him.

"So he told you to get out."

"There was a camera in the far corner. Red light on it. He was watching."

"Maybe," Boz shrugged. "Maybe not."

"Either way, he tried to kill us," Keene said.

"No, he didn't."

Keene could feel his blood pressure rising, which made his head hurt even more.

"What do you mean, no, he didn't? Did you not just come from the same place I did? Did you not see the building blow up?"

"Jon, you were a SEAL. How many demos have you done?"

"Enough to know that that could've killed me."

"First of all," Boz said, "you're wrong. That was a shape charge directed upward. You know it, and I know it. The building was set to blow through the ceiling. Second, he told you he was going to do it. Why didn't you just get out of there? You had enough time."

"Are you kidding me? You're defending this guy?"

"No, I'm not defending him at all. I'm merely stating a fact. I've done enough blast work to know that charge was never meant to hurt anyone. It was designed to bring the building down and burn everything in it. And that's it. Even the blast radius was contained. None of the other buildings around were affected. Other than some glass on the street, there was no other damage."

Keene knew he was right, but it didn't matter. If he'd wanted to find this guy before, he was bent on doing it now.

"Doesn't change anything. Megan's upstairs in a bed with an oxygen mask over her face. Whether he meant for anyone to get hurt or not, she did. And when I find him, he's going to wish I hadn't."

"What if you don't find him?" Boz asked.

"I'll find him," Keene said.

"I'm not convinced finding him is going to change anything."

"What's that supposed to mean?"

"It means that this guy is a messenger. He doesn't know anything."

"You're wrong."

"Why? 'Cause you want me to be?"

Keene didn't say anything. Boz had served and was Special Ops, so he deserved respect. But that didn't change the fact that his judgment was clouded. And Keene suspected why.

"No," Keene said. "Not because I want you to be. I just think you are."

"Because of my belief in God, then."

"What is it with you people!" Keene snapped. "The man is a *terrorist*!" He slammed his fist against the wall.

The door to the room opened, and a nurse stuck her head in. "Everything okay in here?"

"We're fine," Keene said.

"It's all right." Boz spoke softly. "Thanks for checking on us."

The young woman nodded and closed the door, leaving them alone again.

"What's your problem with God?" Boz asked.

Keene just looked at him. Boz, it seemed, was bent on having this conversation. And he just didn't have the energy to have it. He broke away from Boz's stare.

"You know what?" he said. "My head is pounding. I'm going to sleep. We'll get started trying to find this guy in the morning."

CHAPTER 28

Four Days Later

Traffic was already bad and the sun hadn't even risen yet. And it was starting to rain, which made the drive into downtown Washington that much more unappealing. It usually increased drive time by more than twenty minutes. And since she had drunk an entire bottle of wine by herself last night, Marianne Levy was not feeling too great. So she fought her way through the gauntlet of cars, forty minutes past her usual time.

Finally she pulled into the complex and showed the guard her ID. Upstairs her secretary greeted her with a cup of coffee and an itinerary for the day. She was about to move past her when her secretary stopped her.

"Someone here to see you, Ms. Levy," she said.

"I don't recall having a meeting this morning."

"Unannounced, ma'am."

She was about to ask who when she noticed the two Secret Service agents sitting in the waiting area. Then the door to her office swung open.

"That'll be all," she said, moving past to greet her visitor. "Mr. President, to what do I owe the pleasure?" she said.

President Grant moved aside to let her in. "I'd like to talk to you about something."

"Please, have a seat," she said, gesturing to one of the chairs at a small coffee table.

Before she took her own seat, she leaned outside the door and got her secretary's attention.

"Would you mind bringing in some coffee and muffins, please?" Then to President Grant, "Anything specific you'd like, sir?"

"Coffee is fine. Black, please."

"And get something for the agents." She closed the door and took a seat. It was customary when meeting with the president to allow him the first word. But she wasn't big on tradition. "I have a busy schedule today. What can I help you with?"

She watched as President Grant smoothed his pants leg and fidgeted with his tie. Whatever he wanted to talk about with her was obviously something that he wasn't looking forward to. That made her happy.

"Ms. Levy," the president began, "you and I don't necessarily see eye to eye on everything. We've had our differences. . . ."

What is this? An apology? Surely not, she thought. He wanted something, and he'd decided to play nice in order to get it, she was sure.

"And we don't necessarily agree with each other," he continued. "That being said, we do have to work together."

Not for much longer. "Yes, it seems so."

"A few nights ago, I received a somewhat disturbing message."

It was as if time stood still. He hadn't even finished speaking when a feeling of sheer panic filled her.

"Disturbing? How?" she asked cautiously.

"Well, it came through my private e-mail."

She couldn't breathe. All of a sudden, she felt trapped. There were probably agents outside waiting to take her away this very moment. No. It couldn't be. There was no way. She forced back the panic and remained calm.

"Your private e-mail? I wasn't aware that you had private e-mail."

President Grant smiled. "Not too many people are. That's why it's called *private*."

She feigned a chuckle. "Yes, I guess it is. Go on. What did this message say?"

She held her breath waiting for what was coming next.

"Some man calling himself a prophet was on video saying that God was going to destroy the United States."

Immediately a mix of panic and relief swept over her. She said the first thing that came to mind. "Sounds like some religious fanatic." Then, "No offense, sir."

"None taken."

"I'll have someone look into it immediately."

"I'm not sure it has anything to do with anything really. But it's why I asked Bill and Kevin to meet with me."

"I don't understand."

"I realize that I was out of line. I shouldn't have blown up at you the other day in my office. I apologize for that. The American people have spoken on the issue of our law enforcement agencies, and I'll respect that. For now. I still disagree with the entire law. But until it is changed or removed, I will respect it. So I am sorry that I did not come to you before going to them."

She still didn't know where this was leading. And she absolutely didn't trust this apology. The two of them had been political adversaries for over a decade. And she still had no idea what was going on here. Did he know something? Was this a fishing expedition?

"And what is it you asked of them?"

"Nothing that I'm not entitled to, as president. I assure you. I asked them to provide an agent, each. A computer specialist and a field operative."

"For what purpose, may I ask?"

"Just to look into it."

"Do you think there is a credible threat to you or this nation? If so, you are required to inform me, so I can do my job effectively."

"Ms. Levy, you give me a threat assessment every morning. Do you not?"

"I do. Are you suggesting that perhaps it's inaccurate?"

"That's what I'm asking you. With all due respect, of course. Is there anything I should be worried about? Is there anything that perhaps you've been tracking you just haven't felt is worth mentioning?"

Just then there was a knock on the door.

"Come in," she said, perhaps a little too quickly.

The secretary entered, carrying a small tray with coffee and an assortment of muffins. Levy was relieved for this interruption. It gave her a moment to gather her thoughts quickly. And she had to do it fast. The girl would only be there a few seconds. She tried to take a deep breath and calm herself, but her chest felt constricted. There was no way anyone could know what she'd been doing these last few weeks. She was in control of every intelligence agency in the country. What was going on here? She quickly decided that he must not know anything. If he did, she would've already been taken out of there. No, this was a fishing expedition.

The secretary smiled and closed the door on her way out.

"So is there anything I should be worried about?" President Grant said, taking a sip of his coffee.

She had to play this cool. She mustered up her best worried look—not too hard under the circumstances.

"Mr. President, you know what I know."

President Grant pursed his lips and nodded. "Okay, then."

"Okay, then," she agreed.

"So you don't have a problem with me having these agents look into this private matter. Do you?"

"I'm not sure that I would classify this as a private matter just yet. Why don't you send me the video, and I'll have some of my best people look into it?"

"Like you said, it's probably just some poor, misguided soul. I already gave the video to the two agents. No need to worry yourself or your resources on this. I'll make sure Bill and Kevin report back to you if anything they find suggests otherwise." He stood up and grabbed his suit coat. "Thanks for the coffee."

She waited for nearly five minutes after he was gone, a million different scenarios racing through her mind. Was this just an innocent visit? No, it couldn't be. He was baiting her. No, that couldn't be it. If he knew *anything* she would be in a nine-by-nine concrete cell in Gitmo right now. Then what? It couldn't be a coincidence. She couldn't just let it go. She had to find out. She grabbed her phone and punched in the number. It rang only once.

"I thought you weren't going to need me." Ms. Smith said.

"Change of plans."

"Sorry, Marianne. I'm at home. Can't help you right now."

"Then get back here. Now! We have a problem."

CHAPTER 29

President Grant rode back to the White House in silence. He was still upset over the phone call he'd received from Boz a few days ago. An accident? Didn't sound like an accident to him. Keene and Taylor had almost been killed. Boz assured him everyone was fine; it was more Keene's fault than anything. They had spent that night at the hospital with Megan just to make sure. What had he done? What had he sent those kids out to do? And now it was almost a week later and still no word on who or where this man was.

His meeting with Marianne Levy hadn't gone any better. The woman made his skin crawl. And he hated the thought that he'd just given her any information she could use against him. But this Prophet wasn't going away. Grant tried to close his eyes and pray that God would give him discernment in this, but there were too many distractions. He hadn't had a moment of focused prayer in days. And other than a building blowing up in Chicago, he had no substantial evidence this Prophet was real. That, however, was about to be questioned once again.

When he got back he went upstairs to check on Tess. She had been to the doctor this morning already. He'd tried to have her stay home. Being the First Lady had its benefits: she was fully entitled to receive any treatment she needed at home. But Tess argued that the drive and being outside were good for her spirit. She insisted on going there. But that had its drawbacks, too. It made her even weaker after the treatment, because she had to be transported back, a trip that took most of thirty minutes.

Tess assured him that she was fine, just tired, and that he should get back to running the country. He kissed her forehead and told her he would check in on her again around lunchtime. Because he still had a little time before having to be downstairs, he went to his private desk and took out his Bible. He read a few passages and said a quick prayer for his day. He promised that he would spend the night alone, in the Word, and in quality, focused prayer time.

Before he left, he had the notion to turn on the computer on his desk. He had five more minutes. He opened the mail server and watched the spinning wheel of death, as he liked to call it, twirl around as it searched for any new messages. The thing chimed, notifying him he had one new message. There was no subject line, nor was there a return address. Before he even clicked the mouse, he knew what was coming.

A window appeared on the screen with a video player. He clicked the PLAY button and held his breath as it began to play. The Prophet appeared on the screen and began to speak.

"Mr. President, for months now, I have been warning you to tell the American people the messages I've given you. You have ignored these warnings. Why? I know you are a man of God. You know that what I have said the Lord can bring to pass. Why do you hesitate? Why do you not plead with the people to put away their idolatry and return to Him?

Therefore, thus says the Lord: 'You, America, have ignored Me. You have put other gods before Me. I am a jealous God. I have given you all that you have, and yet you do not acknowledge Me. So that you may know I am God, I will remove these other gods. And I will give this nation into another's hands, lest you turn back to Me.' "

The screen went blank.

President Grant cradled his head in his hands and began to weep. He had no idea what to do. How could this be real? Could this Prophet be a true messenger of God? Or was this some deep conspiracy to destroy his administration and ruin everything he had worked for? He *was* a man of God. He *did* try to do what he believed God would have him do, concerning matters of state. He had been open about his faith. He hadn't compromised his integrity in any way. How could this be happening?

He had to collect himself. He was needed downstairs in just a minute. He wiped his eyes and took a deep breath. He would go and honor his appointments for the day. But something had to be done about this. And it had to be done quickly. He reached for the phone and dialed the number.

"It's me," he said when the line was answered. "Tell the networks I would like thirty minutes tonight at seven o'clock."

CHAPTER 30

Bradley Forester III was already into his fourth meeting of the day. As CEO of one of the nation's two largest banks, his day was already in full swing. The meeting that he was about to enter wasn't really a meeting, more a social gathering.

Every other week, he had coffee with the CEOs of the five largest banks and investment firms on Wall Street. They made small talk, going through the gambit of family: kids, wives, mothers-in-law—just for levity's sake—and then they would talk about the important stuff. Many of the men were members of the same social and sporting clubs, so they would take ten minutes to gossip about their golf games and the like. After that, they finally got to business. All together, they'd usually spend about an hour with each other.

He was looking forward to today's gathering. Just yesterday, he had shot a sixty-eight on the course, breaking Tim Crandle's club record of sixty-nine. Crandle, who was his direct competitor as CEO of the nation's largest bank, was his friendly nemesis in all things. Especially golf.

The perfunctory, familial conversation was coming to a close, and it was time to make his friends jealous. He cleared his throat and called for everyone's attention.

"Everyone! If you please, I have an announcement to make."

There were smiles all around, as everyone, even Crandle, knew what was coming.

"As you know, yesterday, I had my usual ten o'clock tee time, and—" He felt the buzz in his pocket. This was unusual. His secretary knew not to disturb him during this time. And since he had all of his phone calls forwarded to her during business hours, even personal calls, there was no reason for this to be happening. He slid the touch screen bar across the screen to unlock the phone, revealing a text message: 911.

Slightly bewildered, he said, "I'm sorry. Please excuse me."

The others shrugged it off and returned to their chatter. But as Forester was dialing the office to call in, one by one the others' jackets and pockets began to buzz as well. Everyone had received the same message: CALL IN. IMMEDIATELY!

Forester was first to make his call, so he got the information first. But it only took seconds for the information to spread across the room. It seemed everyone there was aware of the same thing. Forester hung up the phone and looked at the other men with genuine fear in his eyes.

"You, too?" he asked them.

There was a round of nods. Not because no one wanted to speak. But because they were unable to.

"We have to go," Forester said.

Nobody moved. They were all still stunned.

"Now!" he screamed.

CHAPTER 31

Megan swatted away the doctor's hand for the third time.

"I'm fine!" she said. "Please get that thing out of my face."

"I'm sorry, Ms. Taylor," the doctor objected, waving the otoscope. "But I told you this follow-up was necessary. If I'm to release you from further examinations, you need to let me look and make sure I don't see any blood in your ears or cloudiness in your eyes. I know it's been a couple days now, but I want to make sure."

"Let the woman do her job so we can get out of here." It was Keene.

"You're the reason I'm in here!" Megan reminded him.

Boz came into the room, momentarily diffusing the situation. "Everything okay here, doc?"

The doctor clicked off the little light-emanating instrument and said, "Looks okay. But I'd still recommend a few days of light duty and lots of rest."

"Yeah, I'll take that into consideration," Megan said.

She knew it really wasn't Keene's fault. But she was angry. She'd told him that the place was going to blow up. Heck, the note told them the place was going to blow up! Why she hadn't just walked out and left him there was the real question. She immediately answered it for herself: if anything had happened to him, she would have felt guilty for the rest of her life.

"Hey," she said, hopping down from the examination table, "I'm sorry. Didn't mean to jump on you like that. It's not your fault."

"Yes, it is," Keene said. "And I'm sorry. I shouldn't have put you in that situation."

"I'm a big girl. I can handle myself."

"I wouldn't say a *big* girl." Keene smiled. "I'd say athletic with good muscle tone."

"Ha ha. Funny!" she said. "Can we go now?"

"Waiting on you."

"Any word on the computer from the Internet café?" she asked.

"I just talked to Franks," Boz said. "He said it's fried, and they've got nothing."

"There's got to be something on there," Megan said. "I need to go check it out."

"It's a dead end," Keene said. "Let's go."

"It's only been a couple days," Megan argued. "And I haven't had a chance to look at it yet. Maybe I can find something."

"We've been here for four days. We've been all over this city trying to chase down this guy. I'm telling you. He's gone. Doesn't matter what you find on that computer. You said yourself that he wouldn't risk using it for anything other than sending you that e-mail. The manager said he'd never seen the guy before. We're spinning our wheels here. We need to regroup and figure out what's next."

"Okay," she agreed. "But first, I'm starving. I need something to eat."

They walked down the street to an old-fashioned diner, the kind that looks like a huge, silver train car. Once they were seated, the waitress came and took their orders and disappeared again.

There was a television hanging above grill, with a local morning news program on. The sound was down but the hosts were talking with a guy Megan recognized as an author. His book was on the small coffee table facing the camera. She had been meaning to read it—something about a lawyer who went into the Witness Protection Program.

Keene and Boz were talking, but Megan was watching when the interview was interrupted. A graphic for breaking news flashed on the screen, and the feed was instantly switched to New York City. A reporter was standing in front of the iconic statue of the bull on Wall Street.

"Hey," she shouted to the person behind the counter. "Turn that up."

The young man behind the counter looked at her as if he had been asked to dig a ditch. She pulled her badge out and walked over to him. "I said, turn that up, please."

The kid reached under the counter and produced a remote control. Keene and Boz were already out of their seats standing beside her.

"What's going on?" Keene asked.

The volume on the TV slowly crept up. The reporter looked to be in a big panic.

". . .word here," he was saying, "is that the European market showed no sign of this during their trading session all day. This is coming as a huge surprise, Dave. I haven't had a chance to speak with any of the executives yet, but I'm told someone will be making a statement soon."

The image went to split screen, and a man behind an anchor desk appeared.

"Chris, we haven't heard anything from Washington yet. Can you tell us anything else?"

"Only that this all started about a half hour ago. If you can pan around behind me, you'll see the police tape there. Local law enforcement is on the scene, and they're trying to keep everyone back."

"Okay, Chris, well we'll keep in touch with you there, as we try to figure out what's going on. Thanks."

The screen went full again. This time with the anchor.

"So there you have it, folks. Horrible tragedy in the wake of this sudden and horrifying news. Once again, if you've just joined us, it appears that the CEO of American Financial Mutual bank, Bradley Forester III, has committed suicide by jumping out of his forty-second floor office. This on the heels of the market taking a devastating dive this morning. Still no word on what this means for the immediate future right now. But it's beginning to look like total chaos here in New York at the moment. Now, I believe we have our correspondent in Washington on the phone. Michael, are you there?"

Megan looked at Keene and Boz, who were still-faced. She didn't know what this had to do with anything, but she had a gut feeling it wasn't good. "What do you make of that?" she said.

"Don't know," Keene said. "But I'd bet it has everything to do with this attack. We need to go."

"Where?" Megan asked.

Neither of them had an answer.

"Okay, then," she said. "I'll call and get us a ride. Boz, see if you can get President Grant on the phone and find out anything." Then to Keene, "Jon, you get our food to go."

"What!" Keene said. "You kidding me? Get the food?"

Megan looked at him. "I'm not going anywhere without some food. I'm starving. Besides, remember what you said, 'Never pass up the chance to sleep or eat'?"

Keene rolled his eyes. Apparently, they were back on first names again. "Get on the phone and get us a ride. I'll meet you outside."

CHAPTER 32

Ms. Smith sat on her bed, watching the television above the fireplace and packing her bag again. She'd left the United States shortly after meeting with Marianne and had taken her private chartered plane to Quebec. It was good to get a few nights' sleep at home. She had planned on taking more than just these last few days. Enjoy the quietness of the country. Just twenty miles north of Montreal, her place was far enough out of the city to be private but close enough to get anything she needed quickly. But all of that was not to be.

She had begun to pack, again, after the phone call from Marianne. It appeared there was trouble. She was pretty certain that Marianne hadn't run her mouth to anyone. She was too smart for that. And she definitely hadn't said anything to anyone. So why was the president of the United States in Marianne's office asking about a potential threat? Somebody knew something. And that didn't sit well with her.

Alex was a self-made woman. Born Alexandra Sokolov, she was an orphan. She grew up under the government's care and had figured her life was meaningless. That was until he, Joseph, came for her that day.

He showed up, out of the clear blue, one afternoon when she was fourteen. The headmaster of the girls' home had found her in the library and told her that she had a visitor. This was very strange. No one ever came to visit her. But it sounded exciting, so she followed the headmaster to the foyer, where a man in a suit and tie introduced himself and asked if she'd like to take a walk.

They walked the grounds of the compound, as none of the children were allowed to leave without the accompaniment of one of the staff. But the compound was large and completely fenced in, so there was plenty enough room for a stroll. Eventually they found themselves a long way from the house, in the back of the property in a wooded area, a good four hundred yards away from anyone.

He made no attempt at small talk. Rather he explained to her that he knew who she was, where she was from, who her real parents were, and why she was at the orphanage. He even told her that her real name was Alexandra Sokolov. He had a very compelling story, and she was hooked from the moment he introduced himself. Anything was better than where she was.

Joseph explained to her that he could take her away from there. That he was family and had papers to prove it. He could train her and give her a skill set that would never go unneeded.

"What do I have to do?" she remembered asking.

He answered her by pulling out a pistol with a silencer on it.

"Have you ever seen one of these?"

"On television and in the movies," she answered.

"Have you ever held one?"

"No."

"Here." He took her hand and showed her how to hold the weapon. "Now see that tree right there?" He pointed.

"Yes."

"Shoot it."

She remembered not even hesitating. She pulled the trigger and the gun spat. The recoil sent her arm over her head. That made her angry. Not only had she missed the tree, but she felt like such a weakling for not being able to control its recourse to her arm. Without a second thought, she stiffened her arm and lowered the gun again, taking aim at the tree. She pulled the trigger again and again until it just clicked and no more bullets came out. She had hit the tree six out of nine times.

"Did you like how that feels?" Joseph asked.

"Yes."

"Would you be able to do that to a person?"

Again, she didn't even hesitate. "Yes."

Joseph had smiled at her. He had the warmest and nicest smile.

When they got back to the house, Joseph informed the headmaster that he was her uncle. He produced some papers and a letter from the Canadian government instructing the headmaster to turn Alex over to him.

Naturally, the headmaster made him wait as she made some calls and checked out his story. But apparently, it did. Ten minutes later, she was packed and leaving the house. There would be no more orphanage for Alexandra Sokolov. There would be no more Alexandra Sokolov either, Joseph had explained. From now on, she would be Alex Smith.

The flashing graphic on the television brought her back. She reached for the remote and turned the volume up. It appeared that a banker in New York had committed suicide. But that wasn't what piqued her interest. Soon, the news anchor was connecting the dots and explaining how Wall Street had taken a turn that morning. The entire market was crashing. Some experts were saying it could be worse than the crash of 1929, the event that ultimately led to the Great Depression. Once again, large investments in government-funded companies and programs were going belly-up.

Was this part of what Chin and Marianne had planned? No, it couldn't have been. Something else was at play here. Something was wrong. This had nothing to do with Chin. As a matter of fact, this would jeopardize everything they had done. Marianne was right. They had a problem.

She stuffed the rest of the clothes in the bag and called the private terminal at the airport. She asked to be transferred to the hangar where her plane was being kept. The dispatcher connected the call and told her, "Have a good day. Eh?"

"'Allo," the man said in his French-Canadian accent.

"I need to be wheels up in two hours."

CHAPTER 33

Keene and the team were back in Washington, as per the president's orders. When Boz had stepped outside the diner in Chicago to call him earlier, President Grant ordered that they return immediately. He had received another message from the Prophet.

They had been following the news of the market crash throughout the flight. Megan's ability to connect to a satellite gave them the option of watching live news coverage. And it was bad. Not just bad, horrific. Banks all across the nation had begun to close for the day and lock their doors. ATMs were being emptied by long lines of customers trying to get as much cash out as they could. It was happening again, just like 1929. And as of yet, there was no explanation. One of the correspondents from one of the news channels said that the president had asked all the networks for thirty minutes of airtime before the crash had even happened. The question now was, did President Grant have knowledge of the crash? And if so, how could he let it happen? And even more importantly, could he have helped to stop it? These were all questions Keene himself planned on asking the president in about five minutes.

The Suburban entered the secure area of 1600 Pennsylvania Avenue. The guard outside waved them in, having been instructed to do so the moment they arrived. Chief of Staff Hardy met them at the door to the West Wing and led them in.

"He's in the Oval," Hardy said. "He's waiting for you."

"What's he saying?" Keene asked.

"Nothing," Hardy replied. "Not a single word. He's canceled all of his appointments for the day. He's called for Chief Justice Spencer, Vice President Walker, and Marianne Levy to join us. They're all on their way."

"This can't be good," Megan said. "All three branches of the government represented?"

Keene agreed. He didn't know what was going on inside the president's head, but there were only a handful of reasons why the president would call a private meeting with all three leaders and the head of Homeland Security. And he was sure he wasn't going to like this.

Hardy opened the door to the Oval Office and let them in. President Grant immediately stood and came to them.

"Mr. Keene, Ms. Taylor, are the two of you all right?"

"We're fine, Mr. President," Keene answered for both of them. "What's going on?"

President Grant shook his head and said, "I'll explain in a moment. But first sit down. There's something I need to show you."

He pulled a thumb drive out of his pocket and inserted it into a laptop that was sitting on the desk. He clicked a few buttons and turned the screen around so that everyone could see.

The Prophet's message played while the three of them looked on. When it was finished, he ejected the thumb drive, closed the lid, and looked at his guests.

"I'm not sure when I actually received this."

"How do you mean?" Keene asked.

"I mean, it was sent some time between last night and this morning. I didn't see it until earlier."

"Before or after the stock market?" Boz asked.

"Before."

"And you think it has something to do with this?" Keene said, more a statement than a question.

President Grant sighed. "I have no choice but to," he said.

"I agree," Keene said. "Mr. President, we need to be out there chasing this guy. Not sitting in here. Look what he's already doing."

"Mr. Keene," President Grant said solemnly, "I agree with you—"

"Then let's get going!" Keene said, standing up. "Give that thing to Taylor, and we'll—"

"Just a moment," President Grant interrupted him.

Keene sat back down.

"I was saying," President Grant continued, "that while I agree with you that this video is related to what's happening right now on Wall Street, I cannot say with certainty that this man is responsible for it."

Keene was stunned. He couldn't believe the president was going to defend this guy. Again.

"Then why are we here?" Taylor asked.

"Because I can't rule it out completely," President Grant said. "So I am going to turn this over to you, Ms. Taylor." He dangled the thumb drive. "And I do want you to continue pursuing this man, Mr. Keene. But I want you all to know that I'm going to go in front of the American people and do as he asks."

"What!" Keene stood up again. "Mr. President—"

"Mr. Keene!" President Grant said, raising his voice. "Sit down!"

Keene did as he was told, but his head was about to explode. How could the president go on television and give in to this terrorist's demands?

"Guys, listen," President Grant said, his voice calm once again. "Our country is in real trouble right now. This thing with the stock market, it's happening. And there's nothing that we can do to stop it. You heard what the man said. He said that God was going to remove the idols of our nation. What's our biggest idol? Money! Our economy. Our way of life.

"This could very well be nothing more than a terrorist attack. And I'm willing to concede that fact, if you can provide substantial proof that that's all it is. But in the meantime, our people are going to be losing their minds by tomorrow morning. Our country could be decimated in one week, due to this fallout. Right now, more than anything, the American people need encouragement. And direction. And I'm going to give it to them. Whether you approve or not, Mr. Keene, I will go on television tonight and tell the American people that we have become a godless nation. And that if we have any hope of recovering from this, they had better listen."

"And what if they don't?" Boz spoke for the first time since arriving.

"Then God help us all," President Grant said.

Just then the door opened up again, and in walked Marianne Levy, already in midsentence.

"Mr. President, I thought when we met earlier today—" She stopped short, obviously surprised at seeing the others there. "What's this about?"

Keene had heard about her but had never met her. And what he'd heard about her wasn't pleasant. Even Kevin Jennings admitted to him, once, that he wouldn't cross paths with her. The woman was a commanding presence. And she didn't look very happy.

"Who are you all?" she continued.

"Marianne, thank you for joining us," President Grant said. "These are the two agents I told you about this morning. Jon Keene and Megan Taylor."

Keene was about to say hello but got cut off.

"And you?" she said to Boz. "Who are you supposed to be?"

"He's a personal friend of mine," President Grant answered for him. "He's helping Mr. Keene and Ms. Taylor."

"And what's this about Chief Justice Spencer and VP Walker joining us? What are you trying to pull, Calvin?"

Just then, Hardy arrived with the final two invitees to the meeting.

President Grant wasted no time once they arrived. He motioned for them to sit and started talking.

"Vice President Walker, Chief Justice Spencer. Thank you for joining us. I'll get right to the point. I have reason to believe that there is an imminent and impending threat to our nation's security. Pursuant to article sixteen, section 1a of the Intelligence Enforcement Act, I hereby ask that the powers granted to Director Levy and the Department of Homeland Security be returned to the Executive branch, until said threat is deemed neutralized."

CHAPTER 34

Marianne Levy was beyond mad. She was furious. Never before had she been as blindsided as she had just been in the president's office. She should have known that her impromptu meeting with him earlier was no coincidence. She should have expected that he would try something like this eventually. And now here she was, relegated back to nothing more than a standard cabinet-level position.

President Grant showed them all the video of the man calling himself the Prophet. And though he wouldn't admit it, she knew that the reason he was doing this was not that he thought there was an impending attack. He simply hated her and wanted her out of the way. And he had used this morning's stock market event to convince them. The irony was, there actually was a threat! But it had nothing to do with this Prophet. And it surely didn't have anything to do with the stock market. At least not yet. And it was already in place. There was nothing President Grant or anyone else could do to stop it. And so now she had a choice to make.

She knew when the IEA—the Intelligence Enforcement Act—was brought into law that there was always going to be this possibility looming over her head. Especially since Grant was the one who appointed that stupid chief justice three years ago. But since the days of the peace treaties in the Middle East, she never thought that, outside of someone declaring war on America, she could ever have this happen to her. And Walker, there was a real winner! The only reason he got on the ticket in the first place was because he had the ability to swing Ohio, New York, and Pennsylvania in the election. The man was a complete idiot. He had no idea how to even be an effective senator, let alone vice president of the United States. He would collapse at the thought of actually assuming the role of the president. The whole country would collapse. And that was what she was counting on now, as she planned her next move. She would still get what she had set out to get. Now it was just a matter of tweaking a few details.

And so she made up her mind. She had a new plan. Mr. Chin would now have a decision to make. And she had to see Alex. She had a job for her to do.

★

"Mr. President," Keene muttered. "That was. . ."

"Intense," President Grant finished his thought. "Yes, I agree. But needed."

The four of them sat in the Oval Office, having just finished the ceremony, if you could call it that. It wasn't so much a ceremony as an event, Keene thought. Something of the kind he had never witnessed before. And the look on Marianne Levy's face. It was utter shock and dismay. That brought a quick smile. But he quickly stifled it, knowing the mood was anything but joyous right now.

It happened so quickly, he thought. It was like a roller coaster that shot out of the gate and slammed to a stop two minutes later. President Grant had made his declaration then shown the video to the chief justice and VP Walker. Before the video went to a blank screen, he told them that he had Keene, Taylor, and Boz on assignment looking for the guy. He brought up the explosion at the warehouse in Chicago and then restated his position. Without a second thought, the chief justice and vice president nodded to each other. President Grant then produced the necessary documentation to make the order official, and the two of them signed it without a word. Marianne Levy had stood there, mouth agape. The shock of it all had rendered her speechless.

She did, however, manage to spew a few eloquent curse words as she stormed out of the office. And as she left, she turned to face President Grant and spat, "You'll be sorry you ever crossed me!" And then she was gone.

The president thanked the chief justice for his time and excused him. He told VP Walker that he would speak with him in more detail in a little while. But for now he needed the vice president to step out.

"What now?" Keene asked.

"You three go do your jobs," President Grant said.

"So you still want us to find this guy?" Taylor asked.

"I do," the president affirmed. "But maybe not for the reason that you all think you need to find him."

"What's that supposed to mean?" Keene asked. *Here we go again.*

"It means what it means, Mr. Keene. I do want you to find this man. But"—he held up a hand—"and I do mean *but*, you are not to harm him

123

in any way. Do I make myself clear?"

"Mr. President."

"Mr. Keene," the president held him off again. "I mean it. Do not harm this man. You may not subscribe to my thoughts on matters of faith. I get that. But I am still the president. And until someone invokes some other constitutional amendment to remove me from this office, I will be the one making these decisions. Do you understand me?"

"Yes, sir," Keene said, frustrated.

"I know how you feel about this man," the president said. "But I know deep within my soul that he is not HAMAS, al-Qaida, or any other terrorist. I truly believe that there is something bigger at play here. But I won't abdicate my responsibility in protecting this nation either. That is why I'm giving you permission and the full resources of this office to find him. If I'm wrong, and he is somehow involved in a plot to bring down this nation, we will prosecute him to the fullest extent of my power."

That assuaged Keene's anxiousness a little bit. At least the president hadn't completely lost his mind, he thought. But he still disagreed with the man. This was nothing more than an elaborate terrorist plot.

"But if I'm right," the president continued, "then I—we—are going to need this man's cooperation going forward.

"Now, I have asked the networks for thirty minutes tonight. I am going to give our nation a speech on the steps of the Capitol building at seven o'clock. I would like you all to be there, but I understand if you want to get moving on finding our Prophet."

"What are you going to say?" Boz spoke up.

"I'm going to try and assure everyone we are going to be all right. That we think this stock market thing is just the free market doing what it does. But I'm also going to tell them that they need to take this as a warning. And then I'm going to do something that perhaps no president has ever done."

"What's that?" Keene asked.

"I'm going to share the Gospel with them. And then I'm going to ask them to repent, as a nation. And to turn back to the God who gave them their country in the first place."

CHAPTER 35

The Prophet sat on his couch, weeping. He didn't understand. He had done what he was told to do. And now, he was told, the president was going to attempt to call the nation to repentance. But then he was told that it would not happen. The nation would not turn. That this must come to pass.

"But why, Lord?" he cried in desperation. "Why? If he is to do what You've asked him to, then why? Why have me do all of this? I don't understand."

"*Because it is about much more than just one man's obedience,*" he was told. "*Yes, President Grant is a good man and a true believer. But it is not for him to lead these people through this.*"

"I don't understand," the Prophet cried again. "Show me, Lord."

"*Yours is to do as you are commanded,*" he was told. "*Not to question.*"

"But if not President Grant, then who? Me? I cannot lead them, Lord."

"*No, you shall not lead them,*" came his answer.

"But what of these people?"

"*They have given themselves over to the ruler of this world,*" he was told. "*Long have they forgotten who it is that brought them here and gave them this land. So I shall remove My hand from them for a time.*"

"Please, Lord," he wept. "Let me tell them. Let me tell them all. They can change. Please say we are not too far gone."

"*It is not for you to speak to them anymore,*" he was told. "*You shall be silent until I call you to bring council to the one whom I have appointed.*"

"Oh, Lord!" the Prophet sobbed. "Please, no. Please spare them."

"*Weep for your people,*" he was told. "*Pray for them. For they shall need it.*"

PART 3: JUDGMENT IS COME

CHAPTER 36

Alex Smith stepped off her plane and entered the waiting car. She was back. She had called Marianne to check in as the plane had taxied to the hangar. Though she could not fully discuss things with her over the phone, she knew it was not good. And this brought her a smile. Not because things were not good but because she knew ultimately what it meant. It meant she was about to have a new assignment.

When she was taken from the girls' home by Joseph, it was the happiest day of her life. No more did she have to clean up after herself, do her own laundry, help cook the meals, and study her books. Weapons and stealth became her new studies. Joseph had told her that he was going to make her into something great. And he did.

Four years of intense physical training turned her into one of the world's most deadly assassins. She had worked for many people. Some bad, some not so bad, but all very rich and willing to pay enormous amounts to have certain people removed. And so now she was rich. Very rich. But for her, it wasn't all about the money. Joseph had told her long ago that doing this kind of work would birth something in her. He told her it would bring a fulfillment. A dark, satisfying fulfillment. And it was the power to wield life or death.

She felt the darkness take her soon after her fifteenth birthday. The day she did her first mark. He was a foreign dignitary who liked young girls. Joseph set it up. She would be the mark's "date" for the evening, waiting for him in his room that night.

She had sat there, waiting patiently for the disgusting man to arrive. And when he did, it was exactly like Joseph had said. He had walked over to her, looked her over, and then ordered her to undress as he sat down on the bed.

Joseph had told her that she needed to take his life with her own hands. It would be more satisfying than just putting a bullet in his head. However, he allowed her to have a weapon, in case things went wrong. But they didn't. The man was as predictable as his dossier. He waited for her to get undressed, and then he turned his back to her and asked her to rub his shoulders. That's when it happened. She reached down and removed the short piece of wire she had stowed under the bed. And in one swift motion, she jammed her knee into his back as she wrapped the wire over the man's head, forcing him to stay bent over. She pulled and twisted the wire cable as the fat man flailed and scratched at her arms. But she pulled harder and felt the man's life leave his body.

Afterward, she got dressed and left the room. The excitement and exhilaration she felt was unlike anything she had ever experienced. Then the darkness came. And it took her. She realized she liked it. That was several years ago. There had been many more since. And there was about to be another. She was sure of it.

The driver of the car dropped her off at the main gate, as usual. She produced her badge, given to her by Marianne, and did the security thing. Once inside, she headed straight for the top floor and knocked on the director's door.

"Come in."

She closed the door behind her and took a seat. Marianne was sitting at her desk, her eyes closed and leaning back in her chair.

"You look comfortable," Alex said.

Marianne opened her eyes and looked straight at her. She'd seen this look before. It was the one they all gave. Right before they asked her to do it. She loved that look.

"We have a big problem," Marianne said.

"So you told me. What's going on?"

"Well, for starters, I'm no longer in charge of everything."

"How do you mean?" Alex said, genuinely confused.

"That hack has invoked section 1a of the EIA. He's taken over this office and all intelligence and law enforcement."

"How did he do that?"

"Well," she said, "the provision's there. All he had to do was show a credible threat."

"You mean—"

"No. I don't. He—they—don't know anything. I'm sure of it."

"Then what?"

"This is partly why I called you," Marianne said standing up and then coming around her desk with her finger covering her mouth. The universal *shhh*. "Why don't we go grab some coffee. We can talk then."

"Sounds good. I could use a cup."

The two women left the building, neither saying a word. Outside, a car came around and met them. The driver got out and opened the doors. Marianne told the driver where to take them as they got in and sped away.

The short drive was a silent one. Marianne had always told her that they should never speak inside the car. Though she had the entire system under her thumb, she never wanted to take any chance of someone somehow compromising one of her cars. Once there, they ordered their drinks and stepped back outside. There was a small park less than a block away with a walking path through it.

"It's a pretty day," Alex said. "Shall we take a walk?"

"I think so," Marianne said. Then to the driver, "We'll be right back. Going for a short walk. Wait here for us."

The driver nodded and got back inside the car.

Once she was confident they were out of earshot of anyone and no one was paying either of them any mind, Alex picked back up the conversation.

"So, this problem. . ."

"Yes, it seems there is a man who calls himself a prophet. Some religious zealot, to say the least. Apparently he's been in contact with the president, warning him to speak to the American people and tell them that God is angry with us all."

"Good thing I don't believe in God." Alex laughed. "I might have to be frightened, otherwise."

"I don't care who believes in what," Marianne said. "The fact is, with his warnings and this stock market thing, he's got the man scared. And— unbeknownst to me—the president apparently had three agents working on trying to find this guy when he tried to blow them up in a warehouse in Chicago four days ago."

"So he leveraged that to get you removed."

"Exactly!"

"And what about Chin?"

"It has no effect on Chin. He's ready to move whenever I give him the go-ahead."

"Then what? What do you need me for?"

Here it was. She knew it was coming. But she wanted Marianne to say it. It was, perhaps, her favorite part. When they actually asked her to do it. And Marianne was ripe! The woman was consumed with it; Alex could see it all over her face.

"Two things," Marianne said. "First, he's giving a speech on the steps of the Capitol building this evening. I want you to be there."

Marianne let that hang there, like Alex was supposed to read her mind.

But that's not how it worked. Marianne would have to say the words. This was Alex's second-favorite part, making them squirm as they wrestled with actually saying it. It was one thing to think it. Or even want it. But to say it, that was a whole other thing.

"You want me to be there. . .why?" she prodded.

"Oh, for goodness' sake!" Marianne said, perhaps a little too loudly. Some people stopped to look their way.

They continued walking and remained quiet for a few moments. When it was evident no one was looking or paying attention, Marianne continued.

"Do I have to spell it out for you?" she said in an intense whisper.

Alex stopped walking and looked her dead in the eyes. "Yes, if you want me to do this, then I want you to say it."

Marianne gave an exasperated sigh. "Fine, then yes. I want you to kill the president of the United States."

And there it was. The payoff. She felt the tingle inside, the one that stirred the dark emotion in her. It had been awhile since she'd had a mark. This one was the pinnacle of the assassin's world. But her life had been leading up to this, all along.

For it was Joseph who told her that one day she would be asked to do this. And when it happened, she needed to be ready. She had asked then how he could know that someone would ask this of her. "Because," he had told her, "it is the very reason you were born."

"You'll need to be careful," Marianne was saying. Alex had wandered off into her own thoughts for a moment. But she was back now. "With this being an outdoor speech, there will be snipers on the rooftops and Secret Service agents everywhere."

"This isn't my first rodeo, Marianne," she said. "It'll be done. You know my price."

Marianne nodded. "Yes, no problem."

"And the second thing?" she asked.

"Find this Prophet before they do. And then do the same to him."

CHAPTER 37

Keene, Boz, and Taylor all sat together in an office that Hardy found for them. He told them it was a catchall office for staffers and others who were there doing business for short periods of time. It was small but comfortable. There was a computer and a coffeemaker and a few pastries, but other than that, just a couple chairs and four walls. Keene put a fresh pot of coffee on and grabbed a frosted donut thing and shoved it in his mouth.

"Thoughts?" he said, wiping the frosting crumbs from his lips.

"I need to get back to the bureau and analyze this video," Taylor said. "I need to be on my computer, with my gear."

"I could take you back to see Artie," Keene said.

Taylor gave him a sarcastic grin.

Keene poured himself a cup of the fresh brew and sat down facing them. He had already been trying to devise some kind of plan to use all three of them as effectively as they could. But he still had a few things to work out.

"Okay," he said. "I think that'll be good. Boz, why don't you and I stay back and try to game plan where to go from here."

Boz nodded in the affirmative. "That's fine."

"But," Keene said quickly, "I want us all to be back here before President Grant gives his speech. I want to be on-site in case this nut job decides to show up here."

"You think he will?" Taylor asked.

"Don't know," Keene said honestly. "But I don't want to take any chances if he does. Secret Service will be taking care of protective detail. The three of us can be moving around the area looking for him."

"We don't even have a good description," Taylor said. "Are we supposed to stop every person who kinda looks like this guy?"

"If we have to," Keene said.

"Okay, then I'm going to go get started on this video. Maybe I can get something from it that will help us."

"Okay," Keene agreed. He looked at his watch and saw that it was already after three. "Why don't we break from here and meet at the Capitol at six o'clock. Megan, that'll give you a couple hours with the video. Boz and I can go get cleaned up and talk about what we need to do next."

"Sounds good," she said. "I'll meet you at the east entrance. Give me a shout if anything comes up before then."

Keene gave her a nod as she left. Then to Boz, "My place is about fifteen minutes away. We can go there. Get cleaned up."

"Fine by me, but we should probably talk with Agent Greene first."

"Who?"

"The head of Calvin's detail."

"Oh, yeah," Keene said. "I guess we need to let him know we'll be there."

"If you don't want to get your face shot off."

Keene peeked his head out the door and grabbed the first person who came by. Some staffer or secretary. He didn't know. Didn't matter anyway. "Hey, you," he said. "Tell me where I can find the head of Secret Service around here."

"There's an office down the way and to the right," the young man said. "Someone should be in there who can help you."

"Thanks."

They found the office right where the staffer had said it would be. With a big presidential seal on the glass door. A young man sat behind the lone desk in the room.

"Agent Greene?" Keene asked, peeking his head inside the door.

"He's with POTUS, sir." The president of the United States.

"Special Agent Keene, CIA, on special assignment for *POTUS*," Keene said. "Where are they?"

"Sit Room, sir. Meeting with the JCs and the DOD."

The kid likes his acronyms, Keene thought. "Thanks." Keene backed out of the doorway and turned left down the hall. He knew where the Situation Room was. Then to Boz with a smirk, "POTUS is in the Sit Room with the JCs and the DOD."

"I heard. He's probably a former jarhead," Boz joked.

"Hey, I resemble that remark."

When they got there they were met by another two agents standing outside the door.

"May I help you two gentlemen?" the first agent asked.

Keene flashed his ID again and introduced himself.

"Need to see Agent Greene," he said.

"He's in with the president and the joint chiefs, sir."

"It's kind of important," Keene said. "Can you get him?"

"One second."

The agent lifted his wrist mic and spoke into it. Then placed his finger over his ear as he listened.

"He'll be out in just a moment, sir. You can wait over there," he said, pointing to a small alcove in the hall.

Agent Greene stepped out a moment later and stuck out his hand. "Agent Brian Greene. Nice to meet you, Mr. Keene." Then to Boz, "Boz, good to see you again."

"You, too, Brian," Boz said.

Keene looked back and forth between the two men.

"What can I do for you, Mr. Keene?"

"You know anything about what the president has had me and Boz doing?"

"A little bit, sir. Just that you're on special assignment for him and we're to give you anything you need."

"Good. Here's the deal. I know you aren't all that excited about a speech outside on short notice."

"No, sir, I'm not," Agent Greene interrupted matter-of-factly. "But he insisted. So we're humping it to get it ready."

"Right," Keene continued, "so there's a possibility that the guy we're tracking may show up tonight. I just want you to be aware. I have a picture. Not a great one. We're working on getting something better. But you need to pass it around to your guys. We're going to be on-site, walking. I want Boz and Taylor and me to all be on comm."

"Not a problem, sir. We can get you wired up."

"Anyone sees this guy, they are to report to me. You got that?"

"Yes, sir."

"And unless President Grant is in immediate danger, you do not take a shot at him. Got it?"

"Got it."

"Good. We'll meet you at arrival."

CHAPTER 38

Taylor inserted the thumb drive into her computer at her desk. It was perhaps one of the fastest, most geeked-out machines on the planet. It had every kind of software imaginable and could do just about anything, short of cook and do laundry, though she could probably design a program that could do that, too. And it was able to literally hack into any other system in the world and never leave a trace of her being there, a fact she kept secret from even her boss.

She typed her password in and waited for the window to come up. She tapped away on her keyboard and then hit ENTER. While she waited, she brought up the video. She opened her editing software and began to strip away the layers. One by one, everything in the video disappeared, until she was left with just the man, sitting on the stool, with the bandana over his face. She deleted the body and left herself with just the head. She isolated the bandana and slid it over to a secondary screen, leaving her a forehead and a pair of eyes on the original one. She opened up another portion of the editing software and applied it to the bandana. The image was now sitting in a three-dimensional grid. With her mouse, she could turn the image three hundred and sixty degrees. She clicked a couple buttons and the grid began to map out depth points on the image; how far out the nose stuck, the width of where the lips were, the cheekbones and jawline.

Next she took the picture from the ATM security camera and scanned it into her hard drive. She brought that image up on the third of her four screens and began the process of trying to enhance it as best she could. There wasn't much there, but she had enough to work with.

With that done, she exported the ATM photo and the new three-dimensional image of the bandana into a different program. This one was a facial-reconstruction software. Taking the skin tone of the forehead from the video, and the secondary image of the ATM photo, she typed a few commands and waited. Less than two minutes later, she had a complete, rendered image. She looked back at the eyes from the video. Then turned to the ATM photo. Then to the newly created image. It was perfect. According to Jinx—the name she'd given her computer, after a robot from one of her favorite classic movies, *Space Camp*—she was looking at an exact representation of the man they were looking for.

She saved the image and exited the editing software. Over on her fourth screen, the one she had started out on first, was a message from Jinx, in a dialogue window.

You are now ready to proceed, Megan.

"Thanks, Jinx," she said, patting the monitor.

She looked out the window to her office and made sure no one was lurking around or looking like they were coming to see her for something. Satisfied, she started typing.

The FBI facial-recognition program was one of the best in the world. And it could take anywhere from five minutes to two days to find someone through facial comparison recognition. With Jinx, that time got cut by three-fourths. She clicked the button and watched as the software went to work. Even with the worst-case scenario, Jinx should be able to find him before she had to be back at the Capitol. She leaned back to stretch, when Jinx beeped at her. Sitting up, she looked at the screen. Staring back at her was a Texas driver's license belonging to one Quinn Harrington.

Taylor stood up, kicking her chair back. She pointed at the screen with a huge grin and said, "Ha! I got you!"

CHAPTER 39

In all of her forty-eight kills, Alex had never attempted anything like what she was about to do. This was the granddaddy of them all. Killing the president of the United States. No one had ever done it and gotten away with it. That is, unless you believed in the Kennedy conspiracy. And even then, there was Oswald. Whether he did it or not was not the point. The point was, no one had ever gotten it done without being discovered. Leaving nothing behind. But then again, she had never tried to kill the president before now.

The agents would already be in place by now. Once word was given that President Grant was to give the speech, they would've been flying around like madmen, trying to get the area secured and prepped for him to be there. So she had to think outside the box. The fact that Marianne had given her less than eight hours' notice was something that made her even more excited. There were a couple reasons for this. One, there would be no time for a proper advance team setup. So that meant she had options. And two, it was more of a challenge.

She exited the Smithsonian's National Gallery of Art–East Building and walked along Third Street NW. Off to her left, she could see the steps of the Capitol Building, approximately two thousand feet away. She needed to be closer. Not that she couldn't make a shot from here. It's just that there was no place to take a shot from. Besides, she wanted this to be as up close and personal as she could get.

That gave her an idea. What if, in the midst of an imminent threat, they were to whisk him away? Where would they go? How would they do it? There was protocol for this, she was sure. And she knew who would know said protocol. She found a pay phone and dialed the number.

"I need a coffee," she said when the line was answered. "You want to meet me?"

"Sure," came the reply. "Where at?"

"You pick the place."

"The coffee shop on Lowell?"

"Sure. Give me twenty minutes."

"Okay. I'll see ya there."

She hung up the phone and flagged down a cab. She got in and told the man where to take her.

Marianne was already there when she arrived. The two of them left the coffee shop and started out down the same path they had a few hours earlier.

"I need the evac routes from the Capitol," Alex said.

"Why would you need those?" Marianne asked. "I thought you were going to be there."

"I am. But so is every available Secret Service agent in DC. But when they move him, only a handful go with him."

"Depends on what the situation is. Is he being taken out due to potential threat? Is he being taken out due to imminent danger? Or has there been an attempt?"

"Let's say they believe there's been an attempt."

"Then it would be one of three ways."

"Too complicated. I need to control which way."

"Impossible. They decide right then and there. That way it's completely spontaneous and no chance of being compromised."

"Then I need—"

"However," Marianne said in a menacing tone, "the actual evac procedure from the building to the cars is set. They won't deviate from that."

"Then I need to be there."

"Fine."

"I'll need to have credentials. Something from DHS. Secret Service is going to know their own. Homeland Security could be anyone."

"How will you get out?"

"Don't worry about that. I'll get out. You just make sure I can get in."

"Meet me at six forty-five, north entrance. I'll have what you need then."

"You going to be there?"

"Ha!" Marianne said. "I wouldn't miss this for the world."

CHAPTER 40

The five o'clock news hour came. And with it, more bad news. Reports from all over the country that banks were closing. People could not get access to their money. Riots were starting to break out in small pockets. The country was on pins and needles, waiting for the president to speak, hoping that he could bring some sense to what had happened earlier in the day. The market was a mess. And everyone was saying that it was about to get worse. Grocery stores were being emptied. Banks were closed. Rioting was beginning to start throughout all the major cities. Mayors and governors from all over the country were issuing statements saying that everything was going to be fine. But no one believed it.

The latest news to hit the airwaves was that the price of a barrel of oil had just gone up astronomically. Within the next few days, the price of a gallon of gas was expected to shoot up over ten dollars a gallon. The country was in a full panic. And President Grant was sick to his stomach. He had less than an hour before he gave his speech.

He had informed his staff that he would be writing the speech himself. This came with a barrage of argument. Even VP Walker had tried to convince him that he was letting this get too personal. That he needed to trust the speechwriters to give him a solid manuscript that would calm the American people and show them everything was under control. Grant had laughed at that.

"You think we're in control, Gray? Look around. We're not in control of anything right now. This is happening, man. There is no speech that is going to appease the people. In less than a week, our entire country is going to shut down. Do you understand that?"

"Calvin, look," Walker had pleaded. "You can't know what's going to happen. You need to go out there and assure the American people that we can control this. That we are going to be just fine. And then, if not, we'll deal with it."

"I'm going to deal with it tonight, Gray," he'd said. "And you and everyone else may not like what I have to say, but I am the president. So I will decide what this speech is going to be about. Not you or anyone else. Is that clear?"

"Yes, sir." Walker had stormed out of the room.

Grant knew his friend was angry, but it didn't matter. Walker wasn't someone who shared his deep convictions on faith. Sure, he went to church on Sundays with his family, but that was about it. Walker was what Grant called a weekend warrior. He never spoke ill about God, but he never went out of his way to show he had any strong beliefs either.

None of that mattered. It was nearly time. He looked over the speech again. He made a quick change to one of the lines and then reread it. *Yes,* he thought, *this is exactly what I need to say.*

He called Agent Greene into the office. The agent stepped inside and closed the door.

"Yes, sir?"

"I want you to make sure no one disturbs me for the next thirty minutes. Is that understood?"

"Yes, sir, Mr. President. Any exceptions?"

He thought about that for a moment. What if Tess needed him? What if something else happened that couldn't wait. No, he decided. Even Tess would have to wait. He needed to do this.

"None. Absolutely none. Is that clear?"

"Yes, sir. I'll let you know when we're ready to leave, sir."

"That will be all. Thank you."

"Yes, sir," Greene said, leaving the office.

When the door closed, he pushed away from his desk and stood up. Taking his suit coat off, he draped it over the back of the chair and then knelt down beside the desk. It had been too long since he had found himself in this position. And though his knees rebelled against him for being on the ground like this, it felt good.

He folded his hands and bowed his head and began.

"Father in Heaven. . ."

CHAPTER 41

Boz waited in the living room while Keene finished cleaning up. They had less than an hour before they had to be at the Capitol. That wasn't much time, considering it was a fifteen-minute drive and the fact that they wanted to be there early to get a look around at where the president was going to give his speech.

Then just as he got antsy, Keene appeared, pulling his shirt on.

"I'm good," Keene said. "Let's roll."

Boz looked again at his watch. "You know what? We still have a couple minutes. Can we talk for a sec?"

Keene raised an eyebrow. "Sure. Okay. What's up?"

Boz sat down in one of the chairs there in the den. He had tried to have similar conversations in the past week with him but to no avail. Something or someone had interrupted them every time. Or Keene had gotten mad and walked away. But here they were. No one to interrupt.

"There's something I need to talk to you about. But you just won't let me."

Keene sat down across from him, blank-faced. "Really? You want to do this *now*? We're about to go see if this guy shows up at the speech, and you want to do this now?"

Boz smiled. "Yep. I do. Listen. For the last week, I've followed you around. I've taken your lead on all of this. And where has it gotten us?"

"Oh, so this is all of a sudden my fault?"

"No." He sighed. "I'm not saying that. I'm saying maybe it's no one's fault."

"Here we go!"

"Why are you so bent on dismissing that this guy could actually be who he says he is?"

"Listen to yourself, Boz! You seriously think that God would pick some random guy to just harass the president because all of a sudden

He cares? He doesn't care! This is absurd."

"First of all," Boz said, "God has used random people throughout history to accomplish His will. Secondly, yes, He does care. He's always cared."

"Yeah." Keene rolled his eyes.

"Jon, listen."

"No, you listen. I grew up in church. I went to Sunday school. I learned all the little songs and all the prayers. And when I went into the Marines, I trusted that He would take care of me. And then I got married. And I believed that He had brought her into my life. And so He would take care of her, too. That was supposed to be part of the deal." He sat there with a clenched jaw for a moment. Then continued, "And then some other idiot, who believed in *his* god, and who thought that his god told him to kill everyone who isn't like him, killed her. That pretty much sums it up. Doesn't it? The God you say cares so much, He cares so much that He took her away from me. So don't you sit there and tell me that He cares. If He cared, He would've never let that happen."

"I'm sorry—"

"No, chapy, you wanted to have this conversation. We're having it. You want to know why I think all of this with this guy is a bunch of garbage? Because God doesn't care! And to be completely honest with you, I'm not even sure anymore that He ever existed to begin with."

Boz waited a few seconds when Keene was finished. It was good for him to get it out. Keene probably had never said that to anyone—keeping it bottled up inside for years. Finally Boz said, "What I was going to say was, I'm sorry you've been misled. I wasn't apologizing for the loss of your wife."

Keene sat there a moment and then said, "What's that supposed to mean? Misled?"

"It means what it means. Somewhere along the line, you were led to believe that God is here for our pleasure and that He should do what we want."

"And that makes it so much better."

"Actually, it does. See, your problem is, you think that because God allowed your wife to die, that somehow it was a personal vendetta against you. Or that He somehow abdicated His responsibility. When in reality, what you don't understand is, God loved her more than you could ever love her. And to see her die in pain, like that, brings Him no joy. But you have to understand, there's more to it than that."

"I understand He let her die."

"Yes, He allowed it to happen."

"So you prove my point."

"Quite the opposite. You have to understand that God allows things to happen because He is working all things to their appointed end. And we may not understand why some things happen, but we have to trust that there is a reason for it. God calls us to come to Him, to lean on Him when these things happen. He allows these things to happen because our world is broken. And in due time, He will come back and restore all things to their rightful state. You think He doesn't care. I'm telling you He cares more than you'll ever know."

"Well, He's got a poor way of showing it."

Boz looked back to his watch. The time was getting away from them. "Listen, we need to go. But will you at least continue this conversation with me later? There's a lot more to it. I really want to try to explain and help you understand."

"Tell you what," Keene said standing up, "you promise me that you'll put every effort into finding this guy, as if he was a terrorist, not some freak, and I'll think about it."

"Deal," Boz said. "Now, let's go hear a speech."

CHAPTER 42

Alex knew the only way the president was going to be taken away from the steps of the Capitol quickly was if there was an immediate threat. So she had to make that happen. How, was the question. Once they took him, she would be ready. Since Marianne had given her the evacuation plan, she knew exactly where the president would be taken en route to the motorcade.

She'd spent her young career imagining all the different ways to distract a mark or plan a diversion. She had tried some different weapons, investigated different explosives, tested out certain poisons, all to prepare her for immediate and unforeseen scenarios. Today all of that planning would pay off.

A couple years ago, she'd encountered a young Afghani bomb maker. He was very impressive. After the wars in the Middle East, his country had been left all but devastated. The American troops had pulled out way too soon, leaving the radical factions of his country to move back in and take over the nation. Eventually, the Americans returned but not before the damage had become so extensive the country was hardly recognizable. The years that followed were deadly. And still were to this day. But he had been brought up in a village that had some very talented men when it came to explosives. His grandfather had taught him the trade of bomb making. And he had showed him new ways to conceal an IED, an improvised explosive device.

It was his work that Alex was going to use this evening. While the president was giving his speech on the steps of the Capitol, Alex would be waiting in the stairwell of the hallway. And the explosion, she was sure, would send the agents running, with the president in tow.

Getting the device past security was simple. She had already visited the place earlier today. With the DHS identification Marianne had provided, she was able to walk right in, without even acknowledging the security guard. Not that it would have mattered if he had stopped her. The device was completely unassuming. Just a child's toy. And completely undetectable to all known explosive-detection technology. She wove her way through the corridors to the place she wanted to set the charge. There, in front of the window. She took the item out of the bag and placed it exactly how she needed it.

The room was an upstairs office, unused, like many of the rooms in this building. From the looks of it, the place had probably been left unattended for months. It was perfect. And when the time came, it would do, she was sure, exactly what it was supposed to do. Of course, there might be collateral damage. This was something she wasn't a huge fan of, but given the enormity of the target, she guessed she could overlook it this time.

She checked the device one last time and then left the same way she came in. She took care to make sure no one noticed her coming out, and when she was sure she was good, she casually walked on. The president was scheduled to arrive in less than fifteen minutes. She would need to wait until he was on the steps before getting in place. That gave her, she figured, no more than twenty minutes. She needed to hurry.

★

Agent Brian Greene checked with the other agents on-site, one last time, as the motorcade arrived at the Capitol. All four zones reported all clear. That still didn't make him feel any better. Of course, an impromptu speech like this did work to their advantage on some levels. With little to no planning, it gave potential threats little time to plan themselves. Statistically, the risk should actually be lower. But his job wasn't to play the odds. It was to do everything in his power to make sure the man whose life he was to protect at all costs stayed alive.

He waited for the agents in the lead and rear cars to step out and do a perimeter sweep. Once they gave the all clear, he opened the door to his vehicle and got out. Looking around for double precaution, he opened the back door and motioned for the president to come out. It was only a short walk to the inside of the building. And once they were inside, the first part of the unknown would be behind them. He motioned for his men to flank the president on all sides, and then he gave the go.

★

Keene and Boz arrived at the Capitol building ten minutes before the scheduled arrival of the president. When they got there, Taylor was already waiting for them. She handed Keene a picture and then gave one to Boz.

"Here's our guy!" she said excitedly. "Quinn Harrington, thirty-four years old. Unmarried, no kids. Graduate of University of Texas and then on to seminary. He has a master's degree in theology."

Keene took the photo and studied it. It was definitely the guy. He knew, just by the eyes. "Good job, Taylor. How'd you—you know what? Never mind. Doesn't matter. We need to get this to all the agents."

"Already done. I handed out hard copies and also made it available for download. Every agent and DC police officer has this on his Metro Link right now," she said, referring to the recently developed smart phone required by all government agents and local law enforcement. Then, "You don't think this guy is really gonna show up, do you?"

Keene thought about that for a second. Honestly, he had no idea. He didn't know what to think. They had been looking for this guy for almost a week now and nothing. Not even a crumb. But there was still the fact that the guy left that note in the warehouse, telling them that it wasn't time yet for them to find him. So what did that mean? That eventually they'd get lucky? That all of a sudden he would just decide to come in peacefully? No, Keene couldn't take that chance. This was the perfect place and time to pull something, if someone was so inclined. And his radar was screaming inside him right now. He started to say something when a young, attractive blond woman brushed past him, her head down, looking at her phone.

"Oh, excuse me," she said. "I wasn't looking where I was going."

"Sure," Keene said as he watched her continue on. "My fault," he tried to call after her, but she was already gone.

"Really?" Taylor said.

"What?" He laughed. "I'm not allowed to talk to a pretty woman?"

Taylor remained unmoved.

"Right." Keene cleared his throat. "I don't know if he's gonna be here or not. But something doesn't feel good. We need to be on our toes."

"Agreed," Boz said. "Doesn't sit well with me either."

Keene couldn't believe it. Did Boz actually just take his side on something? "Weren't you the one who said you thought it was a good idea for the president to do this?"

Boz pursed his lips. "Yeah. I was. And I still think he needs to. But I'm with you. I'm not sure it has anything to do with our Prophet, but I've just got a bad feeling about this."

"All right," Keene said, trying to think. "Here's what I want us to do. Taylor, you go meet up with outside perimeter detail. Make sure they all have the picture. Boz, you take the outside by the steps. I'll hang back here and wait for President Grant's arrival. Once he's on-site, we'll decide where to station ourselves. Everyone got a comm?"

Both Boz and Taylor nodded in the affirmative.

"Good. Put them in and let's check in with the detail."

All three put their earwigs in and clipped their wrist mics on just in time to hear the head of the advance team speak.

"POTUS has arrived. Heads up, everyone. We'll move to the building in five, four, three, two. . ."

CHAPTER 43

Men were so easy, Alex thought. And this guy was supposed to be one of the best? Seriously! He didn't even bat an eye. Well, that wasn't true. He did. But not at the fact that she picked his phone and ejected the magazine out of his weapon. *Typical guy*, she thought, *carried it right there on his hip.* She had pocketed both items before they had even separated. And he was too busy trying to get her attention as she ignored him and walked on by. Ever since Joseph had introduced her to this new life, she had always been thankful she was an attractive woman. It just always came in so handy when she was doing a job.

Weaving her way in and out of people, she slipped off to the hallway. She needed to get an idea of the space she was going to be confronted with. As she approached, a guy about her age stood sentry over the doorway. He held his hand up to stop her.

"Sorry, ma'am, this corridor is closed for the evening."

She smiled and pulled out her false ID. "Brenda Jones, DHS. Agent. . . ?"

"Cole, ma'am."

This part was a gamble. One of two things was about to happen. Either this guy was going to shrug it off and let her through or he was going to call her in and clear her ID. She hoped, for his sake, it wouldn't be the latter. Either way, she was going down this hallway. She looked behind them just to make sure they were out of sight and earshot of everyone else in the building.

"Nice to meet you, Agent Cole," she said putting away her badge. "I'm here on behalf of the director. I know you guys have been scrambling all day to get this done. Just helping out. I'm just doing a walk-through of the evac route. Director Levy wants to make sure you all have everything you need."

The agent nodded to her and said, "Yes, ma'am. We were told the director would have a few people on-site. Have a good evening, ma'am."

She moved past the agent and started down the hall. She had gone about halfway when the agent called to her, "Ms. Jones!"

She turned hesitantly, placing her hand behind her back and resting it on her weapon.

"Yes?" she called back.

"The president is on-site. He'll be entering the building momentarily. Just wanted to let you know."

"Thank you, Agent Cole. I'll finish walking through and then be right out."

The agent nodded to her and turned back around to face his post.

★

Keene greeted Agent Greene and the others as they ushered the president into the rotunda. There were some guys there he knew. Many of the Special Ops guys would move on to security detail. And though many of them went into private security because of the money, there were a lot who became Secret Service.

"Good to have you here," President Grant said.

"Glad to be here, sir," Keene said. "Mr. President, you sure you want to do this?"

President Grant looked at him with sadness in his eyes. "Have you seen the news this evening?"

"Been kind of busy, sir."

The president nodded. "The country is in turmoil, Mr. Keene. No one is sure what's going to happen, including me. I cannot go out there and tell them that everything is going to miraculously change. But I can go out there and tell them what I believe. And right now, this country needs that."

Keene didn't bother to say any more. He knew there was no persuading the man to not do this.

"Okay, then. Agent Greene, my other two operatives are outside with your detail. We're going to be walking around just checking faces. That okay with you?"

"Sure," Greene said. "You're all on the comm, so if you see anything, or if we see anything, we can communicate, and we'll move after that—"

"There won't be anything to see," President Grant interrupted. "He won't be here."

Keene felt the air go out of him. "How do you know that, Mr. President? Has he contacted you again?"

President Grant looked at him somberly and said, "I just know."

"Mr. President," Greene spoke up, "if there's something you're not telling us, we need to put the brakes on this thing right now."

"It's fine, Brian," President Grant said. "We will move forward, as planned."

Keene watched as the president gave Agent Greene the nod. That was it. This speech was happening. No turning back now.

"Keene," Greene said, grabbing him by the arm, "I want you to stay close."

"Don't worry, I'm not going anywhere," Keene said. "Let's go."

CHAPTER 44

Several thousand people had gathered in front of the steps of the Capitol. It might have looked like an inauguration, save the grim looks. A podium had been constructed, giving the president a place to speak from. A wire fence had been set up twenty yards away, to keep the mass of people back from the steps. And Secret Service agents surrounded the stage, forming a wall between the people and their leader.

President Grant stepped outside and looked out over the crowd. News cameras lined the fence in front of him. The speech would be on all the major networks, and many of the cable channels as well, he had been told. That was good. He walked up to the lectern and raised his hands to quiet the crowd.

"My fellow Americans, today has been a strenuous day on our country. First, I would like to send my condolences to the Forester family. Our thoughts and prayers are with you tonight as you mourn the loss of your loved one.

"Now, I would like to talk to you all about this stock market crisis. I have been on the phone all day with leaders from around the Wall Street community. And I would love nothing more than to tell you that this is just a hiccup and everything is going to be fine. Unfortunately, at this time, I cannot do that."

The crowds began to erupt in groaning and shouting. This was expected though. You couldn't just tell people worse news on top of bad news and think it would be received well. He waited a second before quieting them again.

"Ladies and gentlemen, please." He waited for them to give him their attention again. "But what I can tell you is this. Our country has always persevered through hard times. I know that many businesses and investors are panicking right now. And there's good reason to. There is no guarantee that this will be an overnight fix. But we can get through it. And I would like to tell you how, I believe, we need to respond.

"In order to do that, though, I need to tell you about something that has been happening over the last several months. . ."

★

Keene listened intently as the president continued with his speech. He was really going to do it. He was going to tell the people about this whack job. And the people were listening as if he were reading them a bedtime story.

"Greene," he whispered into his wrist mic.

"Go for Greene."

"This is Keene. You see anything?"

"Nothing yet. What is he doing? I thought he was going to talk about the market crash."

Keene pinched the bridge of his nose. "Yeah."

There was a crack over the earwig. "Hey, this is Taylor. I've been back and forth all over this perimeter and got nothing."

"He's not here." It was Boz.

Keene still wasn't sure yet, but he was starting to share his colleagues' opinion. "Just keep your eyes open. We don't know that."

★

". . .and so earlier this week, I received another message from this man."

President Grant stopped for a moment and took a deep breath. Here it was.

"Up until this last message, I had ignored the man's warnings. The reason for this is because there was no tangible threat. You must understand that the White House receives hundreds of threatening letters a week. However, I still have a duty, as president, to protect this nation. So I want to inform you that I have invoked the article of the Intelligence Enforcement Act that places all of the authority of the Department of Homeland Security back in the hands of the presidency."

This came with another eruption of the people. It was plainly understood that if this was to ever happen, it would signify that there was believed to be an immediate and impending threat against the country.

"Please. Please! Ladies and gentlemen."

It took several seconds for the people to become calm again.

"I want to assure you. We have no knowledge of an impending threat against this nation. However, and please let me continue when I say this, I do believe we are in a dangerous place."

He waited for the interruption he was sure was coming, but strangely, there was none. Everyone stood quietly, waiting for what was coming next.

"You see, what I haven't told you yet, are the details of this man's warnings. I would like to do that.

"I have made no attempts to hide my beliefs when it comes to God and my relationship with Him. And so I will not apologize for what I'm about to say. Ladies and gentlemen, we have become a godless nation. For too long we have done everything in our power to remove God from every aspect of our lives. And we forget this country was founded upon basic Christian principles. We have become a nation of man's laws, not God's. And in an effort to not offend someone who doesn't share many of our personal beliefs, we have trampled on the very foundation that our forefathers bled and died to establish.

"I cannot tell you what is going to happen to this country. I cannot stand here and assure you that the stock market is going to bounce back over the next week. We may very well be headed for another disaster like the Great Depression of the twentieth century. But I can promise you this. I believe that God is doing something among us right now. . . ."

★

". . .So I want to inform you that I have invoked the article of the Intelligence Enforcement Act that places all of the authority of the Department of Homeland Security. . ."

Okay, Alex thought. She'd heard enough. It was time to get this show on the road. She had been watching the speech from her phone. And she had been down here since she had encountered the agent upstairs. She fully expected that he would be coming to find her in a matter of moments if she didn't come back up. But that wasn't going to happen.

Instead, she picked the lock on the small closet and opened the door before going back up the small flight of stairs and turning the corner. The agent was at the end of the hall, still maintaining his post.

"Agent Cole," she called.

The young agent turned to see her.

"Come here. Quickly! I think I've found something."

The man didn't even pause. He took off at a jog, headed toward her.

"Down here," she said, opening the closet door. "I found something in here you should probably take a look at."

The agent stepped past her and stuck his head inside the closet.

"What? I don't see any—"

She had already pulled the silenced pistol out from underneath her jacket. As Agent Cole stuck his head inside the dark room to see what she had called him there for, she pulled the trigger twice. The gun made a quiet *Phst, Phst.* Agent Cole slumped forward into the closet.

She stepped inside and turned on the switch. A single bulb hung above her, barely illuminating the six-by-nine room. There was a mop bucket over in the corner, so she dragged the body over to it and placed his head inside. Didn't need any blood seeping out from under the door.

Next she pulled out the cell phone again and opened the browser window. This time, instead of returning to the speech, she logged on to a secure network. Her network. She typed in the commands and clicked back off. In just a few seconds, the server would place a call. And that call would then be routed, then rerouted again, through four different satellites, towers, and cell phone carriers. Then it would connect, and then. . .

CHAPTER 45

". . .But I can promise you this. I believe that God is doing something among us right now. . ."

President Grant had no sooner gotten the words out when he felt the need to stop for a moment. He didn't know why. It wasn't that he was at a loss for words. He knew exactly what he wanted to say. But something gave him pause. It made him step back for a moment and think. It was as if he were all of a sudden suspended in time. He could see the people around him, looking at him, and he could see the agents and Jon Keene standing next to him, but it was almost like he was outside of his body looking around. Everything and everyone was moving in complete slow motion. He felt a gentle breeze move across the stage where he stood, and it was warm and comforting. And then from somewhere deep inside, he heard a voice. The voice was gentle and soft but authoritative at the same time. He felt a tear form in his eyes. He had heard this voice before. It was familiar to him, though he hadn't heard it for a while now. He closed his eyes and listened.

★

Keene immediately knew something wasn't right. He turned to Agent Greene who, by the look on his face, felt the same way. They locked eyes. There was a slight panic in Agent Greene's face. Keene was some twenty yards away, so he lifted his wrist mic to his lips.

"Greene, what's going on?"

"I'm not sure," came the reply as he watched the agent move in close to the president.

"You need to get him out of here now!"

"Affirmative."

Keene quickly covered the short distance between himself and the president and heard Agent Greene talking.

"Mr. President, are you okay? Sir, we should go."

The president turned to face both of them. He had an extremely detached look about him. "Everything is fine," he said. "I think we're done here."

"Let's go!" Keene shouted to the other agents. "Something's wrong."

Keene had barely gotten the words out when the explosion rocked the entire street and surrounding area. The blast, which came from the National Gallery of Art–East Building, sent out a concussion wave that barreled people over and reached the steps of the Capitol almost instantly. Glass and debris flew everywhere. People began screaming and running in every direction.

"Go! Go! Go!" Agent Greene shouted as he picked the president up off the floor of the stage and covered him with his arms.

The group of six agents and Keene immediately surrounded the president and began to pull him back inside. Keene thumbed his wrist mic and changed the channel over to two. He, Boz, and Taylor had already discussed that in the event something should happen, they should switch to the alternate channel in order to communicate.

"Boz, Megan, you guys there?"

Nothing.

"Boz, Megan. This is Keene. Come in. Anyone there?"

The agents were trying to move as fast as they could back inside the doors and through the rotunda.

"Boz! Megan!" he shouted.

Some static and then a click.

"Jon! This is Megan, you there?"

"I'm here. Any eyes on Boz?"

"Negative. What's your twenty?"

"On the move with POTUS. Evac route."

Then another click with static.

"This is Boz. You guys on?"

"Here," they both said one after the other.

"What's the plan?" Boz asked.

Keene keyed his mic and said, "I'm in route with POTUS. You two cover the grounds. He's here! Find him!"

"Roger that," Boz said.

"Out," Megan said.

Keene and the team were halfway down the corridor when Keene pulled up short. "Wait! Wait!" he shouted.

Greene pushed the other agents and the president on and stopped.

"What is it, Keene?" he asked.

"That blast was across the street. It wasn't meant to kill him. It was meant to get him out of here and back inside!" Keene looked around quickly. "Where's your agent who was stationed here?"

All of the color drained out of Greene's face at once. He looked down the hallway. The other agents and the president were turning the corner to go down the small stairway that led into the Rayburn House tunnel, a small shuttle-type subway used by the members of the House of Representatives to carry them underground to and from the Capitol and their offices. It was the primary evacuation route. If a threat was indicated, the president would not leave topside, exposed to the outside and the public. He was to be removed via the tunnel into the Rayburn House, where the detail would have the motorcade waiting safely. It was a couple city blocks' distance away from the Capitol, and so it gave the agents time to get the president secluded, away from immediate danger on the outside; and it gave the motorcade agents the ability to get out of the vicinity of the Capitol without the president, in case there was any further aggression toward them.

"Where is he!" Keene screamed.

Greene seemed to snap back. "He was right here. He should've—"

"Call them back! Now!" Keene said. And then he began running down the hallway as the last of the agents disappeared down the staircase.

★

Alex heard the explosion and then felt the ground rumble beneath her feet. *Perfect*, she thought. She had covered the distance at least three times since she'd gotten there. She did the math in her head. Six, maybe seven guys, moving at a quick pace, stopping at every corner to do a quick sweep—should only take them a minute and a half tops.

She looked at her watch, counting down the seconds. They should be here any moment now. And then she heard it. A cluster of footsteps running down the hall. She braced herself. This was it. And she was only going to have one shot at this. She had to let the men pass and then step out from the closet and begin to put them down, one by one. The fact that they would have their backs to her would give her a slight advantage, but she still knew. Some of these guys were former military Special Ops. They would be quick. And they would be accurate when they fired. If they fired. That was the thing. She had to be faster. And she was. She knew it. She had gone through such extensive short-range weapons training that she knew there was only a handful of people in the entire world who were as fast and accurate as she was. She placed her hand on the closet door and turned off the light. The footsteps were now coming down the stairs. She braced herself, ready to dart out and shoot.

But suddenly something changed. The men seemed to stop in mid-stride. Someone was calling after them. She could see them out of the slats of the blinds in the corner of the window of the door. They were turning around. *No!* This was wrong. What happened?

She didn't even take the time to think. Either way, the men had their backs to her. Whether they were facing up the stairs or down the stairs. Made no difference to her. She stepped out and took aim. And then she began to pull the trigger. *Phst! Phst! Phst-phst-phst!*

★

Keene had almost made it to the stairs when he heard the first shot. Still at a dead run, he watched, in horror, as the agent at the top of the stairs crumpled like a rag doll.

"Gun! Gun!" he shouted. He ran harder toward the men.

He heard at least one agent get off a shot but no more. As he got to the stairs, he reached down to pull out his own weapon when he noticed something very wrong. Where was his magazine? His gun's magazine had been ejected. How could this have—and then it all came into picture for him. The woman in the rotunda. She had brushed against him, slightly knocking him off balance. He'd thought nothing of it, at the time, except that she was really attractive, and if he hadn't been there trying to find some psycho whack job, he might've liked to talk to her.

Well, he definitely wanted to talk to her now, he thought, pulling back the slide to check the chamber. And he had a bad feeling he was about to get the chance. He did a quick check around the corner and had to pull back.

Phst, phst, phst!

The wood from the door frame splintered next to his face. And then he heard footsteps, running away from him. Just then, Agent Greene caught up to him.

"I've only got one shot," he told the agent. "My magazine's gone."

"I'll lay down cover, and you grab a weapon from one of them," Greene said.

This time, they came around the corner, guns up and ready to shoot. But there was no one there. He took reached down and grabbed one of the other agent's guns and took off down the stairs.

"You stay here with them," he shouted as he ran. "I'll go after the hitter."

As he started out after the shooter, it registered with him what he'd just witnessed. He had just seen the president of the United States lying on the ground with a gunshot wound to his head.

On the platform for the train, he saw nothing. The shooter had to have run down the tunnel. He knew that with the president giving a speech here, the trains would've been shut down. The shooter obviously knew that as well.

He leaped over the railing and began running down the tunnel. He could hear the shooter's footsteps echoing down toward him. He pushed harder. The tunnel, he knew, wasn't that long, and if he hurried, he might be able to catch up before the shooter reached the Rayburn House.

Just as the tunnel was coming to a close, he slowed his pace a little. He didn't want to let whoever this was get away, but he also knew he was about to come out at another platform. And the shooter could be waiting for him.

Slowing down even more, to a walk, he crept the last few paces with his gun up, waiting to be fired upon. He didn't have to wait long. As soon as the platform came into view, he felt two rounds spit into the concrete just a few inches from his head. He saw the shooter at the foot of the steps. He was right. It was the woman from the rotunda. He fired a couple quick shots but knew he had missed his mark. He dove low, thinking he would hear the woman run up the stairs to make her escape, but that didn't happen. He stood back up slowly, just peeking his head above the raised tracks. When he did, he saw her waiting there, taking aim directly at him. He fired his gun as fast as he could but never got the chance to look to see if he hit anything. Two rounds crashed into his right shoulder and drove him back against the tracks. He lost his balance as the searing pain ripped through his collarbone. And then he fell to the ground.

He heard her run up the stairs.

CHAPTER 46

Atypical to her normal practices, Marianne Levy arrived at the meeting place eight minutes early. She had had conversations with others about her punctuality. Alex, for instance, loathed the fact that she was late for everything. She didn't have a good reason for why she was continually late. Perhaps it was the fact that she just liked the idea of people waiting for her. She checked her watch. Chin would more than likely be late. Alex had complained that he hadn't yet been on time for any of their previous meetings either. Chin, apparently, shared her affinity for making people wait. No matter. It gave her a few moments to reflect on everything.

It hadn't even been a week since the speech at the Capitol. And she hadn't talked to Alex yet about it. The woman was avoiding her. And rightly so. She'd botched the entire thing. Grant wasn't dead, like she had promised he would be. He was, however, in a coma. And his chances of regaining consciousness were less than fifty percent. At the end of the day, she guessed she still had the same result. The man she hated more than anyone on this earth was out of the picture.

Walker had now assumed the office of the presidency. And though she had believed her relationship with him wasn't much better than that with Grant, she hoped he would return her office to her. That, of course, hadn't happened. Instead, the man was drunk with his newfound power and had pushed her even farther away. The bombing of the art gallery, combined with the market crash, allowed him to basically shut down the government and call all the shots. Even Congress had begun to abdicate its responsibilities. All but a few of the senators and representatives had cleared out of DC to go back to their home states, declaring they needed to reassure their constituents. Really, they were all just a bunch of cowards and didn't want to be around if another attack happened.

All in all, the entire country was a mess. The market had plunged even farther. Over a million people had lost their jobs in the span of a week.

Business owners were losing money daily. The price of gas had gone up so much that no one except the very well off could afford to drive. Complete civil unrest was at the doorstep of America. And right now, there was no light at the end of the tunnel.

And then there was Chin.

When she had begun this treacherous journey eight months ago, she couldn't believe how easy it was. She remembered waking up every morning for a week after their initial meeting, thinking it wasn't real. But it had been. And now here she was. On the doorstep of doing something that could never be undone. Forever, the world would be changed.

She heard the cars pull up outside. The doors opened and four men, all in finely tailored suits and carrying automatic weapons, entered the building. Chin followed behind.

"Mr. Chin," she said, bowing at the waist. "Good to see you."

"Likewise, Madam Director."

"Please, take a seat."

The two sat down at the makeshift table across from each other.

"I understand you wanted to discuss further needs," she said.

"Yes," Chin confirmed. "I spoke with your associate about this."

"She did not give me details, other than something about the southern border."

Chin leaned back in the chair and folded his arms across his lap. "Yes, that is correct."

She had already earned a ridiculous amount of money from this venture. Asking for more might seem offensive to Chin, but if he wanted more, then so did she.

"I've already given you invisibility to bring your men into the northern states. I have successfully kept our eyes and ears off your venture. I know that you have your men in place on the Canadian side, ready to bring in your equipment. There won't be a problem crossing the borders there.

"As far as Mexico is concerned, I have some relationships there. But none that would help you to the extent you need. If you want to move more equipment into that country, you'll have to do business with their president, Mr. Ramirez. However, I'm sure with some renegotiation of our dealings, I can be extremely helpful to you in that area. Let's say. . .we add another hundred mil to the hundred you already owe me."

Mr. Chin looked at her with a condescending smile. "Ms. Levy, I came here more out of courtesy."

"I'm not sure I understand."

"Look around you, Ms. Levy. Your country is in a state of panic. Your own government is crumbling. This is no longer about you providing safe passage for our drilling equipment and turning over the property rights.

"When we first met, our deal was that you would provide entry into the country and the secluded protection for our oil workers to drill on your soil. But the reality is this: your country is so far indebted to mine that we own you financially. And the fact that your country is so unstable right now leaves my country only one choice."

Immediately she felt her blood pressure rise. This was not what they had discussed. Chin was reworking the deal. She stood up and pointed at him.

"You listen here, Chin. I committed treason by falsifying those permits, documents, and removing any military or law enforcement from those areas. Do you understand what it takes to deem a section of this country hazardous, environmentally unsafe, and off-limits to the public? We're talking about hundreds of square miles here!

"I have handpicked, fully armed, completely devoted civil military units—which you know I created specifically for this operation—on the borders of those protected areas. They are under the assumption that this is a top-secret, fully sanctioned by *my* government, endeavor with your country. And now you're telling me that this isn't good enough! You are out of line, sir."

"Ms. Levy," Chin continued calmly, "you don't seem to understand. I'm sorry that you've been misled. But things have changed. We no longer intend on coming here and simply secretly drilling for your oil."

Marianne sat back down, stunned. What was happening?

"Ms. Levy, as I said before. This is really a courtesy visit. My country has already moved our men into your southern neighbor's land."

"That's impossible! I would have known about that."

"Improbable, maybe. Impossible, no. I assure you, Ms. Levy. We are very good at staying under the radar. Even yours.

"As it stands right now, we are poised to move against your country very shortly. I came here today to do the honorable thing and inform you. So you could make plans to leave. We appreciate all that you've done for us. We've decided to allow you to keep the money. And we will honor the remaining one hundred million that we owe you. I'm sure you will be very happy. Somewhere. But I highly recommend that you seek residency elsewhere. And soon."

As if he could read her thoughts, he continued.

"You don't believe it is possible that my country would wage war on yours."

She nodded, unable to speak.

"Ms. Levy, my country is one of the oldest empires in the world. We didn't become that by haphazardly making war on other nations. We wait. And we plan. And we wait some more. And we lure our prey into a false sense of security. And then, when they believe that nothing could ever touch them, we pounce, just like the great tiger. Your nation, for more than fifty years now, has borrowed so much money from my nation that we own you already. You cannot operate financially independent of us. Who do you think is responsible for your stock market crashing this very moment? Who do you think is responsible for setting this nation on its current course? We, the Chinese empire. We have orchestrated all of this.

"Your military, what is left of it, is scattered across the four corners of the globe. Do you not understand? You have spent so much time defending other nations' interests these last twenty years, you've left your borders and your people vulnerable."

"But they will come back!" she said. "And when they do—"

"It will be too late, Ms. Levy. By then, our people will occupy your nation. And your country would never risk a ground war on your own soil. We have over three million soldiers. And we will deploy as many as it takes. Your people will bow to our flag. They will learn to coexist with our people. This is the way of our empire."

"You're wrong! They *will* fight you! And you will see how strong and great this country is."

In that moment, she realized how wrong she had been. She didn't hate her country. She hated the people running the country. But none of that mattered now.

Now, she needed to run. Chin was right. There was no way to defend against a direct attack from China. And what was she supposed to do? Warn them? And how would that play out? With her head on a stick. That's how. And if anyone ever found out that she had had any dealings with them previously, the result would be the same, if not worse. This had all gone so very wrong. She needed to leave.

She stood and smoothed the wrinkles from her skirt. She set her jaw and tried to look firmly into Chin's face.

"I believe we're done here."

CHAPTER 47

Keene stood by the bedside of President Grant at Bethesda Naval Hospital. He watched as the man's chest rose and fell in rhythm with the sound of the machine helping him breathe. The gunshot, while not fatal, had caused serious damage. President Grant's brain, they said, had begun to swell almost immediately. And had he not gotten to the facility when he had, he would surely be dead. The extent of the damage was unclear. Also unclear was whether or not he would ever come out of the coma at all. And if he did, the doctors were unsure as to how well he would recover, if ever.

At the time of the shooting, Keene thought his collarbone had been shattered. He had barely even been able to raise his arm over his waist. But after being checked out by the same medical staff, there at Bethesda, he was relieved to find out that the bullet was a through and through shot, just above the bone. Two inches to his left and he might be lying here next to President Grant. Or worse.

He was sore, for sure, but the fact that he kept himself in such great physical shape had already begun paying dividends. Only four days later and he was able to have almost full range of motion in the shoulder. It still hurt like crazy, but he was functional. The doctors said that he should try to take it easy for a couple weeks, but he knew that wasn't an option. He was waiting for a phone call. And depending on what the content of that call revealed, he planned on being back on the streets by this afternoon. He had a killer to find. He quietly returned to the small conference room where Taylor and Boz waited. He pulled up one of the worn fake-leather chairs and sat down. His mind raced with what should be their next move.

"Jon, you all right?" It was Taylor, jarring him back from his thoughts.

"Yeah," he said. "Just thinking."

"About what?" Boz asked.

"I just don't get it. You know? I mean, we finally get a lead on this guy.

We know who he is, where he's from. Got his picture and everything. And then, this woman shows up."

"Maybe she's working for him," Taylor said.

"I don't know," he said, unsure. "It just doesn't feel right."

He quickly noted Boz's sideways grin.

"Don't you start," Keene said. "I don't know how she plays into this, but—"

"But you don't believe for one second that she has anything to do with this guy, the Prophet," Boz interrupted him.

Boz was right. He knew it. He didn't know how or why, but he knew it. This Prophet, while he might not be the one orchestrating what was happening—which was still to be determined—was still involved somehow. Keene was sure. But he was having a hard time connecting the Prophet to anything that had happened at the Capitol. The only thing that could possibly tie him to it was the bombings of the warehouse and the art gallery. But bomb makers are extremely finicky. They don't change up their designs, and these two were as different as night and day. One explosion was meant to destroy a building and not intentionally harm anyone. The other was a diversion, set to do maximum damage, regardless of who was in its path.

"Listen, Boz. I don't know what I think right now. My shoulder hurts like crazy, President Grant is lying here fighting for his life. Our entire country is on the brink of collapsing. And we don't have an answer for any of it."

Boz shifted in his seat again. "Hmph."

Keene was exhausted, and he didn't want to argue. But Boz just wouldn't let it go.

"Okay," Keene said. "Let's just for one minute pretend that you're right. That this Prophet is a messenger. The bomb at the Capitol doesn't fit the fourteen-day timeline. And if that's not what this guy was talking about, then what? Are we still to expect that something is going to happen sometime between now and the next few days? And if that's the case, then who is this woman? Where'd she come from? And why did she take a shot at the president? And how does that fit into all of this?"

Boz seemed to think about it for a second and then said, "I don't know who the woman is. She is obviously a trained assassin. I don't know why she would try to kill Calvin. And I have no idea why the three of us have been brought together. But I do know this: God works in ways that we cannot understand. Calvin's inability to run the country right now may be the very thing needed for God to be able to do what He wants to do here. Do I believe that all hope is lost? No. Do I believe that we can stop whatever it is that's happening? No."

"So what, then? Are we supposed to just sit back and let it all happen?"

"No," Boz said, "we are not. Just because God has set all of this in motion, we do not know, nor can we presume to know, what the end result will be. We are called to seek Him. To follow as He leads."

"So God helps those who help themselves," Keene smarted.

"Funny," Boz chuckled, "you know that that idiom is not found anywhere in the Bible? Actually, it goes against everything the Bible teaches us. In the book of Jeremiah, God says, 'Cursed is the man who trusts in man and makes flesh his strength, whose heart turns away from the Lord.' "

"So," Keene said, "according to God, we're screwed. Which brings me back to where we were."

Taylor, who had been listening the whole time, asked, "Can I jump in here?"

"Why not?" Keene sighed.

"You know, I've tried to keep a relatively unbiased opinion on all of this. And yes, I'll admit. Even as a Christian it's been hard for me to just accept that God is talking to this guy. But I gotta tell you, everything in me says this is for real. I'm with Boz on this."

How was he ever going to find the people responsible for this, when the two people he was being forced to work with wouldn't listen to reason? He rubbed his eyes with the heels of his palms. This was getting worse by the second.

"Then, what?" he finally said. "Where does that leave us? Either way, we have a job to do. We have to find this guy. We're still operating under a time frame. And we have to find this assassin and figure out where she fits into all of this. Or maybe the two of you just think we should just sit back and watch."

"No," Boz said. "I don't think we just sit back here and watch. I think we continue to move forward and find these people. Just because God has allowed all of this to start happening, it doesn't mean that He has abandoned us. He has promised that He would never forsake His children."

"Then how do you explain all of this?"

Boz folded his hands and hunched his shoulders. "Because there are a lot of us who aren't His children."

Just then, the phone in Keene's pocket began to buzz. He stood up and left the room. All three of them had been waiting for this call. When he got outside the door, he hit the button.

"This is Keene."

"It's me, Jennings."

"What's the word?"

"President Walker is giving me full latitude to find out what's going on. You are to continue as you were."

President Walker. *That just doesn't sound right*, he thought, glancing back through the doorway to see President Grant in bed.

"What about Marianne Levy?"

"No one's seen her since she left, after Grant took back DHS. Her office says she's taking personal time."

"What's Walker's take on it?"

"Seriously? You know as well as I do the only reason the man was on the ticket was because he could carry Ohio, Pennsylvania, and New York. Nice guy, yeah. But nowhere near ready to run this country. He has no idea what he's doing."

"Any word on the shooter?"

The line was quiet for a moment. Then, "We think it's *her*."

Keene gripped the phone tighter. "I want everything you have on her, Kevin."

"And you'll get it. Just not yet. Right now, I want you tracking down this Prophet and finding him. He may be able to lead us to her."

"We've spent almost two weeks looking for him, and nothing!"

"That was before. Now you have a name and a driver's license. Find him."

The phone went dead.

Keene entered the room again and sat back down. "That was Jennings."

"What did he say?" Megan asked.

"Exactly what we thought. Walker is giving Jennings full control."

"What about Director Levy?" Boz asked.

"Walker was told she's taking personal time. Who knows? She's probably home, celebrating, trying to figure out how to get DHS back. She's not going to be a problem, though."

"If Walker is going to give over control to someone, shouldn't it be Director Preston?" Taylor asked. "I mean, FBI is supposed to be all things domestic."

"Jennings can be very persuasive," Keene said.

"And the shooter?" Megan asked.

"Jennings confirmed what I thought."

"You know who she is?" Megan asked.

"No. But I've run into her work a couple times. Not literally. I mean, there've been some hits in the past that we believed to be a woman. Russian. No one's ever seen her. All we've ever had was a vague description and a photo we *think* is her. But she's good. Real good."

"Obviously," Boz said. "I mean, she got the jump on you."

"Funny," Keene said.

"Then how do we find her?" Taylor asked.

"We don't. Not yet. Jennings wants us looking for the Prophet."

"I agree," Boz said.

Keene was taken aback for a moment. This actually surprised him. "You do? And why's that? I thought you were—"

"Listen," Boz cut him off. "Whether or not you buy into all of this doesn't matter. This all started with him. He has the answers. And we have less than a week."

"If there even *is* a threat," Keene said. "We don't know! What if all this guy was talking about was this shot on President Grant?"

"Doesn't matter," Boz said. "We can't take the chance. If this guy's telling the truth and something else is coming, we need to find out. Before it happens."

"Why?" Keene said. "According to you we wouldn't be able to stop it anyway."

"Maybe it's not our job to stop it," Boz said, matching his tone. "But it might be our job to warn people of it."

"I agree," Taylor said. "Now we know who he is, and we have his picture. Let's get it done."

As badly as Keene wanted to go against Jennings's orders and hunt down the Russian woman, he knew Taylor and Boz were right. They had to find this guy. If he did have answers, they needed them. And Keene was sure that whatever they found out, eventually it was going to lead them back to the Russian.

CHAPTER 48

Marianne Levy finished packing the few things that she wanted to bring with her in her carry-on. There would be no checked luggage. With three hundred and fifty million dollars—which could have been four hundred and fifty million—she could buy whatever she wanted. When she was finished she set the small bag down in the living room and looked around the house one last time. She would miss this old place.

She had finally heard from Alex. The conversation was quick and via text. All it said was that she was coming here and that she would be there in less than two hours. The two hours were almost up.

She pulled a chair out from the small kitchen table and sat down, her back facing the wall and her eyes facing the door. She let the small handgun rest in her lap. Alex was a trained assassin. And while she had no grand visions of being able to catch her by surprise, she certainly was not going to let the woman catch her in the same way. She didn't get to be the director of DHS by underestimating people. There were only two ways into this room, both directly in front of her. And if Alex had any inclination to shoot her, she would have to come in one of these two doorways.

She heard the faint click of the front door latch. She grabbed the pistol and raised it to a firing position. Then she heard the faint footsteps. Alex was coming through the living room. She had her finger on the trigger, not knowing what to fully expect, waiting for the woman to show her face. But instead, the footsteps stopped just short of coming into view.

"You can put it away, Marianne. I'm not here to kill you."

She kept the gun in position and said, "I have no idea what you're talking about."

"Yes, you do. You're not stupid," came the reply. "And it's exactly what I would do."

Just then, Alex peeked her head around the corner, her hands up, palms out. "I'm not here to kill you," she said again.

Marianne motioned for her to come into full view.

Alex continued walking into the kitchen and grabbed a stool from under the island bar. She sat down and folded her arms.

"You can't blame me," Marianne said. "I mean, I am a loose end. Isn't that what you call it?"

Alex nodded. "Yes, but let's be honest. If I wanted you dead, you'd already be that way. I came to give you these."

Marianne set the small pistol on the table beside her and reached for the small pouch in Alex's hand. She unzipped the thing and reached inside and pulled out three passports. Alex had promised her these a few weeks back. She opened them up, one by one, and thumbed through them. They were all hers. Different names, different nationalities, complete with stamps from several different countries.

"What about you?" Marianne said.

Alex shrugged her shoulders. "I've been doing this for a long time. I think I'm going to retire."

"Retire? Really? Somehow I doubt that. People like you don't retire."

"Yeah, maybe not. But I'm going to at least go away for a long time. Can't stay here," Alex laughed. "And as much as I really like my place back home, I'm going to have to leave it. Can't take the chance. You don't win the Super Bowl and go unnoticed."

"I wouldn't say *won*."

"What's that supposed to mean?"

"Just what I said. He's not dead."

Alex narrowed her eyes at her. "He's in a coma. And if he ever wakes up—and that's a big if—he's gonna be brain-dead. He's as good as dead."

"But not dead."

"Semantics."

"Whatever. Doesn't matter. Chin isn't just coming here to drill."

"I know."

"What? How do you know that?"

"Marianne, for someone as smart as you appear to be, you can be naive. You know that? Or are you so narcissistic that you actually believed that you could get away with all of this and this country would just accept it, after the fact? There's no way. The Chinese are too smart for that. They used you. Face it. They've always intended on coming here. This isn't just about oil and the fact that this country is indebted to them. This is about domination. They are a communist regime. It's their way of life. Take over and assimilate. Just because they've done it through capitalism for the last seventy-five years doesn't mean that they've gotten weak."

"Well," Marianne sighed, "like I said. It doesn't matter. I'm leaving. You're leaving. We won't be here when it happens. Where will you go?"

"Where are *you* going?"

She smiled and nodded her head. "Right. Okay then. I guess I'll be seeing you later."

"No you won't."

"You know you shot that Jon Keene guy, right?"

"Yeah, so?"

"You know he's going to come looking for you, don't you?"

"I doubt it. He's going to have his hands full for a while. But even if he does, that's fine. I've got unfinished business with him."

"How's that?"

"Oh, it's nothing. Let's just say we've crossed paths before. And besides, he's going to come looking for you long before he comes looking for me." She stood up from the stool. "Take care, Marianne."

CHAPTER 49

Keene and Director Jennings sat in the Oval Office, waiting for President Walker. Boz and Taylor were back at her office, trying to get another lead on the Prophet with her supercomputer. Keene and Jennings were here to convince President Walker to increase the threat level. The man was incorrigible. He refused to even entertain that an impending attack could be coming. His focus right now, he said, was getting the American people to stop panicking over the stock market.

"He's not gonna do it, Kevin."

"Probably not. But at least we can say we told you so."

"Fat lot of good that's going to do us if someone blows up New York."

"He's scared. He's just been thrown into the big chair because Grant has been shot, and he has a financial crisis on his hands."

Just then, newly installed President Walker entered the room. Both men stood—out of respect for the office—and shook his hand.

"Now, gentlemen," Walker said, "what can I do for you?"

Keene started to speak, but Jennings put a hand on his shoulder to quiet him.

"Mr. President, we really need to talk to you about this impending threat assessment."

"Jennings, do you have any idea what I'm dealing with right now?"

"Yes, sir, but—"

"No, I don't think you do," he interrupted. "I have a president lying comatose in Bethesda; I've got the FBI crawling all over me about this bomb in front of the Capitol; and our country is on the brink of financial collapse. Do you understand what's going to happen in the next three days if this market doesn't turn around?"

"Yes, sir," Jennings said quickly, taking his opportunity to cut in. "But don't you think it's reasonable to believe that all of this is connected to something bigger?"

"Now you're starting to sound like Calvin."

Strangely, that remark didn't bother Keene. He didn't know why.

"Mr. President," Keene jumped in, "I've been tracking this Prophet guy for almost two weeks. I'm with you, sir. I don't know how any of this plays into the other, but we can't just dismiss it. The guy has been in contact with President Grant for months now. He's been warning us that something like this was going to happen. We need to take him seriously and raise the threat level. The Fourth is just a couple days away."

President Walker furrowed his brow and said, "Mr. Keene, you can't honestly think that someone would try to attack this country on our Independence Day. That's when our security is at its highest! Many have tried. All have failed. Our brave men and women in this country understand that. They will be fully engaged in looking for any type of threat. You're overreacting."

"President Walker, listen to me!" Keene pleaded. "You are naive if you think this country is secure right now. Our brave men and women, as you put it, are busy trying to keep the people of this country from rioting and degenerating into full-on civil unrest. They wouldn't have the manpower or resources to stop an attack right now if they had to. And you don't even know where your director of Homeland Security is! Our military is stretched so far that we have less than eighty thousand troops stateside. I served, sir. I did the things that you people need done but didn't want anyone else to know. So I know how to run a military op. And I'm telling you, we are vulnerable. If this Prophet is even somewhat right, you need to raise the threat level. Let the American people know that there is an imminent threat. Even if we can't prove it."

President Walker placed his hands on the desk and lowered his head. He took a deep breath and looked up again. "Mr. Keene, I can't," he said in a saddened tone. "Do you understand that if I do this, our country will completely deteriorate within hours. Even if nothing ever happens. On the heels of the bomb at the Capitol and the market crashing, people will think the sky is falling. There could be riots. Heck, they're already happening! And it would just get worse. I cannot take that chance. I'm sorry. I truly am. But if you think that this threat is real, then you need to follow up on it. If and when you have solid information, we can talk again."

President Walker stood up and moved to the door. He opened it and said, "Now, if you gentlemen will excuse me, I have some pressing matters to attend to."

★

"He's wrong, Kevin," Keene said, back in the car.

"Maybe. But weren't you the one, just last week, saying this Prophet guy was a kook? And that President Grant was crazy?"

Keene sat there for a moment. Kevin had a good point. He was the one who had been adamantly against all of this. And he didn't know why, but something had changed. The deeper he got into this, the more he had to admit he didn't know what to think.

"I don't know," he said, frustrated. "I mean, here's this guy. Hacks into Grant's private e-mail; Taylor says she can't figure out how—and she's supposedly the best hacker alive. I tried to convince myself that the guy tried to kill us in Chicago, but Boz is right. That charge was set to blow up and out. And. . .the man warned us to get out. Who does that if he's trying to kill you? And then the Russian shows up. I'm supposed to believe that this seminary student has ties to a Russian hitter? Yeah. That's real likely."

"Could happen," Jennings said. "I've seen stranger things."

"Yeah, me, too. But not this. Look, I agree with them that this guy is probably not responsible for President Grant or the bomb at the Capitol. But he knows something. How, I have no idea. But he does. And we've got to find him. If Walker isn't willing to listen to any of us, maybe he'll listen to him. I've just got to find him first. And find out what he knows."

"I agree. And in the meantime, I'll try to meet with Bob Sykes and the rest of the Joint Chiefs. I know they haven't had their eyes and ears focused here. But with Marianne gone, I'm going to need their help. And I'm going to need Taylor to get over to DHS and start digging around in Marianne's files."

"Why's that?"

"Think about it. The director of Homeland Security just disappears?"

"I never thought you, of all people, would care about that."

"I don't. Not that she's gone, anyway," Jennings laughed. "But where'd she go? And why?"

Keene had been so focused on the Prophet, he didn't even stop to consider. . . "You don't think she could have anything to do with any of this do you?"

"I've seen stranger things," Jennings said again.

Keene's phone began to ring.

"This is Keene."

"Jon, it's Megan. Where are you?"

"Headed back with Jennings. What's up?"

"You need to get over here. I think I've found him."

CHAPTER 50

"Okay, so check this out," Taylor said, pointing to her screen. "This is a traffic camera in St. Louis. It's from a red-light camera off an exit on I-44."

She pulled the picture up. It showed a car turning from the light onto the southbound lanes of the interstate.

"Apparently, there is a no-turn-on-red right there. Our guy must've not seen it and turned anyway. When he did, he set off the motion sensor, and it snapped his picture, both front and back.

She zoomed in on the license plate, and then on another screen she pulled up the photo and did the same thing.

"That's him!" Keene said.

"Yes, it is. But this is from five days ago. Now look here."

She clicked around on the keyboard. The two images disappeared, and a video came up.

"This is from a traffic feed in Fort Worth. They have cameras like this in a lot of cities. News crews use it to give local traffic reports. Look. Here's our guy again."

She played the footage. There was the car, moving slowly through rush-hour traffic.

"When was this?" Keene asked. "How did you find this?" He was genuinely impressed.

"Two days ago," she said. And then, "I told you. There's not much I can't do on this thing." She patted the monitor. "And then finally, there's this."

Next she put up another video of a street in what looked like an older, smaller town. Pedestrians walked by casually, as the camera stood sentry over the town square. Seconds later, the Prophet came into view. He strolled casually by the camera and entered a small shop.

"This is one of those city-cams that a lot of towns have. People can go online and just watch what's going on in their town or city. Again, a lot

177

of news crews use these when doing weather or traffic. This is Edinburg, Texas."

"He went home," Keene said.

"He's home!" Taylor affirmed. "Now we at least know where he is."

"He could be gone by now," Boz said. "Just because that's where he's from doesn't mean that's where he lives."

"Maybe," Megan said. "But this is from today. And these are from the last two days." She pulled up similar video feeds, all from the same place. In each one, the Prophet was seen going in and out of the camera's purview. "He may not live there, but he's there right now. And it doesn't look like he's in a hurry to leave."

"Why would he?" Keene said. "He's less than an hour away from the Mexican border. If he felt like we were close, he could just skip across and disappear again."

"So what do we do now?" Taylor asked.

Just then, Jennings stepped into the office. He had been across the hall with Director Preston. "What we do now is split you three up."

"What?" Taylor asked. "Why?"

"Because," Jennings said, "there are a couple things we need done. And I can't have all three of you chasing them down one at a time." He stopped and pointed to Keene. "Jon, I want you down on the border. Boz, I want you with me and Bill when we go talk to the Joint Chiefs tomorrow. And Megan, I need you to take a trip across town and go visit DHS."

"I don't understand," she said.

"I want to know where Marianne Levy is. And I want to know why she's not bullying her way back into DHS. You have complete access to her files and computer and her office. Go see what you can turn up."

"Okay."

"Boz, with your military record, the Joint Chiefs will be more likely to listen to you."

"What are you asking them to do?" It was Keene.

"I'm going to ask them to start calling our boys back here. As many as they can spare. If this threat is real, we need to be prepared."

"It'll take over a week to get our ships back here from the Middle East," Keene said.

"Then we better get them moving. Don't you think?" Jennings said.

Taylor understood the need to split them up. But she didn't want Keene going to Texas by himself. She had a bad feeling that if Keene found the Prophet, there wouldn't be much left of him to question.

"Sir," she said, interrupting, "I know you want me to go to DHS, but shouldn't we be focusing on this Prophet? I mean, what if Jon needs backup? Shouldn't I go with him? I can go to DHS once we find him."

Jennings looked at her with a condescending smile. "Ms. Taylor, Jon can take care of himself. I want you over at DHS." Then to Keene, "Walk with me. Something I want to talk to you about."

Jennings turned and left the office as quickly as he'd come in. Keene started to follow, but Megan grabbed him by the arm.

"Jon, promise me something."

He turned to face her.

"Don't do anything stupid. Remember what you promised President Grant."

"Relax," Keene said. "I'm not going to kill him. Unless he tries to kill me first."

"Just be careful. And stay away from train tunnels."

"You worried about me, Taylor?" He raised an eyebrow.

She didn't know why, but she immediately felt awkward. "No. . ." she stammered, "I just. . . I. . ."

"Go find out what you can at DHS," he said. "I'll keep you both posted on what I find."

Keene turned and left. As she watched him chase after Jennings, she felt something weird in her gut. It was almost as if she was beginning to care about him. Maybe she *was* worried a little.

"I saw that," Boz said.

"Saw what?" she said defensively.

"That look," he said. "You're worried about him."

"I hardly know the man. That's ridiculous."

"Okay," Boz said. "Just remember: this is how it starts."

"How what starts?"

Boz laughed and said, "C'mon. We've got work to do."

★

Keene chased after Jennings who was already halfway out the door. He was slightly conflicted right now. On one hand, he was glad to be flying solo, even if it was only for a little while. He needed the time alone to think. On the other, Boz and Taylor had grown on him. After his wife died, he hadn't been much of a social person. He always kept everything close to the vest. But there was something different about these two. And that confused him even more, because there couldn't be two more diametrically opposite people from him in the whole world. But nevertheless, he liked them.

Probably the craziest thing right now was the fact that he was allowing himself to entertain the idea of what Boz had been saying for days. And he couldn't decide if that made him crazy or just plain sad. For so long, he had harbored this anger that drove him. At first, he had just hated God. Then he decided that there wasn't a God. And then he decided no, there is a God, He was just punishing him for something. And no matter what anyone said, it always came back to one thing for him. How could a supposedly loving God allow this to happen? How could God allow some radical fundamentalist terrorist group to kill his wife? She was the sweetest, most innocent person anyone had ever known. She hadn't done anything wrong. No, there was no God.

And so he shut down. And he became the man he was today. The ruthless, highly trained, deadly operative that he was. The SEALs had turned him into a machine. The CIA had turned him into a weapon. And now here he was, years later, entertaining the thought, once more, that there might be a God. And he still didn't know what that meant. Or if he even liked it. He almost would rather there be a God so he could be mad at Him again. But Boz had been wearing him out. Every time they were alone, the man would try to convince him he had it all wrong. *Who knows?* he thought, frustrated. Maybe he did. But even so, right now, he didn't care.

"Kevin, what's up?" he said.

Jennings continued walking. "Got a call from one of our drug cartel snitches."

"Yeah, so?"

"So he just happens to be on the border in Hidalgo County."

"And that's where this Prophet is," he said, finishing Jennings's thought. "So what'd he say? How's that connected to our guy?"

"He didn't. He just said that there was something there we would want to see. Wouldn't say anything about it on the phone."

"And you want me to go see him."

"Yes. And I want you to do it before you go looking for this Prophet fellow."

"I don't know. The Prophet is gonna have the answers we need. I need to be on him first. Why can't you send someone else? Send Farhetty. He's not doing anything."

"Farhetty's on a plane to Istanbul. I want you to check it out."

"Look—"

"Jon, this is not a discussion. This is me telling you to go see him. You understand? This guy single-handedly gave us the Molinero cartel. He's only contacted us three times. And every time it's been something big. I want to know what he knows."

CHAPTER 51

The sun had already set by the time Keene got home. He, Taylor, and Boz had spent the last few hours of the day continuing to track the movements of the Prophet. It seemed he was indeed in Edinburg and had no plans, that they could tell, to leave anytime soon. They had tracked him several times in and out of town. Where he went when he was out of sight was still to be determined. But at least he was staying put for now.

Independence Day was two days away. And the fact that they had no credible evidence that there was an immediate threat of an attack was hindering them from being able to move forward. President Walker had completely rejected the idea of warning the nation further. He gave explicit orders that if any of them were to pursue this course of action, he would personally see to it that they never saw the outside of a prison cell for as long as they lived. The only thing he was willing to concede was allowing them to continue to pursue new evidence. Jennings had told them he was working on it. But for now, they were to hang tight.

He got a text message from Jennings when he got home that said the informant would meet him in two days, the deadline date. In the meantime, he was to go ahead and try to find the Prophet. He would have a plane waiting for him in the morning. That, at least, made him happy. They knew where the man was. Now it was just a matter of getting there and catching him. He called Boz and Taylor and gave them the update. He wondered if President Walker even knew that Jennings was meeting with them.

It had been a long couple of days. And he'd hardly been home. He wanted a long, hot shower and a good night's sleep. He fixed himself a sandwich, swallowed it in three bites, and headed upstairs to turn the water on. Half an hour later, he felt like a new man. The wound in his shoulder still hurt, but the long shower had helped to loosen the muscles a good bit. He was toweling off when the doorbell rang. He threw on a pair of gym shorts and grabbed his gun. No reason for anyone to be showing up at this hour.

He stood beside the door and was about to call out to see who it was when he heard the voice.

"It's Boz."

He opened the door and walked back into the living room. He sat down and laid the 9mm on the corner table.

"Expecting someone else?" Boz asked, pointing to the pistol.

"Not expecting anyone," Keene said.

Boz nodded and sat down. "So you're headed to Texas in the morning."

"Looks that way. You going with Kevin to see the Joint Chiefs?"

"Looks that way."

Both men sat there in silence for a few moments. Keene finally broke the stalemate.

"I'm not going to kill him, Boz."

"I know. That's not why I'm here."

"Then what?"

"Couple things. First, I wanted to see how you're doing."

"I'm fine. What do you mean?"

"You're not fine. You've got a hole in your shoulder. And I wanted to talk to you about this Prophet guy."

"You trying to shrink me again, chapy?"

Boz laughed at him. "No, I'm not trying to *shrink* you again. Listen. I know you have had a hard time even considering buying into all of this, but I'm telling you, man—I believe with all of my soul that something is happening here. I think you believe it, too, you're just too stubborn to admit it."

Keene just sat there looking at him, stern-faced.

"Tell me what happened to your wife."

Here we go again, Keene thought. "What's that got to do with anything? I told you. She was killed by a terrorist."

"It's got everything to do with everything. It's the very reason you're set on denying that this could all be real."

Ever since he'd left the unit, Keene had worked on his own. Up until two weeks ago, Jennings was the closest thing he had had to a friend. And though it was hard for him to admit, he missed the camaraderie. The last two weeks with Boz and Taylor had brought that to light. But to say that he and Boz were close friends, after this short a period, was reaching. And Boz was close to stepping over the line.

"My personal convictions have nothing to do with this," Keene snapped.

"If there is a threat against this country, then I want to stop it. It's that simple."

"It's not that simple," Boz said. "I get it. You think that God let her die by the hands of terrorists. And since He couldn't stop it, you've dedicated your life to doing what you think He couldn't do."

"You don't know anything! And you're way outta line."

"No, *you're* outta line. You've got this screwed-up view of the world and how it's your job to make everything right. It's not your job!"

"Then who's is it!" he yelled. "His? 'Cause He's done a poor job of it."

"No, He hasn't. That's what I'm trying to show you, if you'd just listen."

Keene dug his fingers into the arms of the chair and set his jaw. Boz had been pressing him to have this conversation since they'd met. And he didn't want anything to do with it, because he wouldn't admit it, but Boz was right. He was mad that this God, if He was real, allowed her to die. And He did nothing to stop it, so Keene had decided he would. And he'd lived the last eight years trying to make sure that he kept some other poor sap from losing someone he loved.

"I've only got one thing to say to you. But it's the very thing that you need to hear."

Keene just stared at him.

"Jesus Christ loves you."

Keene let out a laugh. "That's it? That's all you got for me, chapy? Kindergarten Sunday school?"

"Jon. . . Jesus Christ loves you."

"Seriously—" Keene couldn't help himself. The absurdity of it took him. A couple seconds of laughter gave way to a hard cough. He rubbed his shoulder. "Ouch! Laughing makes it hurt." Then, "You get that from a greeting card?"

"Laugh if you want to. But it's true."

"Okay, chapy. You wanna go there? Let's go there."

Keene sat forward on the chair and gave him a hard stare. "What about my life makes you think your Jesus loves *me*? To be quite honest with you, my life has been one big suckfest after another. Dad left when I was twelve. Mom died when I was eighteen. Had a recruiter boldface lie to me about all the great things I would see and do in the Marines. Two months later I'm getting shot at in Afghanistan. Where was your Jesus then? He wasn't *there*, I can tell you that."

"I'm sorry you—"

"Oh, no, no, no—you wanna know what's *sorry*? How 'bout the fact

183

that I spend six months training for a mission that should've gone down without a hitch, but instead I get a bureaucrat in Washington—trying to make himself look important—who goes and shoots his mouth off to some people he shouldn't have, and I end up walking four of the best men this country's ever seen into an ambush and getting them killed. Or how 'bout the fact that despite all the garbage this world has thrown me, I somehow end up with the most incredible, beautiful woman—inside and out—I've ever known. And she gets ripped away from me because some idiot believed *his* god told him to go hijack a bus and blow it up in front of Times Square! You wanna know sorry? How's that for sorry?"

"You done? You feel better now? Now that you got that out?"

Keene bit his lip and shook his head. "No, I'm not done. Why do you care so much about a God who, apparently, couldn't give two cares about this world, let alone you or me? Tell me, Boz. Where's God when all these wars are going on and people are killing each other? Where's God when you see little kids starving to death or thousands of people being killed by an earthquake or tsunami? Explain to me why a twenty-year-old gets cancer and dies, while a child rapist gets acquitted on a technicality. Where's God in that? Huh?" He slammed his fist on the armrest. "Now I'm done!" He sat back in the chair. "Though I could go on."

Boz pursed his lips and nodded. "So let me get this straight. You blame God for everything bad in the world. Who gets the credit for the good stuff?"

"From where I sit I don't see—"

"No, no, no—you had your time. Now I get mine. All those things you've listed, all these things you've brought up, can be explained by people's choices. The problem is not with God. The problem is with sin. Bottom line: people choose to sin against God. We've been doing it since Adam and Eve. And make no mistake. God is one hundred percent in control. But the problem is, it's really *en vogue* and convenient to blame God for the sins of man. Which, by the way, man is absolutely responsible for."

"Okay," Keene said. "I'll give you that people do horrible things to each other. But what about diseases, earthquakes—those things?"

"Same answer. Sin"

"See. . ." Keene gave a dismissive wave. "You don't have an answer. *Sin!* That's your payoff pitch."

"It's absolutely the answer. What I'm trying to get you to see is that sin is the root of every problem this world faces. The Bible says that because of sin, the whole world is messed up. The Bible acknowledges everything you just said! It's why it says that all of creation groans like the pains of childbirth, waiting for its redemption. It's why Jesus said, 'Behold, I am making all things new.' But the problem is, you're too busy blaming God for earthquakes and cancer, and you've never stopped ask if maybe you're to blame for any of it. You've never stopped and acknowledged your own sin. The fact that your sin, my sin—our sin—is the reason why the world is the way it is. It doesn't make you someone special because you recognize all the problems in this world. It makes you special when you acknowledge One who is the answer to the problems."

"And your answer to the problem is God."

"Yes, it is. This is the very reason why God the Father sent his Son. To redeem what you recognize is broken. And what's more, He came to redeem what you fail to see is broken: you."

"Oh, so now I'm broken?"

"Seriously? Did you hear anything you just said to me a minute ago? Yeah, you're broken. And you're deceived, rebellious, self-serving, self-dependent, self-centered—"

"You done?"

"Yeah, I'm done. . .though I could go on."

The fact that Boz had thrown his own words back at him annoyed him. But he was tired. And his shoulder hurt. And he had a plane to catch in the morning. He guessed everything Boz was saying made sense on some level. But he just didn't feel like dealing with it right now.

"You know what?" Keene finally said. "You're right. I am all of those things. Even more reason why I was right earlier, that your Jesus doesn't love me."

"No," Boz sighed. "It's all the reason why *I'm* right. Because, while you are everything you just admitted you are, the Bible says that Christ showed His love for you by dying for you. Not because you deserve it. But because you *are* all of those things. And because one day, God's going to come to collect a debt that you owe Him and can't pay. But His Son has. If you put your faith and trust in Him. So, I'll say it again: Jesus loves you."

Boz finished talking and stood up. Keene stood up with him and walked to the door. "Listen. I appreciate you trying to look out for me. I really do. And I know you think you know how I feel and think—"

"I didn't come here to make you mad," Boz interrupted. "I know you've got a long day tomorrow. The last thing I wanted was to come over here and get into an argument with you. I just wanted you to hear my heart. And I wanted to know the truth. How long has it been since someone has just shot you straight? How long has it been since someone just outright told you how things are? I know. In our line of work, it's few and far between. Most of the time we get the runaround and are left to figure everything out for ourselves. But I'm your friend, Jon. I'm not going to just leave you hanging out there. On anything. You've got my word. But if you're going to trust me, and my word, you need to know where it's coming from." He turned the handle and opened the door. "Be safe tomorrow. I'll see you when you get back."

Keene closed the door behind Boz and headed upstairs. He wanted to just jump in bed, shut his eyes, and go to sleep. But he knew that if he didn't redress his shoulder, it was going to give him fits tomorrow.

It took him ten minutes to put a fresh bandage over the wound and clean up. He walked the short hall into the bedroom and lay down. He still had Boz's voice ringing in his ears. He wanted to just dismiss it all. Just push it aside and rack out. But he couldn't. Instead, he lay there, thinking about everything Boz had said. Maybe he *was* tired of being angry. Maybe he did want to let it go. Maybe it wasn't God's fault. But where would that leave him?

He thought about that as he finally drifted off to sleep.

CHAPTER 52

Taylor woke up early, got in a quick workout, showered, ate, and was out the door. She had only been to DHS once or twice but never upstairs. And never in Director Levy's office. Jennings had already checked to make sure Marianne hadn't shown up today. She hadn't. The word from her secretary was that no one had seen or heard from her. They had sent a car around to her house to check, but she wasn't there either. Nothing seemed to be disturbed at her house, they had been told. It just simply looked like she wasn't home.

The office was much the same. When she arrived, she got some stares from people. They must have been wondering why all of a sudden someone who didn't work there was rummaging through Marianne's office. They had all been notified, of course. Jennings had made the necessary calls to take care of it. But that still didn't explain the intrigue. The word, officially, was they were treating it as a precautionary measure. In case they decided to elevate it to a missing person status. And if anyone had any information as to Marianne's whereabouts, they were to report directly to Director Jennings. Nobody was buying that, though. Rumors were already flying around the office that Marianne somehow had gotten herself in trouble.

Inside the office, Taylor got to work quickly. She set up her laptop and ran the Cat-5 network cable to Marianne's desktop. She highly doubted that she would find anything there that would be of any value. But nevertheless, she was thorough. And so she began the laborious task of sifting through the files on the drive.

She watched as her program ran and talked to the inferior computer. Little progress bars would streak across the screen as each section took its turn. She checked the time. Keene should already be in Texas. She wasn't sure when Boz was to meet with Jennings, but she assumed they were probably already there. She grabbed her phone and dialed the number. Keene answered on the second ring.

"Hey, just got here. What's up? Anything on Marianne's computer?"

"Nothing yet. I just got started. So nothing on the Prophet yet?"

"I've only been here for about twenty minutes. I showed his picture to the guys around here at the little airstrip but nothing. I've got a couple maps, and I'm going to go check out some different places. But I'm more than likely just going to sit in the center of town, for the most part, and let him come to me."

"Trust me. He probably already knows you're there."

"And how could he possibly know that?"

She had resigned herself fully to accept that this guy was who he said he was. She was a believer. And if her heart had become hardened to the possibility that God would speak once again to His children through a messenger, then shame on her. "How do *you* think?"

For the first time since she'd met him, Keene had no smart comment to shoot back. Instead, what he said actually surprised her.

"Yeah, you may be right. I guess I'm going to have to just try and track him down."

"Uh-huh," she said tenuously.

"Uh-huh what?" Keene asked.

"Nothing. Just never thought you'd—never mind. Anyway, I don't know what Marianne has been doing over here, but if she's done anything questionable, I'll find it. You need to go and get to work. I'll call Boz and see what's up."

"You'll let me know as soon as you talk to him?"

"Yeah. Will do."

She got off the line with Keene and dialed the second number. It rang once and went immediately to voice mail. Seconds later, her phone bleeped with a new text. It was from Boz. He and Jennings were still in with the Joint Chiefs and would be out in a few minutes. The prognosis, he said, wasn't great.

Megan continued to watch the progress bars slide across the screen. One by one they disappeared from the screen as each program finished its analysis. Another one had just done its thing when her phone rang. It was Boz.

"Anything?"

"Just talked to him. Nothing. He said he just got there."

"What's his plan?"

"Said he had a couple maps and some places he wanted to check out but was thinking about sitting there in the town square and waiting for him to show up."

"Nah, he probably already knows Jon's there. He's probably already on the move."

"That's what I said. Listen, Boz, you think Jon's all right?"

"Why? What did he say?"

"Nothing really. Just that when I said the Prophet probably already knew we were on our way, Jon said I was probably right. That sound like Jon Keene to you?"

She heard a soft chuckle on the other end. "Maybe."

"What's that supposed to mean?"

"I don't know. Guess we'll see."

"Anyway, what'd the Joint Chiefs say?"

"The usual. They've got ten operational theaters right now, and unless there is an attack, they can't pull any troops back."

"That's it? They're just going to *not* do anything?"

"They're following orders, Megan. It's what they do."

Boz was still explaining when Taylor saw the screen on the computer switch. One of her programs had found something. Multiple windows began to open up and fill the screen. She clicked through the different windows, trying to see what she was looking at. It didn't look good.

"Hey," she said, interrupting him. "You and Jennings need to get over here now. I've found something."

189

CHAPTER 53

Keene drove his rental out of town to the address that he had. His GPS device informed him he was only fifteen miles away. As he approached the small farmhouse, he pulled the car off the road and decided to take the last quarter mile on foot.

There wasn't much brush for cover, so he tried to just stay low to the ground and move slowly, using the few trees along the way to stop and look. Each time he raised the binoculars, the view was the same. The place looked abandoned.

When he was less than a couple hundred yards out, he looked a final time and saw nothing. He waited for twenty minutes, watching to see any movement. But there was nothing. Satisfied that no one was there, he went to the house.

He looked around back, just to make sure he was right and that there wasn't some kind of outbuilding that the guy might be in. But the only thing back there was a wide-open landscape of dirt and loose brush. He checked the back door and found that it was open. He checked his gun and turned the knob.

A quick sweep of the inside showed him that no one indeed was home. And given the look of the place, if anyone lived there, he did a good job of hiding it. There were some empty cans of soup and a half-eaten loaf of bread. Someone had been there. But whoever it was wasn't planning on staying. And it didn't look like he was planning on coming back.

Keene spent another twenty minutes inside, looking for anything that would lead him to the Prophet, but once again came up empty. If the Prophet had been staying there, he was gone. Not so much as a toothbrush was left.

He left the place and decided to head back into town. He was hungry, and the only confirmation they had of the Prophet being there was video footage from the town square. If there was still a chance of finding him, that was the best one. As he came back into town, a small motel and diner sat beside each other. It was still early enough for breakfast, and Keene was hungry. He parked the car and went inside.

He found a table and grabbed a menu. When the waitress came over, he asked for coffee and said he needed a minute. She brought him a cup and set it down. He reached inside his pocket and pulled out the picture.

"You see this guy around town lately?" he asked her.

"Honey, ain't you been watching the news? You're, like, the third person who's been in here this week. Boss is talking about shutting us down. This market crash's got everyone scared. And with those sherriff's deputies and other cops gone missing, everyone 'round here's been real tense."

"Sherriff's deputies?"

"I guess you ain't heard. Couple days ago, bunch of cops and deputies went missing, all along the border. No one's heard from them. Weird, huh?"

Keene thought about that for a minute. Yes, it was peculiar. Why would a bunch of cops go missing? *Probably just another drug cartel,* he thought, *taking advantage of the chaos going on around the country.* He dismissed it and pushed the picture to her. "Sorry, ma'am. Haven't heard about that. But can you look at this? It's real important."

She studied the photo for a minute and said, "Seems like I might've seen him. Hang on."

Keene watched her walk around the counter and hand the photo to the only other girl working. The other girl took the photo and walked back to Keene.

"Yeah, I've seen this guy. Was in here this morning."

"You know him?"

"Nah, never seen him before today." She cocked her head and squinted her eyes. "What's your name?"

"Jonathan Keene. Why?"

The girl went wide eyed and stepped back a pace. "Whoa! This is too weird. That guy was right!"

Keene sat up in his chair. The hair on the back of his neck stood up. "What do you mean?"

She reached inside her apron and handed him an envelope. "This guy you're looking for? Came in here real early this morning, ordered some breakfast. When he was done, he paid his bill and then handed me this. Said a guy named Jon Keene was gonna come in here today and ask me if I'd seen him. And then he told me to give you this."

Keene opened the envelope and pulled out the single sheet of paper. He unfolded it and read.

> *Mr. Keene, I'm sorry you've come all this way for nothing. As I told you before, I am not the one you seek. I only came here to retrieve a few things. As you read this, I'm already gone. Please do not try to find me. You have other, more pressing things to deal with. When the time is right, I will be sent to you. We shall meet then. For now, you must leave immediately. You are needed in Washington.*
>
> *Until we meet,*
> *The Prophet*

Keene crumpled up the paper and threw it on the table. His head began to pound. He wanted to slam his fist into a wall. He pulled out his phone.

"This is Jennings."

"It's me. He's not here."

"What do you mean?"

"I mean I've spent the morning trying to find him and nothing. Then I get to this diner and show his picture to the waitress and she tells me that he was here. Early this morning. And he gave her a letter to give to me."

"How'd he know you would be there?"

"Good question. Anyway, he's not here. Said he's long gone and told me that I was needed back in Washington."

"Yeah, maybe. But don't know yet."

"What do you mean?"

"I'm here at DHS with Taylor. She's found something. Don't know what it is, but I'm sure it's not good."

"Okay. I'll head back immediately."

"No, you won't. I told you, you need to go see Hector. You're meeting him tomorrow."

"Hector's a thug. We need to be tracking down this Prophet guy. If he's already left, he hasn't gotten much of a head start. I can catch up to him."

"You have no idea where he's going. Besides, that letter may just be a ruse to get you outta town. Stay there and keep looking. If he doesn't turn up, tomorrow you go see Hector, and then you can leave."

"The lady down here says a lot of cops went missing in the last two days. I'll bet you a thousand bucks your boy Hector wants to give us another cartel tip. I don't have time to be running down drug dealers. We have a possible threat to deal with. The deadline is tomorrow!"

"Calm down. I know what the timeline is. You still have to check out the rest of the town and make sure this Prophet isn't there. That's going to take you the rest of the day. Hector wants to meet tomorrow morning first thing. After that you can head home. I've got to go. Taylor's in Marianne Levy's office right now. She's waiting on me. I'll keep you posted."

The line went dead.

Keene clicked off the call and slammed the phone down on the table. At least the food smelled good. He motioned the waitress over and ordered pancakes.

CHAPTER 54

What am I looking at?" Jennings asked her.

Taylor pulled up the files she had found and put them in sequential order for them to go through. They were all different, but they all seemed to connect to one another. "This first one is a petition for a sanctioning of an area of land in Montana. According to this, an area has been set aside for research and has been deemed off-limits to the public. There's even a mandate for Marianne's Civil Military to support in keeping the area secure.

"This next one and the one after that are the same thing. One for North Dakota and South Dakota."

"What are these?" Jennings asked. "And why would Marianne Levy have them?"

"I don't know yet. But it doesn't make sense. Why would DHS be concerned with sanctioning land and keeping people out?"

"Good questions," Boz added. Then he pointed to the screen. "What's that?"

Taylor pulled up the window. "This looks to be like a customs clearance form."

"What's that?" Boz asked.

"This gives whoever has it the ability to cross borders and bring whatever he wants in without inspection. You've got to have some serious pull and connections to make that happen."

"What's it for?" Jennings asked. "And who is it for?"

Taylor skimmed through the paragraphs till she found something. "Says here it's for heavy industrial equipment. And it's for a company called AE Tech International."

"What's that?" Jennings asked.

Taylor switched screens and brought up her Internet browser. In seconds she had what she was looking for. "It's an oil company out of Canada. Chinese based."

"Why would a Chinese-Canadian oil company be bringing heavy industrial equipment across our border and need to circumvent customs?" Jennings asked.

"This isn't good," Boz said. "The Chinese have spent the last ten years putting Canada under their thumb. They already have over thirty drilling sites there. They pretty much already own the country. You know the kind of stink it would cause if Americans found out that the Chinese were drilling here when *we* aren't even allowed to? Canada's one thing. But drilling on American soil is another."

"Isn't this, like, treason, or something?" Taylor asked. "She can't just allow them to come into our country without the proper inspections and authorization to do this—right?"

"It's something, all right," Jennings said. He turned and started to walk out. "I need to go check on some things. You two stay here and see what else you can find out."

"Will do." She nodded.

"Oh, and Taylor. . ."

"Yeah?"

"Find out where Marianne Levy is. I want to talk to her."

When Jennings was out of the room, Taylor turned to Boz. "This isn't good, is it?"

Boz just looked at her and said, "Doesn't look like it. United States–Canada relations have already deteriorated because of this. Who knows what's going on up there?"

"Well, we need to figure out what all of this means. If the Chinese are coming here to drill, there's got to be more paperwork. Could she have done an end run on the entire country?"

"Who knows?" Boz said. "You and I both know that some people are capable of anything. I wouldn't put it past her."

Taylor felt completely betrayed. Marianne Levy had sold out her country. She was going to secretly bring in a Chinese oil company and set them up to drill for the same oil that US companies had been denied access to since, well. . .forever. *If the American people find out*, she thought, *they will be calling for heads in Washington.* "Which is already happening," she said to herself. If the market was going crazy now, what would it do when this came out? What else had Marianne done?

Taylor pushed the open windows aside and continued checking her filters. Halfway down the list another folder caught her eye. She clicked the folder and waited for it to open. When it did, she immediately felt sick to her stomach. Boz, who was standing over her watching, just blew out a long, slow breath.

"You've got to be kidding me," she said, almost in a whisper.

Inside were secure, highly classified documents from the CIA and Department of Defense. A dossier had been put together on an operative. It was complete with a workup of the operative's believed-to-be personal history, a psych evaluation, and a detailed account of the operative's past suspected missions and crime scene photos of the targets. Taylor sifted through the documents, one by one. The list of accomplishments—if you could call them that—was impressive. The operative was listed as *Dangerous, Intelligent, Resourceful, Discreet,* and *Professional.*

"Why would she have this?" Taylor asked. "Better yet, *how* did she get this? Boz, you know about this stuff. This is like high-level CIA stuff, right? I mean, I know Jennings technically works for her, but—"

"No," Boz confirmed. "I worked with the CIA for over ten years. Director Snyder handpicked Jennings as his successor. I may not know Jennings that well, but I knew Don Snyder better than his wife did. And I can promise you, Jennings didn't get that job because Snyder thought he would roll over for Marianne Levy. There's no way Jennings would have given her this. This is the kind of secret Intel CIA directors keep for themselves."

There was a single photograph of the operative. It was a profile view, and it was obviously taken in a hurry and without the operative's knowing. A notation had been made beside the picture, informing that it was the only known photograph of the operative. The shot was from across a street at a train station—somewhere in Europe, Taylor supposed, given the architecture. The order underneath the picture was highlighted in red and listed in all capital letters and read, *TERMINATE ON SIGHT.* Underneath that was a name.

ALEXANDRA SOKOLOV—AKA ALEX SMITH.

CHAPTER 55

Alex Sokolov sat on the bed, staring at the laptop. She had been monitoring the feed now for nearly an hour. The bug she'd placed in Marianne's system was turning out to be very helpful indeed. It's not that she didn't trust the woman, she just. . .didn't trust the woman. She had wanted to make sure she kept tabs on everything she could. And that included the computer of her employer.

Whoever it was over at DHS going through Marianne's files was good. She assumed it was that FBI agent she'd seen with Keene at the Capitol. She'd done a little checking and found out that Megan Taylor was quite special when it came to computers. Perhaps a little too special.

The bug was designed to monitor only the feed. It didn't enable her to operate as a user on the system. However, it did allow her to send a signal to the machine, triggering a nasty little virus—a little something she'd picked up from an Egyptian friend at the University of Cairo—that would wipe out any and all computers connected to that particular server.

She was surprised, initially, when the little alarm had sounded, letting her know that someone was using the computer. She had been in the middle of finalizing details for her departure. The house had to go, as much as she hated the thought. She'd enjoyed the place for nearly a decade now. But with her assassination of the president—she was giving herself the full credit, even though the man was technically still alive—there could be no trace of her whatsoever. The house, her belongings, everything had to go. She had been meticulously wiping down the entire property. She was taking only what she could carry with her. But the little beeping made her stop to see what was happening.

Now here she was, watching and waiting to see what Marianne was stupid enough—no, that wasn't it, narcissistic enough—to have kept on her computer. Everything was fine. Until it wasn't. She should've known. How could she have been so careless? She'd believed Marianne wasn't careless enough to have something like Alex's dossier. That was enough. She should've triggered the virus as soon as she saw the computer come to life. She knew Marianne was gone already. There was no reason for her computer to be on.

Alex cursed herself for allowing this to happen. Maybe Marianne was a liability after all. No matter, that would have to wait. For now, she needed to stop this. She clicked a couple buttons and entered a code. She hit ENTER and watched as the screen began to pixelate. Then the screen began to rain with ones and zeros, and in a matter of seconds everything disappeared. And the screen went blank.

She shut the laptop and packed it in her backpack. Her flight left in less than two hours. She needed to set the charges on the house. If she hurried, she would have enough time to watch it burn to the ground before she left. She spent the next twenty minutes carefully going through the place, checking to make sure nothing was left that could connect to her, in case it miraculously survived the fire. She did one final sweep and closed the door behind her. She had just removed her latex gloves and stuffed them into her pocket when she felt her phone vibrate. She looked at the screen. She was a little surprised. Of all the people she never expected to hear from again, this one was at the top of her list.

"This is Ms. Smith," she said politely.

"Ms. Smith, this is Mr. Chin. I would very much like to acquire your services."

CHAPTER 56

Taylor and Boz were looking at the photo when it happened. The screen just popped, and then everything began to pixelate. She immediately knew what it was.

"Wh—what's happening?" Boz said. "It's all going away. Do something!"

She already was.

The first rule of computers is to never detach a cable or device without properly ejecting it from the computer's hard drive. This process usually consists of using the secondary click on the mouse and selecting the tab for ejecting the hardware *safely*, as the computer puts it. Not following this procedure could often lead to a corrupted, irretrievable drive. The second rule of computers is to never shut down the machine cold, unless it froze up and couldn't be manipulated. Always, always, use the proper shut-down procedure. Not doing so could produce the same result as the mismanaged external hardware. Being a cautious computer nerd, Taylor never skipped the procedure.

Without even considering the downside, she yanked the Cat-5 cable out of Marianne's computer and mashed the power button down on her laptop. Two seconds later, the machine whined to a stop. Ten seconds later, Marianne's computer buzzed, made a couple popping sounds, and then the screen went completely crazy. Starbursts of color shot all over the monitor as the entire screen took on the likeness of a Picasso painting.

"What just happened?" Boz said when it was over.

Megan was furious. How could she not check for a worm like that before starting her search for the files? She had not followed her own procedure, and now this!

"What happened?" Boz repeated.

"That stupid hag had a worm installed!" she said. "I can't believe I didn't check it!"

"Calm down, Megan. You couldn't have known."

"Yes, Boz. I could have. I should have. Now we'll never know what else was there."

"Did you get any of it transferred onto yours?"

"Ha!" She threw up her hands. "I don't even know if my computer was infected. For all I know, this thing is now a glorified paperweight!"

"Okay. Calm down. What do we need to do to find out?"

Taylor took a couple breaths and tried to calm herself. She thought for a moment. "I need to take this back to my office and start it up in safe mode. Our network is secure. And if the worm is operating via the net, it won't be able to function there. If it got onto my computer, I'll be able to quarantine it and remove it. But I have no idea what all it's already destroyed."

"Okay, then. Let's get back to your office."

The door to Marianne's office opened up and Deputy Director Faigan stepped in. The title was extremely misleading, as the man was nothing more than a glorified assistant. He was currently acting as the liaison to Director Jennings. "Ah, excuse me," he said, "but did either of you have anything to do with what's going on out here?"

Megan gave the man a disgusted look. "It's a server worm."

"What's that mean?" he asked.

"It means that anything connected to that server is blown. You can thank your former boss for that!"

The man gave her a quizzical look. "Former boss? What do you mean? I thought Director Levy had just taken personal time. Did something happen?"

"Oh, something happened, all right! You can tell everyone to just sit tight. Director Jennings will be calling to give you all an update. I wouldn't count on seeing Director Levy again, though."

The man's eyes went wide. "Is she all right? Is everything okay?"

"Not if I find her," Taylor snapped.

CHAPTER 57

Keene had spent most of the rest of the day traversing the town and the surrounding areas looking for any trace of the Prophet. He had stopped and shown the picture to anyone who would look. Everyone had said the same thing. *Never seen him.*

He'd tried to call in and see how Taylor and Boz were faring but got cut short both times. Apparently, Boz informed him, Taylor's computer had been infected by something called a worm when she connected to Marianne's office computer. He said they had news but couldn't talk then, and he would call back. Keene had tossed the phone into the seat beside him, frustrated. He just wanted to get back on the plane and go home. But instead, he was here, in this dumpy little town, waiting to talk to a drug snitch about who knew what.

He went back to the roadside inn on the outside of town and got a room. It wasn't the Ritz, but at least it was clean. He turned on the TV to see what was happening in the world outside of Hidalgo County. He fumbled with the remote until he found a news channel. The commentator was talking about the day's events with the market. It seemed as if this whole market crisis wasn't going away. There were a couple clips of President Walker giving a press announcement, asking the American public to be patient. He was asking the American people to set it aside for one day and try to enjoy the holiday. The government would be working round the clock to try to avoid a major financial catastrophe.

"News flash, you big dope!" he said to the TV. "It's already here!"

He clicked the thing off and tossed the remote to the other bed. It was getting into evening, and Boz still hadn't called him back. Keene checked his watch and decided he was hungry. He left the room and walked across the street to the same small diner where he had eaten breakfast.

The same waitress from the morning was there, though she had a fresh uniform on. He waved her over and gave his order.

The food was good, as far as diner food went. He paid his bill and left a generous tip. He had said, "Good luck with business," to her as he left, not even knowing what he meant by it. She must've taken it as encouragement, though, because she gave him a big smile and said, "Thanks."

Looking to his right, he noted the town looked like everything had shut down. Lights were off and cars were gone. Even a small town like this, he realized, had seen the immediate effects of the Wall Street mess.

He decided to take a walk since he had nothing better to do. Besides, there was nothing worth seeing on television, and it was a nice night. The south Texas heat wasn't quite ready to let up for the evening, but at least the humidity had gone down.

Off in the distance, he could see a few small fireworks pop up here and there. Even with the economy tanking like it was and people freaking out, there seemed to still be a few who were at least trying to celebrate.

He'd gone only a few blocks before his phone finally buzzed. It was Boz.

"Where are you? What's been going on?"

"I'm at Andrews with Megan," Boz said.

"What? Why?"

"It's not good. Jennings is headed to the White House right now to talk to Walker."

Keene stopped and felt his dinner begin churning in his belly. "What's happened?"

"Megan found some stuff on Marianne's computer. Seems she'd been setting up a major operation with the Chinese to come here and drill in the Dakotas and Montana."

"What? That's impossible. How could she pull that off?"

"That's exactly what we said. She's been doing it for the last few months. She's forged customs documents, secured land. She even manipulated some military contracts to provide special security and quarantine of those areas. She was selling out the country."

"So what's happening? What's Jennings doing?"

"He's going to show Walker everything. He believes that this is what the Prophet is talking about."

"Why?" he said confused. "I mean, yeah, that could be considered an aggression. But that's not what he said, right?"

"Yeah, you're right. I don't think that's what the Prophet is talking about."

"Then why's Jennings sold on it?"

"Because the first scheduled date for beginning to move on all of this was for the day after tomorrow."

"That doesn't make sense. Treason, yes. Attack on the country. . .that's a stretch."

"I know, but there's more."

Keene could already taste the bile rising in his throat. What this woman had done was disgusting. As much as he didn't want to hear any more, he waited for Boz to continue.

"I told you there was a virus on Marianne's computer. Megan was trying to copy the files when someone launched it from a remote location. She couldn't trace it back because she had to shut her computer down, too. It took her most of the afternoon to just quarantine the bug and remove it from her own computer before she could sift through what was left."

"Yeah, and?"

"Megan was able to see that Marianne made a copy of a couple files the day Grant was shot."

Keene's head began to pound. He knew what was coming next.

"She pulled the evac route and procedure for the president," Boz continued. "We think there's a good possibility she handed that off to someone."

"The Russian." It was a statement, not a question.

"She had the CIA's file on the Russian on her computer. I think Marianne's the one who made the call."

Keene could feel the muscles in his jaw and neck tighten up. "Where is she?" he said in a cold, flat tone.

"She left here on a private charter and landed in Geneva. From there, she hopped two commercial flights to different countries and then disappeared. The last place she popped up was in Mumbai. But I don't think she would stay there. It took Megan most of the day just to track her that far."

"So what now? Why are you at Andrews?" he asked, knowing the answer and not liking it one bit.

"Jennings is sending us to find her. We're leaving for Mumbai in thirty minutes."

Keene pulled the phone away and hissed through his teeth. He took a deep breath to calm himself and put the phone back to his ear.

"So Jennings is just dismissing the whole idea of an attack tomorrow."

"No, he isn't. Listen. The reality of it is this: We've tracked the Prophet for two weeks with no luck. Marianne's tried to have the president assassinated. She tried to sell out the country's oil supply to our biggest debt holder. Our stock market has disintegrated. And we still don't have any idea what's going on. This is out of our control. Jennings wants you to meet with this informant guy tomorrow. Find out what he knows, and if it's anything worth worrying about, we'll follow it. But for now, we have to take what God has given us."

Here we go again, he thought. "You know what, Boz? This is ridiculous! I should be the one going after Marianne. If she did order the hit on Grant, then Jennings should be sending me, an active agent. Not you and Taylor. She's a computer geek! What's she going to do? E-mail her to death?"

"I'm going, too. And don't forget," he said, "I'm more than capable of handling Marianne Levy. And I've got news for you. Megan Taylor might be a computer geek, but she's also a federal agent. She can hold her own."

Keene knew Boz was right, but he didn't want to admit it. "Doesn't matter. You two are the ones who think God is doing all of this. Not me, remember? Maybe *God* wants us to stop Marianne Levy. Maybe *God* has been talking about this all along."

"Maybe," Boz said.

"Then why are you so bent on trying to make something bigger out of it?"

"Because we don't know. And until we do, maybe God has *you* there for a reason. If there is going to be an attack, maybe you're the one God wants there to handle it."

This was insane! He couldn't believe he was having this conversation. "You really believe all of this stuff, don't you?"

The line was quiet for a second. Then Boz said, "You know I do."

Keene stood there for a moment trying to calm himself. Finally he said, "If God wants me here, in the middle of all of this, then why doesn't He tell *me* that?"

"That's a good question," Boz said with a chuckle. "You could ask Him. But the better question is, would you listen if He answered? I'll call you when we land in Mumbai."

The line went dead. Keene forced himself to take a deep breath and exhale slowly. He put the phone back in his pocket and continued walking. When he got to the other side of the town square, he saw a building on the corner. It had a few lights on, and he could see someone walking around inside. He started to go in but dismissed the thought as quickly as it came. He continued walking on. But after a few steps, he stopped. He turned back around and went inside.

The place looked like a grocery store on the outside, but the inside had been completely renovated. The room was dimly lit, and a few candles were strewn around the walls. There were folding chairs covering the floor and a stage at the front with musical instruments covering it. There were signs pointing people where to go with their kids and then other signs pointing people where to go for what the sign called *worship*. The place had a very warm and friendly feel about it. It definitely wasn't like any church he'd ever been in before. There were no pews or huge high-back chairs with purple velvet lining everything. There wasn't even a huge podium for the preacher to speak from, like most churches he'd seen. Just a cool-looking aluminum truss lectern-type thing.

"Can I help you?"

He turned around to see a guy, probably close to his age. The guy wore a T-shirt and a zip-up hoodie. He had on sneakers and jeans.

"Ah, sorry," Keene said. "I saw the lights on and just thought. . ."

"My name's Scott. I'm one of the pastors here."

Keene reached out and took the man's hand. "Jon Keene."

"Never seen you around here, Jon. You visiting?"

"Something like that. I'm from DC."

The man jerked a thumb over his shoulder. "Me and some of the other guys here are having a small-group Bible study back in one of the classrooms. Care to join us?"

"Nah. That's okay," Keene said. "I need to go." Then, "I don't know why; I just thought I'd come inside and look."

"You have a church back home?"

"Lots of churches in DC," Keene said.

The guy laughed. "Yeah. . . That's not what I meant."

"No, not really. I used to go. Haven't for a while."

The pastor seemed to think about that for a second. "Maybe you should."

Keene didn't say anything back. He didn't want to be rude to the man.

"Why are you here, friend?" The pastor narrowed his eyes.

Keene shrugged his shoulders. He really didn't have a good reason. Honestly, he didn't know.

"Okay," the pastor said. "Well, think about this: There is no such thing as coincidence. There is no such thing as chance. The Bible says God has ordained all things. That nothing happens without His willing it or making it come to pass. So let me answer that for you, if I may."

Keene shrugged again.

"You're here because God wants you here. It's that simple. I can't pretend to know the details of that, but make no mistake. You're exactly where you're supposed to be."

"That's funny," Keene said. "Someone else told me that recently."

"Sounds like a smart person."

"Yeah. Maybe."

The pastor looked at him for a second and folded his arms. "Listen. I need to get back in there. But before I go, I feel like I'm supposed to tell you something. I don't know what it means or if it's even what you need to hear. But I'm going to tell you anyway."

"Yeah, what's that?"

"You think you know who God is, but you don't. And the only way to find that out is to spend time with Him."

He reached down and pulled something out from under one of the chairs. It was a Bible.

"Here. My gift to you. You want to know who God is? Read this."

He shook Keene's hand again and turned to leave.

"You can let yourself out whenever you're ready to go. If you're still here when I'm done, we can talk some more."

Keene looked at the Bible. "It's a pretty thick read, pastor. I'm kind of short on time."

The guy was halfway down the hall. He called back over his shoulder, "Start with the Gospel of John. New Testament. Great place to start." He continued walking then stopped and turned around again. "Or who knows," he said with a chuckle. "Maybe you could pray that God would just send you a prophet to explain it!"

CHAPTER 58

When Keene woke up, he realized he had done something he hadn't done in almost a decade. He'd slept in. The clock read 9:45 a.m. He wanted to be angry with himself for sleeping so late, but he couldn't. The reality of it was he'd needed it. His shoulder, while healing surprisingly quickly, was still stiff. The events of the past two weeks had left him running on empty. And he'd tossed and turned all night, knowing that today was the deadline. And no one had any clue what, if anything, was coming.

The shower was small and the water was barely more than a drizzle, but at least it was hot. He worked his big frame around inside the cramped space and let the heat loosen the stiffness. He stood there for ten minutes before finally shutting the water off.

When he left the motel, he noticed that there was an unusual amount of activity going on around the square. Down the street, he saw at least three news vans and people gathering around. As he got closer, he noticed that an area had been set up with a small podium and several microphones. A few sheriff's deputies were gathered around, as well as some other men, dressed in business suits. This didn't look like anything having to do with the holiday. This had a more ominous tone, he thought.

Drawing closer still, he began to hear the statement that one of the men in uniform was giving. Given his age and the brass on his uniform, he deduced that this was the sheriff himself. The man was saying that the missing law enforcement officers had all been found. The bodies had all been hidden, and the men were all killed in the same way. The officers had been located via the GPS trackers attached to their cars. And upon arrival at each scene, it was noted that the men had been killed in the same manner. Each had been shot, execution style. Ballistics would confirm the exact type of weapon used, but they were pretty sure that they were looking at AK-47 rounds.

The thing most disturbing, the sheriff was saying, was that this was not an isolated incident. They now knew similar executions had occurred along most of the Texas border. He and the other sheriffs across the state were forming a joint task unit to investigate and bring whoever had done this to justice.

He finished his statement, and the array of questions began hurling at the man. Reporters shouted over one another and pushed and jockeyed for position, trying to get more information. Keene watched the scene unfold and began to get a sickening feeling in his gut. This was more than just a drug cartel declaring war against the border police. He was sure of it. He had a little over an hour until his meeting with the informant. In the meantime, he had to talk to that sheriff.

★

It was a little after 7:00 p.m., with the time change, when Taylor and Boz arrived in Mumbai. The initial plan had been to stop for the night, check in with Jennings and Keene, and then get started finding Marianne Levy in the morning. That had all changed now.

Taylor had been using the satellite feeds across the Atlantic to dig further on her laptop. She had spent most of the entire twelve-and-a-half hour flight bouncing from one secure site to another, hacking her way in at every turn. She had assured Jennings that no one would be able to trace her and that there would be no way it could come back to him or the agency. He hadn't even batted an eye. "Do it," he said, as he walked away from the tarmac.

The normal commercial flight time to Mumbai was anywhere from fourteen to sixteen hours, depending on stops and layovers. Jennings, however, had called back the Gulfstream-5 that had taken Keene to Texas, saving them the extra couple hours. The good news was they would get there faster. The bad news, they had less time to find the missing director.

Nevertheless, Taylor had lived up to her reputation. She worked under the assumption that Marianne would not be flying commercial, if she left again. So she got a list of every second- and third-tier airport within a two-hundred-mile radius of Mumbai. It took awhile, but seven hours into the flight, she had a hit. A private airstrip south of the city had acquired a charter. The plane was a Bombardier 300 luxury jet. She pulled the manifest for the charter and found that the flight was headed to Dubai. It had one passenger, a female, American. And no checked baggage.

As their own G-5 taxied in, they were notified that the flight crew would need a minimum of three hours to turn the aircraft around: systems checks, refueling, and a new crew. There was no telling how long this chase would go, and they were instructed by Jennings to make sure that they had fresh legs behind the controls. Taylor and Boz decided they would take the three hours to grab some dinner and check in.

A car was waiting for them when they deplaned. The driver introduced himself as the CIA liaison to the region and announced he would take them to a house where they could get cleaned up. The drive was short, and the house was typical for the area. Just another unassuming residence.

"Shower's in there." The man pointed as they entered the house. "There's stuff in the fridge, though I can't promise it's still good." He laughed. "Here are the keys to the car." He threw them to Boz. "GPS has the airport plugged in already. When you're ready to head back, just follow the little lady's instructions."

"You're not staying?" Taylor asked.

"Sorry, ma'am," he said. "No can do. I'm meeting a guy an hour from now." He pulled the blinds back and looked out the window. "There's my ride now." He opened the door and stepped out. "There's an area of town about a mile that way," he pointed down the street, "has some eating places and shops and stuff. If you guys want something to eat, I'd go there. It's pretty safe, but you two will stick out like a sore thumb, so just keep your eyes open."

"I'm pretty familiar with the area," Boz said, to Taylor's surprise. She looked at him with a raised eyebrow.

"Really? How's that, Boz?"

Boz just smiled at her.

"Okay then," she said. "I'm going to shower. Be out in ten minutes."

Boz laughed this time.

"What?" she said defensively.

"Nothing," he said. "Just never met a woman that actually took a ten-minute shower. But, okay."

"Just call Jennings and tell him what we're doing," she said smartly. "And find out what Jon's doing. He should be meeting that guy any minute now."

CHAPTER 59

Keene stopped at the fork in the road. Up ahead, on the left, stood the house. He looked around outside the windows for any sign of danger, but there was nothing. He was the only one—no, the only thing—out here for miles. He reached for his phone and called Jennings.

"I'm here," he said.

"See anything?"

"Just some abandoned house about four hundred yards up. This place is literally out in the middle of nowhere. Not to mention, I'm less than a quarter mile away from the border."

"You recon the area?"

"No time. I had a chat with the sheriff down here about those missing cops."

"Yeah? What's that about?"

"They found them. All of them. More than a hundred border patrol agents, sheriff's deputies, and local cops. All shot, execution style, with the same type of weapon."

"Sounds like the drug cartels are ramping it up."

"What if it's not drug cartels?"

"That's why you're talking to Hector."

"Hector's a midlevel drug runner. We're wasting time. He's not going to know anything."

"Just talk to him. Hector is curious, if nothing else. He's got his nose in everything. If there's anything going on down there, he'll know. And he's real jittery, I'm told. So watch your back."

"You're getting senile in your old age. You forget who you're talking to here?"

"Listen to me," Jennings said coldly. "This kid isn't some ordinary street punk. He's a killer. Don't forget it. I'm not saying you can't handle yourself. Just don't be too cocky to think you're the only one with skills."

"Any word from Megan and Boz?"

"They just called in. They're in Mumbai. But only for another couple hours."

"What'd they find?"

"Small, expensive charter leaving a private terminal to Dubai. American woman. Fits the description."

"It's her," he said between clenched teeth. "Should be me over there."

"You just worry about Hector. I want to know what he wants."

"I gotta go. If he is watching, then he's watching me sitting here talking to you. I'll call you when we're done." He paused for a few seconds then, "And for the record, I still think this is stupid. There's a possible attack happening today, and I'm down here talking to a drug monkey."

"Just find out what he wants. I'll send a plane for you when you call back."

The line went dead.

Keene put the car back in gear and drove toward the house.

★

True to her word, Taylor was out of the shower in just a few minutes.

"I stand corrected," Boz said, bowing his head when she showed up. He was standing in the small kitchen area eating a sandwich. "I had to throw out some cheese, but other than that, the stuff in there is okay. Some lunch meat and bread. Want a sandwich?"

"I'll fix it," she said. "You go get cleaned up. Maybe we can get back early and put some pressure on them to move faster."

"Maybe," he shrugged.

She changed places with him and heard the door to the bathroom shut a moment later. She fixed herself a turkey sandwich with some mustard and found some chips in the cabinet. She sat down in the den and picked up the small remote control sitting on the table in front of her. She clicked it on and thumbed through the channels until she finally found an English-speaking news channel.

The anchor was saying something about the progress of the American president. That he wasn't expected to recover anytime soon and newly installed President Walker had no answer for the American financial crisis that was taking place. Markets all across the globe, he said, were being affected, though with the American dollar having lost so much of its worth over the previous three years, it wasn't as substantial as it could be. Images of footage from riots and protests across the country filled the screen, with the news anchor finally asking the question, "Can America bounce back?

211

Or are we seeing the decline of the West?"

Megan heard the water shut off in the other room. She stood up and took her napkin and empty glass back to the kitchen. Boz would be ready in just a few minutes. She wanted to be ready to leave when he was. She got back to the den area and unzipped her bag. She pulled out some fresh socks and started to put her boots back on when the news anchor suddenly began to talk in a hurried voice. She looked up to see the panic in the man's eyes. She reached for the remote and turned up the volume. The blood drained from her face as she watched in horror the scene unfolding before her. She gasped for breath but felt her chest tighten. All at once a flow of tears came. She couldn't breathe. She choked down the sobs and dug down to find her voice.

"Boz, get in here. Now!" she screamed. "It's happened!"

PART 4: THE 13

CHAPTER 60

Keene had been there with the informant for nearly a half hour. He couldn't believe what he was hearing. Even with the knowledge of an impending attack. There simply was no easy way to believe what the man was suggesting. Was this what the Prophet was talking about? If it was true, it had to be. But how?

"I ain't playin'!" Hector shouted angrily. "They kill my little brother, man! And something bad is about to happen! I'm telling you as a favor." He hung his head and wiped his eyes. "I don't know why your government don't know about this, CIA, but I'm telling you. Someone had to mess up big to miss this."

Keene stood there dumbfounded. There was no way this could be true. An entire army couldn't march on the United States' border and not be detected. He had to call Jennings. He reached for his phone and felt the buzz against his leg. He looked at the display. *Funny*, he thought.

"I was just getting ready to call you," he spoke into the mouthpiece.

"Get back here immediately," Kevin Jennings ordered.

"Yeah, about that," Keene said, "I think I need to stay here awhile. I need to check something out."

"No, you need to get back here immediately. Turn on the TV."

"What's happened?"

"Just do it!" came the reply.

Keene pushed past the group of men and pushed the button on the television sitting on the makeshift stand. It only took a few moments for him and the others to see what was happening.

Every channel had interrupted programming, now covering the breaking news. Plumes of black smoke rose into the sky from devastated buildings. Bridges and highways melted into a pile of searing red metal. Ash and debris covered the entire landscape. Cars were turned over and blown to bits. Then the camera changed. A new city. Same result. Then another. Then another. Finally the images ended. The cameras returned to the news station. A disheveled-looking man in blue jeans and a sweater sat in front of the camera. He opened his mouth and said the words that would change the course of history.

"Ladies and gentlemen, less than ten minutes ago, the entire West Coast of the United States of America was attacked. It appears to be a nuclear strike. Every major city from San Diego to Seattle. The death toll has to be in the millions. . . ."

"You see!" Hector was hysterical. "I told you!" he said. He turned and headed for the door. "Maybe next time, you'll listen."

Keene dropped to his knees and stared at the television. It was as if he were outside of his body, looking around. The room started spinning, and he felt the contents of his stomach begin to churn. He doubled over and threw up on the wooden floor.

He heard the sound of the motorcycles outside, kicking up gravel and dirt as they sped off. And then he heard a voice that sounded far off, calling to him. He realized it was Jennings, still on the phone he had clutched in his hands.

"Jon!" the man yelled again.

He raised the phone to his ear. "I'm here."

"You need to get back here immediately. They've nuked the West Coast. There are reports coming in that they've already entered in through the north. They're coming here. I'm evacuating the president and all nonessential personnel."

Keene was still trying to regain his bearings. "What—what do you mean? The north?"

"The Chinese! Are you listening to me?"

"What's the damage?"

"Looks like somewhere between twelve to fifteen cities. More than likely Russian suitcase nukes. The fallout is going to be pretty bad, but it should contain itself west of the Rockies."

"What about survivors?"

"We're trying to get word for everyone to head east. Get away from the blast radius as quickly as they can."

The Prophet had been right. And they hadn't stopped it. But Keene had been expecting an isolated attack. Maybe one of the major cities, or a subway, or. . .or anything but this. This was a full-scale act of war on the United States. He took a deep breath and calmed himself.

"Hector said that there were upward of a hundred thousand Chinese ground troops south of the border. How did we not know?"

The line was quiet for a moment before Jennings answered. "I honestly don't know. We should've. It had to be Marianne Levy."

"How could she hide it! How could she manipulate our entire intelligence system like that? We're talking about national security!"

"With the amount of anonymity and power that stupid law gave her, there's no telling what she could've done. You need to get back here. I need you here."

"For what! It's already happened. We failed."

"Did you not hear me? Right now the rest of the country's about to be under attack! There are troops moving in."

"Troops! What are you talking about? How could they get troops here?"

"They've been in Canada for ten years drilling, Jon. They have taken over entire towns. Who knows what they've been doing behind closed doors?"

Just then the ground beneath his feet began to rumble. There were a few old pictures on the walls that began to shake. The windows started rattling, and a drinking glass that had been sitting on a counter bounced its way off the ledge and shattered on the floor.

"Hold on," Keene said.

He knew explosions, and this didn't feel like one. Whatever this was, it wasn't another bomb. He ran outside and looked off in the distance. There was a huge black cloud on the horizon about a half-mile wide. And it was getting closer rapidly. In just seconds, the sky grew dark as the sun was masked by an entire fleet of supply planes, artillery carriers, and FC-3 Chao Qi fighter jets—the newest version of the supersonic, fully equipped Chinese combat fighters—flying over his head in perfect formation. The sound was deafening as the hundred or so aircraft flew so close to the ground he could actually see the foreign markings on the underbelly of each plane. They shot out of sight as quickly as they had arrived.

Keene raised the phone to his ear again. "Did you just hear that?"

"Yes. About blew my eardrums."

"I'm not going to be able to fly home. That was an entire fleet of Chinese military planes. Fighters, supply and infantry carriers. They're not coming. They're here!"

Again he heard a faint rumble. He scanned the landscape to see what it was. He couldn't make it out at first, but then it came into view. Another tidal wave of death coming by land. And it was closing in on his position rapidly. He had to move.

"And they've got ground troops, too," he said getting back on with Jennings. "This is bad, man. You've got to get our boys in the air right now!"

"Already doing it as we speak. But we're in a tough spot here. We've got less than eighty thousand troops stateside. And most of them are here on the East Coast. The rest of our country is vulnerable. The 101st in Fort Campbell is the only substantial base we still have west of the Appalachians. Fort Benning and Parris Island are all we have in the South. And they'll all be overrun in a matter of hours if this attack is what it looks like."

Keene started to say something, but Jennings cut him off.

"I'm needed at the White house. Get back here soon as you can. Drive all night if you have to. And stay out of sight."

The line went dead.

Keene tried to take a moment and assess the situation. The Navy, what was left of it—no thanks to the last two administrations—was spread across the Middle East. There were maybe a handful of ships in the DC area. There were, at best, fifty to a hundred combat fighter jets between Andrews and Norfolk, with perhaps a few more at Benning and Parris Island. If another attack happened—as long as it was a conventional attack—and if there was at least some measure of warning, they might have a fighting chance. Especially since the attack on the West Coast had just happened. He was pretty sure that every one of those flyboys were already in the air.

And they were headed west.

He grabbed the phone and called Jennings back.

"What is it?"

"Where are the flyboys?"

"They're already in the air headed out to meet the Chinese fighters."

"Call them back! Now!"

"Why? What's going on?"

"Call whoever you have to call and get them back. Now, Kevin. The Chinese aren't here to destroy us. They're moving in. They want the oil, remember?"

"So?"

"The only way to effectively move in and take over, is if they have no opposition whatsoever. The West Coast was a distraction. They're drawing us in. The highest concentration of anything military we have here is right there on the East Coast. With those boys headed west, DC is a sitting duck. Call them back right now! And get the Navy back here!"

He took one last look at the military convoy headed toward him. They were less than a mile away, at least twelve football fields wide, and rumbling over the Mexican desert, headed toward his homeland. He jumped in the car and sped back the way he had come.

CHAPTER 61

Boz wrapped his arms around Taylor and held on to her as she cried. He could feel his own eyes begin to fill up.

"What are we going to do?" she sobbed. "We should've stayed and found the Prophet."

He held her close and patted her back lovingly, like a father. "There's nothing we could have done to stop this."

She cried even harder. "I just don't understand. Why didn't President Grant tell the people? Why?"

"He tried," Boz said. "This isn't Calvin's fault. You know that."

She pulled away from him and said, "I know. But all those people—"

"Have continuously turned away from Him," he said, interrupting her. He grabbed her by the shoulders and looked her in the eye. "Listen. I don't believe for one second that God wants us to be destroyed."

"Then what is all of this about?" She pointed at the TV.

"I don't know yet. But I know deep within my soul that this is not done and done. The Prophet said that God wants the nation to repent. He doesn't want to destroy us. He wants us to turn back to Him."

"So what do we do?" She wiped the tears away and got herself back under control.

"Pray with me. I have no idea what else to do."

Boz got on his knees and reached for Taylor's hand. She knelt down beside him and took his hand.

"Father," Boz began, "today You have shown us Your sovereign power. And we praise You, that You indeed are Lord of everything. But God, we are so hurt by what we are seeing right now. Our people, our families, our nation is being destroyed. And God, we know that You have warned us to turn back to You."

He stopped for a moment and wiped his eyes.

"Father, please, have mercy on us. Have mercy on us, oh Lord, that we might have the chance to repent and turn back to You. Show us what we need to do. We pray this in Your Son's holy name. Amen."

Just then Boz felt his phone buzz. He clicked the button and said, "This is Boz."

"Mr. Hamilton," the voice said. "Please put me on speakerphone. I would like Ms. Taylor to hear this, as well."

"How did you get this number?" Boz asked, knowing who it was.

"I think you already know that, Mr. Hamilton. Please, do as I have asked."

Boz cupped the mouthpiece and whispered to Taylor, "It's him. It's the Prophet."

He held the phone out and clicked the speaker icon. "We're here. Go ahead."

They could hear the man sniffling in the background. "Please, excuse me," he said, his breath hitching. He sounded as if he had been crying.

"What do you want?" Taylor said sharply. "Why didn't you tell us this was going to happen?"

"I didn't know," he said, sniffling again.

"What do you mean, you didn't know!"

"Calm down," Boz said to her.

"I only told you what I was told. I didn't know anything specific. All I knew was what He gave me to say."

Boz cleared his throat. "Then why are you calling us? It's a little late to stop anything now."

"I'm calling you because He told me to," he said.

"Let me get this straight," Taylor said. "You mean God literally talks to you? Like He did to Isaiah or Moses?"

"You can choose not to believe it if you wish, Ms. Taylor, but yes."

Boz leaned in and said, "This may surprise you, Mr. Harrington, but we believe you."

"So you know who I am." It was a statement, not a question. "Please, then, just call me by my first name. Quinn."

Megan said, "Why are you calling us?"

"Because. God has heard your prayer. And He has searched your hearts and knows that you—"

"Wait!" Megan interrupted. "You mean, just now? When Boz and I were praying?"

"Yes," he said. "Just now."

"That's pretty heavy," she said.

"Yes, it is," he agreed. "God has heard your prayer. I am to tell you that you are correct, Boz. God will not give our country over to be destroyed. Not yet."

"What does that mean?" Boz asked.

"It means that we have work to do," he answered. "He has appointed one who will lead our country back to Him. In the meantime, there are others who have committed some pretty big wrongs."

"I don't understand," Taylor said.

"Though our country has turned its back on God, it is still His creation. He gave us this land. And He loves us. But there are those who have betrayed this nation to satisfy their own personal selfishness. In doing so, they have done more than just turned their back on Him. God is sovereign, but we are still responsible for our choices. They have willfully betrayed Him. He will allow them to be brought to justice. And then. . . He will deal with them."

"You mean Marianne Levy," Boz said.

"And some others. But specifically her," Quinn said.

"And you're telling us it's our job to find them," Boz said.

"For now," Quinn said. "Until something changes."

"What's going to change?" Taylor asked.

"I don't know. I'm only telling you what I've been told to say. I have to go now."

"Why? Where are you going?" Taylor asked. "How will we get in touch with you if we need you?"

"Trust me," Quinn said. "If you need to talk to me, He'll let me know."

There was a beeping sound, and then the line went quiet.

"So what do we do now?" Taylor asked. "We need to talk to Jennings."

Boz dialed the number and waited. Jennings answered after three rings.

"Hey, it's Boz and Taylor."

"You find Levy yet?"

"Not yet, but we believe we know where she is. Where's Keene?"

"Still at the border. He just saw an entire Chinese convoy, fighter jets and all, headed here. We're in the middle of it pretty good right now."

"Is he okay?" Taylor asked.

"He's okay."

"Kevin, you've got to get our boys home as quick as you can," Boz said.

"I'm trying, Boz. Believe me. The Joint Chiefs have already given orders for every naval vessel we have to report to Norfolk immediately.

But it's going to take them at least ten days to get here. We could be completely taken by then."

"Not gonna happen," Boz said. "What about the UK? Are they coming to help? They can have ships here in two days."

"They're saying no. The Chinese own them as much as they do us. Probably worse. They aren't going to lift a finger to help us out. They don't want to be next. And neither does anyone else. They're all waiting to see if the world's greatest superpower falls. Listen, I need to go. You two find Marianne Levy and bring her to me. And bring her alive. Don't you two *dare* kill her before I do. You understand me?"

"Understood," Boz said.

The line went silent.

★

Ten minutes after the call, Boz and Taylor sped through the streets of Mumbai back to the plane. It was a short drive, but it felt like an eternity. Neither one said much on the drive.

As they pulled up to the tarmac, the plane was already out of the hangar. They got out of the car and met the new flight crew. Boz handed Taylor her bag from the backseat and then grabbed his own. She was halfway up the stairs when he called to her.

She turned around and stopped. "What's wrong?"

"I can't go with you."

"What? What do you mean?"

"I can't go," he said. "You heard Jennings. It's going to take our Navy more than a week to get home. We need some help."

"What are you talking about?"

"England is the only country with a military that can help us right now."

"And Jennings said they're leaving us high and dry. We're on our own."

"Maybe not. I know some guys there. Maybe I can change their minds."

She walked back down the small set of steps and stood inches away from him. "Boz, this is crazy! Get on the plane. Marianne Levy is responsible for this. She needs to pay."

"And she will. You're more than capable of finding her and bringing her back. I have a good shot at getting our boys some help quickly. I'm not going to sit back and do nothing."

She sighed and stepped back a few feet. "And how are you going to get there?"

"Give me the sat-phone."

She stared him down for a few seconds, but he wasn't budging. Finally she reached inside her bag and tossed him the phone. She watched him dial the number and wait for the call to be placed.

"Mac, this is Boz. . . . Yeah. . . . You still in Surat?" He listened for a second then said, "Good. I need a pilot and a plane. . . . Mumbai. . . ." Then, "London. . . . Great, I'll be waiting for you."

He hung up the phone and looked at her. "Old friend who owes me a favor. He's going to come get me. I can be in London by morning."

Megan threw her hands up in the air. "They've already said they're not helping us!"

"*They* may have said no." He smiled. "But I know a guy who can change their mind."

"I can't go chasing after Marianne by myself. I need your help."

"No you don't," he said. "I've watched how you handle yourself. Go get her. Bring her back. You're right. She needs to pay for what she's done."

He pointed for her to get on the plane. She realized she was on her own for this part. And a whole new set of emotions began to take hold. How was she going to bring Marianne in by herself?

As if Boz were reading her mind, he reached up and squeezed her shoulders. "You're not just a computer technician, Megan. You're an FBI agent. And a very good one, at that."

Boz was right. Even though her time in the field had been minimal, she was more than capable of doing this. And if Boz could somehow get help, he had to do it. She couldn't stop him.

She set her jaw and nodded to him. She turned and walked up the small set of stairs to the plane. The flight attendant took her bag and closed the door behind her.

She leaned into the cockpit and said, "Let's go."

CHAPTER 62

Jennings rode inside the armored SUV with Director Preston and Bob Sykes, the secretary of the Navy. The other heads of the military, along with the Joint Chiefs and President Walker, were in cars behind him, along with half of the Cabinet. The Speaker of the House and the other half were two cars back and had two separate escorts. Somewhere in the midst of the convoy, an armored medical van carried the fragile body of President Grant and the First Lady. With the attack, it was decided that any type of air travel was too dangerous. Even for Marine One.

With Vice President Walker having become President Walker, there was a vacancy in the office of vice president until Walker could appoint someone. Therefore, Speaker Cunningham was next in line for the presidency, should something happen to Walker. And so, as President Walker was being taken away to the presidential bunker in Virginia along with half of the Cabinet members and President Grant, Cunningham and the other half of the Cabinet were being moved to a secondary facility in northern Pennsylvania. As the convoy sped up the ramp onto the beltway, the two sets of cars split and went in their designated directions.

Prior to leaving Washington, President Walker had gone on television and given a statement. The country was being attacked, and people were asked to take refuge wherever they could find it. It was suggested that people flee the major cities and prepare themselves for the worst. He made no attempt at reassuring the people that the United States would survive this attack. Jennings thought it was a cowardly act, but in all reality, he knew the president was right. No point in trying to sell false hope.

As he suspected, people were panicking and trying to evacuate the city. Cars were jammed bumper to bumper in both directions. And that was the report coming in from around the entire country, as news came in of the advancing Chinese troops. The small number of US troops still in the States had already deployed and were being engaged. For the first time since the Civil War years, the United States was at war on its own soil.

As the truck hugged the shoulder of the packed freeway, Jennings held the phone to his ear, listening to Keene's warning.

"Call them back right now! And get the Navy back here!"

He hung up the phone, knowing that Keene was right. Sykes and the Joint Chiefs were adamant about running out to meet the Chinese. But the reality was, there was no great concentration of troops anywhere in the country. The 101st was running on a skeleton crew; Parris Island and Fort Benning were primarily training bases. And though they did house the majority of the remaining US troops, they could only cover so much territory. The entire country was a giant sitting duck. Sykes had been candid in telling him there was no chance of mounting an offensive against the Chinese army inside the US border.

As of now, there was no sign of an immediate attack on the East Coast. But that wasn't something the president, or any of them, were willing to take for granted. Walker had ordered every available ship and military personnel in the DC and Virginia area to set up a perimeter and stand watch over the East Coast from New York City to Norfolk. Those troops inland would try to hold off the Chinese until the Navy and the rest of the deployed troops overseas could return.

In all actuality, their hands were tied. The idea of bombing the Chinese on American soil was not an option. There was no way the president was going to authorize the destruction of American cities or the death of its own citizens. And the Chinese knew that. A ground war was their only option. And that was bleak, at best. China had over three million foot soldiers. And word was coming in that at least three hundred thousand had already entered the country, either by land or air. It was also learned that a fleet of submarines had surfaced in the Gulf of Mexico and had laid cover for the arrival of an entire fleet of Chinese ships carrying more soldiers and military equipment. Pensacola, Mobile, and New Orleans had already been all but destroyed as the Chinese troops made ground and advanced north. Dallas, Kansas City, Chicago, and St. Louis had already seen air strikes from the FC-3 Chao Qi fighter jets, preparing the way for ground troops. The only hope for the United States was to establish a front that would keep them west of the Appalachian Mountains until they could figure out how to move forward.

The lead vehicle swerved around the last few cars on the exit ramp and took off toward the secure bunker. The convoy followed and sped ahead. Less than twenty minutes later, they arrived at the foot of the giant hill that housed the bunker. They radioed to the guard shack up ahead, so as to not be shot as they approached at such a high speed. They only slowed down briefly, long enough for the four armed sentries to identify the vehicles' passengers. Once inside, they got right to work. Jennings spoke first.

"Okay, people. Let's hear it."

A first lieutenant approached and handed him a stack of printouts. "This is everything we have so far, sir."

Jennings took the copies and passed them around. The report was everything they already knew. The entire country was being invaded. They all took a seat around the giant conference table and looked to President Walker.

"Sir?" Jennings said, trying to prompt a response.

Walker just stared back, stone-faced.

"Mr. President?" Bob Sykes said, raising his voice, obviously impatient with the president's lack of decisiveness.

"Yes, yes," Walker said, rubbing his temples. "Okay. Obviously, no one saw this coming. So how do we fix it?"

Jennings was instantly mad. *Fix it?* "Mr. President, I don't know if you've noticed, but the Chinese have declared war on us, sir! You don't just *fix* this!"

"I wasn't suggesting we could snap our fingers and make it go away, Director Jennings," President Walker said.

"Sir," Sykes said, "our options are limited. Unless we are willing to literally level half of our country, the only thing we can do is engage them on the ground."

"Then let's get to it!" Walker said.

Sykes looked at Jennings with a contemptuous glance. No one had wanted to say it, but Jennings wasn't about to play politics or exchange platitudes. Not when this was happening. He cleared his throat and started to speak. But Sykes beat him to it.

"Mr. President, for the last twelve years, your predecessors have made it their life's work to defund and dismantle this country's defenses. President Grant has tried time and time again, since being in office, to reverse that. And I'm not sure what party you actually affiliate yourself with, sir, but you have done nothing to help him along the way. You people up on the Hill have acted like we're invincible. You've been naive and ignorant. Everyone here knows that, as a senator, you sponsored or cosponsored at least four bills that reduced the size of our military. And now it's come back to bite you. You're no more fit to run this country than my niece! And if I and everyone else in this room had our way, you'd be charged with treason for what's happening right now!"

"You watch your mouth, Mr. Secretary!" Walker shouted and jabbed a finger at him. "I'm still the president!"

"You're an empty suit with a title!" Sykes yelled back. "You're no president, sir."

Walker's face began to redden, and his hands began to shake. He sat back down in his chair and buried his head in his hands. The room was silent for almost a full minute. Finally Jennings spoke up.

"Look, Gray, we all know you didn't ask for this. For goodness' sake, man! None of us did. But, as you said, you *are* the president now."

Walker lifted his head and looked around. "Everyone, please leave the room. I need to speak with Secretary Sykes and Director Jennings."

Without a word, the room cleared, leaving only the three men. When they had all gone, Walker continued.

"Kevin, Bob, you may not believe it, but I love this country. And yes, I may have been wrong on some policies, but I am willing to admit it. And I'm also willing to admit that I'm in over my head here."

Jennings looked at Sykes.

"However," Walker continued, "I will not stand for the two of you disrespecting this office. I am the commander in chief, and it is my responsibility to see that we do everything we can to stop these Chinese from taking over our country. So here's what's going to happen: I'm putting the two of you in charge. Jennings, you will directly oversee our entire operations. You will work with Bob and the Joint Chiefs. Bob, do you have a problem with that?"

Sykes shook his head. "Not at all, sir. I think that is a great idea. We have the experience and the knowledge to get this done. Jennings is more than competent."

"Then that'll be all. Please, if you would, leave me for a moment."

The two men nodded and turned to leave the room. As they made for the door, Walker called back, "Jennings. A moment please?"

Jennings closed the door behind Sykes and waited.

"You know," Walker said, "I heard once that Grant actually wanted you to be his running mate. I would've thought he'd asked you."

"He did," Jennings said. "I said no."

"Why?"

"Because," Jennings said, "I don't do politics. Politics is what got us into this mess in the first place."

He closed the door behind him as he left.

CHAPTER 63

Keene continued to push the rented Taurus harder and harder, trying to make up time but to no avail. Ever since he'd left Houston, he'd been forced to try back roads, not knowing where he was going, relying on his own sense of direction. He only hoped he was still running parallel to the I-10.

He pulled the little car over to the side of the road to think and try to get his bearings. He'd already passed Baton Rouge and was nearing the Mississippi border. With any luck, he'd be in Biloxi in a couple hours.

He felt the rumble first. Then he heard it. Finally he saw the convoy cresting the small hill in front of him. Americans!

Getting out of his car, he stood in the middle of the road, waving his arms. The lead vehicle stopped inches from him. A head popped out of the driver's side door and shouted, "Clear the way, sir."

Keene reached into his back pocket to pull out his ID and was instantly met by ten M-16 assault rifles. "Easy, soldiers!" he said calmly, slowly holding his hand out. He flipped open the wallet showing his badge. "Jon Keene," he said. "CIA. Where's your superior?"

The young man who'd been driving the lead truck eased out of the vehicle and approached him, taking the wallet and ID. He examined it for a moment then tossed it back to Keene. Turning to his men, he said, "At ease." The men behind him lowered their weapons. The young soldier trudged off to a few vehicles behind and came back with another younger-looking soldier.

"What's a spook doing out in the middle of Louisiana?" the new guy asked him.

"Well, normally," Keene began, "I'd tell you that's classified. But I think we're all a little past that now."

"Yeah," the young man agreed. "I guess so. Name's Kitterick, Paul. First Lieutenant, 81st Training Wing, Biloxi."

He shook the young man's hand and said, "Jon Keene, CIA."

"Jon Keene?" Kitterick said quizzically. "I've heard of a Jon Keene. Heck, we've all heard of a Jon Keene. Real mean dude, former SEAL. Led some kind of Black-Ops team. . . What was it. . .? Oh yeah, START-6. You that Jon Keene?"

Boz had tried to bring it up with him. Even Megan had asked a time or two. But that was a chapter of his life he hadn't wanted to talk about. He had tried to distance himself from his military career. He was a CIA agent now. He had let go of that life long ago.

The Specialized Tactical Assassination and Recovery Team—START-6—was the unit he and five others had been a part of together. He was the commanding officer of the team and answered only to the president. The unit had gained fame throughout the entire military. Until the ambush in Pakistan. All the do-gooders on the Hill had felt it necessary to bring their morality into question through hearings. And Keene had been their main target. He'd led the mission that had gotten four of his own men and six civilians killed. It was a mistake he should've been able to prevent. But he hadn't. He'd missed it. He'd disappeared for almost four months after that. Until Jennings found him. The unit had been disbanded, Jennings had told him. And he wanted Keene to come work for him and the CIA. That was a long time ago, and he'd tried to forget about it ever since.

"Hey," Kitterick said, jarring him back, "you *that* Jon Keene?"

"I used to be," Keene answered. "Where are you guys headed?"

Kitterick smiled a broad grin and turned to his men. "Hey, fellas! We got us a real celebrity here! This here's Jonathan Keene. *The* Jonathan Keene! START-6!"

The men broke into a round of whooping and hollering, with a smattering of applause.

"Keesler was hit about two hours ago. Took out everything. We're about all that's left." He pointed to the fifty or so military vehicles, carrying roughly four hundred men. "We've gotten word, through radio, that just about every base we got between the Rockies and DC was hit. There are some small pockets of guys left in each base. Everyone's trying to mobilize and head to the rally point."

"Where's that?" Jonathan asked.

"101st Airborne, Fort Campbell."

"Why there? Why not Fort Benning?"

"Benning got hit super hard. The Chao Qis. But they're going to be okay. We just can't get there. The whole I-10 is destroyed behind us. North up the I-59 is the only option we've got. Fort Campbell's the next largest base we got west of DC. Pretty much all the major cities west of there have been attacked. We all figure Fort Campbell is high up on the list. You should come back with us, Captain," Kitterick said.

"Can't," Keene said. "My orders are to get back to Washington."

"Well, you can't go that way," Kitterick said. "Like I said, everything behind us is bad. It's a miracle we made it through. No way you're getting through in that!" He pointed to the beat-up Taurus.

Keene looked around, trying to weigh his options.

"Tell you what, Captain," Kitterick continued. "Chain of command in this United States military is jacked up one side and down the other. Most of us don't know who's in charge. Half of the men I've talked to have lost most or all of their superior officers. When the Chao Qis hit, they targeted officer's quarters and command centers. The communication we're getting from Washington is minimal. You're the highest-ranking officer in any division I've heard from. Anyone who's actually got some rank is overseas. And until they get back to bail our butts out, you're our best hope of figuring out what to do here. So how about you ditch the go-cart and jump in? You can take the I-40 once we hit Nashville and head to DC if you still want to."

"You guys go on ahead. I'll find my way. Thanks."

Kitterick looked somberly at him. He grabbed him by the elbow and began to lead him away from the men. "Can I talk to you for a sec, sir?" he said.

Keene followed him out of earshot of the rest of the men.

"All right, Captain. I'm going to shoot you straight, here," Kitterick said, barely above a whisper. "These guys are a bunch of scared kids. They all know who you are. Who am I kidding? Everyone who's ever worn a uniform after you, knows who you are." He jerked his thumb over his shoulder. "You can't get to DC going that way. Your best bet is to jump in with us, head to Tennessee, and once you get there, you've got multiple choices as to how you get back to Washington. But right now, these men need you. They need to know that there's hope on the horizon. You can give them that just by being in the truck with us."

"I already told you," Keene said, "I can't do that. You're their commanding officer, now. Lead them."

Kitterick threw his hands up in the air. "Fine! Go ahead and turn your back on your country!" He turned to walk back to the truck.

Keene was on him in a flash. He spun the young lieutenant around, picked him up by the collar of his uniform, and bounced him off the stop sign that stood there managing the cross street.

"You let me tell you something," Keene said. "I've sacrificed more for this country than you and any fifty of those men over there. You understand that?"

The young Lieutenant swallowed hard. "Sir, there's no doubt in any of our minds that you haven't sacrificed for this country. But look around you."

Keene let go of the young officer.

"These men just watched everything they know get destroyed by twenty Chinese aircraft. They're scared. I'm not going to lie to you. I'm scared. But the reality is exactly what I told you. You're not getting back to DC that way." Again, he pointed at the road behind them. "You're a soldier. And a leader. We're still mostly a training wing of the Air Force. Very few of us have seen any real time, including me. We need leadership, sir. Even if it's from someone who doesn't want to be here."

Keene looked over the shoulder of the young lieutenant. The faces of the men before him told the whole story. They were scared. And lost. Without someone to issue basic orders and give them a game plan, these men were as useless as a bunch of sheep looking for a pasture to graze. "What's your ETA to Fort Campbell?" he asked.

A broad smile crossed the young officer's face. "Twelve hours, sir, if we saddle up and move out now, provided we can find clear roads the whole way. We'll need to stop for basic provisions at the first available place."

"How's ammo?"

"We're a training base, mostly, sir," Kitterick repeated. "So we had a lot of stuff on base. We took everything we could get our hands on. We should be okay, unless we come across something major."

Keene took his phone out and checked it. No service. Kitterick saw the phone and said, "Pretty much all communication has disintegrated over the last two hours. With all the cities being hit by the Chao Qis, the cell towers are gone. Sat-phones and two-ways are about all that work right now."

"You got one?" Keene asked.

Kitterick turned the volume up on his radio pack on his belt and clicked the mic. "Paulson, bring me the sat-phone."

The door to one of the trucks opened, and another young man carrying a rucksack joined them. He pulled the phone out and handed it to Kitterick, who gave it to Keene.

Keene punched in the number and waited.

"It's Keene."

"Where are you? Been trying to reach you for a half hour."

"Cell towers are down. No service. I'm on a sat-phone. I've run into a training division from the 81st in Biloxi. They're headed to Fort Campbell."

"Good," Jennings said. "Benning got hit hard. They had over a hundred thousand there on base. Most of them were families and civilians."

Keene clenched the phone in his hand and felt his jaw tighten. "How many survivors?"

"We're still waiting to get the final word, but it looks like quite a few. When Pensacola got hit, they were able to get an early warning out to Benning. They had enough time to get out. They took a lot of damage, but they were able to fight back. Looks like they took out half a dozen Chao Qis and kept the Chinese from sending in a ground attack."

"Well, at least it was something," Keene said. "So where are you?"

"We're in the bunker. Walker has given me and Bob Sykes control over everything."

"What's the situation?"

"Sykes is trying to get our boys back here as quickly as he can. But it's going to take awhile. We can get bodies back here in fifteen hours, but they have no support. It's going to take at least a week to get everything over there mobilized and moving here. In the meantime, we need to just do our best and try to set up a front line and hold them off."

"So what's the plan?"

"The plan is to mobilize everything we've got and get them to the 101st in Fort Campbell. It's the next biggest, active base we have, and the Chinese are probably going to hit it soon. If we can mobilize everyone there, we're going to try and push back. Once we get word from Fort Benning, we'll reassess. It's our only chance for right now."

"That's suicide. And you know it."

"It's all we've got. The 101st is stacked with weapons. They have twenty-five thousand infantry on base and more on the way. Until our boys get back here with reinforcements, that's the plan.

"Effective immediately, you have been reinstated to active duty and field commissioned to general. Sykes and I are calling the shots from here, but you're in charge out there. You do whatever you need to do. You got it?"

"General! You can't just make me a general! Whose idea was that?"

"The Sec-Nav. That's who." Jennings said. "He's giving you full command."

"And what does he expect me to do?" Keene said. "Just take out a couple hundred thousand Chinese foot soldiers?"

"That would be nice. Listen, just get to the rally point and take command. The plan is to get word out to citizens for them to try and get east of the Appalachian Mountains any way they can. Like you said, the Chinese don't want to destroy this country. They want to take it over. It's not going to do them any good if they blow up the whole place. Right now they're trying to shock and awe everyone into submission. The mountain range will give us a good natural blockade. The only way they'll be able to get east of that will be to fly over or come through the passes. We can defend that. But before we do, we need to get as many Americans as we can on this side of it. By then, our boys will be back and we can take this fight back to them."

Keene knew he was right. It was the only option. And though he wasn't excited about being thrust back into his old life, he would rather be in charge than taking orders from someone else.

"This is nuts."

"I know. But it's all we've got," Jennings said. "Keep this sat-phone with you and stay close. If anything changes, I'll let you know. Let me know when you get to Fort Campbell. Good luck and Godspeed."

Godspeed. . . Yeah right! Keene thought. He looked up to the sky and thought angrily, *You and I are going to have a talk, real soon!*

"Who was that?" Kitterick asked when Keene threw the phone back to him.

"Keep that thing close." He pushed past him and went to the rented Taurus and grabbed his bag. He walked to the front of the convoy and jumped on the hood of the first vehicle. He cupped his hands over his mouth and shouted for everyone to gather round.

He took a second to take in the scene. It had been over eight years since he had addressed a team of soldiers. "My name is Jon Keene, recently promoted to *General* Jon Keene." Again, he thought about how ridiculous that sounded. "Some of you know who I am. That means absolutely squat! This isn't some nostalgic who's who in the military hall of fame. As of now, I am your commanding officer. Anyone who doesn't follow my orders to the T, I will personally shoot! Any questions?"

A thundering "No, sir!" resounded.

"Good! Then let's move out! Absolutely no radio chatter, unless initiated by me. Got it?"

Again, there was a resounding chorus. "Yes, sir!"

"Good," Keene said. Then, "Move out!"

He grabbed Lieutenant Kitterick by the shirt collar again. "Just so we're clear," he said, "we don't stop for anything, or anyone, unless I say so. Got it?"

Kitterick nodded. "Yes, sir." He smiled and said, "Thank you, General. Congratulations on the promotion."

"You can congratulate me if we make it to Fort Campbell alive," Keene said.

CHAPTER 64

Taylor wasn't much of a phone guru, but basically it all boiled down to microchips and Scriber Identity Modules—SIM cards. In other words, computer parts. And she knew computers better than anyone she'd ever encountered. And right now she was rebuilding her phone, so to speak, to make it satellite capable.

With the Chinese blitzkrieg, all standard forms of communication in the United States were down. No Internet, no cell phones. Televisions were still working in some areas but only those that were satellite fed. And only those in homes that still had power. According to the *World News Report*, a European news program she had caught before taking off again, the Chinese had specifically targeted cell towers and power plants in their shock-and-awe campaign of air-to-surface missiles in all of the major cities west of the Appalachian Mountains. The response from around the world was mixed, she learned. Many countries were sympathetic, but—like the reaction to the onslaught of the Nazis in the early stages of WWII—most countries simply didn't want to get involved. Others, who were outspoken with their disdain for America, celebrated that someone was finally taking the country down. Either way, the United States of America was on the precipice of being completely overthrown. It had all happened in a single day. And here she was on a plane headed for Dubai, trying to jury-rig her phone so she could make contact with Jennings.

She dug through her bag and found the small clip she needed. She pulled the back of the phone off and got into the motherboard circuitry. She placed the clip where she needed it and powered on her computer. Within seconds she was connected to the satellite feed through her laptop. She looked at her phone, which now showed a full signal. She dialed the number.

"This is Jennings."

"Director Jennings, it's Taylor, sir."

234

"Kind of busy. You and Boz find Marianne yet?"

"That's what I'm calling about. But I wanted to see what's going on back home, sir."

She could hear Jennings exhale a long, slow breath. "It's not good. We've lost all major communications. We have no idea what the death toll is. There has been no attempt at communication from the Chinese. All we know right now is that they are methodically hitting the major cities and then dropping ground troops in behind the air raids. We estimate that there are already two hundred thousand of their infantry in country and probably more on the way."

"What about Jon? Have you heard from him?"

"Jon is fine. He's met up with an Air Force training wing from Biloxi. He's going with them to Fort Campbell. That's where our troops are rallying. From there we're going to try and mount a defense."

"Wow," she said.

"Yeah, wow," Jennings echoed. Then, "Marianne Levy. Any word?"

"We think we've tracked her to Dubai. No extradition treaty, not that it matters that much right now. But it's probably why she chose it. She can disappear, and even if we did find her, we can't bring her back."

"Oh, I'll bring her back," Jennings said. "You let me worry about that. I want that woman here! You and Boz find her."

"Yeah, that's what I was saying before. . . ."

"What is it?" Jennings said, obviously impatient.

"It's just me going to Dubai."

"What do you mean, it's just you?"

"I'm flying solo here. Boz is headed to London."

"What in the world for?" Jennings said, his voice rising.

"He said he has some friends there he thinks can help. He said he had to go, and he would be in touch with you as soon as he could."

"You have a way to contact him?"

"No, sir. He's got a standard phone based out of the United States. Same as every other American. Unless he gets access to a sat-phone, we've got no way of contacting him."

"Well," Jennings said, "the good news is, from what I know about Boz, he is a very resourceful person. Who knows? Maybe he can muster up a miracle for us. I mean, he is a preacher, right?"

"Yes, sir."

"You just do whatever you have to do to find Marianne Levy. You understand?"

"I'm on it, sir."

"Oh, and Taylor?"

"Yes, sir?"

"Bill Preston says you're not just a computer geek. He says you're probably one of the best agents he has in the bureau."

"Thank you, sir."

"I don't have to tell you that an FBI agent entering the United Arab Emirates while the United States is under attack is probably not going to go well at customs."

"Already taken care of, sir." She hesitated for a moment. "I've already hacked into the Customs and Security Exchange there in Dubai. I also brought along a couple different passports." She let that hang there for a second. Then, "I won't bother you with how I came into possession of those."

"I don't frankly care. I've got six myself. I'd probably think less of you if you *didn't* have a couple of your own."

"Right. Anyway, I shouldn't have any problems entering the country. And as soon as my feet hit the ground—"

"And when you do find her," Jennings interrupted, "I expect you to secure her. And if you have to, you dig a deep, dark hole and throw her into it until I can get the two of you out of there. You understand me? I do not want her getting away."

"Understood."

She pulled the phone away as she heard the click, ending the call. She set it on the small table beside her and disconnected the little clip. Then she tilted the screen up to face her and began tapping away at the keys.

"Okay, Marianne," she said. "Where are you?"

CHAPTER 65

Do you have *any* idea the amount of strings I had to yank to pull this off?" the man said to Boz as he came aboard the small jet.

"Nice to see you, too, Mac," Boz smacked his friend on the back as they hugged. "I really appreciate this."

"No problem, mate," the old Brit said. "I owe you."

"If you saved my butt twenty times between now and tomorrow, you'd still be saying that!" Boz laughed. "Let it go, already!"

"Yeah, you're probably right." Mac shook his head.

It had been almost twenty years since they'd met. Mac was a former Royal Air Force pilot turned world-class spy for Her Majesty the Queen. MI-5, to be precise. At age forty-five and nearing retirement, his cover had been blown—and some very unpleasant people arranged for Mac's family, a wife and a seventeen-year-old son, to be kidnapped and held for ransom. All of which was in retaliation for Mac's involvement in bringing down a wealthy oil sheik with a propensity to deal in illegal arms and heroin. Because of the sensitivity of the mission, the location in Pakistan where the family was being held, and the low probability of success, Don Snyder, then CIA director and a great friend of the family, called in a twenty-seven-year-old Army Ranger whose team was already in the country. With very little time for planning and no true exit strategy, Boz and his men snuck into the village under the cover of night and took out the entire compound where the family was being held. They managed to retrieve the family and not set off a single alarm anywhere within the city. Sixteen hours after the fist ransom demand had been made, Mac was reunited with his family. And to this day, he'd never forgotten it.

"Tell you what," Boz said as the plane took off. "You get me to London in half the time it's supposed to take, I'll consider us even. For real."

The smile faded from Mac's face. "That's a real spot your boys are in over there. Isn't it? I'm sorry to see it."

"Yeah, it is."

"And those fools back home aren't willing to lift a finger to help you. That right?"

"That about sums it up," Boz said. "I was hoping I could change some minds."

"You know you can't change stupid!"

Boz laughed at his friend's candor. "I know. But I've got to try."

"Let me ask you something," Mac said. "Are you going on behalf of your country as a diplomat? Or are you trying to actually get something accomplished?"

Boz smiled. He knew what his old friend was asking. Was he actually going to try to change the minds of the English prime minister and his parliament? Or was he going to do something that could get himself, and whoever followed him, thrown into prison?

"I'm trying to get something accomplished," he said seriously.

"Have you spoken to him yet?" Mac asked.

"Not yet. I thought it'd be better just to show up and ask."

"You're crazy, mate! You know that? Crazy!"

Mac reached behind Boz's seat and pulled out a small satchel. He unzipped it and pulled out a sat-phone and handed it to Boz. "Call him," he said. "He'll want to know you're coming."

Boz handed the phone back to him. "I don't want to give him time to think about it. I'd rather just show up and ask."

This time it was Mac who laughed. "If I know my son, I've got fifty quid says he's already planning on doing it anyway!"

CHAPTER 66

The trip north had been mostly uneventful. Keene and the convoy stayed on the interstate as much as they could, only taking side roads when they came through Hattiesburg, Meridian, and Tuscaloosa. Keene had sent a scout one mile ahead for the duration of the trip. Now as they approached Birmingham, they could already see the plumes of black smoke rising from the hilltops. Keene had put the brakes on everyone and set them in formation. He jumped out of the truck and called for a navigation specialist. A few minutes later, they had assessed the map and decided on how to proceed. About a mile and a half north, there was a secondary road that would take them out and around the city.

Jennings had informed them that most of the Chinese infantry hadn't made it this far inland yet. Most of the concentration was in the northern and western cities, even though the Chao Qi fighters had already done their damage throughout the country.

Still, Keene didn't want to take the chance. Even a small unit of five hundred infantry could pose a threat. It would cost them close to an hour of drive time, but they wouldn't have to engage the enemy if there were Chinese there. Slowly, they approached the city and got off at the exit. Twenty miles north of the city, they connected back to the I-65 and proceeded on toward Nashville.

The last three hours of the trip were long and slow. Nashville was the biggest city they were to encounter. As they got near, they slowed even more to allow the scout vehicle to advance farther ahead. Keene had no intention of driving into an already established enemy hold. Even though the 101st was in Nashville's backyard, the city was a major thoroughfare for interstate traveling, having three major interstates running through its core. He doubted the Chinese would be brave enough to try and set up a foothold there with Fort Campbell so close by, but he still wanted to be cautious.

Before they had even gotten to the I-840 bypass that would take them out and around the entire city and connect them over to I-24, the scout had returned with bad news. The city had already been devastated, and the road was out about a quarter mile south of the I-840 exchange. Once again, Keene decided to stop everyone.

"Hold 'em up," he said, keying the mic on the walkie-talkie. "Someone bring me a radio."

Immediately, the long train of military vehicles came to a stop in the middle of the interstate. Keene stepped out and took the tactical radio.

"Hundred and first, this is General Jon Keene accompanied by the 81st training wing from Biloxi. You read me? Over."

A few seconds passed with no response. He repeated the process again and waited. The phone burped and cracked and then a static-laced voice cracked from the other end.

"This is the one-oh-one. Over."

Keene pressed the receiver button again. "We are sixty miles southeast of your position. You got eyes on the city?"

The line clicked a couple times, and then the voice came back. "Roger that, 81st. Got you on radar. The city has been hit pretty bad. Everything north of your position is impassable."

"How'd you get left alone?" Keene asked.

"We didn't. We've just got some pretty nice toys here, sir. By the time Pensacola and Fort Benning got hit, we'd had enough warning that we were able to defend ourselves. They hit the city first. Came in from the south. We took down three of the Chao Qis that advanced on the base, but the damage was already pretty much done to the city. They tried to air-drop some infantry and vehicles in at the airport, but we shot that down, too."

"Hoo-rah!" Keene said.

"Yes, sir!" came the reply.

"So how am I going to get me and all these boys up there?"

"Thompson Station Road, sir. It's about half a click from where you are. It'll bring you back around to the I-840 bypass. You're clear all the way in from there."

"Roger that. We'll be there shortly."

"Sir?" The voice crackled.

"Yeah?"

"We're under direct order from the Sec-Nav to bring you in once we heard from you. We have two Blackhawks scrambling right now. They'll be at your position in fifteen minutes."

"Unless those birds can carry all of us—the last time I checked, they couldn't—I'll see you in an hour. Out."

Keene turned off the radio and circled a finger in a big winding motion above his head. "Let's move out, people!"

He jumped back in the truck.

CHAPTER 67

Taylor sat in her rented Mercedes in front of the International Bank of Commerce on Al Rigga Street in Dubai's financial district. It was odd, she thought, that in the United States, Mercedes was a symbol of status and wealth, while in other nations it was nothing more than the typical rental. They were as common as a Toyota back home.

It was shortly after opening hours, and the traffic going in and out was steady. She had spent the entire rest of the flight hacking her way through a money trail that was sophisticated, well thought out, and extremely well hidden. Just not well enough. If she was right, and she believed she was, this was where Marianne would turn up.

Three hundred and fifty million dollars. That was the amount she was able to trace. Of course, with banking fees—wire transfers and commission on monetary exchange—the final sum was somewhere around three hundred and twenty-six million. Still, a generous amount by any standard. But nowhere near worth the damage the woman had caused.

She kept thinking about how this fit in with what the Prophet had said. While she wanted, just as much as anyone back home, to find this woman and make her pay for what she'd done, she couldn't help but wonder if somehow it could've all been stopped. The Prophet had warned them to have President Grant go and tell the American people to repent and turn back to God. And President Grant was going to do that. So why, then, was all this still happening? She stopped for a moment and silently thanked God that she didn't have any family back home. She was an only child, and her parents had passed away a couple years ago. But her heart was still broken for her fellow citizens. And because she had been running nonstop for the last two days, she realized she hadn't even allowed the weight of what had happened back home sink in. She glanced up from her laptop and took in the area again. Still no sign of Marianne.

The last thing she wanted was to take her focus off the bank. But she became overwhelmed with emotion as she sat there, considering the enormity of what had happened. She needed some strength. She needed some reassurance. She reached into her bag and pulled out her Bible. She thumbed through a few passages she had marked. They always seemed to lift her up and restore her hope.

She thumbed through the passages for about fifteen minutes, taking a moment every few seconds to glance back at the front of the building. She was about to put the Bible away but stopped. She had only been familiar with a couple verses of the chapter, but she felt like God's Spirit was pressing her to go there and listen to what was written. She flipped through the pages and looked for the passage. Isaiah 55. She had only started reading, but by the time she had gotten to verse four, her heart began to fill with joy.

Behold, I made him a witness to the peoples, a leader and commander for the peoples. Behold, you shall call a nation that you do not know, and a nation that did not know you shall run to you, because of the LORD your God, and of the Holy One of Israel, for he has glorified you.

Seek the LORD while he may be found; call upon him while he is near; let the wicked forsake his way, and the unrighteous man his thoughts; let him return to the LORD, that he may have compassion on him, and to our God, for he will abundantly pardon. For my thoughts are not your thoughts, neither are your ways my ways, declares the LORD. For as the heavens are higher than the earth, so are my ways higher than your ways and my thoughts than your thoughts.

For as the rain and the snow come down from heaven and do not return there but water the earth, making it bring forth and sprout, giving seed to the sower and bread to the eater, so shall my word be that goes out from my mouth; it shall not return to me empty, but it shall accomplish that which I purpose, and shall succeed in the thing for which I sent it. For you shall go out in joy and be led forth in peace.

She wiped her eyes and thought about what she had just read. She closed her eyes and prayed, *Father, I believe with all my heart that You have brought all of this to pass for a purpose. And Your word says that our ways are not Your ways, and our thoughts are not Your thoughts. But, Lord, I believe You have shown me this scripture today for a purpose. I know that Isaiah was speaking to Your people. But aren't we Your people, too? Please, Lord. Let this scripture be a promise for us today, also. Please, Father, spare our nation and lead us back to You. I ask You in Jesus' name. Amen.*

As she lifted her head and opened her eyes, she got an overwhelming sense of peace and affirmation. She wasn't sure yet what was going to happen, but she definitely knew that God had reassured her that He was in control. And while everything was in chaos right now, eventually He would still the chaos and bring restoration.

She closed the Bible and placed it back in her bag. She decided that sitting inside this cramped car wasn't going to get her anywhere. Besides, she needed to use the restroom. She decided to go see what the inside of the International Bank of Commerce looked like.

She entered the double doors and found a spacious lobby. Along one wall was a station of kiosks with computer monitors and automated banking. The other held typical teller stations for everyday banking. At the far end of that wall stood a set of elevators, manned by an armed guard. In the center of the room was an information desk with two men, dressed in finely tailored suits, sitting, monitoring the goings-on of the large room. At the back end of the room were signs for public restrooms, and in front of that was another, larger kiosk that housed a snack vendor. She could already smell the aroma of the fresh hot coffee.

She tried to think of something clever to ask the men at the desk but decided against it. She didn't want to attract any more attention than she already was. She smiled curtly at the men and moved toward the restrooms. When she was finished, she stepped up to the counter and ordered the largest cup they had. The man handed her a coffee and her change and nodded. As she turned around to leave, she pulled up short. Across the room, the doors to the front entrance were opening. And another American was entering.

She'd changed her hair. And the clothes were casual not business professional. She wore oversized sunglasses to hide her eyes, and her collar was pulled up to shield her face. Taylor immediately sat down beside the snack kiosk in one of the several chairs that were there for customers. There was a newspaper sitting on the table, so she opened it and hid herself as the woman walked past her, only several feet away, and stepped up to the elevator guard.

Taylor shifted in her seat slightly to get a better look at the elevators. The woman had some kind of ID badge and was now placing her hand on some device the guard had produced. Megan had seen them before. Portable ID scanners. They could be programmed to receive hand- and fingerprints, retina scans, or even voice analysis. This one seemed to be simple enough. The woman only had her hand on the thing for a moment before the guard stepped aside and gave her a key card. This was for the elevator itself, Taylor presumed. She watched as the woman disappeared into the elevator and the doors closed. She waited a few seconds and then stood up, took one giant last gulp of the coffee, and threw it away. She nodded to the guy at the information desk as she left.

When she got to the car, she pulled her laptop and phone out. Looking up at the entrance door every second or two—determined not to miss her coming out—she went to work attaching the small clip to her phone. She logged in to the satellite and placed the call.

"This is Jennings."

"Can you talk?"

"Hang on."

She heard the voices in the background get quieter. And then she heard a door close.

"Okay. What do you need?"

"I've found her."

"Do you have her in custody?"

"Not yet. I tracked her to a bank here in Dubai. I'm waiting for her to come out. I'll follow her and see where she goes."

"I don't care where she goes. I care where she ends up."

"I got that. I just wanted to know if you could tell me if the CIA has any assets here in Dubai. Or if there's a house, somewhere I can take her. I don't think you want me dragging her into my hotel."

The line was quiet for a second, and then Jennings said, "Give me ten minutes, and I'll call you back."

"I may not have ten minutes. She just went in. I almost walked right into her. If she comes out, I'm going to have to move quick."

"Okay, then just call me back when you can. I'll have what you need then."

"Will do." Then, "Any word?"

She heard Jennings take a long breath and blow it out again. She could imagine him standing there pinching the bridge of his nose.

"It's not good. The Chinese fighter jets have hit every highly populated city and military base in the country west of the Appalachian Mountains. The only reason, we believe, they haven't advanced on the East Coast is they're waiting until they can get infantry in place. That, and it's really the only defense systems we have left in country. We have a handful of ships between Andrews and Norfolk. We have roughly sixty F-35 and F-22 jets combined. The problem is, we don't have enough pilots here to fly them.

But the Chinese don't know that. So they're staying in the Midwest, for now. But it's only a matter of time before they hit us. We're sure."

"What about Jon? Any word from him?" As she asked, she felt a small lump in her throat.

"He's okay. He checked in a couple hours ago. He's at the 101st Airborne Division, north of Nashville. They've got a fair amount of troops there and a ton of artillery. Now it's just a matter of getting them mobilized."

She was relieved to hear Jon was all right. For now. "So what's the plan?"

"It's thin, but Jon is waiting for the rest of the scattered divisions to show up. From there, we're going to try and mount an offensive. The plan is for us to communicate to as many citizens as we can to find their way east of the Appalachians. If Jon and those guys can hold the Chinese off enough to get that done, we can defend the East Coast. By that time, we should be seeing our Navy and a ton of our boys coming back in."

"How long?" Megan asked.

"Minimum a week. More like ten days."

Holding the Chinese off for ten days was highly improbable. According to Jennings, they had already dropped infantry throughout Chicago, Detroit, Indianapolis, Columbus, and Cincinnati in the north. The Midwestern cities were the same. And with the Chinese moving in artillery on the heels of the air attacks, the American people were cowering, waiting to see what would happen. As soon as the Chinese realized they weren't going to get any resistance, they would press on, bringing in even more ground troops and more artillery. They had a couple days at best.

"Sir, you and I know that we don't have ten days."

"I told you, it's pretty thin."

"What about all the people in the central part of the country?"

"We're going to set up blockades with air support at all the Appalachian mountain passes. Even if it takes people two weeks to get to one of them, we'll get them through. But there are those who will stay. They won't resist. And the Chinese don't want to come in here and destroy the country. They just want the land and the resources. Once they have people under submission, they'll just continue moving forward."

"What about Boz? Any word from him?"

"I haven't heard from him. But no one is going to help. They can't. The Chinese would crush anyone who tried to help us. They've already bullied the Mexicans. We know now that they've been using Canada for the last ten years to bring in their military. They probably threatened Canada with the same attack if they resisted. It's brilliant, actually. No one's on our side on this one."

"Not even the UK?"

"Especially not the UK. The English prime minister is the softest politician they've had in twenty years. And with the damage the last administration did to our relationship with them, they're acting like they don't even know us. We have to hold out till our troops get home. And even then, we're going to need an act of God."

Taylor felt her breath hitch. She thought back to what the passage had said in Isaiah: ". . .*and a nation that did not know you shall run to you, because of the Lord your God.*"

"Don't worry, sir. I think we're going to get one," she said.

Just then the doors to the bank opened. Marianne Levy walked out, checked her surroundings, pushed the sunglasses up on her nose, and took off walking down the street.

"I have to go," she said quickly. "She's on the move."

CHAPTER 68

It was just before lunch when Boz and Mac entered the pub at Pickford's Wharf on Clink Street. It was a decent place—good food, good ale, according to Mac. Neither of that mattered to Boz right now. He wasn't much hungry, and he didn't want to be all that noticed anyway. Mac's son Eli was already enough of a celebrity, depending on who was around at the time. Mac had said that this was a good place to meet. Not a lot of nosy people and not a typically frequented place for guys like Eli.

As they waited, Boz watched the small television hanging above the bar. It was a BBC news program, and the discussion was the same one on every news station around the world: the Chinese invasion of the United States. The topic was how it could have happened and whether or not anyone was going to come to the aid of the suffering country. And it was getting heated. There was a disagreement as to whether or not Prime Minister Bungard and the Royal Navy should run to the aid of their former longtime ally.

Boz turned away from the screen to see that his friend had arrived. He stood and took the younger man in a bear hug.

"Eli Craig! How are you?" he said as they broke their embrace. Boz stretched his arm out and offered a seat.

"We're not here to talk about me," Eli said, sitting. "What's the word? They aren't telling us anything."

"The word is, we're in a bad way," Boz said somberly. "It's a long story, so I'll have to start at the beginning."

"Go on, then." Eli sat back in his chair and grabbed a handful of peanuts.

Boz recounted everything that had happened, from the first phone call he had received from Calvin three months ago to the meeting in the Oval Office with Keene and Taylor. He told him everything he knew about the Prophet and how he thought all of it was directly connected. He continued on with the Marianne Levy situation, the assassination attempt of President Grant, the attack, and finished with the bear hug they'd shared just a moment ago.

"So let me get this straight," Eli said. "You get a real-live prophet telling you to tell the nation to repent and no one does anything about it?"

"We tried. President Grant was going to tell the nation when he was shot."

Eli looked across at him. "Hmmm."

"Hmmm. . .what?"

"I think he waited too long, mate. You and I both know that when God says do something, you don't piddle around. Now do you?"

"Calvin's a good man, Eli. He was just trying to make sure this wasn't some crackpot."

"Right, but he knew better, he did."

Boz sighed. "Yeah, we both did. But that's neither here nor there. Ultimately, this was God's plan. No way this wasn't happening if He didn't want it to."

"Right. There's that." Eli nodded. "What are we to do about all of this now?"

"One of the last things we heard from this Prophet guy was this: when the time was right, he would find us. So I have to believe that God is not completely going to give the United States over without giving us a chance to right the ship, so to speak."

"And that means you want to fight back."

Boz nodded.

"Ah. . .there's my old boy!" Eli said, smacking the table. Then, "Nuclear propulsion has come a right long ways in the last ten years. But your boys are still going to need at least a week to ten days to get back. That's if they're already en route."

Again Boz nodded.

"And my boys could be there in two. But we aren't allowed to come help our little offspring nation, now are we?"

Boz shook his head.

"What are we to do about that, you suppose?"

Boz shrugged.

"Right. Well, it's a good thing one of us has been thinking, mate! If you don't know what to do, I guess I'll have to tell you now. Won't I?"

"You know I can't ask you officially, Eli. I'm not here as an emissary."

"Boz, you're not just my brother in Christ. Far as I'm concerned, you're my family. And one thing we take seriously around here is family."

"What about your men? What about your prime minister?"

Eli made a sour face and waved his hand. "*Pffft!* First of all, that tired ol' windbag is about as useless as a screen door on a boat. Second, I've got twenty ships, with twenty-five hundred sailors and soldiers on board each one, standing by waiting for me to tell them to set sail. Also on those twenty ships, I have seventeen Tornado GR4s and twenty-five JSFs," he said, referring to the Royal Air Force and Naval fighter jets. "And I've got pilots for them as well."

Mac nudged Boz and held his hand out. "Fifty quid. I told you. I know my boy!"

Boz waved the man off with a smile. Then to Eli, "You know you could be exiled, or worse. You'll lose everything."

Eli leaned forward and placed his elbows on the table. "Three things," he said. "One, I wouldn't be alive if it weren't for you. And I mean that in both senses of the word. Two, I've worked hard to earn my position in MI-5. Before that, I worked hard to earn the respect of my men in the Royal Navy. They trust me. And besides that, they *want* to go. I've talked to every ranking officer of every ship standing by. They and their men are ready and willing to go when I say."

"What about your director general?" Boz asked, referring to the head of MI-5.

"Ah," Eli said, waving a hand, "he hates Bungard. He said if he were thirty years younger, he'd do it himself."

"And three?" Boz asked.

"Oh, right," Eli said, remembering his list. "And three, I've been praying about it since I heard about the initial attack on the left coast."

"And?"

"And I think you're right. I don't think God's done with the United States yet."

Boz nodded, and they all stood up. "What's the plan?"

"The plan is we go get in my car and take it to my ship." Eli grabbed his keys off the table and stood up. "And then we go kick the Chinese back to the Great Wall. And then, I say we knock that thing down, too. Just to prove a point!"

CHAPTER 69

It was late in the evening when Keene had his first opportunity to sit down at the table with all the senior ranking officers who were on base. He had spent the majority of his time with Major General McIntyre, the commander of the 101st, finding his way around and getting something to eat. Since his arrival with the 81st, several more units and divisions had reported. Some were still scattered to the west and making their way in, while a few more were to the north and east waiting for orders. All in all, they estimated around eighty thousand troops in country. A good portion of those were already on the East Coast, particularly at Fort Benning. The latest report showed there had been few deaths at Benning, though there were many injured.

Keene looked around the room. Some faces he knew. But most of them he'd never met. That was logical, seeing as how there were officers from every branch sitting around the table. And the fact that he'd been out for so long. He finally gave a loud whistle to get everyone's attention.

"Ladies and gentlemen. We've got work to do."

The ten or so commanding officers quieted down and came to attention.

"For those of you who don't know me, my name is General Jon Keene. As you know, President Walker has given complete operational command to Director Jennings of the CIA and Secretary of the Navy, Bob Sykes. I have been put in charge of this operation. Which means that I'm running this soup sandwich."

That earned him a few grins.

"So here's the deal: Right now, the Chinese are dropping in troops in every major city that the Chao Qis have already hit. Our job is to get everything we've got and can move, and head east. Once we get to Knoxville, we'll split. Most of us will head north to Albany. Some of us, however, are going to meet up with infantry from Fort Benning.

"Jennings is working on a way to communicate to the citizens to head east. The idea is to get as many people east of the Appalachian Mountains as we can. We can defend the mountain passes. They're a big funnel. The only way to get foot soldiers across them is to airlift them in or come through those roads. Once we have those passes secure, we'll have regular patrols covering the secondary roads that would also give them access. The units we're going to meet up with from Benning, this will be their primary objective, as well as holding the southern front and allowing the Chinese to move northward. By that time, our boys will be back from the Middle East.

"I spoke to Jennings just a few moments ago. He told me that the forward base in Afghanistan is all but packed up and loaded. They will be landing at Andrews over an eight-hour period, starting twenty-one thirty hours in two days. They will have some air support but not enough if the Chao Qis decide to engage. Other companies are double-timing it to do the same in Pakistan and Iraq. They're going to be coming in light. Pretty much just bodies until the Navy gets our gear back. Any questions so far?"

A hand shot up. Keene pointed to him. "Major General McIntyre?"

"Thank you, sir," the officer said. "We have a lot of gear here at Fort Campbell. And we have the means to fly a lot of it. If we could get some air support for transport. . ."

Keene nodded. "Unfortunately, we're not going to get much. Jennings is afraid to send us anyone right now. If DC is attacked, they're going to need everything they have. And they're expecting it. The Chinese know they have to take DC in order to take the country. They can level New York, Chicago, and every major city in this country. But Washington is our heart. We lose that, we just lose."

"So then we're grounded," McIntyre said.

"Not entirely. I'm sure you've met Majors Hurt and Caldwell," he said pointing to the two Air Force pilots. "Majors?"

Major Hurt cleared his throat and leaned forward. "Thomas and I were two of the first to go out and meet the Chao Qis before getting called back. We took some minor damage to our aircraft, so we were rerouted here. I spoke with Corporal Murray and his mechanics. We're flight ready as we speak."

"So," Keene continued, "Jennings says he expects the Chinese to come through Montreal once they secure the Midwest. When they come, they're going to come hard. They'll most certainly hit with an air attack first. That means the Chao Qis will come from all directions. Unless we can stop them. And that's the point of us securing the passes. If we have anti-aircraft artillery set up, we can help out until our troops can engage them. If we can make it to Albany before they cross over the northern border, we can do some serious damage. Maybe even push them back a little.

"We need to get every truck, cargo plane, tank, and whatever else we can find packed up and ready to move in five hours. Once we get east of the mountains, we should be clear of any enemy encounter. From there, we need to hump it to Albany. We'll send as many cargo planes as we can with artillery and men. Majors Hurt and Caldwell will give air support. And everyone flies under the radar. I don't want a single bird in the air above seven hundred feet. Commander, I want those Chinooks, Apaches, and Blackhawks loaded down with as many airborne as they'll carry. The rest will have to go by road.

"The men from the forward Afghan base will make land in forty hours. It's a little over fourteen hours to Albany. That gives us a little over twenty-six hours to get there and set up base."

"Sir, if we know the Chinese are coming through Montreal, why doesn't Sykes just order a hit on the city?" one of the officers asked. "We could cripple their offensive."

Keene nodded. "You're right, we could. But you're talking about leveling one of the largest cities in Canada. Jennings and Sykes aren't willing to do that. Too many civilians."

The group of officers became angry and started talking all at once. And Keene agreed with them. The United States had already received its own fair share of damage. And Canadians were just sitting idly by. Although they were weak militarily and couldn't afford the Chinese turning on them, their lack of action spoke volumes. Nevertheless, the apathy of the Canadian government didn't justify the slaughter of Canadian citizens. So Jennings and Sykes forbade any attack on Canadian soil.

"Listen," Keene said, calling everyone back to attention. "Albany is already being evacuated. Civilian casualties will be far less than if we hit Montreal. That's the plan."

"How do we know for sure they won't move in sooner?" another officer asked.

"We don't," Keene admitted. "But the Chinese are meticulous in their planning. And they aren't stupid. They know if they move in from the north right now, they'll be spread too thin. They will have to wait until they can bring up more infantry and artillery from the south. They will come in from all three sides. That's why it's important for us to get those mountain passes covered and get Fort Benning up and completely operational again. If we can shut down their attack from coming over the mountains, and if we can keep them from advancing north from Atlanta, we have a good shot at holding them off once they come from Montreal."

Keene looked around at the officers sitting around the table. He knew that they knew what he was asking them to do was a long shot at best. But it was all they had. Right now, securing the eastern part of the country was their only option. With the West Coast gone, people living east of the Appalachian Mountains made up nearly eighty percent of the remaining population. They had a little over five hours before the first transport was to leave. They had work to do.

"That'll be all," he said, dismissing them. "I'll be in my quarters if anyone needs me."

Keene left the building and walked back across the street to the officer's quarters building. He was exhausted from the nonstop driving from the Mexican border. He decided he needed a long, hot shower and at least an hour of sleep. It might be the last time he had either again for quite a while.

He stripped down and turned the water on as hot as he could stand it. Twenty minutes later he came out feeling slightly better. His shoulder was healing fine but still hurt like crazy. He thought about the Russian. He had crossed paths with her at least four times now. This was the first time, though, they had ever come face-to-face. He vowed as he changed the bandage that if he made it out of this alive, he was going to hunt her down.

He finished dressing the wound and came out of the bathroom and sat down on the bed. He took his watch off, set his alarm for ninety minutes, and set it on the small bedside table. He stared at the book sitting beside the lamp. He argued with himself for a couple minutes before he finally picked it up but then set it back down. He looked up and said, "I think it's about time You and I had a talk." He gave a chastising laugh at himself. *I can't believe I'm doing this*, he thought. He looked up again. "I've hated You for a long time. You know that? And I've been perfectly fine with that. But then You bring all of. . .of this!" He was starting to feel the anger well up inside him. "Wasn't it enough that You took her? And now You throw me into this! Some crazy idiot who says You talk to him and says You're going to destroy this country because people have turned away from You?"

He stood up and started pacing back and forth. "And then President Grant, a man who is faithful to You—" He jabbed a finger into the air. "I mean, he was going to stand up in front of the country and tell everyone what *You* supposedly want. And You let him get shot in the head! Is this what You want?"

A soft knock came at his door. He opened it to find an MP standing there.

"Everything okay in here, sir?"

"I'm fine." He closed the door again and walked back over to the bed and sat down. His head was pounding, and that shower had drained him of every last bit of adrenaline that had been keeping him up.

"Listen," he said, looking up again. "I don't know what You want from me. Boz says You have a purpose for all of this. I sure wish I knew what it was. 'Cause right now, this is about the most screwed-up thing I've ever heard of. I mean, look at this! One moment I'm trying to find this guy to find out what You've told him. The next thing I know, I'm in command of our entire military forces—which by the way, really? Suddenly I'm the most qualified guy to do this?—trying to save a country that, quite honestly, I don't think stands a chance. So if You've got something to say to me, then why don't You speak to me? Huh? Why don't You just tell me what You want!"

The room fell silent. He looked down at his watch and saw that twenty of his ninety minutes had already passed. The Bible was still sitting there. He blew out a long sigh and picked it up. "Boz said You speak to us through this. Since You won't talk, maybe You'll say something to me in here, huh?" He started thumbing through the pages. That pastor from Texas said to start in the Gospel of John. He didn't even know where that was, so he just continued to turn pages until he saw a heading that caught his eye. "A Letter to the Exiles", in the book of Jeremiah. He recalled that Jeremiah was one of those people the Prophet quoted in his video to President Grant. He lay back on the bed and began to read. And he didn't know why, but he felt his breath catch and his pulse quicken as he got to verse eleven: *"For I know the plans I have for you, declares the LORD, plans for welfare and not for evil, to give you a future and a hope."*

He stopped and reread it. And then he reread it again. And he didn't know if it was because he was so tired or because he just wanted to believe it, but a sense of calm and peace began to come over him. He had barely finished verse fifteen when his eyes fell shut and he drifted off to sleep.

CHAPTER 70

Taylor threw the phone on the seat beside her and put the Mercedes in gear when Marianne got into the cab. She pulled out of the parking spot and followed a couple car lengths behind as the cab turned onto Al Jazira Street and then onto Salahuddin Road. From there the car turned onto the main road, E11, and headed south.

Going this direction, Taylor had a pretty good idea where they were headed. Many of the luxury hotels and long-term rental apartments were located in a section of the city known as Palm Jumeirah, a set of man-made islands that, from the air, looked like a giant palm tree. The daring project had made international news while under construction and added more than three hundred miles to the Dubai shoreline. The fact that they were headed in that direction now didn't surprise her, but it did give her a little pause. This was one of the most highly trafficked areas of the city. How she was going to get to Marianne and not make a big scene was going to be tough. Once she saw where the woman was staying she could maybe make her move at night, but that would have to be determined by where Marianne was staying and what the nightlife was in the area.

A little less than fifteen minutes later, the cab exited the highway. Megan continued to follow at a safe distance. Finally she pulled over and watched the cab enter the Ottoman Palace Resort. She watched as Marianne got out and went through the entrance. Quickly Megan pulled up and jumped out. She threw her keys to a valet and told him she'd be right back. She had no idea if the young man even spoke English and could understand her. But she wasn't waiting around to find out.

It took her a few seconds to spot Marianne once she got inside. She was walking through a garden area into a courtyard that led to the luxury apartment villas. Taylor stayed with Marianne as she made her way through the walkways and palm trees, hanging back far enough to remain unnoticed. Finally Marianne slowed down and reached inside her pocket.

Now she knew where Marianne was. Getting to her wasn't the problem. She could go right now and knock on the door. The problem was going to be getting Marianne out of there unnoticed. And Taylor had no idea if Marianne had anyone else in the place with her. She sat and watched for a few moments before deciding. She would come back tonight and take Marianne then.

She watched Marianne's place for another few minutes before turning around and leaving the same way she came, hoping her Mercedes would still be waiting for her.

★

Alex Sokolov sat on a lounge chair, across a courtyard from Marianne's villa. She had seen the FBI agent at the bank and decided to just watch. Once Marianne had gone inside, she decided to leave and come here.

When Chin had called her a few days earlier she had already decided she was done. She had enough money to retire. What was left to do but hang it up and enjoy life? And then Chin called.

While she admitted there was no greater feat in her profession than what she had done in Washington, she hated loose ends. And Marianne was one. Chin didn't necessarily care about the loose ends. What could Marianne do to him? He and his government had already orchestrated war against the United States. There was nothing Marianne could say or do to make that any worse. But just like any good capitalist, Chin wanted the money. He never said whether or not his government wanted the money, just that he wanted it. She figured it was the latter, given the terms of their agreement. Chin was giving her a cool fifty million. And even though he promised to bring the entire force of the People's Liberation Army down on her if she took a penny more, she doubted he would. That would mean he'd have to involve people she was sure he didn't want knowing about the money.

Nevertheless, it was never about the money for her. It was always about the kill. But fifty million was a hundred times more than any contract she'd ever taken. And that would just be plain stupid not to do it. So here she was.

She had to admit, she hadn't expected to see the FBI agent, or anyone else for that matter. But nevertheless, the agent was here. She was good, Alex thought, to be able to find Marianne this quickly. But the agent had a problem. She was most definitely sent here with orders to bring Marianne back. And that meant she would have to figure a way to get her out of there without causing a scene. She, on the other hand, did not have that problem. Her job wasn't to take Marianne anywhere.

She stood up and walked to the villa.

★

Taylor was halfway to the car when she decided to go back. She had been lost in her thoughts when she realized she hadn't paid attention to any of the security. She stopped and looked around, noticing small cameras here and there. That was something she was definitely going to have to be aware of. She turned back around and headed to Marianne's villa. There was a small courtyard there, and she was sure it would be monitored. She needed to see where the cameras were and what kind they appeared to be if she was going to hack in there and make sure they could be erased.

She had just returned to the same corner she was at before when her heart nearly stopped. She backed away quickly, so as not to be seen. Slowly she peeked her head back around the corner. There, standing at Marianne's door, was the Russian assassin, Alexandra Sokolov.

She backed away from the side of the building and went around the other way. There was no path there, just trees and shrubs. But that at least gave her some cover. There was a small patio on each of the villas on this side. She quietly crept ahead and looked for a spot to see from. She moved around another small bush, getting a little closer. She crept low, trying to stay out of sight.

The sliding glass door to the villa gave way to the view of the spacious living area. Taylor couldn't see anyone anywhere, but she could hear movement inside. She angled her body to get a better position. Nothing. She needed to move closer, but she would be exposing herself. She decided to take the chance. It wasn't like someone would normally be crouching out in the midst of the bushes and trees. Unless she made any sudden movements, she was sure she wouldn't be seen. She got as low to the ground as she could and crept around to the other side of a giant palm tree that stood at the end of the patio. She gently raised her head and looked.

Past the den sat a small kitchen area with a table and four chairs. Marianne was tied up to one of them. There was tape over her mouth, and her cheeks were streaked with black lines from her running mascara. The woman's eyes were a mixture of fear and sorrow, and the tears flowed freely from them. The Russian sat so that she was facing Marianne, her back to Taylor. The Russian seemed to be talking about something, though Megan couldn't hear anything.

After only a few more seconds, Marianne's eyes grew wide, as she began shaking her head back and forth. The Russian raised her arm, revealing a silenced handgun. Suddenly, Marianne's demeanor changed. It was as if she knew what was coming. Taylor watched her shoulders rise and fall, as the woman took a deep breath and let it out again. Then she closed her eyes and relaxed against her restraints. The Russian checked to make sure the silencer was secured. She leveled her gun and fired twice.

Marianne's head snapped back and then slowly rolled to one side. The Russian stood up and moved the dead woman's chair out of the way. She produced a laptop and set it on the table. Taylor couldn't read the screen, but it was obvious, after only a few seconds, that it wasn't the Russian's computer. She would type, stop, then smack the table in frustration.

Megan knew that there was nothing she could do for Marianne. The woman got what she had deserved. But there was a chance that she could maybe track this Russian. But she would have to get out of there right now. She needed to be back at her car when the Russian left. She backed away slowly. Once she was sure she was clear of the villa's view, she stood up and ran back to the front entrance. The Mercedes was right where she had left it. The young man she'd thrown the keys to was standing behind the desk. She winked at him and passed him an American fifty-dollar bill. He handed her the keys and smiled. She jumped in the car and pulled out onto the street outside the exit. She found a spot where she had a clear view of the main entrance. When the Russian left, she'd be on her tail.

CHAPTER 71

Keene awoke to the sounds of engines. Lots of them. He looked over at the bedside table and saw that his alarm was not set to go off for another thirty minutes. The entire base was being packed as quickly as could be, but he didn't expect them to be ready this quickly. He jumped out of bed and found his boots.

He was halfway to the central command office when Major General McIntyre found him. The man seemed to be in a big hurry and was waving at him from across the way as he hurried to meet him.

"Just got word, sir," McIntyre said. "The Chinese surfaced ten miles off South Carolina. Three submarines."

"What are they doing?" Keene asked.

"Well, it looked like they were going to hit some of the East Coast."

"What do you mean *were?*"

"Parris Island was able to catch them coming in. Before the submarines surfaced, they had two F-35 Lightning IIs in the air. They successfully took them out."

"Then what's the problem?"

"The problem, sir, is that there are three carriers coming in from the south of Florida's coast."

"The F-35s have stealth capability, yes?" Keene said, motioning for the man to follow him as he walked toward the command center.

"Yes, sir."

"How many do they have on base?"

"Six, sir. With pilots, fully loaded down and ready to deploy."

Keene thought for a moment. He hadn't expected the Chinese to come in from the south yet. He figured another day, at least. Once they made land, it would only take them a day to move into DC. Those carriers couldn't be allowed to advance any farther.

"Okay," he said. "The Chinese are coming quicker than I thought. If they were planning on making land by this morning, that means they're more than likely going to hit Albany earlier than tomorrow night. Those Lightning IIs take out the carriers?"

McIntyre shook his head. "No, sir. Brigadier General Halstead didn't want to risk sending what little air support they have that far out without talking to you first."

Keene nodded as they pushed through the door to the command center. As he entered the room, a corporal handed him a sat-phone.

"Brigadier General Halstead for you, sir."

Keene took the phone. "This is General Keene."

"General!" the woman said. "From Marine to SEAL, then CIA, and then back to Marine. Impressive!"

Keene feigned a smile at the jab. "How you doing, Karen?"

"Obviously not as good as you. Good to have you back, Jon. What's the matter? The CIA wasn't adventurous enough for you?"

"I'm not back," he said. Then, "What's going on over there? Heard you had some company."

"Yeah, three Song Class tubes popped up just a few miles off shore."

"Intentions?"

"Never found out. It was pure luck we even saw them coming. Their technology has advanced over the last five years. Soon as we knew what it was, we sent up the F-35s."

"And the carriers?"

"Infantry and air support."

"Well, I don't think it'd be a good idea to let them make land."

"No, sir."

"Can your F-35s take them out before they can get planes off the decks?"

"We believe they can."

"Any chance they're a decoy of some sort? To draw us out?"

"Don't think so. We were able to get a little bit of warning before the Chao Qis hit us. We took minimal damage. But as far as they knew, we were disabled. We didn't counterattack at all. Just laid low."

"Good. And your pilots feel good about it?"

"Yes, sir."

"Then get them in the air, general."

"Yes, sir."

"You guys take care of yourselves over there. You and Benning are the only thing standing between the Chinese and the southeast coast."

"You got it, *general*." Then, "Good to have you back, sir."

"I'm not back," he said again as the line went dead. He handed the phone back to the corporal and said, "Let's move, people!"

Over the next several hours, Keene worked with the other commanding officers, organizing and detailing procedures for moving the entire base out. The C-130s were loaded down with as much gear as they could handle and still fly efficiently at the low altitude. It was determined that they could make the trip to Albany and back in less than six hours. Knowing that the majority of the troops were going to be traveling by road, and the amount of time it would take, they decided that they could afford to make two trips with the C-130s. This was good, because it meant that they didn't have to leave nearly as much behind.

Majors Hurt and Caldwel finished checking their aircraft. As soon as they gave the all clear, Keene sent them up. He wanted Hurt and Caldwel to make sure the airspace was clear before sending up the C-130s. It took less than five minutes for the fighter pilots to make a sweep and give the go-ahead. Within minutes the C-130s were lined up, ready to take off.

Keene and Major General McIntyre had decided that McIntyre would stay behind and supervise the second cargo shipment, once the C-130s returned. From there, McIntyre and the rest of the men and women would meet up with the other regiments and armored divisions being assembled from Benning and Parris Island. McIntyre would then take command of the southern region. Keene would take command of the 101st Airborne division and lead the offensive in the north. As the first wave of soldiers began to move out, Keene grabbed McIntyre and took him aside.

"I guess this is it," McIntyre said.

"Yeah, guess so," Keene agreed, looking around once more. "You guys keep your heads down and your eyes open."

"You, too, Jon."

Keene shook the man's hand and headed for the lead vehicle. He jumped in, nodded to the young man behind the wheel, and grabbed the radio. He keyed the mic and cleared his throat.

"Listen up! We may be traveling at night, but that doesn't mean we're invisible. We need to move fast and as quietly as we can. Until we get to the other side of Knoxville and through those mountains, we're going dark. I don't want to hear a peep or see even a penlight, unless it's absolutely necessary. Understood?"

Once everyone had confirmed, he placed the mic back in its clip on the dashboard and signaled to the driver to proceed.

CHAPTER 72

Taylor had been sitting in the Mercedes for nearly three hours. The sun had already begun to set, and it was getting dark quickly. *What in the world is that Russian doing in there? Could I have missed her?* she thought. She doubted it. The way the resort was situated on the island and the way the island itself was designed, there was only one way in or out. She had to come through here. So what was the holdup?

Perhaps, Taylor thought, the Russian had her own villa there. If that was the case, she could be sitting there for a long time. She decided to call Jennings and see what his thoughts were. Once again, she pulled out the laptop and connected the phone.

"What's going on?" Jennings asked.

"Well, it's good and bad, sir. I found her."

"And?"

"She's dead."

"What do you mean she's dead!"

"The Russian."

"What?"

"I followed Marianne to a villa she was staying in. When I got there, the Russian was there. I watched her kill Marianne."

"How?"

"Execution. Double tap to the head. She couldn't see me, but I saw the whole thing."

"Okay, then," Jennings said. "You're done."

"Not done, sir."

"How's that?"

"The Russian, after she killed her, was going through Marianne's computer. A laptop. She obviously couldn't find what she was looking for because she looked agitated. I'm outside the resort now. There's only one way in or out of this place. I want to track her."

"Taylor, this woman is one of the most highly trained assassins in the world."

"I'm aware of that, sir. But two things: One, she tried to kill President Grant. I'm not about to let her get away with it. Not if I have a chance to stop her."

"And two?"

"I'm smarter than her."

She heard Jennings exhale into the phone. Finally he said, "I've literally got a war going on over here. As much as I wanted Marianne brought to justice for this, she got what she deserved."

"Maybe. But I can't just let this woman walk away."

"Don't get yourself killed. I can't help you over there."

She understood that was about as much of a blessing she was going to get from him. "Yes, sir." Then, "What's happening back home?"

"Jon has just about every force we have mobilized and on the move. They'll be in Albany in a few hours. We know the Chinese are advancing on us from Montreal. If we don't stop them there, they'll be able to have the entire country secured in less than a week. By the time our boys get back from the Middle East, it'll be too late. And then the only option we'll have from there is to engage in full-on war on our own soil."

Taylor felt a lump rise up in her throat. How had it come to this? "And if we succeed?"

"Then we can at least know the eastern states are secure. We can move forward from there."

That wasn't comforting to her. But at least there was hope. "Director Jennings, let me ask you something."

"Yeah?"

"Are you a man of faith?"

The line was quiet for a few seconds before he answered. "I grew up going to church. But I'll admit I haven't been someone who regularly turns to God for much. But here lately, I've been reconsidering my options."

Taylor laughed to herself. "Yeah, I imagine a lot of people are right now."

"Yeah, I imagine so."

Taylor thought for a moment about what she was going to say next. She didn't want to come off as being sanctimonious or pious, but she really felt like she needed to say it. "Listen, sir. I know you've got enough to think about. But this Prophet, he warned us this was going to happen. And now it has. But I believe we have a chance to right this thing. We're going to have to tell our people about this. And then we're going to have to make some major changes. So think about that. 'Cause right now, you're the one calling the shots. Jon is going to stop this invasion. I know it. And I have no idea what Boz is doing or where he is right now. But I can tell you this: I believe, with everything that I am, that this isn't over. We still need to find this Prophet. If there's any chance of us turning this thing around, he's the key."

The line was quiet for a few seconds.

"Well, I'll let you in on a little secret," he finally said. "I'm inclined to agree with you. And that's why I want you to forget this Russian and get back here. So you can help us find him."

Megan was relieved to hear he agreed. But she didn't want to let the assassin off so easily. She had her, right there. She thought for a moment and then said, "Okay, but you've got to promise me that we won't forget about her."

"You have my word. Trust me. If it weren't for our current situation, she'd be my number-one priority."

"So how do I get home?"

"Let me make a few calls. All of the transport planes leaving the Afghan region are making stops in Berlin to pick up supplies and refuel. You can meet one of them there."

"Okay, I'll check back when I'm in the air to Germany."

She disconnected the wires once again and put the phone away. She started to pull out of the parking space when she stopped suddenly. The Russian had just exited the main reception area. She was leaving. Taylor quickly argued with herself about just leaving or going ahead and following the woman. Since there was only one way off the island, she decided she would at least follow her that far and then decide. She watched as the Russian got into the car the valet brought around and sped through the main gate.

She let the woman drive past her, along with two other cars, and then pulled out. The trip around the point of the island and back to the mainland was quick. Taylor decided she couldn't let it go. She at least had to see where the woman went. She stayed back and watched as the woman turned her car onto the E-11 main road.

The Russian seemed to be making Taylor's decision for her. After ten minutes, it became apparent the woman was headed toward the airport. Taylor figured that as long as the Russian continued on this route, she would follow her, since she was going to the airport anyway. If the woman veered off this course, she would decide what to do then. But it never happened. And now they were getting very close to the exit.

Taylor assumed the assassin wouldn't be flying commercially. And that meant that she would be turning into the private terminal. Just like her. That wouldn't be good. The Russian would see her coming in behind and assume she was being followed. Taylor had to do something quick.

She remembered from the drive out of the airport that she only had about another two miles of main road before having to turn into the airport entrance. She decided to gamble. If she was right, the woman would be going to the private terminal and she would have the jump on her. If she was wrong, then she would just head to Berlin. The Russian would have to wait.

Traffic was steady on the highway, so she got over in the far lane and accelerated. She didn't move too fast, as to draw attention to herself, but swift enough to overtake the Russian's car, two lanes over. Within a few seconds, she was a good bit ahead of the woman. Once she felt comfortable that she was far enough ahead, and the Russian couldn't see her, Taylor gunned it. She continued on and made her way to the exit that led into the terminal.

The private terminal was big, for a private terminal, but still manageable. Taylor figured she had no more than fifteen minutes to find the woman's plane before it took off. She raced to where her own plane sat and pulled out her laptop. It only took her a few seconds before she was into the airport's mainframe. In another two minutes, she had it narrowed down to two hangars. One plane going to Geneva, the other to Thailand.

She quickly weighed the options in her head. She only had a few more minutes. The Russian would already be at her hangar by now. Thailand was definitely a place to disappear to. You could get lost there easily. However, an almost-six-foot-tall attractive blond woman would stick out like a sore thumb in Thailand. Geneva, on the other hand, now that was a place where someone with the Russian's physical attributes could blend in. She checked the computer screen one last time. The hangar was only a few hundred yards away. She jumped out of the car, checked her weapon, and started walking.

Halfway there, she stopped. She had just got done telling Jennings she was smarter than this woman. But this was reckless. If this assassin were worth half her salt, she would expect this, even if she weren't *expecting* this. Taylor thought for a moment and an idea came to her. She ducked behind a fueling truck and pulled out her phone. Within seconds she was connected to airport security. She identified herself as a foreign agent and asked if there was a way to ground all flights, explaining that she had reason to believe an explosive device was hidden somewhere on the grounds, possibly on an aircraft. The mere mention of an explosive device, she knew, would indeed ground every plane there for at least an hour, while the security protocols were followed. She also knew that this would make the Russian suspicious. And that was what she was counting on.

She quickly got off the call, making an excuse, and watched as one by one the planes moving freely among the tarmacs and runways began to slow down and come to complete stops. Within seconds, she heard sirens and knew her plan had worked. She moved out from behind the fueling truck and back to her own hangar.

The night sky gave her decent enough cover. Most of the stars and the moon were obscured by a heavy cloud ceiling. Other than the few lights on the buildings themselves, it was dark. And that was good because she didn't want anything drawing attention to the three police cruisers that were sitting unattended at the end of the small lot.

It is pretty universal for law enforcement officers to leave their cars unlocked because in an emergency, the last thing they need is the hassle of trying to get into a locked car in a hurry. So Taylor was confident that the cars would be unlocked. Apparently, the fine officers of the UEA Airport Police didn't share these tenets. All three vehicles were locked. But she only needed to get into the trunks, so she pulled a little black case from her pocket. Though she had never needed to do it, the FBI had trained her how to pick a lock and had given her the little kit she now held in her hand. She had been told to never go anywhere without it. And right now, she was thankful that she had listened. The first trunk gave way with just a few pokes and twists of the little tweezers-like blades. She quickly looked around. Not there. She moved onto the second car. Same thing.

"Come on!" she said in a frustrated whisper. She picked the lock on the third car and lifted the lid. "Finally!"

She took what she was looking for and hurried back to her car, being careful not to be seen. She threw it into the backseat and hurried off toward the hangar she believed the Russian was leaving from.

She made it to the hangar and hugged the side. Slowly, she inched her way forward, getting closer to the open hangar doors. She found a few crates to take up a position behind and waited.

It only took two minutes before the Russian woman appeared. And she did so carrying her pistol. She had it dangling at her side, as she carefully glanced around outside the hangar. Was the woman just being curious? Or did she sense something wasn't right? She took another look around and stepped back inside, out of Taylor's view. The woman's awareness was probably fully heightened. The Russian knew something wasn't right. And that was what Taylor was hoping for.

Taylor knew that it wouldn't be long before security made its way through, checking every building and plane. When that happened, the Russian had two options. Stay put and pretend nothing was wrong or get out of there and come back later. Given the fact that the woman was one of the most wanted assassins in the world, Taylor assumed she wasn't going to stick around. She carefully backed away, not making a sound. Once she was sure she was clear, she hurried back to her car.

There was only one road in and out of the private terminal. Taylor knew from hacking into the mainframe that only four planes were scheduled to have taken off this evening. Automobile traffic in and out of the terminal should be minimal. She was counting on this, because if she made a mistake, the wrong person could get badly hurt. She said a quick prayer that she would be right and sped off out of the terminal.

The road between the main terminal and the private one was a little over a mile long. Barren desert was the only thing on either side of the road, with the exception of a small building that looked like an equipment shed halfway between. A few fuel trucks and other machinery were parked beside and around the small building. Taylor pulled her car in behind them to hide it. She got out, retrieved the spike strip she'd stolen from the cop car, and took up a position only three feet from the road behind another truck.

She had only just gotten set when she heard the approaching vehicle. The road was long and straight, so Taylor assumed that the car would be traveling at a good speed. And it was. As she peeked out from behind the truck, the headlights of the car were getting closer at a rapid pace. Timing was going to be everything here. She had only a window of a few seconds to step out, make sure it was her target, and then take action.

She waited until she could sense the car was almost on her position. She watched the road in front of her until she saw the beams of the headlights get narrower and narrower. Finally, at the last second, she stepped out and confirmed it was the Russian. She threw the spike strip out into the road. She jumped back behind the fuel truck in time to see the Russian woman jerk the wheel.

Megan watched as the car jetted past her, unable to slow down. It hit the spike strip, just as she had intended. The car slid to the right and then up onto two wheels as the driver lost complete control, rolling three times before coming to rest upside down. Glass from the windows had blown out in every direction. When it came to rest, the car was a crumpled heap and a mess. Taylor raised her gun and ran to the car.

When she got there, she couldn't believe what she saw. There was blood on the airbag that had exploded and pieces of torn clothing were on the shards of glass still hanging from the driver's side window. But the Russian was gone. Had the woman been thrown from the vehicle? She turned to look around the area when she felt the *thwak!* in the door beside her.

She jumped over the nose of the car and scurried behind the mangled front end of the other side. The Russian had survived the crash and was shooting at her with a silenced pistol.

Thwak, thwak, thwak!

The shots hit the front of the car again. She tried to stay still and listen, to see if she could hear the woman moving around. She had to be injured, Taylor told herself. No way someone could just walk away from a crash like that unscathed. She sat still for a second. Finally she heard the crunch of the dirt and gravel. And it was moving away from her. The woman was trying to run.

She jumped out from behind the car and fired three shots in the direction she had heard the footsteps. She knew she probably hadn't hit anything, but she wanted to confirm the direction of the shots. She crouched back down and looked carefully through the rims of the wheels. She saw the muzzle flash and then heard the *thwak!* again as the Russian's bullet hit the rear of the car. Her aim was getting worse.

Megan stood up again and fired exactly where the muzzle flash had come from. She heard a guttural "Ugh!" and then what sounded like someone falling and dragging herself along the gravel and dirt. Finally the dragging stopped.

Megan took the small flashlight out from her back pocket and clicked it on. She was taking a big risk here, but she had to. She was sure, from the sound of it, the Russian was down.

She played the beam of the light across the ground in front of her and waited for another burst of *thwaks!* But they never came. She stepped out from behind the car.

She had gone about thirty feet off the road, into the desert, when she saw her. The woman was lying still on her stomach. Her gun was a few inches from her head. She had one hand above her, the other by her side. One leg was bent and the other straight, as if the woman had been trying to crawl away. She kept her gun trained at the woman's head and used her foot to roll her over.

The Russian flopped over onto her back. She had a four-inch piece of glass sticking out from her neck. She had, apparently, been thrown from the vehicle. Right through the driver's window. The woman's entire left side was soaked with blood. The wound in her neck was bubbling as she labored to breathe. She began to cough, as blood spat from her lips and onto the desert sand beside her head. A smile creased her lips as she tried to say something, but Taylor couldn't hear it. She kicked the woman's gun away and leaned down, placing her own gun directly over the woman's heart. The Russian coughed and tried to speak again.

"My name is Alexandra Sokolov," she said.

"I know who you are."

"I underestimated you." The Russian tried to smile but it only led to a coughing fit.

"Yes, you did."

The woman coughed again, heaving up more blood. "I killed your president," she laughed.

Megan felt a tear roll down her cheek. "He's not dead."

The woman's breathing was becoming more shallow. She only had a few seconds left. Taylor stood up to leave, but the woman grabbed her ankle. She leaned back down.

"I–I'm sorry," the Russian said and exhaled.

Megan watched as the Russian's eyes went wide. She could see the fear and the terror in them. "I'm sorry, too," she said as the woman's grip fell away.

Alexandra Sokolov was dead.

CHAPTER 73

It was less than four hours from sunset when the last of the troops and supplies arrived in Albany. There had been no further advancement from the Chinese. They seemed to be, for the time being, satisfied with occupying the central part of the country. This made sense, though. If their main objective was oil, they already had what they'd come for. All of the oil presumed to be in the United States was between the Rockies and the Mississippi River. With no resistance other than a few pockets of militant citizens, the Chinese had taken the country in less than three days. Keene knew, though, it was only a matter of time before they came for the rest. If there was one thing he knew about a military strike, it was you don't quit until you've completely subdued your enemy. There was no way the Chinese were not going to try and take Washington. It was the head of the beast. And the only way to kill the beast was to take off the head. So it stood to reason, the next twenty-four hours could determine the future of the United States of America.

Albany was a ghost town. Jennings had been successful in his grass-roots campaign to get the word out to citizens. Between public radio and the Emergency Broadcast Network, word was spreading throughout the nation that there was sanctuary for Americans if they could get east of the Appalachians. Fort Benning and the other divisions were reporting in that people were arriving in droves to come through the mountain passes or up from Atlanta. There had been some attempts by the Chinese to advance on those checkpoints, but the American forces had been ready this time. More than fifteen Chao Qi Chinese fighter jets had been taken down, along with twenty or so pockets of Chinese infantry who had tried to push through the mountain passes. It seemed, for now at least, America was getting her legs back under her.

Keene had spent the last couple hours, since arriving in Albany, coordinating the defense strategy. Most of the commanders and their troops

271

had already been deployed to strategic points within a fifty-mile radius. Keene had spoken with Jennings, who had already mobilized and sent north everything he could spare to help reinforce Keene's men. However, he and Keene both decided on leaving a good number of men in the DC area in case the Chinese somehow managed to pop up off the eastern coast again. The Chinese had incredibly advanced radar and stealth technology. As little as two nuclear subs surfacing off the coast could do irreparable damage.

The problem Keene was facing now was twofold. He knew the ultimate target was Washington. The Chinese would absolutely come for it. And in order to get ground troops in, they had to come from the north. So Albany was definitely a logical place to set up the defensive front. However, if they were able to stop the advancement—and he definitely planned on stopping the advancement at any cost—there was nothing keeping the Chinese from another complete nuclear strike on the eastern United States. In all reality, if the Chinese were there for the purpose of the natural resources, then there was nothing to deter them from completely annihilating the rest of the country. They had already proven their intentions on the West Coast. The loss of life would be catastrophic. And that would be game, set, and match. That, Keene told himself, could not be allowed to happen. So the question, then, was how could he make sure it didn't?

He grabbed the sat-phone and dialed the number.

"We're all set. I sent out two recon units to put eyes on what's going on up there. They should be back any time now."

"Good," Jennings said. "I just got off the phone with Taylor."

"How is she? Everything okay?"

"She's fine. Levy's dead."

Keene let that hang there for a moment. "She killed Levy?"

"No."

"Then what? Who?"

"Alexandra Sokolov."

"What! I thought she was working for Levy."

"You know how it is, Jon. Loose ends."

"How do we know it was her?"

" 'Cause Taylor saw the whole thing."

"How? What happened?"

"Oh, it gets better. Taylor's not your average computer geek."

"I'm beginning to see that."

"She followed Sokolov to the airport, where she did something completely stupid. She's starting to remind me of you."

Keene decided to take that as a compliment.

"She somehow lured Sokolov *back* away from the airport," Jennings continued, "and ran her car off the road. Sokolov was thrown from the vehicle but survived. She and Taylor exchanged fire and—"

"So Megan shot her?"

Keene listened as Jennings quickly recounted the rest of the conversation he'd had with Taylor. Though he was happy that both the Russian and Levy were taken care of, he found himself worried about Taylor. And though he wasn't sorry Sokolov was dead, he wished he had had a chance to question her.

"She say anything—the Russian?"

"Said she was sorry."

"Too late for that now," Keene said, disappointed that they would never get anything else out of the assassin. "What about Boz?"

"Haven't heard anything. Don't know what's going on. Maybe he just decided to get somewhere safe."

Keene had only known Boz for a short time, but he believed he knew him well enough to know that Boz wouldn't just bail on them. Or on the country. He decided to let it go. "I've been thinking. If—scratch that— *when* we push the Chinese back, it's not going to sit well with their command. You and I both know there's only one reason why they're going to continue to advance."

"They need to take Washington," Jennings answered for him.

"That's right. And if they can't take it, what's the next best thing?"

"Yeah," Jennings said. "I've been thinking about that, too."

"Kevin, we've spent the last twenty-four hours drawing our citizens east of the mountain range because we've told them it's the only place they would be safe. The Chinese have already shown that they are willing to use a nuke."

"I agree," Jennings said. "I've already discussed this with President Walker."

"What did he say?"

"Nothing. The man has completely shut down. I actually think he's suffering from some form of shock. I'm having the medical staff look at him right now."

"Any improvement on President Grant?"

"Not much. His breathing is still labored, but they're saying that his brain function seems to be increasing."

"That's good." Then, "Even if this works, they have to take out Washington."

"I know it. So how do we stop it?"

Keene had been thinking about it since he'd arrived in Albany. "They could launch a small surface-to-surface missile. But the warhead won't be that big. They wouldn't take the chance of bringing it by the ground. Too easy to stop that. That leaves only three ways they can get it there. One, it's already there. I doubt that that is the case. They wouldn't have been able to keep that quiet. Someone, somewhere, would have seen or heard something."

"I agree."

"Two, they bring it in by nuclear sub."

"I don't think they can," Jennings said. "We had those U-boats in South Carolina taken out, literally, seconds after they surfaced. They can't take a chance of that happening again."

"I agree," Keene said. "So that leaves the third option."

"They fly it in."

"They fly it in," Keene repeated.

"So then the next question is, from where?" Jennings said.

"From somewhere near Montreal," Keene answered. "They'll have a Stealth loaded up somewhere away from the advancing troops. They won't take the chance that it gets compromised. And it's not going to be Montreal airport because they know we can air strike that place easily if we begin to push them back." He thought for a minute and then continued. "I need you to find every airstrip between here and Montreal that can handle an H-8 Stealth."

"Remember what I said about Taylor doing something stupid?" Jennings said.

"Yeah, she reminded you of me."

"Exactly."

"Just find me that airstrip. You can yell at me later."

"I'll call you back."

They spoke for another minute before Keene ended the call and sent word out that he wanted a satellite video conference in ten minutes with every commanding officer of every division they had standing by. He found a young corporal who led him to a room where the conference would be set up.

"Get me Colonel Givens," Keene told the corporal, referring to the executive officer who served directly under McIntyre at the 101st. "Tell him I need him here five minutes ago."

"Yes, sir."

Givens popped his head in less than a minute later. "You wanted to see me?"

"Yes, Colonel." He gestured for the man to take a seat. "I'm giving you command of the operation."

"Sir, I—"

Keene held up a hand to hold him off. "I've already talked about it with Jennings. He agrees. Listen." Keene closed his eyes and rubbed his forehead. "I'm not the guy to do this. I've been out for too long. Too much has changed. You know these men. They serve under you. I'm a CIA agent. And I'm good at it. And that's why I'm giving command over to you. From this point on, you will coordinate directly with the Sec-Nav. In just a few minutes, we're going on a video conference. Sec-Nav will be on, and he will lay out the operation. Got it?"

Colonel Givens nodded. "Yes, sir. Permission to speak freely, sir?"

"Go," Keene said.

"I appreciate all you've done. I won't let you down."

"I know you won't, Colonel."

"But I also know you wouldn't give up command like this unless you had a good reason. What's going on?"

A thin smile creased Keene's lips. The colonel was perceptive. "This is classified. So it stays between me, you, and Jennings, until otherwise stated."

"Yes, sir."

"The Chinese won't stop, even if we stop them here. They have to take out Washington. Otherwise, we're still a threat. Do you understand what I'm saying?"

"I think so, sir."

"Good, then I need you to find me the five best men here. SEALs and Rangers. We're going to make sure that the Chinese don't have a plan B."

"Let me look through my roster, sir. I'll have them back here in twenty minutes."

"After the conference," Keene reminded him.

Just then the corporal returned. "They're ready for us, sir," he said. He opened the laptop on the table and clicked a few buttons. In just a few seconds, several little windows appeared with officers in them. The Secretary of the Navy, Bob Sykes, was in the last window.

"Hello," the Sec-Nav said. "For those of you whom I've never met, I'm Secretary Sykes. . . ."

The conference lasted only a few minutes. Keene officially handed off command to Colonel Givens, and then Sykes laid out the plan of operation from this point forward. When they were done, everyone signed off, and the computer was shut down.

"I'll be back with your men in just a few minutes," Givens said.

Keene nodded and picked up the sat-phone.

"You find my airstrip?"

"I've pulled satellite imagery from a couple different fields close to Montreal from the last forty-eight hours. There's only one that can handle an H-8—Massena International-Richards field. And there seems to be a lot of activity there. The whole town has been leveled. The only reason they'd hit a town like that with so much force is if they wanted it all to themselves. It's roughly sixty miles southwest of Montreal and just across the river in New York."

"That's it," Keene said. "Far enough away from Montreal but close enough to send it up if need be."

"Yep. And listen, I can't say for sure, but one of the images captured looks like an aircraft. It's covered by a tarp or something. But analysis on the dimensions and the shape of it fit an H-8."

"Okay, then. I'll let you know what we find."

"Good luck, Jon. I'll say a prayer for you and the men."

Of all the things his boss had ever said over the years, that was the single most unexpected thing he had ever heard. "I didn't know you believed in all that stuff."

"I'm starting to rethink a lot of things," Jennings said.

"Yeah, seems to be a lot of that going on around here." He hung up the phone.

Givens returned a few moments later. He had five men in tow as he entered the room. "General Keene, this is Ramirez, Horn, Kirkpatrick, Jenkins, and Foust," Givens said, introducing the men.

Keene looked them over. He knew the type: highly trained, specialized operatives who were possibly the most physically and mentally fit human beings on the planet. "Thank you for coming gentlemen. Colonel Givens, that will be all."

The colonel left without another word. When the door was shut, Keene motioned for them to take a seat. He had already pulled up the satellite imagery that Jennings had found. He turned the laptop around for the men to see.

"This is Massena, New York. And that," he said pointing, "is an airstrip big enough to hold a Chinese H-8 Stealth. Do you understand what I'm saying?"

The men all looked at the photos of the decimated town and said, "Yes, sir."

"Good, 'cause no matter what happens, we are going to make sure that H-8 doesn't ever leave Massena. Got it?"

"Yes, sir."

"Gear up, gentlemen. We're rolling out in fifteen."

CHAPTER 74

Boz stood at the front of the bridge of the HMS *Queen Elizabeth*, the flagship of the Royal Navy. They had been at sea now for over a day and were getting close to American waters. Boz had been on a lot of carriers before, but this by far was one of the most sophisticated pieces of machinery he'd ever seen. The propulsion and navigation systems alone were state-of-the-art technology. Not even the Americans had anything like this yet. Of course, with the previous two administrations cutting the defense budget by nearly two-thirds, it was no wonder the Brits had finally bested them. And the *Queen Elizabeth* was just the tip of this spear. The HMS *Prince of Wales*, the *Queen Elizabeth*'s counterpart, was right on their tail, along with twenty-three other warships.

Prime Minister Bungard had been livid when he had gotten word. Pretty much his entire Royal Navy had been hijacked. He had assumed immediately that it was Eli Craig who had arranged all of this. He wasted little time getting Craig on the phone once word got out. He had threatened to hang Craig at the Tower of London when he got back. Bungard said he would bring Craig, and every participating commanding officer with him, up on treason charges and would have them imprisoned for life.

Eli had kept his calm throughout the short conversation but quickly reminded the prime minister that—as he had so eloquently put it—over half his navy had mutinied on him. How did he think that was going to go over at Parliament? The prime minister quickly quieted down after that. Eli continued by telling him that what was done was done and that it should've been Bungard's decision in the first place to help the Americans. Eli had continued, charging that Bungard was a coward and a disgrace to King William and their country. And then he gave the final blow. Eli told him that once the Chinese heard that England was coming to the rescue of the United States, it wouldn't matter to them who had made the decision. The fact was England was about to wage war on China. The mother country was coming to the aid of her child. And whether Bungard liked it or not, he was in this now, so he'd better figure out how to make this look like it was his idea all along. Or it would be Bungard who was the one being strung up at the Tower of London. That was the end of the conversation, as Bungard slammed the phone down. Within an hour, information came back to the HMS *Queen Elizabeth* that Bungard had called a special session of Parliament and announced that, along with key strategic leaders—namely, Eli Craig—he had ordered the Royal Navy to lead a covert operation to come to the assistance of the United States.

Though it was well known the Chinese had perhaps the best stealth technology available, the Brits had some pretty good stuff of their own. For the last ten years, teams of Russian, German, and defected Chinese scientists had been acquired to develop what had been first installed on the *Queen Elizabeth*. When the ship had been commissioned and officially put out to sea, the Royal Navy ran a myriad of ghost operations, testing out the new stealth technology, which had proven nothing but successful. Over the next few years, every ship in the navy had been outfitted with it. And unless the Chinese had developed something new in the last six months, Eli assured Boz that no one should see them coming. Short of someone flying directly over them or another ship literally crossing their path, they were invisible.

There were two problems with that, Boz realized. One, no one knew they were coming. Not even Keene. And there was no way to get word to them. Once the *Queen Elizabeth* and the fleet had gone dark, that was it. There was no communication outside of ship-to-ship coms. The second problem: they had no idea what they were headed into. They were now only hours away from the American coast and they would have to stay dark until the last possible moment. Once the fighter aircraft took off from the decks, they would be completely visible. And then, it was no turning back. Boz only prayed that they wouldn't be too late.

The sun had already set, and the cloud cover was thick. Hardly a star in the sky. Eli had just returned to the bridge as Boz was looking out on the horizon.

"Pretty dark out there, mate."

"Yeah, I can't decide if that's a good thing or a bad thing."

Eli waved it off. "That's a good thing. Gonna help us see the coast when we come up on it. Less light up there means we'll be able to see the landscape better."

"And who knows what we're going to see," Boz said quietly.

Eli put his hand on Boz's shoulder. "It's never as bad as you think.

You told me that once. Remember?" He turned and pointed to the fleet behind them. "We've got a lot of boys back there who are completely sold out. They know that if America falls, the entire world could be next. This isn't just about your country. It's about theirs. And they aren't going to let that happen."

Boz nodded. He knew his friend was right. The Chinese might not be looking for a world war, but if America fell, they'd get one. Every country on the planet—aside from China's current allies—would be gearing up for an invasion. And more than likely, they wouldn't wait. They'd be proactive. And with the nuclear capabilities of other nations, and China's track record of being irresponsible on every other level of diplomacy, it wouldn't take long before someone decided that launching them all would be the only option. He hoped and prayed that wasn't what God was going to allow to happen.

"It's just sad that it's had to come to this, Eli."

"I know, mate. So if God allows us to get out of this alive, we'll just know we have a lot of work to do."

Boz patted his friend on the shoulder and left the bridge. He went downstairs and out onto the deck. He walked up and down, looking at the aircraft that were already positioned to take off and head into battle. He felt a huge weight pressing down on him. Boz looked down at his watch. Only two hours left. He found a small bench and sat down. He folded his hands and closed his eyes. And began to pray.

CHAPTER 75

Jennings sat at a conference table with Bob Sykes and President Walker. They had coms up on every unit they had deployed in the southern and Albany regions. The first of the American troops had returned from Afghanistan and had landed at Andrews. They were immediately deployed to the Albany front. More would be returning over the next several hours as the fleet of C-class cargo planes came in, though it would still be several days before the majority of the equipment and troops would make it back. Jennings hoped they could last that long. He was sure they were about to find out. The sun had been down for an hour now and the wait was on.

Jennings thought back to the days of the American Revolution, when war was done differently. Men would line up in regiments in fields, according to ranks, and then march on one another. It wasn't until a few farmers and hunters realized that they couldn't win the war by conventional methods that everything had changed. From that moment on, war was no longer conducted in a gentlemanly way. No longer did the armies of generals stand and face one another in open fields, and only during the daytime. Raids on troops and forts began to happen at unexpected times, during the night and on Sundays. The enemy was being targeted in close quarters along roads and in the thicket of the forests. Guerrilla warfare was born.

Jennings looked over at Walker, who was fidgeting and biting his fingernails. Sykes, on the other hand, looked calm and collected. The two men couldn't be more different. Jennings, for the second time that day, said a silent prayer. He thanked God that at least Walker had the wherewithal to remove himself from this part of it.

The three men sat in silence for another ten minutes before the first radio call came in. A series of mortars had been fired on the forward unit in Albany. The Chinese infantry had engaged.

Within seconds, the entire command center at the bunker was in full swing. Sykes began to call out orders and check in with the other stations and regiments. They, too, had been engaged. The mortar shells and gun-fire could be heard as they filled the room over the coms monitoring the northern front. Sykes and the Joint Chiefs began barking out commands to the troops. Seconds later, the other half of the coms lit up. The Chinese had coordinated their attacks on the southern front to happen at the same time.

The Chao Qis came first with a massive air attack. Most of Albany and half of Atlanta were leveled in less than an hour, clearing the way for the Chinese infantry and armaments to move. The American troops were taking heavy fire. Jennings listened, as the People's Liberation Army pressed forward.

The next two hours were painful. While the northern front was hold-ing its own, the southern front was having trouble. With Florida being accessible from the Gulf or the Atlantic, the Chinese continued bringing up ships from the south. Sykes was forced to send what air support he had left to Major General McIntyre, to aid the men and women from Fort Benning and Parris Island, leaving Washington vulnerable. No doubt a thought-out strategy by the Chinese.

Within an hour of Syke's decision, four Chinese cargo ships appeared off the coast of Delaware, having sneaked past the already weak American coastal blockade. As soon as they were noticed, Sykes sent out four Apaches and two Blackhawks, but the ships had already gotten into Delaware Bay. The Apaches were able to inflict some damage, but the ships had already run aground. The Apache and Blackhawk pilots quickly learned that the ships weren't ordinary cargo ships. They had been outfitted with surface-to-air defense missiles. Within seconds of the Americans' arrival, the Chinese launched an attack. The Apaches and Blackhawks continued to evade and attack, but the Chinese ships, carrying infantry, vehicles, and WZ-10 attack helicopters, were being unloaded at an extraordinary pace. It only took a few minutes for the Chinese to get the WZ-10s in the air. The Blackhawks and Apaches, outnumbered and outgunned, were forced to retreat back to Andrews. The pilots had estimated anywhere from three to five thousand Chinese foot soldiers on each vessel. With less than a hundred miles separating them from Washington, DC, it appeared the Chinese would successfully invade the nation's capitol, regardless of whether or not the Americans held off the northern and southern attack.

CHAPTER 76

The sun had been down for half the night. Keene and his new team had been on the road for six hours. The drive was a little over two hundred miles. But that was taking the interstate almost to the Canadian border before turning west. They couldn't risk that. So the only option was to travel two-lane and county roads through the mountains. The drive that should've taken five hours was now taking seven.

They had been able to maintain contact with the forward base in Albany for only the first two hours. After that, they were out of range. And the mountains, though giving them a quiet approach to Massena, were wreaking havoc on communications. Not even the satellite phone would work. The last thing Keene had heard was the Chinese had advanced. And though he was confident in the US soldiers, he was well aware that they were hugely outnumbered. And they definitely didn't have the artillery that the Chinese had on hand. It was going to come down to skill. And that gave him hope, knowing the US forces were the most efficiently trained military in the world.

Now that they had made it through the mountains, Highway 56 would take them into Massena. Keene noticed that the sat-phone was showing signal, so he tried to call in. He knew the moment Jennings answered, it wasn't good.

"It's chaos here. The Albany front is holding okay, but the southern front is getting overrun. Sykes sent everything we could spare that way. The idea was to give them as much air support as we could. But it's bitten us in the rear end."

Keene felt his stomach fall. "What's happened?"

"Four Chinese cargo ships beached off the coast of Delaware twenty minutes ago. And we don't know if they're the only four. But they have infantry, WZ-10s, and artillery. Washington's a sitting duck right now. And we can't call back the air support from Benning and Parris Island, because it's the only thing that may keep them from getting taken."

Keene felt the bile rise in his throat. "They knew you would do that."

"They know everything!" Jennings said. "We can't make a move without them already having an answer to it."

"They've been planning this for years. We're having to operate out of reaction." He tried to force down his anger. "I know we've said it's off the table, but we may be forced to step it up."

"There is no way that President Walker, or anyone else in this bunker, is going to authorize using that kind of force. We're talking about American lives here. On our own soil! No way."

Keene knew he was right. It just simply wasn't acceptable to think of using any kind of weapon of mass destruction on American soil. And with the previous administration's disarmament campaign, they no longer had the range to hit China itself, not that that would have been an option either. There were over a billion people in their country, and their government didn't care about any of them. It would do no good to attack China when, it appeared, their entire military was here. This whole thing was getting worse by the second.

Just then, he heard something in the background. Jennings told him to hold on. He listened, straining to hear what was happening, but the surrounding noise was too much. He cupped the mouthpiece of the phone and told Ramirez to pull over. Ramirez let off the gas and pulled to the shoulder of the road.

"Jon, you there?"

"Yeah, I'm here. What's going on?" he said anxiously.

"Hang on," Jennings said again. Then, to someone there in the command center, "Put that on the com!" Then, back on the phone, "Listen to this!"

Keene listened as Jennings held the phone out to pick up what the com was saying. A huge wave of relief swept over him, and he caught himself whispering, "Thank you, God." And the weird thing was he actually meant it.

He pulled the phone away from his ear and put it on speaker. "Listen to this, guys." He held the phone up for the men to hear. What came over the little speaker was the best thing Keene had ever heard.

"Mr. President, this is Eli Craig of His Majesty's Royal Navy. I understand you've run into a little problem."

"You could say that," the president said.

"Well, I believe I can help you with that. I am currently two miles off the coast of your eastern seaboard. And I've brought a friend."

"Mr. President, this is Bozwell Hamilton. I've been working with Jon Keene and President Grant. Who's calling the shots?"

"Boz, this is Jennings. I'm here with the Joint Chiefs and Secretary Sykes. They're running the op."

"Okay," Boz said. "We've got twenty ships with close to fifty thousand men, including pilots and aircraft. Where do you want us?"

Keene and the other men in the truck broke out in excitement. They exchanged high fives and let out a few cheers. Keene told the men he'd be right back and stepped out of the truck.

He walked along the shoulder of the road a few paces and sat down. For the first time in over a week, he felt some relief. The whole ordeal was so overwhelming that he just sat there with his head in his hands for a moment. He hadn't even realized he was still holding the phone until he heard Jennings yelling for him.

"Jon!" Jennings said for the third time.

He snapped back to and put the phone to his ear. "I'm here."

"Did you hear all of that?"

"Yeah, most of it. Enough."

"Boz had already figured we'd be splitting the troops north and south. They've already sent their fleet in both directions. They'll be at Parris Island in less than an hour. And they're already coming ashore in Boston. They'll be in Albany in less than two hours. That's if we even need their infantry. They've got enough air support to possibly take out the Chinese completely."

"What about DC?"

"Five ships, including two carriers. They're coming in behind the cargo ships the Chinese beached. They should be able to overtake them in the next hour."

Again, Keene felt a wave of relief. But it only lasted for a moment, as he was quickly reminded why he was here on the side of the road. Immediately he felt the urgency of what they needed to do. "Kevin, if DC's safe, then—"

"Then you've got to hurry!" Jennings finished his thought. "Once they realized they're beat, they'll send it."

"I'll call you back."

Keene put the phone away and started to run back to the truck. He stopped short and looked up into the night sky. "I think You and I still need to have a conversation about a few things," he said, "but for now, I'll just say thanks."

He jumped in the truck and said, "Let's move it! We're under a major deadline now."

"What's the timeline?" Kirkpatrick asked from the backseat.

"That's the problem," Keene said. "We don't know."

"So, like, five minutes ago," Foust said.

"Yeah. Or sooner!"

Ramirez pulled the gear lever and slammed on the gas. They were still fifteen miles from the city limits. Every second from this point forward was critical.

As they got closer, Keene told Ramirez to pass up the road they would eventually take and proceed toward the city. He wanted to at least get a quick look at what they were headed into. A quarter mile out Keene ordered Ramirez to kill the lights and stop. Keene pulled his field glasses up and scanned the area. The others followed suit. As they took in the scene, they all expressed their disgust at what they saw. The entire area had been leveled. It was obvious that the Chinese had intended to use the place and wanted no resistance whatsoever. Massena looked worse than any other city that had been hit. And the fact that it was a smaller town made the devastation all the more apparent. Ramirez turned the car around and went back the way they had come.

They had decided earlier that the best way into the airport was through the Racquette River, which ran along the southern border of the city and eventually right by the airfield. Ramirez turned off Highway 56 and onto County Road 40, which ran along the river. They decided that they would come ashore on the banks where a road called Aviation Road intersected the main road that traveled along the river. Aviation Road, appropriately named, would lead them directly onto the airport grounds. From there they could recon the area and find the H-8 stealth bomber.

A quick survey of the perimeter as they came into town from the river showed the Chinese did, in fact, have several checkpoints set up around the main roads into the city from the south. And though Foust and Horn wanted to take them out, Keene wouldn't allow it. He reminded them that the H-8 was the target and that they needed to go in quiet. They couldn't take the chance of someone not reporting in during a regular check. It would only sound the alarm and announce their arrival. So they continued on, heads down and silent.

As they approached the bank of the river by Aviation Road, a patrol vehicle passed by. Keene held up a fist for the men to get down until the vehicle passed. A moment later, he gave the all-clear sign, and they continued forward. They stowed the inflatable under some fallen brush and climbed the bank. After a quick check to make sure no one was coming, they followed Aviation Road in, as it led them toward the airstrip.

A small group of buildings sat at the end of the road, mostly maintenance and a small hangar. A few vehicles and soldiers were milling about, but nothing they couldn't deal with quickly. Across the field to the east was the main terminal. That's where most of the action was happening, Keene could see through his field glasses.

It appeared that the Chinese had already gotten word their military was being pushed back. At least fifty or more men were scrambling back and forth around the terminal. The tarp that Jennings had said he'd seen in the satellite photo was clearly visible. Within seconds, Keene's fears were confirmed. As the tarp was being cleared, the sight gave way to the huge aircraft it had been hiding. The H-8 sat glimmering under lights that had been set up all around it. As he watched, he saw a group of men exit the terminal pushing a huge cart. He was too far away to confirm what was on the cart, but he didn't need to. He knew what it was. And it was minutes away from being loaded into the plane.

"Kirkpatrick, how long for them to load it?" he asked.

"Bomb that size, rigging it into the drop mechanism, thirty minutes tops," Kirkpatrick answered.

That didn't leave much time. But he had an idea. He took out the sat-phone. When Jennings answered he said, "What's happening?"

"It's good. Boz has really saved our behinds on this one. The Chinese are being pushed back hard right now. Most of their forces south have just retreated. They had a larger contingent coming in from Albany, so it's taking longer, but we've got them on the run!"

"Good. How long would it take you to get an air strike on my location?" he asked.

"Hold on."

Keene could hear him talking in the background. Finally Jennings came back on.

"Twenty minutes if I send them now."

"Send them. I'll have the target painted."

"So it's there?"

"Yeah, and they're loading it now. Tell the flyboys no matter what happens, do not let that H-8 get in the air."

"Don't worry, I will."

Keene hung up the phone and looked at the other five men. "Okay, here's the plan. . . ."

In less than a minute, Keene had laid out what everyone was going to do. Since Jenkins was the shooter, Keene wanted him in the best position. And that meant that they were going to have to advance on the small buildings up ahead. That position would give Jenkins a clear line of sight to the terminal and the entire field. And the shot range was right in his wheelhouse of eight hundred meters. Once Jenkins's position was secured, Keene and the others would make their way across the field toward the terminal and the H-8. Foust would take up a position at the north end of the field and point the laser at the target for the air strike. They only had fifteen minutes left, but they needed to place charges on the building and blow it. Once Keene and the others made it to the terminal, it was game on. They didn't have time for tactics. If they were engaged, they were to take out whomever they came across. Because it was already the middle of the night and everyone there seemed to be focused on the aircraft, Keene hoped they could get to the terminal with little to no interaction. The men checked their weapons and moved forward.

They noted six men as they approached the small cluster of buildings at the end of the road. Foust, Horn, and Ramirez took the first three, while Keene, Kirkpatrick, and Jenkins neutralized the others. Keene almost felt bad for the poor young men. They had no idea what had hit them, once again proving Keene's assertion that the American soldier was the best-trained weapon on the planet. The whole process took less than a minute. They had seventeen left.

Keene and his team took off at a dead run toward the terminal. Halfway across the airfield, Foust broke off and headed north. The others continued moving at breakneck speed to the target. Three and a half minutes later, they approached the terminal.

They decided to come in from the back side, which would use up precious extra seconds, but they couldn't just walk head-on into what was going on there. Keene held up his hand and checked his wrist mic. "Six, this is one. All clear?"

Jenkins came back immediately. "One, this is six. All clear."

"Five, you set?"

Foust answered. "Five is up and set. Target is painted."

Ten minutes to go.

Keene motioned for Ramirez, Horn, and Kirkpatrick to spread out. Each of them had a small shoulder bag filled with explosives. They were to try and set as many charges as they could. Keene wanted to help out the air strike by lighting up the sky for them before they even got there. There were a few foot-patrol soldiers on this side of the building, but it was still pretty much unattended. Keene nodded to the other men as they approached the building. The foot soldiers were taken out immediately with ease. Not a shot was fired. But the raucous inside seemed to be ramping up anyway. The men had just finished placing the explosives on the building's perimeter when Keene felt his stomach twist. The H-8 was firing its engines.

Keene motioned for the other three men to move back to the field. They still had five minutes before the air strike would be there, and the H-8 was readying for takeoff.

"Six, this is one. We're on the other side of the building. What's happening?"

"Ah, looks like they're loaded and ready to fly, one. What's the call?"

Keene thought for a minute. "Can you take out the plane?"

"I can shoot at it," Jenkins said. "But I don't know the aircraft well enough to know if I can disable it or even damage it. But one thing's for sure: if I take a shot, they're going to know we're here."

"Roger that," Keene said. "Hang on."

Just then Foust came on the radio. "One, this is five. Contact made with air support. ETA, two minutes."

"Roger that," Keene said smiling. Then to the others, "Okay, boys, let's light 'em up! Once the building blows, take out anything that moves."

Keene and the others stayed low in the grass and went around to the front side of the building. The air strike was coming any moment now, but the H-8 had already started to taxi out onto the runway.

"Six, can you take out the pilot?" Keene asked.

"I've got a three-quarters view," Jenkins said. "He has to turn to make the taxiway though. I can hit him then."

"Do it," Keene said. Then, "When six takes the shot, blow the building. Five, you keep that target painted. I don't care if the pilot is out or not. I want that H-8 grounded."

"Affirmative," Foust replied.

Keene watched as the huge bat-looking aircraft slowly made its final turn out onto the runway. Jenkins came on the radio. "And. . .in three, two, one. . ."

Keene watched as the stealth bomber suddenly jerked to the left and stopped. Then, slowly, it began to roll off to the side of the runway, into the grass. He lifted his wrist mic.

"Now!"

The small terminal never had a chance. The charges that Keene and his men had placed around the perimeter did more than their job. The entire place exploded in a giant fireball. Gunfire immediately followed as Chinese soldiers sprayed fire in every direction, not even knowing who or what they were shooting at. Keene and his men were being given perfect cover, as the flames from the building lit up the night sky around it, revealing the Chinese soldiers. It was, Keene thought, almost like target practice.

Every few seconds Keene would see someone else go down, like he'd been hit by an invisible linebacker. Jenkins. The sniper was now concentrating his fire on soldiers. Keene called for the men to pull back. The air strike was coming any second.

Just as he'd given the order, he heard the whistling, screaming through the sky. He turned to see the H-8, a hundred yards away, go up in a giant plume of smoke as two F-35 Lightning combat jets streaked by, five hundred feet above the deck. Foust had succeeded keeping the laser on the H-8. It was now nothing more than a smoldering heap of twisted metal.

As Keene and the men continued to advance on the terminal, Keene began to notice something. At the far end of the terminal, the only place they hadn't bothered to set charges—the angle of the building made it nonessential, though Keene was rethinking that now—a group of men were loading into three SUVs that had been parked at that end of the parking lot. With the majority of the gunfire concentrated at the other end of the building, they were going pretty much unnoticed. Except for Keene. He noticed. And though they were fifty yards away, the men were being well lit by the flames from the far end of the building. Keene stopped short and focused his stare. He knew the man at the center of the group who was being hurried into the car. And he was about to get away. No way Keene could allow that.

He keyed his wrist mic and yelled to the other men, "Kirkpatrick, see to it that you guys finish this. Foust, soon as the area's secure, you get to that nuke and disarm it. Got it?"

"Where are you going?" Ramirez shouted over the gunfire.

Keene was running to the parking lot now. The SUV had already sped out of the terminal. There were several cars parked. Keene opened the door to the first one he came to, a Ford F-150 pickup truck. He checked the console and the visor. No keys. He was about to jump out when he noticed the keys were in the ignition. He cranked the starter and spun the tires.

"Keene," Kirkpatrick said again, "we've secured the terminal."

"Good, get to that nuke and make sure it's not on a timer."

"Roger that. Where are you going?"

He fishtailed the truck off of Aviation Road. The SUV was already half a mile ahead. "To catch the man responsible for all of this."

CHAPTER 77

Kirkpatrick signaled for the others to approach slowly, as they made up the last fifty yards back to the terminal. The air strike had done more than its job. It had taken out the entire front of the terminal and anyone standing within a twenty-yard radius. The few men that had been left had either scattered or had stupidly tried to fire back at them. All of the five men Givens had assembled for Keene, however, were expert marksmen. The remaining soldiers never stood a chance. In less than a minute after the strike, the only sound that could be heard was the roaring of the flames pouring out of the building.

Kirkpatrick held them up as they got within a few yards. He wanted to make sure that there wasn't anyone hiding somewhere thinking about a last-ditch effort at being a hero. He pulled his wrist mic up and called to Foust and Jenkins. "Six, five, this is two. All clear?"

Both men gave an affirmative.

"Okay. We're holding here. I'm still not sure if anyone is holing up somewhere waiting to take a potshot at one of us. Make your way to our position."

Again, both men acknowledged.

It took two minutes for the two men to meet up with the others. Once they were there, Kirkpatrick laid out the procedure.

"Ramirez, you're the techie here. How much time do you need to disable that thing?"

Ramirez shrugged. "If it's not already set to detonate, five—maybe ten minutes."

"And if it is?" Foust asked.

Ramirez shrugged again. "Then however long is left on the timer."

"Nice," Kirkpatrick said.

The men moved quietly but quickly toward the H-8. It was less than a hundred yards to the plane. Jenkins and Foust walked backward, keeping an eye on the terminal behind them, just in case.

The H-8 was still smoldering as they approached. The entire nose of the plane had been bent sideways, leaving the rear of the plane sticking up into the air. The left side of the aircraft's wing was completely torn off, exposing the wiring and fuselage, though there was no threat from it. The strike had been a direct hit. Any fuel left in the plane would have already burned.

The good news was the underside of the plane was fully exposed. The bomb trap, though, was wedged shut. Horn quickly dug through his bag and pulled out two pry bars. He handed one to Foust, and they got to work.

The bad news was they no sooner had started to pry the trap open when they heard the screeching of tires as vehicles turned onto Aviation Road and Administration Building Road, the only two ways in or out of the airport. The Chinese weren't done. It was obvious the other soldiers from the checkpoint stations would've heard the goings-on. They just didn't know how many to expect. Keene had thought that, other than the few checkpoints, the majority of the manpower would be centered there at the airport. Keene had been wrong. Kirkpatrick raised his night-vision glasses to see at least four trucks heading their way. And two of them had .50 caliber machine guns mounted on them. Jenkins already had his rifle propped against the wreckage and was taking aim.

"Take out the gunners first," Kirkpatrick ordered.

"Roger that," Jenkins said as he squeezed the trigger.

He quickly repeated the process four more times, taking out both gunners and the drivers of the trucks. The vehicles all stopped two hundred yards out, immediately returning fire.

Just as the first rounds whizzed past them, the trap popped open. Ramirez and Foust quickly reached in and pulled the housing down. It was stuck at first, so both men used a leg against the belly of the plane for leverage. Kirkpatrick, Horn, and Jenkins continued to lay suppression fire. The men in the trucks were all scattering and moving out to flank them.

"How much time?" Kirkpatrick yelled over the gunfire.

"I'll have it loose in two minutes," Ramirez yelled back. "The air strike pretty much did all the work for us."

"Make it one," Kirkpatrick yelled back.

Kirkpatrick, Foust, and Jenkins all began to advance on the terminal again, each one heading out in a different line. Jenkins went straight south, Foust went east, and Kirkpatrick went west.

Some months earlier, Oakley, the well-regarded sunglasses company, had secured a government contract to make a military-grade, night-vision version of their famous sport line of glasses, and every member of the US military was issued two pair. Each man on the team had his on and could see the ground ahead like it was daylight. The Chinese soldiers had nothing of the sort. Once again, Kirkpatrick and the men were able to eliminate the attackers efficiently and quickly. In just over three minutes, all twenty or so Chinese soldiers had been neutralized.

Kirkpatrick took out his final target and said, "Clear!"

Jenkins and Horn came back also, "All clear!"

The three men retreated back to the mangled H-8. Ramirez and Foust had the nuke out of its housing and lying on the ground. The bomb was approximately three feet long and fourteen inches round, in the shape of a tube. It had wires coming out of it and a display screen on the front. The timer had been activated. It had twenty-six minutes on it.

Kirkpatrick reached inside his backpack and grabbed a small blanket out and laid it on the ground. "Give me a hand here," he said. The four men picked the heavy tube up and set it on the blanket. He zipped up his bag and slung it over his shoulder. "We need to move," he said. "No telling how long we have before more of them show up. Ramirez, you can start on this thing when we get in the boat." The four men each grabbed a corner of the blanket and hoisted the bomb up. In two-by-two formation, they took off running back to the bank of the Racquette.

They had just gotten back in the water when three more vehicles carrying more Chinese soldiers raced by them, heading into the airport. The five men used their paddles to push off and away from the bank. Foust started the little engine and twisted the throttle sticking out of the back of the engine. The inflatable quickly sped away.

Ramirez went to work immediately on the bomb casing. He traded his night-vision Oakleys for a headlamp and handed two flashlights to Foust and Jenkins. The timer read fourteen minutes.

"How long, once you get it opened?" Foust asked.

"Only a minute or two," he said, continuing to work. "But I'll need to be still. Can't do it on this water."

"We're almost there," Kirkpatrick answered.

Another hundred yards and the small inflatable came to rest on the bank again. Again the four men grabbed the blanket and hoisted the bomb. They made their way out of the boat and up the bank to County Road 40, where they had left the truck.

Ramirez tossed the keys to Foust, who popped the tailgate of the big SUV so the men could set the bomb inside. Kirkpatrick ordered the others to stand around the truck with him, watching for anything approaching. For the most part the county road was deserted anyway, but they couldn't take any chances. Particularly now. The display read ten minutes.

"Got it," Ramirez said, lifting the main faceplate. "Now I just need to—uh. . .this isn't good."

"What?" everyone said in unison.

"Anyone speak or read Chinese?"

"C'mon!" Kirkpatrick yelled between clenched teeth. "Are you kidding me?"

"No, I'm not," Ramirez said seriously.

Kirkpatrick reached inside the vehicle and grabbed one of the satphones. The number had already been programmed in, in case something happened to Keene and they needed to call in. He hit the call button and waited.

"This is Jennings."

"Director Jennings, this is Lieutenant Kirkpatrick."

"Where's Jon Keene?" Jennings asked with a worried tone.

"I have no idea, sir," Kirkpatrick answered. "But we have a bigger problem right now!"

CHAPTER 78

Taylor was forty thousand feet in the air on a C-32 transport with two hundred American soldiers when the news came in from Washington. The Royal Navy had unexpectedly come to the rescue of the United States, via the help of one Bozwell Hamilton and retired Admiral Eli Craig. Immediately the men had begun to whoop and holler, raising fists in the air and shouting cheers. Taylor had immediately bowed her head and thanked God.

As they approached Andrews, she looked out the small window to see two fighter jets off to the right of the plane. They were being escorted in, one of the marines told her. She didn't know if that made her feel safer or more like a target.

Once they landed, Taylor was taken to a car, where she was told she would be transported to the bunker where Director Jennings and the command center were. Jennings had ordered that she be brought there the moment she landed. When she got in the car, she was once again surprised. Sitting beside her and in front of her were two three-star generals. They introduced themselves and shook her hand. One of them even gave her a friendly jab in the shoulder and said, "Good work, Agent Taylor!" obviously aware of the details of her last twenty-four hours. She said thanks, but she really didn't feel like she'd done anything special. Marianne had gotten herself killed, and Alexandra Sokolov had died from her injuries in the crash. She guessed she still had a hand in bringing the two women to justice, if you could call it that. Even though they were dead, she still felt sorry for them, wondering if somehow in the last seconds of their lives they had reconciled with God. But she doubted it. And that's what really broke her heart.

More news came in over the radio as the car approached the bunker. The Chinese were being pushed back. The US forces and their British counterparts had turned the tables. The Chinese were on the run.

The guard at the base checked them in as the car pulled forward and into the narrow tunnel in the mountainside. Inside, they were led out of the vehicle and into the elevator, which took them nearly twenty stories down. Once outside the elevator, a second set of checkpoints were there. They went through the process again and finally were escorted into the secure facility. She waited for the Secret Service agent to swipe his card and for the little LED light to turn green. It did, and he opened the door without a word.

The room was eerily quiet. Jennings was standing with his back to her holding a sat-phone. The other men turned to look at her as she walked in but otherwise paid her no mind.

"What's going on?" she asked, worried.

Jennings turned to see her and held up a finger.

"Keene's team is trying to disable a Chinese nuke. It's set to go off in four minutes," Sykes said. The look on his face told the rest of the story.

"Where is it?" Taylor asked.

"Upstate New York. Keene and his men went there to stop them from flying it into DC."

Her heart immediately sank. Jon was in upstate New York with a nuclear bomb? "What's the problem?" Taylor asked. "Aren't they trained for this kind of thing?"

"Keene is," Sykes said, "but he's not there."

Now she was worried and confused. "What do you mean? I thought you just said—"

"I don't know what's going on up there right now," Sykes cut her off. "I have no idea where Keene is. All I know is that his team is there, trying to stop the thing from going off and taking out half of upstate New York, Ottawa, and Montreal."

Megan was listening, but she was already pulling her laptop out of her bag. "Someone give me the number of that sat-phone!" she said. Jennings and everyone else turned to look at her. *"Now!"*

Jennings quickly rattled off the number of the phone to her. Within seconds she was tapped into the feed of the call. "Who am I speaking with?"

"This is Lieutenant Kirkpatrick, ma'am."

"That phone got a camera on it, Lieutenant?"

"Yes, ma'am."

"Turn it on. Now."

Megan watched her laptop screen as Kirkpatrick fidgeted with the phone.

"We're down to two minutes and forty seconds here," Kirkpatrick said.

The image came up on her screen. "Okay, what are you looking at? Show me. And put me on speaker."

Kirkpatrick did and tilted the phone down toward the bomb. Quickly, she took a screen shot of what Kirkpatrick and the men were looking at. "Okay, first thing you've got to do is remove the neutron trigger."

"Ma'am, this is Captain Ramirez. I'm a bomb technician. I can disarm the device. The problem is I can't read the symbols to make sure they haven't wired something weird."

Taylor had already assumed this. It was the reason she had taken the screen shot. "I'm already running it through a software program," she said. She clicked a couple buttons and said, "There. I've just sent it back to your phone, Captain. It should be on your screen."

"Got it!" Ramirez said.

Everyone sat motionless and silent for the next minute. According to Kirkpatrick, they had less than two minutes to get the nuke disarmed. Everyone watched the clock on the wall as the second hand ticked down. One minute and thirty-two seconds later Ramirez came back on the line.

"All good! Package is secure."

Everyone in the command center clapped and cheered. Jennings walked over to Taylor and gave her a big kiss on the forehead.

"Taylor, you are possibly the second best asset I've ever had."

She smiled. "Yeah, who's the first?"

Jennings's smile faded as he let out a sigh. "Jon Keene."

"Where is he?"

"Don't know. Haven't had time to ask." He turned from her and picked up the phone again. "Lieutenant, you still there?"

"Yes, sir."

Taylor pointed back to her laptop. "I've got him here. You don't have to use that thing," she said pointing at the sat-phone.

Jennings hit the button and put it on the table. "Where's Jon Keene?"

"Don't know, sir. Once we secured the airstrip, he took off. Said he saw someone he needed to chase after."

"Who?"

"No idea, sir. He didn't say. He just put me in charge and took out of there."

Sykes whispered something in his ear. Jennings stepped back and looked at him with disdain. "He's my best man, Bob. And he's the reason why everything we've done tonight has been successful. No way!"

Taylor stood up and spun Jennings around to face her. "What? What's going on?"

"It's going to be all right. Jon can take care of himself."

"What are you talking about?" Her pulse began to quicken again.

Jennings gently grabbed her by the arm and led her aside. "Listen, Jon is *the* best operative this agency has ever seen. I don't know who he's chasing, but if he left those men to go do it, then I have to believe the target was worth it. But we have to get that nuke back here under our supervision. We can't just let it sit there."

Just as he was finishing, she heard Sykes speaking into the laptop's microphone. "Okay, gentlemen. You are to proceed back here immediately. Under no circumstances does that device leave your immediate sight. Do you understand?"

"What about General Keene?" Kirkpatrick answered.

"Keene is on assignment. Your orders are to report back here with that device. Understood?"

"Understood."

Megan heard the click, signaling that the connection had been severed. "What does he mean? On assignment?"

"Military's first code of conduct," Jennings answered. "Never leave a man behind."

"I don't understand."

"Sykes just told them, in so many words, that there was more to the assignment than they were aware of. That Jon is still operating. Otherwise, they would've gone looking for him."

"Is there?" she asked, agitated. "Is there more?"

"Not that I'm aware of," Jennings said apologetically.

"Then where is he? Why did Jon leave his men and go chasing after someone?"

"I have no idea."

CHAPTER 79

Keene had been following the three SUVs now for almost an hour. The cover of night had kept him from being seen. The F-150 was solid black, and with a cloudy night providing no light from the moon or stars, the truck was the perfect vehicle to tail his prey. He had heard about the new night-vision Oakleys that the military boys had been using for the last six months but had never seen or used them until tonight. *Pretty impressive*, he thought. He'd been driving for an hour now with no headlights in the pitch dark, and he could see as well as if it were broad daylight.

He had no idea what road they were on or where it was leading, but he knew it was out in the middle of nowhere. He hadn't seen another car since they left the airfield. He was sure, though, wherever it was they were going, it was going to be someplace secluded. The man he was following would take extra care not to be found.

He'd crossed the man's path once before. At the time, the man was just a Ministry of State Security agent—China's security and intelligence agency—though it was possible he had been connected to the PLA at the same time. China often used high-ranking military officials in their intelligence agency. The agents were pulling double duty, so to speak. Regardless, the man was military now.

Finally the three SUVs began to slow down. Keene knew only that they had been driving west then north. And though they hadn't crossed any kind of border station, that meant they were now in Canada. Keene let off the gas and watched up ahead as they turned down another road. He couldn't see much because the road was blocked by a hillside. He crept slowly to the turnoff. The three SUVs were just ahead, but there were brake lights. They were coming to a stop. Keene pulled the truck over to the side of the road and got out. He checked his watch. The sun would be up shortly. Whatever it was he was going to do, he needed to do it fast.

He checked his ammo and took off walking down the dirt road. After a hundred yards or so, he came around a small bend in the road and saw a house—a cabin, perhaps—nestled up against the hillside in a clearing beyond the tree line. It was probably used for hunting or just a weekend escape, he thought. It was the kind of place you'd bring your family to get away. From everything. Including civilization.

He noted four armed guards outside the house. Two on the porch and two standing fifty feet in front of the house, facing the road he was currently walking down. The tree line was about to give way to the clearing. He decided to hole up there for a few minutes and watch.

After five minutes, another two men came around from the back of the house, both armed. That brought the count to six. And there was no way to tell how many were inside. But a thin, pinkish-orange line began to crease the horizon. He was going to have to move quicker than this if he was going to get in there. He quietly moved down the tree line to the far end of the house. From there, he had a profile view of the property. After assessing the situation for a moment, he decided it would be better to take out the guards in the back first. The others would come around back eventually, looking for them.

He waited until the two guards from the rear went back around to the front. *Must be a regular patrol schedule*, he thought. This was the third time they'd done it since he had been watching. As soon as they were gone, he shot out from the trees and made his way to the back of the house. He checked his weapon and made sure the sound suppressor was in place. The first guard came around the side of the house. Keene let him get three steps past the edge of the house before he fired. He turned around just in time to see the other one come. Both men were dropped before they knew what hit them. He grabbed the two men's bodies and dragged them over to the center of the property.

Given the timing of the rotation, the two guards he'd just taken out should've gone back around front by now. That meant that the two from the front were probably going to be coming around the back any second now looking for them. He was right. He'd no sooner finished the thought when the first guy came around. Keene took him just as he made the corner. The other one came within moments of the first one.

With all four house guards down, Keene made his way slowly back around to the front. The two men stationed away from the house were still there, unaware their counterparts had run into trouble. Funnily enough, their job was to make sure that people like him never got to the house. *Oh well*, he thought. *That's what you get for hiring two-bit hacks.* He raised his MP5 and sent off four quick shots, two each to the guards fifty feet away, with their backs to him. The men dropped right where they stood. He stood still, holding his position for a good two minutes, just to make sure no one else was going to come running out of the house for him.

When no one came, he made his way silently up and onto the porch. He tried the knob. Unlocked. He turned it slowly and pushed the thing open. Nothing.

Inside, the door opened up into a spacious living area. A hallway led to the back, and a stairway led upstairs. He didn't see anything so he decided to go upstairs and clear that area first.

At the top of the stairs, there was a small landing area that fed into another hallway with doors lining it. Bedrooms, if Keene had to guess. He checked each one but found nothing. He had the entire upstairs cleared in two minutes.

Back downstairs, he moved down the hallway from the front door. A small kitchen sat off to the right and another room off to the left. Sitting there, at a desk, with his arms folded on top was the man he had come to find. He raised his weapon and stepped into the room.

"Mr. Jon Keene," the man said. "I wish I could say it is good to see you again."

"You're going to need some more guards, Chin," Keene said.

"That's General Chin," the man corrected him.

"Yeah, so I've heard. Since we're playing semantics, it's *General* Keene." He motioned with the barrel of his gun. "C'mon. Let's go. Get up. Slowly. And keep your hands where I can see them."

"Once again, you have been a pain in my side," Chin said.

"Yeah, sorry to rain on your parade." He pointed again. "C'mon. Let's go."

"I assume you have neutralized my nuclear device."

Keene was starting to get agitated. Was he just going to have to shoot the man right here? "Yes, it's been neutralized."

"Pretty smart, you figuring out where we were."

"It wasn't that hard, Chin. You guys are pretty predictable. Now, let's go. Or I'm going to shoot you right here."

"As opposed to. . . ?"

"As opposed to taking you back to DC and putting you on trial for waging war on my country," Keene spat.

"Yes, that probably is what your people would like to do. Isn't it?"

This time, Chin pushed back his chair and stood up.

"But you see, Mr. Keene, this isn't over. You may have pushed my men back. For now. But do you not understand that we already occupy two-thirds of your nation? And by this time tomorrow, I will have over one million soldiers in your country. It's only a matter of time before we take the rest."

One million soldiers? How was that possible?

As if reading his mind, Chin continued. "Your neighbor to the south, Mexico, has been generous in helping us bring our men across. While you and your friends in Washington have been busy trying to keep us out of Albany and the south, I've been bringing in troops nonstop for two days."

The clock in Keene's head was ticking. And the alarm was about to sound. This was taking too long. He needed to get Chin out of there now.

"You see, Mr. Keene, you have suggested two options here. One, you kill me. Two, I come with you to Washington, and they eventually kill me. I think I'd rather go with option three. You see, I don't get killed in option three," he said smiling.

And there it was. The alarm was raging full force inside his head. He felt the man's presence first. He hadn't heard him coming up behind him. And he should've known better.

He turned, just in time to see the club come at him. It hit him square in the collarbone. Right where the Russian had shot him. White-hot pain shot through his arm and up into the back of his neck as he dropped the MP5 and went to his knees. He tried to catch himself, but it was no use. The second blow was to the back of his head.

He fell face forward and slammed on the hard wooden floor. He heard Chin laughing as his eyes rolled back into his head and the blackness took him.

CHAPTER 80

Nine Weeks Later

Taylor and Boz sat with Director Jennings watching the video again for the fourth time in the last hour. She had used every bit of her knowledge and technology available to determine where it had been shot. But there was just no way to know. Nothing had turned up.

She wiped her eyes and said, "I'm sorry, guys. I've been at it nonstop for two days now. There's just nothing there. I can't tell you where it was filmed. And even if I could, the deadline is in four hours."

Boz placed a hand on her shoulder. "It's okay, Megan. We know you've done all you can do. At least we know he's alive. We'll find him. I promise."

Jennings stood up. "I'm going to go get some coffee. Anyone want some?"

"I'll come with you," Boz said. "Need to stretch my legs anyway. Megan, you want anything?"

She shook her head and wiped away another tear. She wasn't willing to let it go. She just couldn't. As the two men left the room, she hit PLAY and watched again, hoping to see something, anything, that would help them.

The camera came into focus on an open field slightly smaller than a football field. The entire perimeter had been wrapped in electric razor wire, and there were armed guards surrounding it. A makeshift prison. Inside the wired perimeter were close to five hundred men, all lined up, all sitting with their hands on top of their heads, fingers interlocked. And sitting at the front of the group was Jon Keene. He looked beaten nearly half to death and had been stripped down to nothing but his boxer shorts—no doubt to show the severity of his wounds.

The scene abruptly changed to an office where General Chin sat, his hands folded across a desk. He cleared his throat and began to speak.

"President Walker, it has been a little over two months now since our engagement. You and your leaders in Washington have shown great resolve these past days. However, we, the People's Republic of China, have decided that we have successfully completed our mission. We have what

303

we came here for. Our industrial sector has already begun setting up drilling and extraction factories.

"Therefore, we have decided not to continue our advancement against the rest of what's left of your country. However, there are pockets of individuals, such as the ones you have witnessed. We cannot and will not tolerate this. The People's Republic of China has conquered this land west of your Appalachian Mountains. We will not stand for insubordination. It is now sovereign Chinese soil and should be treated as such. But we are not monsters either. And because of that we have decided to open our communications and allow you to speak to those of your country who either chose not to seek sanctuary in the east or just weren't able to. You will tell them to lay down their arms. You will tell them this territory is now occupied by the People's Republic of China. And you will tell them they will stop this rebellion if they wish to live. Otherwise we will be forced to gather the insurgents and demonstrate our sincerity, as we will now demonstrate for you."

The camera changed feeds again back to the field. A small gate opened up and four guards entered the field. They grabbed four men sitting next to Keene and brought them forward, so that they were standing right in front of the camera. One of the guards spoke something in Chinese, and then all four fired, shooting the four men in the backs of their heads. Screams from the other men rose up. Several even stood to rush the gate but to no avail. Keene tried to put his hands up in an effort to stop the men, but he appeared to be so weak from his injuries, he couldn't stop them. Another command was given from one of the guards, and the men who had stood up were also shot. The camera feed changed back to General Chin.

"So you see, Mr. President, we are very serious in our resolve. We will not tolerate any resistance.

"You *will* speak to your people instructing them to follow our orders. If you do not, we will immediately begin hunting down and eliminating these threats. The first and foremost of these will be Agent—or should I say General—Jon Keene, whom you saw in the compound. We will not hesitate to level entire cities if we need to, in order to spread our message. You have forty-eight hours to decide whether you will comply. Instructions on delivering this message will be made available to you at this time."

The feed changed once again, and another man appeared. He introduced himself as Yuan Li, the minister of communications for the People's Republic of China. The video lasted another three minutes as Li gave instructions as to how President Walker was to make his announcement to the American people.

Boz and Jennings returned as the video was coming to a close. Both men sat down and stared at the screen.

"Anything?" Boz asked.

"No," Taylor said, still trying to control her emotions. "I've watched it over and over again. And every time those men get shot—" Her breath hitched. "I. . .I just don't know. I can't find anything."

"It's okay, Taylor. No one expects you to," Jennings said.

Taylor grabbed a tissue from the small box sitting on the desk. "So President Walker is going to go through with it?"

"He doesn't have a choice," Jennings said.

"What about the rest of the country?" Boz asked.

"We find a way to move forward," Jennings said. He looked at his watch and said, "C'mon. Walker wants us upstairs for a meeting before his speech."

"Us? What for?" Taylor asked.

"Don't know," Jennings said. "He didn't say. Just that he wanted you two there."

Taylor grabbed her stuff and stood to leave. She thought about Jon again. She hoped that he was okay. She prayed that he would just survive. That somehow, he would get through this, until they could find him and bring him home. She followed Boz and Jennings to the elevator.

CHAPTER 81

The secure bunker had four levels underground. The first two were for general operations, the third was for the command center and a medical wing. The fourth was for housing with one hundred rooms to be used as living quarters and one room reserved for the president.

Taylor stood behind Jennings as he nodded to the Secret Service agent before entering the room. The agent waved them on, and Jennings opened the door. President Walker stood and greeted them.

"Thank you all for coming," he said. He motioned for them to have a seat.

"What can we do for you, Mr. President?" Megan asked.

President Walker pursed his lips and rubbed his jaw. "You know, not a lot of people think I'm qualified to do this job."

Taylor looked to see Boz and Jennings giving him the same look she was. The one that said, *Yeah, no kidding.*

"Doesn't matter what they think," Jennings said. "You're the guy."

"I may not be as qualified as Calvin, but I'm not an idiot," Walker said.

Jennings started to say something, but Walker cut him off.

"I'm also not so arrogant to ignore the fact that you all tried to warn me that something like this could happen. But there's no sense in us dwelling on the past. We have to worry about the future."

"Yes, sir," all three of them said.

"So I want you to tell me about this man who calls himself the Prophet. Is all of this connected to him?"

Taylor looked to Jennings, who looked over at Boz.

"We believe so, sir," Taylor said.

"How?"

Megan and Boz recounted the entire event. From the initial contact that had been made with President Grant, all the way to where they currently sat in his bunker residence.

Walker looked on steadily as they finished. Finally he said, "So what now?"

"No one knows," Boz said. "The Prophet said he'd find us when the time was right."

"What does that mean?" Walker asked.

"We don't know," Jennings said, echoing Boz's thoughts.

"But in the meantime," Megan said, "it would be wise of you to tell the people."

Walker sat back and folded his arms. "You want me to tell the people of this country that God did this to us?"

"The Chinese did this to us, Mr. President," Boz said sternly. "God allowed it. Big difference."

"Listen," Taylor interrupted. "We're not exactly on easy street here, President Walker. I don't know what God's plan is for us, going forward. But I can promise you, it would go a long way to help us if you told everyone that we need to humble ourselves before Him and ask Him for His guidance in moving forward."

"In the meantime," Jennings said, "Boz and Megan are continuing to look for this Prophet."

President Walker stood up, signaling that the meeting was over. "I have a speech to give in a little while. I better get ready. Thank you all for coming up here."

Taylor followed Jennings and Boz to the elevators.

★

President Walker closed the door behind his guests and went back to the sitting area. He reached behind the pillow on the couch and pulled out the book again. The last few days had been extremely hard for him. He had been struggling between resigning and allowing the Speaker of the House to assume the presidency or just toughing it out. He hadn't made his decision until five minutes ago, listening to Jennings and his two agents.

Just yesterday he had gone downstairs to sit by Calvin's bed. He and Calvin had been longtime friends. But their relationship had been strained the last few years. They seemed to be as different as oil and water. But Walker still, and always had, respected the man. Calvin was a great leader and a man of his word. He was respected among the American people and foreign dignitaries. Well, except for the Chinese, obviously.

He had been sitting by the bed, just thinking, when Tess, President Grant's wife, had come into the room. She had been brought here along with President Grant when they first moved everyone. Her residency in the bunker was just a few doors down from his. She came over to him and sat down beside him. They had talked for a little while. She had asked about his family and how he was coping with everything going on. She had been so sweet. Here she was, battling cancer; her husband lay unconscious from a gunshot wound; and she was asking him how *he* was doing? He had been completely taken aback. And then she reached into the drawer beside Grant's bed and pulled out his Bible and gave it to him.

"Calvin has a lot of highlighted passages in there," she said. "Perhaps you may want to look at some of them. I know whenever he has gone through something that has weighed on him, this has brought him through it. Maybe you'll find it useful."

He had taken the Bible, not really knowing what to say. He tried to find the words when she spoke again.

"But you can't keep it," she said, smiling. "Calvin's going to need that back when he wakes up."

"Yes, ma'am," was all he could muster. He hadn't known why, but the whole thing had overwhelmed him at the time. And now here he was, thumbing through the pages again.

He had been reading all night and hadn't stopped until Jennings and the others had come to see him. And even though he had grown up going to church, it had never really made any sense to him. It was just something that you did on Sunday. Go to church, then go to lunch afterward, then go home and watch whatever game was on the television until everyone fell asleep on the couch or their favorite chair. But this was different. He'd never spent time reading a Bible. He hadn't even known where to start, but Calvin had lots of notes in the margins and tons of passages highlighted. He hadn't realized how long he had been sitting there reading until he felt his eyes burning and had looked at the clock. And for the first time, he had begun to understand some of the things that that preacher had been talking about all those years.

He checked his watch again. He had fifteen minutes to get downstairs. The speech was not something he was looking forward to, but it was necessary. He couldn't allow the Chinese to just openly kill American citizens. Not if, by doing what they asked, he could spare them. He closed the Bible and grabbed his suit coat.

Downstairs the command center had been set up. Minister Li's instructions were clear and simple. The Chinese had provided a satellite link for them to connect to. The signal was also connected to the satellite feed that would broadcast the speech to the citizens in the East.

He checked his notes and was led to the podium, where one of the guys wired him with the mic. He looked into the camera and waited for the red light. When it flashed on, he began.

"Ladies and gentlemen, it is with a heavy heart I address you today. Our country has suffered a great blow. For those of you who have yet to find your way to the eastern states, please hear me. General Chin and the People's Republic of China have taken control of everything west of the Appalachian Mountains. They have claimed the entire territory as sovereign Chinese soil. As of now, we have no choice but to concede this defeat.

"I have spoken with General Chin. He has assured me that he wants no more violence. Nor do we. But I must tell you that those of you who continue to resist this occupation with violence and insurgence are inciting more violence. The Chinese do not wish to harm you. However, if you continue on this path, they have made it clear that they will continue to destroy the great cities of the Midwest and those who stand in their way, until you stop. Many more innocent people will die as a result of your actions. Please, please, stop. If you can somehow make your way to the eastern states, do so. We will welcome you in safely. But if you choose to stay, you must obey them.

"Now, I want everyone to listen to me. This country has been a great nation and a friend to many others for a long time. But recently we have become an enemy to ourselves. We've allowed ourselves over the years to become something that our forefathers never intended us to become. The day President Grant was shot, he was going to speak to us all about this. At the time, I didn't see it. But I do now. And I would like you all to hear what I believe he was going to say. You see, this country was founded upon a belief system. That belief system was that all of us were endowed with certain rights. And those rights were given to us by God. And our forefathers believed that with every ounce of their beings.

"Over the years, we have, much like the Israelites from the Old Testament often did, allowed ourselves to move away from God, putting our faith and trust in many things. And in doing so, we have abandoned the very principles that once made America great. And that is our fear and reverence for God."

The light on the camera flickered.

"Excuse me," President Walker said into the camera. He looked to the technician. "Is everything okay?"

"The Chinese have cut the feed to their satellite," the technician said. "But you're still live on ours."

He nodded and continued. "Listen, friends. I have no idea what lies ahead for us as a nation right now. But I can tell you this: President Grant knew that we were headed for troubled waters. To some degree, I even think he saw this coming. And he was going to warn us. Well, it's too late for a warning now. The damage has been done. But it is not too late for hope. I do not believe that God has brought us here just to leave us in this condition. But I've also recently learned that each time that the Israelites allowed themselves to be led astray, they humbled themselves before God, and He restored them. Now I'm not saying that if we do that, God will indeed restore our nation to what she once was. But I do know that if we don't, He will not.

"I find it ironic that—on our own Independence Day—we were shown how much we actually needed to be dependent. I also find it ironic that it was in this very month, September, so many years ago, when the pilgrims landed on a strange new land that would become our nation. A nation birthed out of thirteen colonies founded on Christian principles and values. And now here we are. After generations of prominence and greatness. Fallen. And now, having come through the devastation, after getting our legs back under us, we find ourselves once again back in the thirteen where we started. It's as if God is showing us the contrast from what we once were, to what we have become.

"Perhaps this is His way of taking us back, to remind us. To remind us of how we came to be. Back when we fled tyranny because we wanted to worship Him, not remove Him from every aspect of our lives. . .from our government. Friends, we have a choice to make today. Will we return to what made us great? Or will we continue down the road that has left us where we sit now?

"Let us be reminded today of how He has brought us all here, to this place, in this time. And let us humble ourselves before Him, in hopes that He may grant us a great nation once again. God bless you all, and may God bless, once again, the United States of America."

EPILOGUE

Keene could barely keep his head up as the two guards dragged him back to his cell. He had been with the interrogators again. It was the fourth time this week. He didn't know how much more his body could take. This had been going on for two months now. He didn't even know what the point was. They didn't want information from him. That was obvious. All they ever did was beat him and scream at him. It really was just plain old torture. No reason, other than to make him suffer.

It was all because of Chin. During the time that Chin was with the MSS, Keene had stumbled across him. Chin and his goons had taken hostage a US ambassador in South Korea and were trying to get military information out of him. Keene and his team had been sent in to retrieve the ambassador. Though they had secured the ambassador and taken out all of Chin's men, Chin had gotten away. Keene had never forgotten the man. And now Keene was his prisoner.

The guards opened the door to his cell and threw him in. He landed on his side on the hard concrete. A fresh batch of blood rose up from his stomach as he spat it out. He still didn't know where it came from. As much as they had beaten him these last few weeks, he couldn't believe he still had any blood left to bleed. And just when he thought he'd never see the outside of these walls again, Chin had him brought upstairs to a field two days ago, where there were at least five hundred other men being held captive. They had sat him down in front of all of the other men. And then they did the unthinkable. They picked four of them and executed them. He knew right then that that wouldn't be all. He had tried to stop the other men from getting up, but he was just too weak. And so he watched Chin's men shoot them, too.

He had no idea what time it was anymore. His internal clock had stopped working three days ago. He just didn't have the strength or the energy to fight back. He told them, each time when they started the beatings, that they wouldn't break him. But that was a lie. He had broken about the same time his internal clock stopped working. He was just so beaten up and exhausted that he didn't have the energy to cry out or beg them to stop.

He assumed it was getting onto nighttime because he felt the dampness begin to set in on the floor. He tried to think back to even just a few weeks ago, when he and Megan and Boz were all together, trying to figure out what this whole thing about the Prophet was about. He wished he could see them. He wished he could tell Boz that he'd remembered everything that Boz had said to him. That what Boz said had made him think.

Suddenly all of the emotions that he'd been trying to hold back finally came to the surface. He pulled himself into a ball and began to rock back and forth. He felt the first tear run down his cheek since losing his wife. And then another. And then it was as if everything inside of him let loose. He wrapped his arms around his cold, mostly naked body and began to weep.

He stayed like that for at least five minutes before he was able to get control of himself. Finally he wiped his eyes and found the strength to sit up onto his knees. He placed his elbows on the thin mattress that they had given him to sleep on and folded his hands.

"God," he said, "I don't know what You want from me. And I know I've been angry with You for many things, and I'm sorry. I had no right to be angry with You. I heard everything Boz said. And I'm trying to believe it. I'm so sorry I've pushed You away. Please forgive me. I'm not asking You to get me out of here. But I can't take them beating me like this anymore. I have nothing left to give. Please, make it stop. Please just let me die. Please, Jesus, forgive me for my sins and let me come home to You. Just make it stop."

He felt his arms give out as his head fell to the mattress. He closed his eyes and drifted off.

They usually let him sleep for four or five hours. Just long enough for him to regain some strength. But this was too early. He couldn't have been asleep for more than an hour. But even though he couldn't see the gate, because of his swollen eyes, he could hear it. And it was opening. They were coming for him again.

He felt the hand on his shoulder. But it was different this time. The touch was gentle. Not forceful. He raised his head to try and make out the figure that was standing before him.

"Mr. Keene!" the man whispered.

"Who are you?" he said in a cracked voice.

312

"Here, drink this," the man said, handing him a bottle of water.

He took it slowly at first then began to let it flow freely over his mouth. It was the first real drink of water he'd had in days. Only sips had been allowed before. He poured some over his eyes to wash away some of the dried, crusted blood.

"Hurry," the man said. "We don't have much time."

Keene still couldn't make him out, though he looked somewhat familiar. "Who are you?" he said again.

"God has heard your prayer," he said. "I've come to take you home."

The man put his arm under his shoulder and lifted him to his feet.

"Hurry," he said again. "We haven't been given much time to get out of here. And you have much to do."

"Wait," Keene said. He tried to look at him. "I know you. How did you get in here?"

The Prophet smiled. "I told you I'd find you when the time was right."

ROBBIE CHEUVRONT is the worship/associate pastor and an elder of The Journey Church in Lebanon, Tennessee, and cofounder of C&R Ministries with Erik Reed. He is also a songwriter and formerly toured with BNA recording artists, Lonestar. Robbie is married to Tiffany and has two children, Cason and Hadyn, and is currently pursuing a theology degree.

ERIK REED is the lead pastor and an elder of The Journey Church in Lebanon, Tennessee. He graduated from Western Kentucky University with a BA in Religious Studies. He also graduated with his MDiv from Southern Seminary. Erik is married to Katrina, with two children, Kaleb and Kaleigh.

SHAWN ALLEN is the teaching pastor of the Hartsville campus and an elder of The Journey Church. He is married and has two dogs, Charlie and Pepper. Shawn is a graduate of Bethel University and is currently enrolled at Southern Seminary.

Robbie Would Like to Thank:

First and foremost, my heavenly Father. God, you are so gracious to me. I have so much to be thankful for. Your grace and Your mercy toward me are undeserved, and I am so humbled before You. You have blessed me beyond words, and I praise You for who You are. You are my God and King. I love You and serve You with all that I am.

Next, I would like to thank my incredible wife, Tiffany. Every day with you shows me just how much God has blessed me. I thank Him that He would choose you for me. I would be lost without you. I love you with all my heart. You are an amazing woman, mother, and wife. I do not know what I did to deserve you, but I'm never looking back. I cherish you with all that I am.

To my children, Cason and Hadyn: Daddy loves you! You two make me laugh when the days are long and stressful. I pray that you would live your lives for Christ and never stray from His side. He is all you will ever need. Run to Him for EVERYTHING. I love you!

Erik Would Like to Thank:

There are so many people to thank for the love, patience, friendship, and joy they bring into my life. However, I do want to especially highlight one person in this book who has made a lasting impact on me. That is my grandmother, Dorothy Reed. My grandmother and her late husband, Earnest Reed (my grandfather), grew up in an era when America faced some enormous challenges. They experienced the Great Depression and WWII. They saw an America that had no fear of discussing God and even recognized its deep need for Him. But they also witnessed the decline and near disappearance of this. Yet in spite of the culture's shift and change, they remained steadfast. My grandfather passed away when I was five years old, and I never got to know him that well. But my grandmother tells us about him, still. She loves Jesus and has taught her children and grandchildren what it looks like to love Jesus, too. My thank-you is to her for her patience, love, and unwavering commitment to pray for her family, lead by example, and live to make much of Jesus Christ. I love you Gan-Gan.

Robbie, Erik, and Shawn Would Like to Thank:

Our publisher, Barbour Books: You guys are incredible. That you would take a chance on some unknown goofballs like us is beyond anything we could have imagined. Thank you for being patient with us these last couple years, as we have tried to learn the ins and outs of your world. Telling a story is easy. What you all do is. . .well, let's just say we're glad we have you! Thank you for everything you all do.

To Jamie Chavez, our editor: Jamie, you are a disturbingly talented woman! Your work speaks for itself. We are honored to have worked with you and hope to do so again in the future. We love your straightforwardness. We love that you see any project that you work on as your own. Thank you for everything.

To our church: Journey Church, we love you all so much. You all make being in ministry so much fun. You are such an unselfish group of people. You serve tirelessly to see the Kingdom moved forward. God has blessed us to have you as our church. We are humbled to be in covenant with you as your pastors. Let us always stay focused on Christ, moving forward with the Gospel and forward as a church.

There is a long list of people that help us do everything that we do. Our church, our families, and our lives would not be what they are without you all. Thank you, Kendria Spicer, our admin assistant at The Journey. Thank you to our fellow Elders; it is a blessing to serve along side such Godly men. Finally, to all our Journey volunteers and ministry leaders, and our friends: Thank you all for being in our lives. We thank God for you every day. We love you all!

If you enjoyed **The 13: Fall**,
be sure to read the gripping follow-up novel—**The 13: Stand**.

Coming Fall 2013

Here's a sneak peak. . .

The Room was just like any other room: adequately furnished, old hardwood floors
that had scuff marks on them from all the years of tables and chairs being scooted
across their surfaces, and a few unassuming paintings hanging slightly crooked on
each wall in order to give the room a more. . .homey feel. An antique desk stood
against one wall with an Aresline Xten chair—the world's most expensive office
chair. Opposite the desk stood two other chairs—for guests—which could have
been bought from Walmart. The old man didn't know. Nor did he care. His second wife had bought them. He would never think of sitting his old frame down in
anything but the Aresline. *The Room,* as it was called, was the perfect place for this
meeting. And for one reason. One that only those who had been there were aware
of. Its location. The old man checked once more to make sure he had everything
he needed and then went back up the stairs to the main house.

The main house sat just off Durant Road, a few miles out of downtown;
an old, fully restored Civil War farmhouse sitting back, nestled in the tall pines.
Unless someone knew exactly where it was, they would probably just miss the
little, narrow dirt road that led the three quarters of a mile through the wooded
area leading to the house. The old man had bought the house twenty-five years
earlier for his third wife. She had thought it cute and a good place for her daughter to stay as she finished nursing school. He hadn't cared much for the house
itself, but the grounds behind it were perfect for the project he had been planning. And though the project was going to cost close to a quarter of a billion
dollars, he didn't care. He had the money. Old money. The kind that came at the
expense of hundreds of thousands of unsuspecting Americans. Tobacco.

The old man had since divorced his third wife. And his fourth. His current
wife—wife number five—had extended family all over the country. So now the
house was used for visiting friends and family. But, for the most part, it remained
empty. And that was a good thing. Because it allowed the old man to conduct his
more *sketchy* business away from inquiring minds. Because behind the house, buried fifty meters below the surface, was *The Room.* Constructed of three-foot-thick,
steel-reinforced concrete walls, *The Room* was the northern wing of an eighteen-
hundred-square-foot, state-of-the-art survival shelter, stocked with provisions for
up to ten people to live on for as long as five years and complete with its own water
and air filtration system. All constructed and designed by one Gavin Pemberton III.

Pemberton—or the old man, as he was called by his friends—had offered
his place for tonight's meeting. An offer that was readily accepted by all parties
involved. *One couldn't be too careful these days,* he thought. No one ever knew
whether the Chinese were going to come over the mountains at any second, or if
that imbecile, Walker, was going to negotiate more land over to those communists.

Sure, Walker had promised that he was going to see to it that they did everything they could to ensure the United States' return to greatness. The only problem was, the idiot was trying to change everything great about what was left of the country.

Pemberton saw the headlights from the cars bounce off the trees, swinging back and forth as the small dirt road curved and twisted, as he kicked back and forth in the old, wooden rocking chair on the wraparound porch. Moments later, the cars stopped in front of the old, yellow farmhouse and emptied their lone passengers. The cars then left. And without a word, the old man stood up and motioned for the two men to follow him around the side of the house to the backyard.

A small toolshed-looking structure sat at the edge of the yard, leaning against the row of trees. No one would ever guess that underneath the almost thirty-foot-tall pines sat one of the most secure facilities on earth. The old man silently stepped inside and found the hidden keypad behind the workbench. He punched in the numbers and stepped outside again.

Within seconds, the concrete slab in front of the toolshed began to grumble. He reached out and pulled one of the men back. "Wanna watch where you're steppin' there, hoss." With almost surprising swiftness, the concrete slab released a *phst!* and began to rapidly move to the side, revealing a set of stairs that led down into the dark earth.

The old man began to descend the stairs. "Better shake a leg, fellas," he called over his shoulder to the two men still standing there. "This thing's gonna reset itself and close in about ten seconds."

The two guests followed their host down the dark stairwell.

Once inside *The Room*, the old man gestured for his guests to take a seat. He, of course, took the Aresline. Once everyone was seated he began.

"Good to see you, Judge. Thanks for coming, Governor."

Both men nodded and exchanged pleasantries.

"Milton said that this was urgent. And that it was something that needed my direct attention," the governor said.

The old man looked at the other man. "You tell him anything, Milton?"

"Nothing specific. But I think we all know why we're here."

"Do we?" It was the governor.

Pemberton pursed his lips and folded one of his long, skinny arms up under the other one, resting his finger in the cleft of his chin. "Lemmie ask you something, Joe. When you were a little boy, when you thought about what you wanted to be when you grew up, what was it?"

The governor thought about it for a moment. "I wanted to be a fireman."

"So then, why aren't you a fireman?"

The governor shifted in his seat. "Well, I guess because. . .well. . . Look, I just wanted to help people, really."

"And that's why you ran for governor," Pemberton said.

"Yes," the governor answered.

Pemberton leaned forward. "And that's why I got you elected. Because I saw something great in you, Joe. It's why I spent the kind of money I did on you, boy. Because I knew that you couldn't be shaken. That you'd do whatever you needed to do in order to maintain the greatness of this state."

"Thank you, Gavin. I appreciate your kind words."

"And I know that you ain't gonna kowtow to any special interest groups," Pemberton continued. "It's your beliefs on God, is what's got me fired up!"

"I don't understand," the governor said. "Gavin, you know my position on that. I'm an atheist."

"Exactly!"

"Perhaps I can shed some light here," the judge said.

Pemberton swept his arm out in a gesture, giving the judge the floor.

"Joe, it's been over four months since the Chinese attacked. We all know how close this country came to almost losing everything. If it weren't for sheer, dumb luck and an exceptional operative named Jon Keene, we'd all be wearing red and pledging allegiance to the People's Republic of China.

"Gavin and I have been talking for a while now. President Walker is adamant about his decision to stand still at this time and not take aggression toward the Chinese. That's ludicrous, in our minds. Once our boys got back here on our shores, and with the help of the Royal Navy, we should have gone full throttle back at them. We should have pushed them right back through the border towns they crossed over and right into the Pacific Ocean. Not just stop and negotiate new borders. What kind of President does that?"

"A coward! That's who!" Pemberton snapped.

The governor nodded to that. It was no secret that the governor had publicly made his objections of President Walker. That he had called him "misguided" and accused him of "playing upon the fears of people who ignorantly placed their hope in something that didn't exist" by giving credence to the man who called himself *the Prophet*.

"Listen, Joe," the judge continued, "they may call this part of the country the Bible Belt, but I'm here to tell you that there are a lot of people who couldn't give a care about changing the kinds of things Walker is talking about changing. The man's gone mad! People down here don't want that kind of change. We liked our country just fine the way it was before Walker and Grant let it get sold out right out from under their noses."

"So what do you want me to do about it?" the governor said.

"We want you to be our president," Pemberton said.

The governor laughed a throaty, short laugh.

"We're serious," the judge said.

"And how do you plan on making that happen?" the governor said, still chuckling.

The judge stood up from his chair and went to the wet bar. He poured himself two fingers of Pemberton's thirty-year-old scotch. He glanced over to the other two to see if they, too, wanted one. They both nodded and the judge poured the round.

Sitting back down, he continued. "Joe, I've been on the North Carolina Supreme Court for eighteen years now. I've seen a lot come and go. I've seen laws that should have never been laws remain laws. And I've seen laws that were rock solid get thrown out like yesterday's table scraps.

"I say that to say this: in 1869, the US Supreme Court ruled that a state did not have the right to secede from the union. But here's the thing: it was against the law for us to secede from England when we wanted our freedom. They said it was against the law when the South tried to secede from the North. But the bottom line is this: our own Declaration of Independence lays out the grounds for when the people of this country should rise up and defend what they know to be right."

He pulled out a small piece of paper and unfolded it. Retrieving his reading glasses from his pocket, he smoothed the page and began to read aloud.

" 'When, in the course of human events, it becomes necessary for one people to dissolve the political bands which have connected them with another, and to assume among the powers of the earth, the separate and equal station to which the laws of nature and of nature's God entitle them, a decent respect to the opinions of mankind requires that they should declare the causes which impel them to the separation.' "

The governor cleared his throat and tried to say something, but only a squeak came out. He coughed and pounded himself in the chest. "I'm sorry, I guess that scotch went down the wrong pipe. Milton, Gavin, I've known you two for a long time. You both are like a second set of granddads to me. But gentlemen, what you are suggesting is treason."

Pemberton shot out of his chair. "Treason? Treason! I'll tell you what's treason. Letting the gal-dern Chinese set off ten suitcase nukes on our West Coast is treason! Sitting back and watching them come unimpeded across our border was treason! Presidents Grant and Walker aren't fit to run a shoe store, let alone this country. And I *won't* sit by idly and watch them ruin everything my family and I have worked for almost three hundred years to achieve."

"Calm down, Gavin," the judge said.

Pemberton drained his glass and slammed it down on the desk before taking his seat again.

"Joe, what Gavin is saying is there are those of us who have already been moving towards a solution. This thing has come together quickly, I must say. But in the end, it was inevitable. We can't sit back and let some wacko religious zealots manipulate this country into changing what we are. We have to act now."

The governor twirled his finger around his glass. He took a big swallow, stood up, got himself a refill, and sat down again. "So this isn't just some fly-by-night fancy that you two have cooked up?"

Pemberton leaned forward onto the desk. "Son, I've got no less than two hundred of the top business minds in these southern states ready to pour resources into whatever we need to make this happen. Milton has been in meetings with justices from every state supreme court from Virginia to Georgia. We don't like Grant's idea of running this country. What's left of it. We need to take it back. We need to kick these Chinese back to where they came from. And we don't need some crackpot calling himself a prophet dictating government policy. We're doing this. And we want you at the helm."

"Why me?"

"Because," the judge said, "you already have executive experience and people love you. And like you said, you don't even believe in God. Why would you base your country's future on what some kook who says, 'God says. . .'?"

The governor finished his second drink and grabbed the other two men's glasses. He poured them all another round and sat down. "You realize what you're asking, right?"

The old man and the judge nodded.

"I mean, this is going to make a lot of waves."

They nodded again.

"I'm serious, gentlemen. I mean this could cause an all-out second civil war. Are you prepared for that?"

Pemberton raised his glass. "Son, we're not just prepared for it." He slowly tipped it back and took a sip. "We're counting on it!"